Sherlock Holmes
and
Doctor Watson:
The Early
Adventures

Volume II

Sherlock Holmes
and
Doctor Watson:
The Early
Adventures

Volume II

Edited by
David Marcum

Belanger Books
2019

CONTENTS

Foreword

Adventures

(Continued on the next page . . . .)

The following adventures appear in the companion volumes of

Sherlock Holmes
and
Doctor Watson:
The Early Adventures

Volume I:

Volume III:

COPYRIGHT INFORMATION

Editor's Foreword:
They Were Young Once Too . . . .
by David Marcum

W hen I was a kid, every one of my literary heroes was older than me. It wasn't something to ponder or resent – that's just the way it was. I started reading mysteries in 1973 at age eight with the exceptional adventures of *The Three Investigators*, and while their ages were never definitely stated – they didn't drive yet, for instance – it was clear that they were several years past me. Then, not long after that, I found *The Hardy Boys*. Frank and Joe were definitely eighteen and seventeen respectively, driving cars and planes and speedboats, and traveling all around Bayport and to New York, and anywhere else in the world that they wanted to go – Down South, Out West, Canada, England, Mexico, Iceland, Greece, Morocco, and everywhere else too. I don't think that I believed all of that adventure would suddenly come my way when I turned seventeen or eighteen – but I don't recall *not* believing it either.

Not long after finding The Hardy Boys, I realized that what I was reading were the *Revised Texts*, cleaned up and severely shortened from the stories that were originally published from the 1920's to the 1950's, before the revisions began. In those earlier books, Frank and Joe were sixteen and fifteen – but that really made no difference to me, as that was still older than I was, and all just some mysterious vague maturity that I hadn't yet reached.

The path where I found my other "book friends" (as my son would call them years later) led me to encounter other series characters like Sandy Steele and Brains Benton and Tod Moran, and adventure books by Troy Nesbit and Capwell

1

Wyckoff, to name just a faction. I collected and read about Tom Swift, Jr., but he never interested me as much as the pure mystery and adventure stories. I read some Doc Savage (although not enough), and became a friend-for-life of Tarzan, and also a Star Trek fanatic. One thing that they all had in common was that they were older than me.

In high school, I discovered some of the other Great Detectives – Nero Wolfe and Ellery Queen and Hercule Poirot. All older. In 1980, when I was fifteen, I happened upon Clive Cussler's Dirk Pitt, showing me that "grown-up" books could be incredibly fun after all, and not boring as I'd feared. At one point in *Iceberg* (1975 – the second Pitt book published, and the third chronologically), Pitt is described as being thirty-two years, four months, and twelve days old. At age fifteen, that was just a vague out-there age, lumped in with all of those other ages that were beyond my experience. Years later, after having re-read that book at least two-dozen times, I somehow still see Pitt as older than me, although now I'm more than twenty years older than he was in that story. That perspective is entrenched in my head.

When I was ten years old in 1975, I first encountered Mr. Sherlock Holmes and Doctor John Watson, who have been my greatest heroes ever since. They were older than I was, of course, as was every other figure in the books that I liked, so it was no big deal. But I didn't realize then what a stubborn issue the mistaken perception of Holmes and Watson's ages would turn out to be.

Holmes and Watson are recognized everywhere. Certain items related to Holmes – a deerstalker, or a pipe, or a magnifying glass – are identified all over the world with detectives in general and Holmes in particular. Many people have some idea of Holmes and Watson even if they've never read a Holmes story or seen a Holmes film or television episode. Others may have seen some of these films, and from them believe that they have a true idea of Our Heroes. But usually they don't.

There is a persistent and incorrect idea, reinforced by countless film misrepresentations, that Holmes and Watson were always staid and dull British chaps of middle years (or older), with Holmes a spry, cranky, and impatient eccentric (at best), and Watson a white-haired and portly *Boobus Brittanicus, a la* Nigel Bruce. Students of the true and Canonical Sherlock Holmes know this to be a falsehood.

When we first meet Holmes at the beginning of *A Study in Scarlet*, on January 1st, 1881, he is still twenty-six years old (although he'll turn twenty-seven in just a few days, on January 6th.) Watson, already a wounded war veteran, is only twenty-eight. Granted, Holmes is brilliant, and has already established a practice as a consulting detective, and Watson is a qualified doctor who has been to war and seen terrible things that most will never face, not even counting his injuries and subsequent disability. That is to say, they are exceptional men. But the thing that gets lost and forgotten is that *they were only in their twenties then.*

I'm a civil engineer, and there are several employees at our firm who are just about the same age now that Holmes and Watson were when they met on January 1st, 1881. Sometimes, knowing these coworkers pretty well, I try to imagine Holmes and Watson at that age, instead of as the middle-aged (or older) versions that so often want to spring to mind. I see how these coworkers behave in meetings, or carrying out responsibilities, or deal with those who are older and either know more, or who now know less as time and technology have moved on. It's a very instructive thing to observe, and they respond, as Mr. Spock says in *The Wrath of Khan*, "each according to his

3

gifts". I try to picture how Sherlock Holmes in his twenties would act, and also how he would be perceived, especially by those who are a little older.

Much is often made of how Scotland Yard and the other officials didn't want to take Holmes seriously, especially in those early days. There's a tendency to explain it away as if they thought that Holmes was too eccentric, or his methods too unusual. But consider that it might also have been a function of their age. Who among us has had a young doctor, fresh from school and in his or her twenties, and wondered if this person has enough knowledge and experience and seasoning to *really* know what's what. Then think about Holmes in that same light.

There has been a marked reluctance to portray Holmes and Watson anywhere near these younger and often appropriate ages in television and film. There is always a middle-agedness in media performances. When I was younger, and everyone was older than me, it just seemed natural. I was fortunate – or not fortunate, depending upon one's perspective – to see practically no screen versions of Holmes whatsoever while growing up, thus cementing in my head the Canonical version that I found in the original adventures. (This was before cable television and VCR's, and way before DVD's, so finding Holmes on screen occurred almost not at all.) I obtained my first Holmes book, an abridged copy of Whitman edition of *The Adventures*, in 1975, and then promptly shelved it, unwanted. It was only a few weeks later, when I saw part – but only a part – of *A Study in Terror* (1965) during a Saturday afternoon re-run, that I was tempted to explore The World of Holmes more deeply. The Holmes of the film seemed intriguing, and I was prompted to retrieve my sole Holmes book and start reading. Soon after I found more Canonical titles, and then pastiches like Nicholas Meyer's *The West End*

Horror and *Enter the Lion* by Sean Wright and Michael Hodel. I discovered that my local library had some old 1940's Basil Rathbone radio shows, so I was able to *hear* Holmes for the first time. (And even then, with intelligence beyond my years, I knew that Nigel Bruce was just plain wrong.)

But I didn't *see* Holmes on screen for a long time. In 1979, my dad took me to the local movie theater – and we were the only ones in attendance – to view *Murder by Decree* starring Christopher Plummer and James Mason. Both actors were excellent, and Plummer absolutely defined the heroic aspects of Holmes that I've always admired with his outrage at the government's conspiracy, taking his anger right to the face of the corrupt Prime Minister. James Mason was fine too – or so I thought at the time. But hindsight has educated me, for when the movie was filmed in 1978, James Mason was sixty-eight years old – playing a man who was actually thirty-six during the events during that Autumn of Terror, 1888.

I went for great stretches without any visual Holmes input. There was once a story on the CBS Evening News that happened to be on while I was in the room and talking with my parents. I glanced over to see that it contained a very short clip, to make some point within the story, from Rathbone's 1939 *The Hound of the Baskervilles*: "*Murder, my dear Watson,*" he said. "*Refined, cold-blooded murder.*" It was a five-second blink-and-you'll-miss-it scene, but it was my first time at *seeing* Rathbone as Holmes, after several years of hearing his radio performances. He was perfect. He was wearing the deerstalker, and he *looked like Holmes was supposed to look.*

Little did I realize that in *The Hound*, his first time out as Holmes, he was already too old for the part. He was in his late-forties then, while Holmes was only thirty-four when *The Hound* actually occurred. Rathbone and Bruce at least tried to do Holmes and Watson correctly in their first two films, *The*

Hound and *The Adventures of Sherlock Holmes* (also made in 1939), with Bruce darkening his hair and the stories set in the correct era, but a few years later, in the twelve films that they would make for Universal, they gave up all pretense of doing it right. Both acted like their own ages – in their fifties by that time, with Bruce possibly seeming even older with his white hair and bumbling muttering behavior.

Other Holmes films have also cast actors well-along in middle age, further solidifying the common belief that Holmes and Watson were always just somehow *older*. Arthur Wontner, who was a perfectly visualized Holmes, played him in five films when he was between fifty-seven and sixty two – and with a rather genial, soft-spoken, and sometimes bemused attitude. Peter Cushing took on the role of Holmes on multiple occasions: In the 1959 version of *The Hound* (when he was forty-six), in the 1968 BBC television show *Sherlock Holmes* (when he was fifty-five), and in 1984's *The Masks of Death* (when he was seventy-one). Granted, this final portrayal is supposed to show an elderly Holmes, but when *The Hound* occurred, as mentioned, Holmes was in his middle-thirties, and in Cushing's BBC version, he was a couple of *decades* too old. As part of his BBC series, Cushing also filmed *A Study in Scarlet*, one of only a handful of film versions of this Canonical tale. It ignored the meeting between Holmes and Watson, and instead jumped straight to The Lauriston Gardens Mystery. Perhaps that's just as well, since Cushing was fifty-five then, and would have needed to be a fine actor indeed, with some structures pulling his skin quite tight, to pull off a portrayal of a fellow in his twenties.

Another version of Holmes and Watson's first meeting occurred in the television episode "The Adventure of the Cunningham Heritage" (October 1954), which showed Watson being introduced to Holmes before veering off into another mystery entirely. This was from the thirty-nine episode series, *Sherlock Holmes*, (1954-1955) which has been hailed as being light-hearted (for the most part) and set in the early days of Holmes and Watson's friendship. But the stars, Ronald Howard and C. Marion Crawford, at thirty-six and forty respectively, were also too old if they wanted to seem like young men – and the older images of Holmes and Watson were again perpetuated.

The same is true for other actors. Douglas Wilmer was in his mid-forties when he starred in the excellent 1964-1965 BBC series. (I wish that more of these episodes had survived.) Ian Richardson was forty-nine when he played the mid-thirties Holmes in 1983's *The Hound of the Baskervilles* and *The Sign of Four*. Jeremy Brett was already fifty-one when his first performance as a mid-thirties Holmes in "A Scandal in Bohemia" aired in 1984. He would continue to appear as Holmes for the next ten years, as both his mental and physical abilities substantially declined. As he unfortunately (and irritatingly) foisted more and more of his own health issues onto his portrayal of Holmes, along with the insistent doctrine that he was portraying a very accurate Holmes, a great many people accepted that his version, with mental illness and older unhealthy features included, was the correct one, and it's been a difficult legacy to shake ever since.

Sadly, with its many flaws, Jeremy Brett's performance as Holmes has been the last time whatsoever that a television series about Sherlock Holmes has been aired in either Great Britain or America since 1994. There have been a few stand-alone films, such as a version of *The Hound* starring Richard Roxburgh (2002), and some other films with Matt Frewer, Jonathan Pryce, and Rupert Everett. In theatres, Sir Ian McKellan played an intentionally elderly Holmes, while Robert Downey, Jr. was forty-four and then forty-six when he played, in two back-to-back films, a middle-aged Holmes who was decidedly damaged goods. Screen representations of the younger Holmes just aren't to be found.

Noted Sherlockian Bert Coules has scripted a series of television programs featuring an age-appropriate Holmes and Watson in their twenties, solving cases early in their friendship. Hopefully, these will be produced, so that, for the first time since 1994 and the end of the Brett performances, a Sherlock Holmes television series will once again be on the air.

In the meantime, the public image of Our Heroes is often that of elderly fellows, rather than the way that they were presented in most of The Canon. We meet Holmes and Watson when they are twenty-six and twenty-eight, respectively. Five of the Canonical tales occur when Holmes is in his twenties – "The *Gloria Scott*", "The Musgrave Ritual", *A Study in Scarlet*, "The Resident Patient", and "The Speckled Band". (Take a moment to recall "The Speckled Band", set in 1883, one of the most famous Holmes tales. Can you see it? Do you remember the terror that is conveyed? Now imagine being Holmes and solving that case . . . and only being twenty-nine years old.)

There are twenty-five Canonical adventures wherein Holmes and Watson are in their thirties, and twenty-eight when they are in their forties. Only two, "The Lion's Mane" and "His Last Bow" occur later. In the first, Holmes is fifty-three, and in the second he is sixty. And yet, so many times he and Watson are shown as older men, sixty years or more if they are a day.

In some screen adaptations, this cannot be helped. Unlike the amazing BBC radio adaptations of The Canon starring Clive Merrison and Michael Williams, overseen by Bert

Coules, where the actors can play Holmes and Watson at any of the correct ages through the use of their voices, visual actors cannot jump so easily from their mid-forties in one episode to their twenties in the next. Allowances for this, such as in episodes of the Wilmer and Cushing and Brett series, must be made. But still, some occasional effort ought to present all those times that Holmes and Watson *weren't older.*

Luckily, even though visual mediums continue to reinforce that incorrect idea, the printed stories can present the younger versions of Holmes and Watson.

Since the mid-1990's, I've maintained an ever-growing chronology related to the complete lives of Holmes and Watson, containing both The Canon and thousands of traditional Canonical pastiches. It's currently over nine-hundred dense pages, and likely to cross a thousand soon, and the years before Holmes and Watson initially "officially" meet on January 1st, 1881, are extremely full of narratives about what else occurred. (One should not be surprised that their paths crossed a few times in a few extra-Canonical stories before being introduced that fateful day in the laboratory at Barts Hospital.)

The entries in my chronology for 1881, 1882, and 1883 – the years covered by this new collection – cover over sixty pages, spreading from the events of *A Study in Scarlet* that occur on the morning of January 1st, 1881 to the evening of December 31st, 1883, as related in the opening and closing frame-tale segments of "The Adventure of the Vintner's Codex" by Lyndsay Faye.

These are dense years, explored broadly and deeply (but not yet completely) by many pasticheurs. For instance, there are fifteen versions (so far) of the meeting in Barts Lab, all providing extra details and perspectives to this momentous

9

event, while not contradicting the "official" version in any way:

- *A Study In Scarlet* – Dr. John H. Watson
- *Sherlock Holmes of Baker Street* (Chapter 6, pp. 53-56) – William S. Baring-Gould
- "A Study in Scarlet" (BBC Radio Broadcast) – Bert Coules
- *The Private Life of Dr Watson* (Epilogue) – Michael Hardwick
- "The Adventure of the Cunningham Heritage" – Sheldon Reynolds *Sherlock Holmes* (Television Episode – *Opening Segment*)
- "I Meet Dr. John Watson" (Chapter 2, pp. 19-24) – Michael Harrison *I, Sherlock Holmes*
- "The Detective and His Boswell" (Chapter 1) – Runa93
- *Death on a Pale Horse: Sherlock Holmes on Her Majesty's Secret Service* (Part II Chapter 4, pp. 89-94) – Donald Thomas
- *At the Mercy of the Mind* Chapter 90 – Gwendolyn Frame
- *When the Song of the Angels is Stilled* (Chapter 51, pp. 363-367) – A.S. Croyle
- "Only A Mild Acquaintance" (Chapter 1) – music97
- "A Pocketbook of Insanity" (Chapter 1, Segment 3) – Wraithwitch
- "The Bishop and the Horns of Plenty" (p. 87) – Karl Showler *Sherlock Holmes and the Watson Pastiche*
- *The Secret Diary of Mycroft Holmes, Esq.* (Chapter 17) – Westron Wynde (S.F. Bennett)
- *Worth and Choice* (Chapter 6) – KCS

And that doesn't even count all the other stories that are set earlier in the day of January 1st, before this meeting, all relating what else was happening then in addition to the few short paragraphs that Watson provides in the Canonical account later published in the 1887 *Beeton's Christmas Annual*.

There is an amazing array of traditional, Canonical, and excellent Holmes adventures to found under the collective umbrella of "fan-fiction", with nearly all of them published under many curious and unique *nom-de-plumes*. With the paradigm shift that allowed so many delvers into Watson's Tin Dispatch Box to find a way to publicly release stories without the restriction of going through the narrow and obstructive channel of traditional publishing, an explosion of narratives has been revealed over the last few decades. Too many of those who declare themselves to be arms-wide-open Sherlockians are cheating themselves to an incredible degree by ignoring some really excellent examples of Holmes's adventures – often as good or better than those from traditional publishers, and sometimes better than The Canon itself.

Below is a list of some – but definitely not all – of these traditional and Canonical "fan-fictions" (as well as the modern literary agents who revealed them), covering the years from 1881 to 1883:

- "Barman" – Sigerson
- "What Providence Brought Together" – KaizokuShoju
- "Only A Mild Acquaintance" – music97
- "The Violin" – Haley Moore
- "Vexing Visitors" – MONKrules
- "No Dogs Allowed" – KCS
- "The Houseplant" – KaizokuShoju
- "A Man's Limits" – KCS
- "Brown" – Monty Twain
- "Beginnings" *London Crime: The Detective and The Doctor*
- "The Art of Boxing" – Protector of the Gray Fortress
- "Lunch Money" – Monty Twain
- "The Most Winning Woman" – TeriyakiKat
- "A Pocketbook of Insanity, or Watson's First Case" – Wraithwitch
- "Sherlock Holmes – My Limits" – Monty Twain
- "Another Curse of Our Indian Possessions" – medcat
- "The Pursuit of Justice" – Lands End
- "Photograph" – MONKrules
- "The Case of the Baker Street Flatmate" – Bemj11 *Tales of Scotland Yard*
- "The Dreaded Band" *London Crime: The Detective and The Doctor*
- "Irregular Protectors" – Ancalime8301
- "The Unelucidated Casebook of Sherlock Holmes: The

Framingham Forgery" – infiniteviking
- "The Second List" – Be3
- "Contradictions" – Pompey
- "A Pound of Flesh" – Alone Dreaming
- "The Other's Limits" – Anony9
- "A Study in Tea Leaves" – Chewing Gum
- "The Case of the Startled Bay" – Westron Wynde (S.F. Bennett)
- "Bedside Manner" – Capt-Facepalm
- "The Tenants of Baker Street" – Protector of the Gray Fortress
- "Perfectly Insufferable" – Jack of All Suits
- "Combat" – shedoc
- "The Worth of a Friend" – pebbles66
- "Pocket Watch" – Capt-Facepalm
- "Deadly Loose Ends" – Blues Scale
- "A Man About the House" – pebbles66
- "A Row" – Monty Twain
- "My Heart's In the Highlands" – Capt-Facepalm
- "The Adventure of the Barchester Clergyman" – callensensei
- "Lines On the Face" – lew daney
- "All Hours" – Nanatsusaya
- "Baker Street Lodgings" – Wraithwitch
- "To Be Valuable" – Bartimus Crotchety
- "Decidedly So" (Chapters 2-4) – rabidsamfan (C.H. Dye)
- "Mind Over Memory" – KCS
- "The Case of the Thursday Rendezvous" – Alone Dreaming
- "Reveries" – smallrose
- "Watson's Finances" – Miss Roylott
- "Lost" – Monty Twain"
- "Will You Be My Friend" – bluedragon1836
- "Experimentation" – Bartimus Crotchety
- "These Are Deep Waters" – Igiveup
- "The Case of the Mottled Eyes" – Louann Qualls
- "Burden of Proof" – Capt-Facepalm
- "Dark Clouds" – Natalya Ilyinishna
- "The Whistle in the Attic" – wordybirdy
- "Found Pages (4)" – Dan Antidormi
- "Pain and Music" – Alone Dreaming
- "The Pink Reticule" – Tristan-the-Dreamer
- "Cold" – Bartimus Crotchety
- "Unexpected Complications" – E Phoenix
- "It's Christmastime in the City" – KCS
- "A Christmas Stocking" – Daniel A. Antidormi
- "Irregular Christmas" – callietitan

- "Their First Christmas" – Aleine Skyfire (Gwendolyn Frame)
- "Simple Gifts" – KCS
- "Friend" – KaizokuShoju
- "One Year" – KaizokuShoju
- "A Winter's Tale" – charleygirl
- "Surprising The Master" – xXBleedingRosesXx
- "Things Are Not As They Should Be" – MJ Azilem
- "Juxtaposition" – Bartimus Crotchety
- "The Case of the Attempted Vendetta" – Vishakha Sharma
- "The Beast of Hampton Moors" – Mike "The Baron" McManus
- "Hazards" – Pepipanda
- "Recruiting an Irregular" – juniper
- "The Egg" – Jon'ic Recheio
- "First Blood" – charleygirl
- "The Winning Woman" – Maryann Boyle Murray
- "February, 1882" – Crystal Rose of Pollux
- "Matters of Humanity" – Chuxter
- "The Case of the Black Group" – C.H. Baker
- "The Rescuer" – IrregularHonor
- "Peaceful Mornings" – Protector of the Gray Fortress
- "Prize Fighter" – KaizokuShoju
- "Back to the Beginning" – Curreeus
- "The Adventure of the Woman With the Cane" – Nitzchild
- "A Row with Mrs Hudson" – EchoValley26809
- "The Call of the Chickadee" – You Float My Boat
- "Unbidden Ghosts" – ScarletteQuill
- "Trains" – Chuxter
- "The Adventure of the Dubious Fiancé" – Gaia1
- "The Breaking Strain" – Bartimus Crotchety
- "Untitled Halloween Story" – Law-Abiding Citizen
- "Memories" – medcat
- "Yes, Guv'Nor" – Ivy U Rhizzpi
- "A Friend and Associate" – MemorieLane
- "Duet" – Ketari Fang (Addy-kin)
- "Seaside Poison" – xMORIARTYx
- "Mrs Hudson's Misadventure" – IrregularHonor
- "Are You Feeling Adventurous?" – MadameGiry25
- "Professional" – Arhie
- "Three Weeks" – sherlockiantreky
- "Rose" – Gyroscope
- "Enchantment" – IrregularHonor
- "Untitled Air on G" – prettybrokenthings
- "Reflective Thoughts" – Jfreak

13

- "The World Stares" – shell less snail
- "Chaotic" – Hades Lord of the Dead
- "In Writing Only" – Hades Lord of the Dead
- "Not A Sidekick" – Aisho9
- "The Soft Underbelly of Civil Conversation" – aragonite (Marcia Wilson)
- "Colourful Experiments" – Jfreak
- "Painkiller" – Lemon Zinger
- "Moment of Panic" – Taleya
- "A Stronger Fear" – KCS
- "Humming To Ourselves" – Monty Twain
- "Death Waits For Nothing" – Rose H. McKellen
- "The Case of the Missing Box" – InTheRealWorld
- "A Little Bit of Fun" – PoeticPerson
- "Honor the Light Brigade" – beargirl1393
- "Deprivation" – Lemon Zinger
- "The Crime that Never Happened" – Ronald Carpenter *Sherlock Holmes: The One True Detective*
- "Who Would Kill Marwood?" – aragonite (Marcia Wilson)
- "Observations of a Lodger" – shedoc
- "The Catalyst Client" – Loki's Campaign Manager
- "The Baker's Bread" – Alan Downing *Armchair Mysteries of Sherlock Holmes*
- "The London Littoral" – aragonite (Marcia Wilson)
- "Rest in Torquay" – jenny starseed
- "The Fascinating Case of the Circular Cord" – Dennis L McKiernan
- "Stealth Tactics" – KCS
- "Diagnosed" – Science of Deduction
- "The Olive Affair" – Boston Manor
- "Essential" – Protector of the Gray Fortress
- "Between Pride and Insult" – You Float My Boat
- "Scar" – Alaylith
- "Irrational" – MONKrules
- "Unfortunate Mannerisms" – Lennon Drop
- "Afoot!" – ihedge
- "A Moment of Being" – charleygirl
- "Why The Case of the Velvet Female Thief" – Velvet Green
- "Hope" – Bowen Cates
- *On Afghanistan's Plains* – Pompey
- *Agreement and Disputation* – KCS
- "Lost and Found" – Arwen Jade Kenobi
- "In Good Hands" – Nunewesen

- "A Calculated Risk" – Msynergy
- "No Secret So Close" – Addy-kun
- "Loyalty" – Monty Twain
- "221 Words and a 'B'" – MD Hammer
- "The Art of Deduction" – Deana
- "The Adventure of the Secret Threat" – Kaizoku Shoju
- "Extrasensory Perception" – Dean King
- "Boom" – Knife86
- "When Master Met His Match" – Werewolf Master
- "Rainy Days and Board Games" – wordybirdy
- "The Best of Sherlock Holmes" – vraindall
- "Reminiscences of Miss Helen Stoner" – Miss Roylott
- "Holmes's Speckled Band" – Tehstrangeness
- "Untitled" – tunclr4
- "The Case of the Irregular Irregular" – Eyebrows2
- "Sherlock Holmes and the Pocket Watch Murders" – Forgotten Phoenix
- "Heredity" – Ingrid Matthews
- "The Problem of the Biggin Hill Duel" – Adrian Luciens
- "Summertime Wonderland" – The Liberal Admitted
- "The Case of the Baker Street Irregular" – Arctic Squirrel
- "The Sport of Kings" – Kadal
- "A Case of Twelve" – wordybirdy
- "The Pugilist, the Doctor, and the Detective" – Eyebrows2
- "The Adventure of the Blind Prophet" – Phantom Cavity
- "Realization" – Tristan-the-Dreamer
- "Indoor Shooting Practice" – Monty Twain
- "The Adventure of the Haunted House" – AnnCarter
- "Sherlock Holmes and the Mad Fakir" – shedoc
- "A Nagging Question" – Protector of the Gray Fortress
- "Terror" – anony9

For those who have to have their stories somehow legitimized by appearing by way of "acceptable" mediums, here is another tremendously incomplete list of Holmes and Watson's adventures, also set between January 1st, 1881 and December 31st, 1883, that have appeared in novels, short story collections, and television and radio broadcasts:

- "The First Cases" – Anon. *My Name is Sherlock Holmes*

15

- "The April Fool's Day Adventure" – Denis Green and Anthony Boucher *The Lost Adventures of Sherlock Holmes* and *The New Adventures of Sherlock Holmes* (Radio Broadcast)
- "The Adventure of the Slipshod Charlady" – John Hall *The MX Book of New Sherlock Holmes Stories" – Part I: 1881-1889*
- "The Speaking Machine" – Jim French *The Further Adventures of Sherlock Holmes* (Radio Broadcast)
- "The Italian Gourmet" – Roger Ricard *A Sherlock Holmes Alphabet of Cases" – Vol. II (F to J)*
- "The Darlington Substitution Scandal" – Denis Green and Anthony Boucher *The Forgotten Adventures of Sherlock Holmes* and *The New Adventures of Sherlock Holmes* (Radio Broadcast)
- "The Wandering Corpse" – John Taylor *The Unopened Casebook of Sherlock Holmes*
- "School For Scoundrels" – Jim French *The Further Adventures of Sherlock Holmes* (Radio Broadcast)
- "The Adventure of the Willow Pool" – Denis O. Smith. *The Chronicles of Sherlock Holmes Vol. IV*
- "The Adventure of the Temperance Society" – Deanna Baran *The MX Book of New Sherlock Holmes Stories – Part IX: 2018 Annual (1879-1895)*
- "The Diary of Anthony Moltaire" – Jim French *The Further Adventures of Sherlock Holmes* (Radio Broadcast)
- "The Adventure of the Traveling Orchestra" – Amy Thomas *The MX Book of New Sherlock Holmes Stories – Part I: 1881-1889*
- "The Adventure of the Double-Edged Hoard" – Craig Janacek *The MX Book of New Sherlock Holmes Stories – Part IV: 2016 Annual*
- "A Scandal in Tite Street" – Mike Hogan *Sherlock Holmes: Murder at the Savoy & Other Stories*
- "The Kingdom of the Blind" – Adrian Middleton *The MX Book of New Sherlock Holmes Stories" – Part I: 1881-1889*
- "The Case of the Ruby Necklace" – Bob Byrne *The MX Book of New Sherlock Holmes Stories" – Part V: Christmas Adventures*
- "The Jet Brooch" – Denis O. Smith *The MX Book of New Sherlock Holmes Stories" – Part V: Christmas Adventures*
- "The Adventure of the Naturalist's Stock Pin" – Jon L. Breen *More Holmes for the Holidays*
- "The Adventure of the Knighted Watchmaker" – Derrick Belanger *The MX Book of New Sherlock Holmes Stories – Part V: Christmas Adventures*
- "Christmas Eve" – S.C. Roberts *The Misadventures of Sherlock Holmes*
- "The Haunting of Sherlock Holmes" – Kevin David Barratt *The MX Book of New Sherlock Holmes Stories – Part I: 1881-1889*

- *You Buy Bones* – Marcia Wilson
- "The Adventure of the Dover Maiden" – Jim French *The Further Adventures of Sherlock Holmes* (Radio Broadcast)
- "The Adventure of the Velvet Lampshade" – Peter K. Andersson *The Cotswolds Werewolf*
- "The Case of the Thistle Killer" – Charles Early *Sherlock Holmes* (Television Episode)
- "The Case of the Honest Wife" – Lyndsay Faye *The Strand Magazine* and *The Whole Art of Detection*
- "The Stolen Relic" – David Marcum *The MX Book of New Sherlock Holmes Stories – Part V: Christmas Adventures*
- "The Adventure of the Serpent's Tooth" – Jim French *The Further Adventures of Sherlock Holmes* (Radio Broadcast)
- "The Singular Adventure of the Abandoned Bicycle" – Alan Stockwell *The Singular Adventures of Mr Sherlock Holmes*
- "The Adventure of the Pawnbroker's Daughter" – David Marcum *The MX Book of New Sherlock Holmes Stories" –Part I: 1881-1889*
- "The Eye Witnesses" – Alan Downing *Armchair Mysteries of Sherlock Holmes*
- "The Adventure of the Surrey Giant" – Paul W. Nash *The Remains of Sherlock Holmes*
- "A Christmas Goose" – C.H. Dye *The MX Book of New Sherlock Holmes Stories – Part V: Christmas Adventures*
- "The American Ambassador" – David Scott *Holmes Redux*
- "The Case of the Vintner's Codex" – Lyndsay Faye *The Strand Magazine* and *The Whole Art of Detection*
- "*Matilda Briggs* and the Giant Rat of Sumatra" – Ian Charnock *The Elementary Cases of Sherlock Holmes*
- "The Pearl of Death" – GC Rosenquist *Sherlock Holmes – The Pearl of Death*
- "The Adventure of the Paradol Chamber" – Alvin F. Rymsha *Sherlock Holmes: The Lost Cases*
- "The Mysterious Disappearance of the Good Ship *Alicia*" – Gerald Kelly *The Outstanding Mysteries of Sherlock Holmes*
- "Sherlock Holmes and the Tick Tock Man" – Roy Templeman *Sherlock Holmes: The Chinese Junk Affair and Other Stories*
- "The Case of the Vanishing Blueprint" – Liz Hedgecock *The Secret Notebooks of Sherlock Holmes*
- "The Plain Gold Wedding Ring" – Nick Cardillo *The Feats of Sherlock Holmes*
- "The Helverton Inheritance" – David Marcum *The MX Book of New Sherlock Holmes Stories – Part IX: 2018 Annual (1879-1895)*

- "The Great Zeffarini" – Richard Stone *Mysteries Suspended*
- "The Problem of Woolthshrap Prison" – Thomas G. Waddell and Thomas R. Rybolt *The Chemical Adventures of Sherlock Holmes*
- "The Case of the Vain Vixen" – Gayle Lange Puhl *Sherlock Holmes and the Folk Tale Mysteries" – Vol. I*
- "The Two Footmen" – Michael Gilbert *The New Adventures of Sherlock Holmes*
- "A Simple Solution" – David Marcum *The Strand Magazine*
- "The Adventure of the Defenestrated Princess" – Jayantika Ganguly *The MX Book of New Sherlock Holmes Stories – Part I: 1881-1889*
- "The Paddington Witch" – John Taylor *The Unopened Casebook of Sherlock Holmes and* (BBC Radio Broadcast"
- "The Adventure of the Christmas Visitor" – Denis O. Smith *The Chronicles of Sherlock Holmes Vol II*
- "The Night in the Asylum at Torence" – Herman Anthony Litzinger *Traveling With Sherlock Holmes and Dr. Watson*
- "The Battersea Worm" – John Taylor *The Unopened Casebook of Sherlock Holmes and* (BBC Radio Broadcast"
- "The Adventure of the Monstrous Blood" – Craig Janacek *Light in the Darkness*
- "The Adventure of the Old Russian Woman" – H. Paul Jeffers *The Confidential Casebook of Sherlock Holmes*
- "The Coffee House Girl" – David Marcum *The MX Book of New Sherlock Holmes Stories – Part XIII: 2019 Annual (1881-1890)*
- "Sherlock Holmes and the Mummy's Curse" – H. Paul Jeffers *Ghosts in Baker Street*
- "The Moriarty Gambit" – Fritz Lieber *The Game Is Afoot*
- "The Gray Goose" [Author Unknown] *The Stories of Sherlock Holmes* (South African Radio Broadcast)
- "The Affair of the Friendly Tramp" – N.M. Scott *Sherlock Holmes – To A Country House Darkly*
- "On the Wall – Lenore Glen Offord *The Baker Street Journal*
- "The Seaside Horror" – Magda Josza *The Private Diaries of Dr Watson*
- "The Case of the Frightened Bookkeeper" – Howard Merrill *The Further Adventures of Sherlock Holmes* (Radio Broadcast)
- "The Adventure of the Inn on the Marsh" – Denis O. Smith *The MX Book of New Sherlock Holmes Stories – Part I: 1881-1889*
- "Sherlock Holmes and the Bradfield Push" – Hugh Ashton *Secrets From the Deed Box of John H. Watson MD*
- "The Endell Street Mystery" – Malcolm Knott *Sherlock Holmes: The Soldier's Daughter*
- "Watson's Christmas Trick" – Bob Byrne *Sherlock* Magazine

- "The Case of the Schweinitz Portrait" – Floyd R. Horowitz *The Baker Street Journal*
- "A Volume In Vermillion" – Kim Newman *Sherlock Holmes Mystery Magazine* and *Moriarty: The Hound of the D'Urbervilles*
- *The Surrogate Assassin* – Christopher Leppek
- *Murder at Sorrows Crown* – Steven Saville and Robert Greenberger
- *Sherlock Holmes and the Raleigh Legacy* – L.B. Greenwood
- *The Case of the Revolutionist's Daughter* – Lewis S. Feuer
- *Mrs. Hudson and the Spirit's Curse* – Martin Davies
- "Denoument" - Donald W. Jackson *The Baker Street Journal*
- *Mrs. Hudson and the Malabar Rose* – Martin Davies
- *Sherlock Holmes and the Case of the Edinburgh Haunting* – David Wilson
- *Sherlock Holmes and the London Zoo Mystery* – Willoughby Lane
- *Sherlock Holmes and the Portsmouth Plot* – Boston Manor
- *Sherlock Holmes Lost Adventure* – Laurel Steinhauer
- *Sherlock Holmes and the Somerset Hunt* – Rosemary Michaud
- *Sherlock Holmes Uncovered: The Eccentric Painter"* – Steven Ehrman
- *The Case of the Howling Dog* – Allen Sharp
- *The Adventure of the Bloody Tower* – Donald MacLachlan
- *Sherlock Holmes Uncovered: The Viking General* – Steven Ehrman
- *Holmes in the West Country* – Patrick Campbell
- *Test of the Professionals: Leap Year* – Marcia Wilson
- *Test of the Professionals I: The Adventure of the Flying Blue Pidgeon* – Marcia Wilson
- *Test of the Professionals II: The Peaceful Night Poisonings* – Marcia Wilson

This current collection of adventures – and there will never be enough of them to completely tell the whole story of Holmes and Watson – provides valuable additional information about those early years in Baker Street.

As usual, I've arranged the stories in this collection in chronological order. As a die-hard and passionate Sherlockian Chronologicist, I really believe that it adds to the enjoyment to progress through a volume of adventures while matching them with what was occurring at the same time in the lives of Holmes and Watson.

As with every project that I attempt, I want to thank my true love, soul mate, and wonderful wife (of over thirty years!) Rebecca, and our wonderful amazing son and my friend, Dan. I love you both, and you are everything to me!

Once again, I can't find words to express the gratitude I have to all of the contributors who have used their time to create this project. I'm so glad to have gotten to know all of you through this process. It's an undeniable fact that Sherlock Holmes authors are the *best* people!

Additionally, I'd also like to especially thank:

- Derrick Belanger – I'm very glad to have gotten to know Derrick, even though we've never actually met in person – yet. We've both been involved in many projects since we first started communicating back in the fall of 2014, initially discussing Sherlockian matters, and then progressing to writing stories and producing books, sometimes with Belanger Books, and others with different connections. As always, I'm having a wonderful time, and I can't wait to see what happens next. Thanks so very much!

- Brian Belanger – Brian is an incredibly talented and very busy graphic artist, and he's having fun on the same scale that I am by being able to play in the Sherlockian sandbox. He constantly amazes me with his gifts, and I can't wait to see what he'll come up with next. Many thanks!

20

Finally, last but certainly *not* least, **Sir Arthur Conan Doyle**: Author, doctor, adventurer, and the Founder of the Sherlockian Feast. Present in spirit, and honored by all of us here.

As always, this collection, like those before it, has been a labor of love by both the participants and myself. As I've explained before, once again everyone did their sincerest best to produce an anthology that truly represents why Holmes and Watson have been so popular for so long. These are just more tiny threads woven into the ongoing Great Holmes Tapestry, continuing to grow and grow, for there can *never* be enough stories about the man whom Watson described as "*the best and wisest . . . whom I have ever known.*"

David Marcum
August 7th, 2019
The 167th Birthday of Dr. John H. Watson

Questions, comments, and story submissions
may be addressed to David Marcum at
thepapersofsherlockholmes@gmail.com

Sherlock Holmes
and
Doctor Watson:
The Early
Adventures

Volume II

The Adventure of the
Substitute Detective
by I.A. Watson

In my early months in residence with Sherlock Holmes, my experience of his caseload was rather sporadic. I was slow in recovering from the wound I had taken at Maiwand Pass and a subsequent fever at Peshawar when my life was despaired of. I took constitutionals, visited the Army and Navy Club, and wrote a little, but not much else. I was gradually drawn into my flat-mates' odd world of crime and detection, piece by piece.

Some of my experiences were comprehensive, as was my introduction to the career of a consulting detective – that is, an expert to whom other investigative professionals refer when a matter is too difficult or baffling. The demise of Enoch J. Drebber was a salutary revelation about the science of detection, so much that I made copious notes for a planned essay on the affair. [1]

On occasion I played a role or was an observer in Holmes's other investigations. I saw first-hand what the detective could accomplish in The Adventure of the Impossible Coin, The Murder of the Amorous Balloonist, The Significant Misfortunes of a Malarial Thespian, and other singular events.

At other times my involvement and understanding of Holmes's cases was incomplete and second-hand. I cannot with authority describe The Problem of the Inverted Pygmy, The Mystery of the Baboon's Heart, The Second Death of Reverend Mayhew, The Disturbing Matter of the Wrong Wedding Cake, or The Scandalous Bridge Tournament that led to the near-detonation of Woolwich Arsenal. Those enquiries will likely remain unrecorded forever.

Holmes and I were coming to know each other. We discussed his cases in confidence and I gradually came to understand something of his methods. I became familiar with some of the wide cast of informers, specialists, and agents he had gathered, and with the Metropolitan Police officers who were his most regular applicants. Of the Scotland Yard men, the most prominent were Inspectors Gregson and Lestrade, rival investigators to whom the most difficult investigations were awarded. It seemed to me that both men's first action in any case was to turn to Mr. Sherlock Holmes.

It was Tobias Gregson who called at 221b Baker Street on a blustery October morning, shaking the rain off his coat and stamping over to the hearth.

"I told him that Mr. Holmes isn't here," our landlady protested to me, hovering at the doorway. "He said he'd see you, Dr. Watson."

"Thank you, Mrs. Hudson. Would you send the girl up with some tea?"

The formidable landlady disfavoured Gregson with a last sniff and retreated to prepare refreshments.

"Holmes has been absent for several days now," I instructed my visitor. "I have not seen him for almost a week."

"Where is he?" Gregson demanded. "He is needed."

"I have only his note warning me that his work has taken him away, and that he may be gone for some time. This is not the first occasion when he has vanished on some investigation."

The jowly, portly Detective Inspector growled. "He is a very inconvenient fellow."

"You appear to find him of use," I noted. I confess that my voice carried a note of criticism. Gregson and the other

Scotland Yarders received the credit for the cases that Holmes helped them solve. The injustice of it niggled me, and I was determined that one day I would set the record right.

"He has a mind that works in odd ways," the inspector allowed. "It sometimes comes at a problem from a different angle. That's why I need his view on the work I have in hand."

"I will be happy to pass word to my fellow lodger that you need to speak with him, or to give him any note you might wish to leave."

Gregson warmed his hands on the fire, uncomforted. "That's no good. The Commissioner is breathing down my neck now, before the papers catch hold of what's happening. Once the broadsheets get their teeth into it . . . well, I need to get to the truth." The inspector's eyes sparked with venal inspiration. "Holmes keeps note-books about the criminals of London, doesn't he? Long lists of which men are coiners and which men are confidence tricksters – and who the best cracksmen are. If I could look through those journals . . . ."

"I'm afraid that would be an unconscionable breach of privacy," I insisted. I have no doubt that five minutes' glance at the pages of Holmes's index would have enhanced Gregson's career significantly, but I had no intention of allowing such an invasion. "Also, Holmes is careful to obscure his information by means of codes and abbreviations, to protect his sources and ensure anonymity for those who require it."

"But there must be a file somewhere that details the best thieves, the sort of men who can enter a locked premises, open the best safes on the market, and depart again unseen without leaving the slightest trace!"

"You are referring to the Kirby Jewellers robbery," I surmised. That crime at least had made its way into the press. Five nights earlier, somewhere between eight and six, a packet of uncut diamonds valued at two-thousand guineas had been extracted from a sealed strong-room without witness or sign of forced entry.

"That's one," Gregson confessed. "There are three others, the details of which have not yet been made public. The first was ten nights back, when a thief entered the premises of the stockbrokers Lumley and Chayne and abstracted Swedish bearer bonds valued at three-thousand *krona* – eleven-hundred pounds. Since the break-in at Kirby's, there has been an assault on Hepple's Currency Exchange, where foreign notes to the value of almost two-thousand pounds were taken, and most recently, just last night, another outrage. An heirloom tiara of the O'Tierney family was being maintained and polished at Esperson's Jewellers and was removed from their new combination safe. The security guard saw nothing."

"That does sound like a case that might interest Holmes," I agreed. "Unfortunately, I have no way of contacting him and no idea what he is doing. I'm not even sure he is in England."

Gregson's beefy jaw worked as he struggled with this setback. "We know they were the same criminal," he confided in me. "Look at these."

He handed me four deckle-edged calling cards, each containing but a single word in copperplate font: *One*, *Two*, *Three*, and *Four*. Hand-inked beneath the printed script was the word "*Rec.d*" and then the recorded sums of money equivalent to the value of goods stolen.

"The fellow is leaving receipts?"

"He is laughing at us!" Gregson hissed. "Laughing at Scotland Yard!"

I had to confess that the thief seemed to be mocking his hunters. "I will certainly let Holmes know of the problem when he appears," I promised.

Gregson was clearly under serious pressure to get results. "I cannot wait. If you will not allow me to check Holmes's books then you must help me some other way, Dr. Watson. You have gone about with him when he has chased his prey. You must know who he would go to, who he would ask about things like this. You must have seen the secret of how he finds felons."

"I have some little acquaintance of certain individuals, but I am certain they would not receive me as they do Holmes. There are some who speak with him because they owe him favours. Others because he pays them well. Still others are informers because they fear Sherlock Holmes's closer attention to their own affairs. I cannot approach these men as Holmes would."

"There must be something you can do. The matter is urgent."

I reviewed the resources that the world's only consulting detective might call upon. My eyes strayed to the rug upon which the inspector stood, and I recalled a very different visitor who sometimes occupied that space, ragged cap in hand, trousers torn at the knees, grubby-faced and mischief-eyed. The young rogue's name was Wiggins, and he led an irregular troupe of street-urchins who sometimes served as Holmes's eyes and ears.

"I will make some enquiries," I told Gregson. "I cannot promise success."

"Anything is better than nothing," the policeman responded. "There was no sign of how the burglar got in – None! Four perfect robberies in less than two weeks. When the news breaks, so does my career!"

He agreed to return the next day to hear if I had uncovered any word. After I saw him out, I resorted to Mrs. Hudson to discover how Holmes alerted his street Arabs, and to set them on.

That afternoon I received another call from the forces of the law. This time the querent was Inspector G. Lestrade, Gregson's great rival for the public's laurels. Thin where his opponent was stout, rodent-faced where Gregson was jowly, sallow rather than florid, Lestrade was in many ways the temperamental and intellectual opposite of his fellow officer.

"The two of them are the best that Scotland Yard can offer," Holmes had once told me, in the tones that a medical man might use to impart the need to sever a limb to save the patient. "Gregson is marginally the brighter, but Lestrade the more persistent. Gregson is the fox-hound, hasty and boisterous, Lestrade the terrier, temperamental and implacable. One believes everything, the other nothing. Between them they manage to occasionally catch the right man. But they are the best."

"Where is Sherlock Holmes?" Lestrade demanded as Gregson had before. "There is a case that would benefit from his review."

I explained again that the detective was gone away, beyond my means to contact him.

"That won't do," the inspector protested. "What does he mean sneaking off like that when there are matters of public importance to address? I have a dead soldier and a mysterious fakir, and a note from the Foreign Office demanding to know what has happened!"

"You have my sympathies," I condoled. "However, I cannot produce Holmes for you. You might have to address this case by yourself."

Lestrade shook his head. "You don't understand . . . ." Then he paused and looked at me speculatively. "Or you might understand. You were an army doctor who served in India, were you not?"

I confessed to holding such posts in the Fifth Northumberland and the Berkshires. [2] "I was out on the Sub-continent for a little under two years, although the last three months of it were in a hospital bed, thanks to a Jezail bullet."

"Then you must know about these Indians and their magic men."

"I've seen a fellow do the rope trick and some snake-charming, if that's what you mean."

"And the rest? They say that the Indians invented thugs."

"The Thugee? They were suppressed thirty years ago, Lestrade. It's history now." [3]

"Is it? Because I've heard sailors on our wharves speak of such killers. They wear a yellow sash, don't they, that they can use as a strangling cord? And they carry a special dagger, a personal weapon for ritual murder."

"That's how they were sometimes described. The old laws of the Mughal Empire awarded death sentences for murderers who shed blood – strangulation is a bloodless death and allowed a legal loophole. Hence the *rumāl*, the yellow headscarf, which could be a throttling cord. Their status weapon was the *katar*, a short blade with a strange *H*-shaped grip. Their drug of choice was *datura*, [4] a nightshade, which makes its victims sleepy."

"So you *do* know about them," Lestrade celebrated.

"I know *of* them. Enough to tell you that they are long gone. India has its troubles, but not Thugee."

Lestrade was not satisfied. "The dead man is a retired Colonel, Logan Fisk. He was attached to the British force in Bangalore."

"I can't say I know it. Bangalore is in Kamatarka, in the southeast of the Sub-continent. My experience was up the west coast and across into Afghanistan. India is a vast place, Inspector, thirteen times the size of Britain, and it has many different terrains and cultures within it."

"This Fisk, he was found burned in the ruin of his house, but it is clear from the remains that he was cut up first. Tortured, perhaps?"

I was out of my ambit. "If Holmes were here, I'm sure he could – "

"But Holmes isn't here!" Lestrade interrupted. "So we must do the best we can. You are a doctor. Won't you come and examine the body? You've had some martial experience, so you know knife wounds, and you've accompanied Holmes to coroner's inquests and autopsies."

"That hardly makes me a substitute for Sherlock Holmes," I protested.

"Doctor Watson, this Colonel Fisk was only recently returned from India. Several men testify to the presence of a mysterious fakir or hindoo Thug lurking around his home. The mandarins of the Foreign Office expect answers about the murder. You are the only fellow I know who has experience of the place where Fisk spent ten years in military service and who knows something of the people out there. And you understand forensic investigation. Won't you help agents of your Queen and Country solve this mystery?"

This was an appeal for which there could be no denial.

What would Sherlock Holmes do? I was acutely aware of my lack of experience in his investigations. I felt like a sham accompanying Lestrade to Logan Fisk's recently leased and re-named Cubbon Lodge [5] on the Upper Thames, and raking over the remains of the burned-out shell.

"The fire was discovered about three-twenty this morning," he told me, as if I was Holmes. We shouldered our way through the police fire-fighters who were tidying away their pump-engine and coconut matting. "The house-boy gave the alarm, being woken by the smoke. The flames began in the gun-room, we think. That's where we found Fisk's body. The domestics all got out through the back."

There were four servants, huddled miserably in blankets as they must have been since early morning. They were a cook and gardener couple, a housemaid, and the alert page boy. All had been in service only three weeks, hired when Fisk had first taken the cottage upon his return from Bangalore.

I heard what they had to say on the mysterious Indian. Each had been separately approached while they were away from the lodge-house by a tall, swarthy, turbaned foreigner with good English who had tried to question them about their employer. Money had been proffered. His questions had been about the layout of the house, about what visitors Fisk had received, about the Colonel's daily routine, and about when and where he went when he left Cubbon Lodge.

None of the staff admitted to taking a bribe and supplying the stranger with answers. All of them had reported the approaches to Colonel Fisk, who had questioned them closely about the Indian. Fisk had found it significant that the fellow had worn a yellow neckerchief.

"It wasn't just them that were questioned," Lestrade told me. "Fisk's luggage and furniture came back with him on the boat, of course. It seems that the same foreigner accosted some of the crew who unloaded it. That's where accounts of the weird dagger come from, those meetings on the docks. And this fellow disappeared without a trace when somebody tried to follow him, which is why they thought him a *hoodoo*-man."

We viewed the body, but it was a charred ruin. The best I could offer was to confirm that, yes, there were signs that some cuts had been made to the epidermis *pre-mortem*, and they were consistent with cruel knife-work. I suggested that the body be examined for poisons, though I didn't know if any such traces would survive a roasting. Holmes would know.

It occurred to me to ask the servants the same questions that the Indian had. They revealed that Fisk was an employer of irregular habits. He left the house without notice and was sometimes gone overnight – the gardener thought there might be a woman involved. His only visitors were four military men, old comrades who had retired with him. All of them had shipped home together at the end of their service. They had come to dinner on four occasions. One or two of them had called at other times.

A uniformed constable drew Lestrade's attention to something the fire-fighters had spotted. On the charred wall of the former gun-room were the burned ash rectangles where a series of Fisk's framed pictures had hung. The servants confirmed that these were old prints from the Colonel's Indian service and daguerreotypes of people he had known there. We were able to trace three gaps in the burned silhouettes, where nails were knocked to hang pictures but no frame had burned.

"They were removed before the fire was set," I realised.

Nobody could remember what those particular images had been.

"I wish I could be of more help," I assured Lestrade when we had finished pacing the ruined cottage and questioning the survivors. "I suppose you have a watch set for this supposed fakir?"

"Of course. But you know the docks. London Basin is the busiest port in the world. At any time there are hundreds, probably thousands, of mysterious foreigners teeming about there. Plenty of them wear turbans and dress strangely. How can we tell one from the other?"

"Perhaps you should go back to the Foreign Office fellows who set you on?" I suggested. "Why are they so particular to have this crime solved? I mean, yes, one wants to catch the fellow who murdered a retired soldier, but what draws so much political attention?"

Lestrade reluctantly agreed to brave the superiors who had placed him on the case. He did not relish exposing his lack of progress to them.

So pitiable did he look, stood in the ashes of Cubbon Lodge, that I agreed to discuss the matter again with him tomorrow. It was the least comfort I could offer.

Perhaps Holmes would have returned by then?

I was checking Holmes's volumes of Hart's Army Lists [6] regarding Colonel Fisk when Gregson appeared the next day. The inspector was even more ruddy-faced than before, giving me concern for his health.

"A letter has been received by the O'Tierneys," he revealed. "A ransom note of sorts. If they do not purchase back their family tiara, it will be cut up for its gems and gold and sold separately."

"The thief is bold," I admitted. "How would such a fee be paid?"

"In uncut gemstones, delivered to a distinctive rock on the coast and left there. It is a well-selected spot, bleak and open, which would make it difficult to lie in wait for the criminal."

"Everything else that he stole is untraceable," I observed. "Bearer bonds, foreign currency, and small diamonds. Now he converts the one notable piece of loot into something that cannot be tracked either."

"It means he needs no intermediary to 'fence' the plunder. The chap is devilishly cunning."

"Is there any further development on how he might have accessed the sealed rooms and safes?"

Gregson looked sullen. "Ordinarily I would look at the man who holds the keys. But four such dishonest stewards? And three of them family men who were at home during the times of the thefts, attested by kin and servants. And yet somehow the burglar defeated the finest locks, even a combination safe, and came away with his prizes, all unseen."

"The night-guard at Esperson's?"

"Wide-eyed and vigilant, he says. He seemed credible enough when I questioned him." The inspector scowled unhappily. "Have you been able to discover anything through Holmes's contacts?"

Wiggins had reported to me only an hour before, but the street-urchin had not relished the idea of answering to the Scotland Yard officer in person. "The burglar's deeds are known amongst the criminal classes, if not by the general public. There is much discussion in low quarters as to his identity. The consensus is that he must be new in town, some outside talent. Quiet enquiries are being made by the villainous fraternity, either to recruit or remove him."

"Not one of the regulars, then?"

"If there had been a fellow of such talents on the loose in London for long, would we not have encountered him before?" I pondered. "And don't forget the numbered calling cards, the receipts. That is something new."

"Then . . . he might not even be *in* Holmes's indexes." Gregson sounded crestfallen. "We *must* find Holmes."

I had learned much of my fellow lodger's habits in our months together. "Holmes has a talent for disguise, sharpened by some time as a thespian, and an ear for accents. He can pass as a barrow-boy or old tar, as a grumpy major or a gullible toff. He can vanish into the *demi-monde*, hearing and seeing all but

36

never raising suspicion. He knows the back alleys and hidden courtyards of London as well as any man alive. He has many contacts, aides, allies in every walk of life, cultivated to assist him with whatever endeavour her undertakes. We are unlikely to be able to discover him."

Indeed, I had ventured to suggest that Wiggins and his Irregulars might locate Sherlock Holmes, but the ragamuffin had refused. "If Mister 'Olmes is 'iding out, then 'e's got good reason for it," Wiggins assured me. "'E won't go thanking us for givin' 'im away."

"And if he isn't hiding?"

"Then why is them fellows watching 'is 'ouse?" the lad challenged me.

"What fellows? Where?"

Wiggins had pointed them out to me, a surly-looking fellow selling bootlaces along the far side of the street and an idler with a newspaper who wandered past every ten minutes or so.

I had suggested accosting the blighters and seeing what they were about. Wiggins advised against it. "If Mr. 'Olmes don't want 'em to know 'e's onto 'em, it's best to let them bide, sir. But the lads'll follow 'em when they goes off and see where they ends up."

For this reason I did not mention the surveillance to Gregson. Indeed, the bootlace vendor and the pavement reader had both vanished while the Scotland Yard man was visiting.

The choleric detective was still unhappily baffled. "Something must be done. I need some break in this case – before it breaks me!"

"Holmes would study the scenes," I considered. "He might inspect the locks for signs of scrapes where tools were used, and from that deduce the distinctive technique of the cracksman. There may be some tread-mark, some disturbed object, some grease-smear or lost thread that opens up lines of investigation."

"Well, *he* might," Gregson grudged, "but he isn't here to do that, is he? We've been over the sites many times, pulling everything apart for clues. There's nothing!"

I imagined Holmes's comments on the police searches. But in the great detective's absence, what else was there to do?"

I was at a loss, but felt I must make some suggestion. "There may be another burglary. If so, then seal the scene. Bring in a scent-hound to discover any trail. Seek witnesses from people whose business takes them out at night – the cabbies and night-soil collectors, even the streetwalkers. Perhaps you might even find some old criminal who has served his time for burglary and see if he can suggest how the deed was done?"

Gregson snorted at the idea of resorting to housebreakers and harlots, but he was become desperate. Whatever reply he might have made was interrupted as the page announced another visitor.

Inspector Lestrade had arrived. He and Gregson eyed each other like dogs who disliked intruders on their territory. Gregson was by the hearth so Lestrade took position by the bow window.

"Holmes is not here," Gregson deigned to inform his fellow officer. "Still."

Lestrade' sharp close-together eyes glowered. "I see that. I'm here for Dr. Watson."

"You're still no further with the Fisk murder, then."

"And you're stuck on the burglaries."

"I have a number of lines of enquiry."

"So do I."

Gregson shrugged, as if his rival was not worth his time. "Thank you for your comments, Doctor. I must be off. *My* case was given me by the Chief Constable himself."

"Mine came by fiat of the Foreign Office," Lestrade topped him. "Colonel Fisk was a man of consequence, well known to several senior civil servants to whom he had directly reported during his time overseas."

I remembered the army lists. "Fisk led a small unit of detached men on intelligence operations. He spoke the native tongue well enough to pass as local. He was commended for his work during the riots and uprisings of the Madras Famine."

I shuddered as I spoke. No one could pass through India as I had and not hear of the great famine that had struck during '76 to '78 in the southwestern provinces of Madras and Bombay, and in the princely states of Mysore and Hyderabad. The shortages covered 257,000 square miles, starved 58,500,000 people. Five-and-a-half-million died. And yet during the famine, the Viceroy Lord Lytton exported a record 6.4 million-hundredweight [7] of wheat to Britain, and the supposed Famine Commissioner for the Government of India made harsh cutbacks in who received aid. [8] It was hardly the Empire's finest hour.

"I don't know what he was up to out there, but it got him a medal, and it means that there's important people paying attention to this case," Lestrade insisted.

Gregson relented enough to allow one mildly sympathetic glance at his fellow officer. "They don't realise how tough it can be to crack some cases," he admitted.

"Has the coroner done his work?" I ventured.

Lestrade looked discomfited. "Yes. There was something in the colonel's blood and stomach – *datura*. The Thugee's drug."

"Your fellow was poisoned then, not stabbed to death," Gregson suggested.

"Datura doesn't usually kill," I enlightened him. "It makes one delirious, perhaps to hallucinate. A man might seem drunk or lunatic. Soldiers sent to quell a seventeenth century rebellion in Jamestown, Virginia, famously made a salad of it without realising its properties, and spent several days as naked madmen." [9]

"The substance was used to incapacitate, then. Or to make Fisk vulnerable to questioning."

"But the method of his death, the slow knife-torture, was the mark of the Thugee," Lestrade insisted.

"You have not found your inquisitive Indian, then?" I asked.

"Indians we have found, and plenty of them. The one Indian we especially seek . . . who can say? We may have questioned him and let him slip away again."

Gregson's compassion was exhausted. "I daresay a proper search will turn the fellow up, and then the full story will come out. My own mystery is a much harder nut to crack."

"Your mystery? The only question is how long you will flounder until Sherlock Homes turns up!"

It was clear that no more was going to come of the discussion, so I threw the detectives out and returned to my own work.

A little after five that same afternoon, I received a note of hand from a small girl who knocked anxiously at our back door to deliver her missive. I recognised one of Wiggins' barefoot accomplices and tipped her a half-crown for her efforts.

The letter was hardly more than a note, an edge-scrap torn from some pocket-book, but I recognised Holmes's handwriting:

Walk south along Baker Street at 7 p.m. sharp. Jump into the cab that stops for you at Portman Square. Speak to the person to whom the cab delivers you – S.H.

Intrigued by those odd instructions, and reasoning that the precaution was to abstract me from Baker Street without my being traced, I followed Holmes's directions to the letter. As the hall clock struck seven, I parted from Mrs. Hudson and began my perambulation.

I immediately saw the bootlace merchant, still lurking in a doorway across the way. He was stooping to disguise his height, as Holmes often did, but this fellow was broader, stockier. Upright he would have topped six foot. He kept a workman's cap pulled well over his brow.

As I followed the pavement, I became aware of the man with the newspaper, idling along behind me. There was also a covered dray standing further up the road, with a suspiciously alert-looking driver.

My shoulder-blades tingled, as they did in the Maiwand Valley when some murderous Afghan was aiming his Jezail rifle at my back. It was not a comfortable walk.

A smart two-wheeler rattled down behind me, swerving round the parked dray, and pulled up featly beside me by the green garden of Portman Square. "Cab for Doctor Watson!" the driver called.

I leaped aboard. At once the coachman shook his reigns and set the cabriolet [10] surging forward at speed. The dray sprang after us, confirming my suspicion that it was also part of the watch.

I checked the cabbie who cornered us into Portman Street to see whether it was Sherlock Holmes in disguise, but was

41

disappointed. Unless the dedicated detective had shaved his head and pulled out several teeth, he was not the madman driving this hansom.

"Jus' 'old on, sir, an' I'll 'ave these fellers off'a us in no time!" he promised. He slid the cab round a tight turn into one of the old cobbled service roads behind George Street. The narrow alley had back gardens on one side and stable blocks on the other and was scarcely wide enough to pass. The larger pursuing dray would have had even more trouble, but as it began to navigate the passage one of the stable doors opened and a resident began to navigate his trap out, completely blocking the vehicle that followed us.

"That was deliberate," I recognised. "Holmes set it up."

"Yus, sir." The cab drew away from our thwarted pursuers. We swerved across Oxford Street, down Park Street where we blended with dozens of other cabs taking people on their evening constitutionals, and onto Piccadilly. "Mr. 'Olmes says you are to 'op off 'ere," he told me as we pulled in beside Green Park. "You're to 'ead along Queen's Walk, all the way into St James' Park. Go to the Blue Bridge and wait in the middle. Talk to the fellow what comes to see you."

"Not to Holmes?"

The cabbie shrugged. "That's as I were told, sir."

"And I don't suppose you were told who those men watching in Baker Street were? Or what they wanted?"

The driver had no further useful information, except that he was to continue on through the city as if he were still conveying me, to further frustrate pursuit. I tipped him, slipped onto the kerb, and passed into the heavily-treed Green Park where my passage would be screened from the road. [11]

It was a fine autumn evening and the park was well populated with promenaders. I made my way along the straight footpath of Queen's Walk, trying to apprehend whether I was being watched or followed. There were too many bypassers to have any real chance of knowing. I wondered whether Holmes was also watching me – there was a limping newspaper vendor there, a portly doorman, a shabby tinker, a strolling ostler. Was I the bait to let him spy out some enemy who was spying on me?

I slipped from Green Park across the newly-opened Mall [12] into St James', leaving the path and threading through the trees onto the lawn, to better get an idea of anyone who was following me. I cut down to the lake, trying to look like any visitor who wished to go and visit the pelicans. [13]

There were people crossing the suspension bridge, of course, and quite a few idlers tossing bread to the birds. I positioned myself halfway across and waited for contact.

After ten minutes I was beginning to wonder whether something had gone amiss. The whole affair seemed slightly ridiculous. Was this a prank? But then a well-tanned barrel-chested fellow approached me and asked, "Doctor Watson?"

I admitted to my identity. "And you, sir?"

"Sargeant Farnley, sir, late of the _____shires."

That was Fisk's regiment. "You have recently come from India," I surmised, feeling a little like Sherlock Holmes.

"Yes sir. I was with the garrison at the Bangalore Cantonment. [14] I returned home just a short while ago, after discharge."

"On the same ship as Colonel Fisk?"

"The *Homer*, sir, yes." The retired sergeant paused, looking stiff and uncomfortable. "I was instructed to give you my testimony, sir."

I realised that on the bridge in full view of the evening strollers we could see any approach and were as anonymous and private as if we had met in some club – perhaps more so. "Instructed by Sherlock Holmes?"

"Yes sir. Mr. Holmes tracked me down at the boarding house where I had taken lodgings and was kind enough to fund my removal to a different one. He asked me to repeat to you the account that I gave to him of some events in Mysore last year."

I noticed that the old soldier was keeping a careful watch on the lines of approach, much as my orderly Murray used to do back in our service.

"You knew Colonel Fisk?" I ventured.

Farnley nodded. "I was one of the staff in his headquarters, the Intelligence Office. The Snoopers Shop, we called it."

I wondered how much Farnley was allowed to tell me about such matters. My limited experience of those spy-wallahs was that they liked to keep their secrets.

Something odd occurred to me. "Fisk returned to England with four brother officers. Were they all Snoopers?"

"Yes sir. Colonel Fisk and Captains Levett, Shackleman, Dennis, and Selby."

"And how many others were officers in their unit?"

"No others, sir. That was all of them. The unit was closed down."

That seemed stranger still. "They were all commended, decorated, for their effort during the Famine, for work against rebels in the hills of the Western Ghats." [15]

"Aye, sir, we were."

"You were there? You'd better tell me what Holmes wanted you to repeat."

"Yes sir. Well, you know how the famine hit the southwest. People like skellingtons, too weak to even brush the flies off their eyes. Thousands dying, and others turning to banditry and raiding to survive. It were a busy time for the Intelligence Office."

44

"Your chaps would pass themselves as natives and go amongst the crowds, listening and watching. Visiting informers."

Farnley nodded. "And a bit more than that, sir. The Snoopers liked to get ahead of trouble if they could, by making it happen a bit early."

I frowned. "You mean they fomented rebellion so as to weed out the troublemakers?"

"Well, maybe. It weren't my bit of the job. We NCO's just took out the squads what did the arrests. I wasn't part of the interrogation team."

Another aspect of the intelligence division that I disliked was their use of what, in other circumstances, would be described as bloody torture. I doubt that Her Majesty would be pleased to know that such things were done in the name of Queen and Country.

"Well, sir, one of the prisoners blabbed about an organised cell of rebels over in the Animali Forest – that's up in the Ghats, forty miles east of Madurai, something over two-hundred miles off Bengalore. There'd been quite a bit of trouble there, including some railways lines pulled up to stop the trains. These rebels were better organised than most, it seems, and they'd holed up in some old temple or stronghold from the Thugee days."

"Had they now?"

"Yes sir. And they were better equipped, too, than the raggedy desperates who were raiding the farms and granaries, which meant they had money behind them. Proper weapons and a bit of leadership – those were bad signs."

I agreed that they were. "What did Colonel Fisk do?"

"It took a bit of time, but he eventually worked out where they must be. There was some old accounts in journals from the time when the Thugs were suppressed that gave him clues, evidently, and I know some natives were brought in for hard questioning. Eventually, just a month before rainy season, [16] we set off with an expedition to Animali, the five officers and about a hundred of our company for support. And me."

"To hunt these bandits in a former Thugee stronghold."

"We had a devil of a time finding it, despite the old diaries. You know the terrain, sir, with no track lasting longer than a season. I don't know if you've seen the hills there, with thick forests and stalking tigers and venomous snakes, but it's hard going even if you're sure of your route. We lost three men in there just to reach the site. But at last we found this old ruin, something of a stone temple maybe, judging by some carvings that showed some right goings-on. The place was half-reclaimed by the jungle, but it was a rebel camp alright."

I thought back to the scant line of information in Fisk's Hart's entry. "The Colonel led an attack."

"He did. We came in by night and took them just as dawn came up. But they was expecting us – it being hard to sneak a hundred men through that sort of terrain – so it all became a horrid mess. I suppose we weren't used to going into prepared positions that were held as well as any proper fortress. Those rebels were properly armed too, with Pattern 853 Enfields – not the Indian Service ones we gave to our native regiments after the Mutiny, that were deliberately less good, but the proper British versions. [17] We ended up in a right old firefight."

I could well imagine it, that confused exchange of lethal shots where all semblance of co-ordination and order was lost and there was only mayhem and death. I had seen it and survived it – barely.

"We won in the end," Farnley told me. "It was a heavy butcher's bill. We lost forty-three men and nineteen wounded as eventually recovered. Captain Dennis was hit in the shoulder but he survived. But we killed close to two-hundred rebels, in the fighting or by execution after. We caught their leaders too, including some princeling with an Eton education and ideas above his station."

"So Fisk was commended for suppressing the dangerous bandits, but censured for the heavy cost in lives," I supposed.

"Well, that too, sir. But when they questioned this prince chap about where the money came from, I mean money to buy all those guns – and they had a field piece as well, though it was never used – well, after some persuasion with hot tools his 'ighness revealed that there was a Thugee loot cache in the old temple. There was actual treasure hidden in a secret room!"

I raised my brows. "Did you discover it?"

"Well, the officers tried to keep it quiet, but you know how troops are. There were guards in on the interrogation, and soon news was all around camp. But Colonel Fisk kept discipline. 'There's procedures about this, boys,' he told us. 'There'll be a prize share for all when we bring this back to the Cantonment.' And then we found the secret door to a room no bigger than a cupboard really, but there was gold and silver, jewellery and gems, like a maharajah's store!"

There had been no record of that in Hart's. "What became of it?"

"We took it back, of course, under strict guard. Captain Shackleman, he said he thought it must be worth fifty-thousand pounds, and three-quarters of that would come to the men who found it. The NCO's would be in for a tenth, and by then there was just two of us still alive, and even the privates would get maybe four-hundred pounds apiece. [18] We all thought as we'd be rich men."

"I take it that was not the case?"

Farnley shook his head bitterly. "I don't know the full story. Politics, I suppose, but this princeling was somebody important, and it didn't go down well with the Indian posh-

47

knobs that he'd been tortured, killed, and robbed. Things was already tricky with the famine and that, and by then the government back in England was looking closely at how things were being handled. So in the end the treasure wasn't confiscated by the army and divvied up with prizes like it should have been. It was handed back to this prince's relatives, to shut them up, I suppose."

"How did Fisk take that?" I wondered.

"Not well, according to camp gossip. Cut up rough, he did, and evidently made threats to the higher-ups, saying he knew things that they'd want to keep quiet and that. I suppose he did. The Snoopers knew where all the bodies were buried. But it didn't do him no good. Within months he'd got his discharge papers and all his cronies with him – and the rest of us, because we might be 'disaffected' – by which they meant sore at being cheated of spoils of war we bled and died for. And so we were shipped home on the *Homer*, and here we are."

"So there might be Indians, wealthy and powerful Indians, with reason to dislike Colonel Fisk?"

"I reckon so. Him and his buddies. But I'm not waiting around to see what happens next. Mr. Holmes has arranged for a train ticket to be waiting for me at Paddington, and then I'm gone from London for good. I'm not hanging about to get tortured to death."

"You think the man who killed Fisk might hunt for others? For you?"

Farnley shrugged. "I don't know who killed the Colonel. But I know his pals are dangerous men, and angry ones. When we was on the *Homer*, Captain Levett had a quiet word with me. Did I want to make some money when we got back home, to make up for what was owed us, what we'd had stolen from us? There was a place for loyal men with proper training and

48

discipline if I cared to try my hand. Well, I didn't care to try it and said so – it sounded very dodgy to me, sir."

"They were planning something illegal?"

"I didn't ask for details, sir. The Snoopers aren't squeamish about burying loose ends. I just said no and determined to lie low until I could vanish. When I heard about the Colonel, I was frightened worse. And then Mr. Holmes found me, and if he could, then the Captains could. So . . . that's my story, sir. And why I'm off and away, while I can."

"Did the Captains talk to anyone else returning on the *Homer*?"

"I don't know, sir. If they did, they'd be quiet about it." He glanced along the bridge, as if nervous to see Snoopers creeping up on him. "I need to be off, sir."

I thanked the fellow and let him go. As he hastened away towards Horse Guards, I pondered his remarkable testimony. I began to see why Holmes might have felt it better to disappear. Four well-trained and experienced intelligence agents on some kind of spree might well object to a competent investigation into their present activities. The watch set on Baker Street suggested that they knew of his interest.

I wondered why Holmes might have needed me to hear Farnley's story. Was my friend worried for his life and wanted another person to know what he had discovered? Or . . . .

The revelation came to me belatedly. A squad of well-trained Snoopers, versed in infiltration and all kinds of dirty deeds, were now loose in London. Lestrade was investigating the murder of their former commander. Gregson was hunting some likely-new gang of burglars who were performing incredible heists and leaving receipts for the cash they took. Were they seeking to steal fifty thousand pounds-worth of compensation?

Somebody in the Foreign Office had presumably made the decision to return the Thugee horde to that princeling's family for political expedience. Somebody there knew what the discharged Snoopers were capable of. Gregson had been set on to the hunt but had not been warned of the tigers he was stalking.

Holmes was warning me to warn the Scotland Yard men. They faced not two cases but one.

"Levett, Shackleman, Dennis, and Selby," Gregson repeated. "Where are they, Lestrade?"

"Vanished," the other detective inspector answered. "We assumed they were hiding from this mysterious fakir. Instead they may be out there plotting more crimes."

"These were men accustomed to passing amongst the people of India in native dress," I pointed out. "Any one of them might be the fakir."

"Why would they kill Fisk, though?" demanded Gregson. "Did he try and stop their burglaries?"

"This sergeant that Dr. Watson spoke with feared for his life enough to leave London," Lestrade noted. "Farnley presumably knew what his officers were capable of."

I revealed another worry. "If the Snoopers really feel that they are owed fifty-thousand pounds by an ungrateful nation, then there is plenty more thievery to come."

"And we still have no proof that Levett and company were actually behind any of it – the thefts or the Cubbon Lodge fire," Gregson complained. "Still, now we have suspects we can begin to – "

"To search in all the places this Thugee fellow has already searched!" Lestrade interrupted him.

The two detectives glared at each other across the length of the Baker Street fireplace. They shared the same frustration but not much else.

"It occurs to me that Holmes's disappearance has not prevented him from investigating this case," I observed, to keep the peace. "His absence is likely entirely due to his involvement. The watchers on this house – gone now, so we cannot question them – are a sign that these felons wish to get Holmes before he gets them. And yet Holmes was able to locate Farnley, the man whose testimony links your two mysteries together. Surely even now he is working to bring your cases to resolution."

The idea both comforted and annoyed the Scotland Yard men. "I don't doubt but that proper routine work would have come to the same conclusion in the end," Lestrade sniffed. "Holmes is merely unhampered by Judge's Rules and judicial oversight."

"This is all theory anyhow," Gregson criticised. "These officers were behind the thefts? That does not explain by what magic they walked through locked doors and came unseen into top-rate vaults. These off-the-books soldiers might have skills, yes, but why would they be taught safe-cracking?"

"And why drug and torture Fisk before he died, to resemble a Thugee execution? Or burn his house?"

I had no answers for those questions. I was fumbling for something else placatory to say when Mrs. Hudson rapped on the door. She entered looking a little pale, and our maid and page were with her.

Behind them came three strangers, all of a military aspect, despite their new civilian clothing. They carried .422-calibre Beaumont Adams service revolvers like my own, and they ushered our staff to join the inspectors and me in our sitting room.

"I'm sorry, sirs," Mrs. Hudson apologised as if there had been a spot on our breakfast tray tablecloth. "These gentleman were insistent to come up here and see you."

Lestrade saw the guns and would have charged the intruders anyway, but Gregson held him back. "Steady," he advised his rival. "There's no chance."

I had come to the same conclusion. The trio had spread out around the room, one by the door and the others covering us from opposite corners. They held their weapons like professionals and looked exactly as deadly as one might expect from a crack military unit.

"What's the meaning of your intrusion, sirs?" I demanded.

One of the men levelled his pistol at me. "I think the conclusion should be fairly obvious, Dr. Watson. You have picked an unfortunate fellow-lodger with whom to share your chambers."

"And you are pointing firearms at members of the Metropolitan Constabulary," Gregson warned them. "Do you think we don't know who you are, Snoopers? Levett, Shackleman, Dennis, and Selby . . . . where's the fourth of you?"

One of the intruders sneered at the florid policeman. "Selby? Selby's dead. Selby had second thoughts about our retirement operation."

"Another murder to your name!" Lestrade accused them.

The speaker amongst the renegade officers seemed to find that amusing. "What's one more, Inspector? If you know those names, then you know about Animali, about what we endured there. And about how we were betrayed by our superiors and our government."

"Soldiers sometimes suffer," I admitted. "It's no licence for mutiny, or for crime."

"Is it not? We'll have to disagree. We are owed, for service to our nation, for the blood of comrades, for the stupidity of our leaders. You're an old India hand, Doctor. You saw the poor choices that were made in the retreat from Kabul, the bloody mess at Maiwand. We saw the greed and ambition of politicians and of generals who might as well be politicians kill millions of the natives of Madras and Bombay. What now of our moral claim that we British are better suited to rule the Sub-continent than the indigenous princes? We did our murder more efficiently, I suppose. But in the end we faltered and appeased the princes and maharajahs, though it was not the great and noble who paid the cost. It was men like those you see here, and the common troops under us."

I could not tell whether the man was condemning the Empire for its behaviour or for flinching from absolute tyranny.

I indicated that Mrs. Hudson and our maid should take seats on our couch. "I apologise for the disruption," I told our landlady.

"It's not your fault, Dr. Watson," she told me resolutely, and cast a scorching stare over the invaders on her domain. "I imagine Mr. Holmes will deal with them right enough."

"What do you hope to accomplish by coming here?" Lestrade demanded of the soldiers. "Even if you silence us – especially if you silence us – you will never escape."

"That's true," I agreed. "Holmes is on to you. He is closing in."

"He got to Sergeant Farnley," our captor agreed. "That was annoying. But you three haven't worked out yet how we managed our robberies."

"I'll take your confession," Gregson assured them. "Anything you say will be taken down and used in evidence against you."

I glanced at each of the three armed men who occupied our home. "This is how you did it," I realised. "No lock-picking necessary! You simply came to the houses of the men who had the keys, who knew the guard routines. You held them at gunpoint while one of you visited the business premises and perpetrated the theft. Did the families even know that they were hostage for your successful burglaries, or was it just the key-holders themselves? Did you make those men fear for their loved ones if they ever admitted what you had done?"

Gregson's lips pulled back in a snarl. "You forced them to be your accomplices!"

"Of course!" Lestrade spat. "These aren't house-breakers. They're spies, torturers, and strong-arm bullies. That's how they did their jobs – by threat of force."

"If you like," our captor agreed. "But it's worked well for us so far, and we have much more to raise for our retirements before we're done. The quiet men in the Foreign Office who did us dirty will bitterly regret their weaselling. And threat of force will work for us again here, now."

"He wants to hold us 'ere until Mr. Holmes turns himself over to them," Mrs. Hudson guessed. "They couldn't find him, so they'll make him come to them."

"Holmes set a watch on this place just as we did," another of the soldiers spoke – I learned later that it was Levett. "He had those tramp-children on lookout. He'll know soon enough that we came here, and if he's smart he'll know better than to involve more police."

"I regret for the necessity," their leader told me. "Especially I apologise to you, Dr. Watson. I'd have preferred not to harm a brother officer. But we must be ruthless. Holmes cannot be allowed to carry on hunting us. Already our men are unnerved by the Thugee spectre."

My head jerked up. Of course Holmes would adopt a disguise to pursue these renegades. What better way to obfuscate identification than to assume an identity that suggested the vengeance of that princeling's family, or the vengeful last remnant of the suppressed Thugee? Holmes's delight in the theatrical sometimes got the better of him.

"Then the fakir did not kill Fisk," Lestrade concluded. "It was you men."

Another smirk from the Snoopers' leader. It was enough confirmation.

"Nobody killed Fisk," I suggested to the intruder who'd done most of the speaking. "*You* are Fisk. You killed Captain Selby. You drugged and murdered him when Selby cavilled at the plan, and chose the method of death to turn the manhunt on the Indian who was chasing you. You burned your own house down to cover your tracks, keeping only certain prized mementoes that you could not bear to sacrifice."

The Scotland Yard men's relentless accusing gazes grew harder yet.

"We also had to know if Selby warned anyone about our plans," Levett added.

I sneered at Fisk. "You are no brother officer of mine. You're a disgrace to your regiment and to the service."

"The regiment and service disgraced themselves first," Colonel Fisk snapped back.

There was a rap on the door, and a deep Cockney voice called out, "Oy, in there! I'm sent up by Captain Dennis, to bring you this 'ere Indian bloke!"

Fisk gestured wordlessly to his comrades. I was impressed by their instant and co-ordinated response. Levett checked the window then took position covering all of us hostages. Fisk and Shackleman flanked the door, covering anyone who entered. Only then did their leader call, "Come in."

A scarred pugilist of a docker pushed the fake Thugee through the door. The Indian wore a turban and a long coat over native fig and a yellow scarf. The prisoner looked as if he had taken a heavy blow to the head. He swayed from side to side, only kept upright by the bruiser who held his bound wrists.

"Captain Dennis says this is the fellow what you put out that reward for," the wharf-scum crowed.

Fisk grabbed the Thugee by his coat lapels and pushed him roughly to the floor. "Mr. Sherlock Holmes," he crowed.

"Actually, no, Colonel Fisk," said the docker in quite different tones. "That would be me."

He produced from his coat a small round bomb with a burning fuse and tossed it directly at Logan Fisk's feet.

"Grenade!" the soldier shouted, diving for what cover there was behind Holmes's work-table. Levett and Shackleman moved almost as quickly, trying to find places to evade the spraying shrapnel of the deadly gunpowder-filled sphere.

"Now, Watson!" Holmes called at me. He jumped over to Fisk and downed the distracted fellow with a perfectly-positioned haymaker.

I launched myself out of my chair and caught Levett amidships, recalling my rugby days and having no mercy. The soldier tumbled down still grasping his gun, so I rattled his teeth for him and stamped hard on his radius until it snapped.

Lestrade and Gregson were slower off the mark, but as Shackleman comprehended that the bomb was a dud as fake as the fakir that the disguised Holmes had led in, the Scotland Yard men swarmed the last rogue and brought him down with fists and boots. His Beaumont Adams skittered across the floor. Mrs. Hudson halted it under her shoe.

56

Less than a minute after Holmes's entry, the Snoopers were pinned down and Lestrade and Gregson were holding them quiet with the guns they had dropped. "There's a fourth man who was keeping watch outside," Holmes advised them. "I incapacitated Dennis first. A number of my Irregular assistants are sitting on him."

Lestrade looked at the Indian who was getting up from the rug and wiping fake blood from his face. "And who is this?"

"An old stage associate from my day on the boards. He consented to play the role of the Thugee for this performance, since I had to star as the brutish dock idler. Mr. Crowther, thank you for your portrayal. Here is your fee. Please do not drink it all at once, old chap."

"You knew they were coming for us," I realised.

"Yes. I apologise to you all for that. I had underestimated their ruthlessness and how little they would care for the conventions of civilised England. It seems that I still have things to master in this consultancy business. Once I knew of their intent, I had to act quickly to thwart them."

"They'll get the reward they deserve from the Empire now," Lestrade promised, "at the end of six feet of noose."

"I regret little," Fisk told us. "Only that I didn't kill you in time, Sherlock Holmes."

"A regret I trust you will share with many others in the years to come," I told him.

"You do not then regret your choice of friend, Watson?" Holmes asked me, with the slightest note of trepidation.

"I consider myself privileged to uphold the honour of our nation and the rule of law," I assured him, "and to have your confidence that I would act when the time was right."

"Sturdy fellow! Inspectors, you have your men, and they will lead you to their lesser accomplices and their ill-gotten gains. This matter is effectively closed, and is no longer of interest to me. I require a change of clothes, a good shave, and a good bath, and then another problem. Mrs. Hudson, I apologise again for this unwarranted interruption in your domestic routine."

I reviewed the array of captured criminals in our sitting room and recognised that my recovery days were unlikely to be always idle. There are worse forms of therapy than thwarting traitors to crown and country.

"Yes, well," our landlady replied to Sherlock Holmes, "I'd better see about getting a fresh pot of tea sent up. That one will have gone quite cold."

NOTES

1 – This would eventually become *A Study in Scarlet* (1887), Dr Watson's first published account of the great detective's work.

2 – Holmes historians generally reconcile different references in Watson's military career by assessing him as first being an assistant-surgeon to the Fifth Northumberland Fusiliers, dispatched to India at the outbreak of the Second Afghan War, and then being attached to the 66th Regiment of Foot, the Berkshires, before the Battle of Maiwand on 27th July, 1880.

3 – The Indian Thugees and Dacoits were organised criminal fraternities that survived by robbery and ransom. They traditionally perpetrated ritualised mutilation and murder on their victims. Ziau-d din Barni's *History of Firoz Shah* (c.1356) includes an account of Sultan Jalaluddin Khilji arresting and deporting one-thousand Thugs, and reads as if the organised criminal fraternity was already a matter of common knowledge. The power of the gangs was finally broken by the British administration's *Thuggee and Dacoity Suppression Acts*, 1836–1848, which increased the penalties for Thugee crimes, and by military action.

4 – *Datura stramonium* is also known as Jimson's Weed, Jamestown's Weed, Devil's Snare, Devil's Trumpet, Devil's Weed, Devil's Cucumber, Thornapple, Moon Flower, Talolache, Hell's Bells, Tolguacha, Stinkweed, Locoweed, Pricklyburr, and False Castor.

5 – Fisk presumably named his house after Lieutenant-General Sir Mark Cubbon KCB (1775-1861), the British Commissioner of Mysore state, or more likely after Cubbon Park (now Sri Chamarajendra Park) in the heart of Bangalore, named after the administrator.

6 – These annual and quarterly lists of the members of the British Army and their accomplishments began in 1840 and continue to the present day. The original format has never altered through two-hundred editions.

7 – 320,000 tons.

8 – In 1878, the Famine Commissioner for the Government of India, Sir Richard Temple, imposed stricter qualification standards for relief, and more meagre relief rations. The "Temple wage" for a day's hard work in the Madras and Bombay relief camps was one pound of grain plus one *anna* (one-sixteenth of a rupee) for a man, and a slightly

reduced amount for a woman or working child. Viceroy Lord Lytton supported Temple against critics, arguing that *"Everything must be subordinated to the financial consideration of disbursing the smallest sum of money."*

By early 1877, Temple proclaimed that he had put *"the famine under control"*. Critic William Digby noted that *"A famine can scarcely be said to be adequately controlled which leaves one-fourth of the people dead."* In the second half of 1878, an epidemic of malaria killed many more who were already weakened by malnutrition.

The long-term consequences of the mishandled situation included migration of many Indians to British tropical colonies as indentured labour, and the foundation of the Indian National Congress, which began a new generation of Indian nationalism and eventually led to independence.

9 – Watson is referring to Robert Beverly Jr's *The History and Present State of Virginia, Book II: Of the Natural Product and Conveniencies in Its Unimprov'd State, Before the English Went Thither* (1705), which describes the 1676 "Baker's Rebellion". His colourful account reveals that:

> *. . . some of them ate plentifully of [the weed], the effect of which was a very pleasant comedy, for they turned natural fools upon it for several days: One would blow up a feather in the air; another would dart straws at it with much fury; and another, stark naked, was sitting up in a corner like a monkey, grinning and making mows (grimaces) at them; a fourth would fondly kiss and paw his companions, and sneer in their faces with a countenance more antic than any in a Dutch droll.*
> *In this frantic condition they were confined, lest they should, in their folly, destroy themselves – though it was observed that all their actions were full of innocence and good nature. Indeed, they were not very cleanly; for they would have wallowed in their own excrements, if they had not been prevented. A thousand such simple tricks they played, and after eleven days returned themselves again, not remembering anything that had passed.*

10 – In Victorian taxi terminology, a hansom cab or cabriolet was a two-wheeled vehicle, while a Clarence or growler was four-wheeled with an enclosed cabin. These were all hackney cabs. A hackney coach was a six-seater.

11 – Of the connecting chain of four parks that run northwest to southeast across the heart of London – Kensington Park, Hyde Park, Green Park, and St. James' Park – Green Park is the only one that contained no memorials or buildings in Watson's era. Earlier monuments had been removed and buildings demolished. The park consists almost entirely of mature trees rising out of turf and the only flowers are naturalised narcissus. It is bounded to the south by the road called Constitution Hill, which divides it from the grounds of Buckingham Palace. This is the site of Edward Oxford's 1840 attempt to assassinate the four-months pregnant Queen Victoria.

12 – The famous ceremonial route was installed along the north edge of Green Park as part of royal architect John Nash's 1826-1827 renovation for the Prince Regent (later King George IV), but was not opened to the public for sixty years. The Mall had therefore only been available to general traffic for two years at the time of our present narrative.

13 – The fifty-seven acre St. James' Park includes a lake with two islands, Duck Island and West Island. The Blue Bridge crosses the water and affords spectacular views across the lake to Buckingham Palace to the west and eastward to Horse Guards Parade and the Westminster Palace Clock Tower (where Big Ben is housed. The tower is nowadays called the Elizabeth Tower). The original 1857 iron suspension bridge was replaced by the present bridge in 1957.

Although the park has long since ceased to be the royal zoo where King James I (1603) kept camels, crocodiles, an elephant, and an exotic bird aviary, a colony of pelicans donated by a Russian ambassador to Charles II in 1664 still thrives there today, and is a key feature of the lake.

14 – From 1806-1881, the Bangalore Cantonment was a thirteen-square mile military base extending from the Residency on the west to Binnamangala on the east, and from the Tanneries in the north to Agram in the south, the largest military garrison in South India. Stationed in the cantonment were three artillery batteries and regiments of the cavalry, infantry, sappers, miners, mounted infantry, supply and transport corps, and the Bangalore Rifle Volunteers, along with their families and support staff. The area was a small city in itself and included clubs, churches, bungalows, shops, and a hospital. It was directly under the governance of the British Raj rather than the local Durbar of the Kingdom of Mysore as Bangalore city was.

15 – The Western Ghats or Sahyadri (Benevolent Mountains) run 990 miles north to south along the western edge of the Deccan Plateau,

61

covering 62,000 square miles with an average elevation of 1,200 feet, rising to the peak of Anamudi at 8,242 feet.

16 – India's monsoon season begins around the end of May and continues until early October. It is particularly vicious in the area around the Western Ghats, making some roads impassable.

17 – After the Indian Rebellion of 1857, the native regiments' Enfield rifles were replaced with the Pattern 1858 Indian Service version which reamed out the rifling of the Pattern 1853 and replaced the variable distance rear sight with a fixed sight, which greatly reduced their effectiveness. The weapon's increased bore gave it a tendency to explode. British troops retained the superior previous 1853 model.

18 – £50,000 in 1881 would be around £4.4 million in modern currency. £400 then would be worth £35,400 today. The standard wage of a British private solder in 1881 was around £30 per year before stoppages.

The Adventure of the Resident Patient
by Sir Arthur Conan Doyle

In glancing over the somewhat incoherent series of memoirs with which I have endeavored to illustrate a few of the mental peculiarities of my friend Mr. Sherlock Holmes, I have been struck by the difficulty which I have experienced in picking out examples which shall in every way answer my purpose. For in those cases in which Holmes has performed some *tour de force* of analytical reasoning, and has demonstrated the value of his peculiar methods of investigation, the facts themselves have often been so slight or so commonplace that I could not feel justified in laying them before the public. On the other hand, it has frequently happened that he has been concerned in some research where the facts have been of the most remarkable and dramatic character, but where the share which he has himself taken in determining their causes has been less pronounced than I, as his biographer, could wish. The small matter which I have chronicled under the heading of *A Study in Scarlet*, and that other later one connected with the loss of the *Gloria Scott*, may serve as examples of this Scylla and Charybdis which are forever threatening the historian. It may be that in the business of which I am now about to write the part which my friend played is not sufficiently accentuated, and yet the whole train of circumstances is so remarkable that I cannot bring myself to omit it entirely from this series.

I cannot be sure of the exact date, for some of my memoranda upon the matter have been mislaid, but it must have been towards the end of the first year during which Holmes and I shared chambers in Baker Street. It was boisterous October weather, and we had both remained indoors all day, I because I feared with my shaken health to face the keen autumn wind, while he was deep in some of those abstruse chemical investigations which absorbed him utterly as long as he was engaged upon them. Towards evening, however, the breaking of a test-tube brought his research to a premature ending, and he sprang up from his chair with an exclamation of impatience and a clouded brow.

"A day's work ruined, Watson," said he, striding across to the window. "Ha! The stars are out and the wind has fallen. What do you say to a ramble through London?"

I was weary of our little sitting room and gladly acquiesced. For three hours we strolled about together, watching the ever-changing kaleidoscope of life as it ebbs and flows through Fleet Street and the Strand. Holmes had shaken off his temporary ill-humour, and his characteristic talk, with its keen observance of detail and subtle power of inference, held me amused and enthralled. It was ten o'clock before we reached Baker Street again. A brougham was waiting at our door.

"Hum! A doctor's – general practitioner, I perceive," said Holmes. "Not been long in practice, but has had a good deal to do. Come to consult us, I fancy! Lucky we came back!"

I was sufficiently conversant with Holmes's methods to be able to follow his reasoning, and to see that the nature and state of the various medical instruments in the wicker basket which hung in the lamplight inside the brougham had given him the data for his swift deduction. The light in our window above showed that this late visit was indeed intended for us. With some curiosity as to what could have sent a brother medico to us at such an hour, I followed Holmes into our sanctum.

For three hours we strolled about together . . . .

A pale, taper-faced man with sandy whiskers rose up from a chair by the fire as we entered. His age may not have been more than three or four and thirty, but his haggard expression and unhealthy hue told of a life which has sapped his strength and robbed him of his youth. His manner was nervous and shy, like that of a sensitive gentleman, and the thin white hand which he laid on the mantelpiece as he rose was that of an artist rather than of a surgeon. His dress was quiet and sombre – a black frock-coat, dark trousers, and a touch of color about his necktie.

"Good evening, Doctor," said Holmes, cheerily. "I am glad to see that you have only been waiting a very few minutes."

"You spoke to my coachman, then?"

"No, it was the candle on the side-table that told me. Pray resume your seat and let me know how I can serve you."

"My name is Doctor Percy Trevelyan," said our visitor, "and I live at 403 Brook Street."

"Are you not the author of a monograph upon obscure nervous lesions?" I asked.

His pale cheeks flushed with pleasure at hearing that his work was known to me.

"I so seldom hear of the work that I thought it was quite dead," said he. "My publishers gave me a most discouraging account of its sale. You are yourself, I presume, a medical man?"

"A retired army surgeon."

"My own hobby has always been nervous disease. I should wish to make it an absolute specialty, but, of course, a man must take what he can get at first. This, however, is beside the question, Mr. Sherlock Holmes, and I quite appreciate how valuable your time is. The fact is that a very singular train of events has occurred recently at my house in Brook Street, and to-night they came to such a head that I felt it was quite impossible for me to wait another hour before asking for your advice and assistance."

Sherlock Holmes sat down and lit his pipe. "You are very welcome to both," said he. "Pray let me have a detailed account of what the circumstances are which have disturbed you."

"One or two of them are so trivial," said Dr. Trevelyan, "that really I am almost ashamed to mention them. But the matter is so inexplicable, and the recent turn which it has taken is so elaborate, that I shall lay it all before you, and you shall judge what is essential and what is not.

"I am compelled, to begin with, to say something of my own college career. I am a London University man, you know, and I am sure that you will not think that I am unduly singing my own praises if I say that my student career was considered by my professors to be a very promising one. After I had graduated I continued to devote myself to research, occupying a minor position in King's College Hospital, and I was fortunate enough to excite considerable interest by my research into the pathology of catalepsy, and finally to win the Bruce Pinkerton prize and medal by the monograph on nervous lesions to which your friend has just alluded. I should not go too far if I were to say that there was a general impression at that time that a distinguished career lay before me.

"But the one great stumbling-block lay in my want of capital. As you will readily understand, a specialist who aims high is compelled to start in one of a dozen streets in the Cavendish Square quarter, all of which entail enormous rents and furnishing expenses. Besides this preliminary outlay, he must be prepared to keep himself for some years, and to hire a presentable carriage and horse. To do this was quite beyond my power, and I could only hope that by economy I might in ten years' time save enough to enable me to put up my plate. Suddenly, however, an unexpected incident opened up quite a new prospect to me.

"This was a visit from a gentleman of the name of Blessington, who was a complete stranger to me. He came up to my room one morning, and plunged into business in an instant.

"'You are the same Percy Trevelyan who has had so distinguished a career and won a great prize lately?' said he.

"I bowed.

"'Answer me frankly,' he continued, 'for you will find it to your interest to do so. You have all the cleverness which makes a successful man. Have you the tact?'

"I could not help smiling at the abruptness of the question.

"'I trust that I have my share,' I said.

"'Any bad habits? Not drawn towards drink, eh?'

"'Really, sir!' I cried.

"'Quite right! That's all right! But I was bound to ask. With all these qualities, why are you not in practice?'

"I shrugged my shoulders.

"'Come, come!' said he, in his bustling way. 'It's the old story. More in your brains than in your pocket, eh? What would you say if I were to start you in Brook Street?'

"I stared at him in astonishment.

"'Oh, it's for my sake, not for yours,' he cried. 'I'll be perfectly frank with you, and if it suits you it will suit me very well. I have a few thousands to invest, d'ye see, and I think I'll sink them in you.'

"'But why?' I gasped.

"'Well, it's just like any other speculation, and safer than most.'

"'What am I to do, then?'

"'I'll tell you. I'll take the house, furnish it, pay the maids, and run the whole place. All you have to do is just to wear out your chair in the consulting room. I'll let you have pocket-money and everything. Then you hand over to me three quarters of what you earn, and you keep the other quarter for yourself.'

"This was the strange proposal, Mr. Holmes, with which the man Blessington approached me. I won't weary you with the account of how we bargained and negotiated. It ended in my moving into the house next Lady Day, and starting in practice on very much the same conditions as he had suggested. He came himself to live with me in the character of a resident patient. His heart was weak, it appears, and he needed constant medical supervision. He turned the two best rooms of the first floor into a sitting room and bedroom for himself. He was a man of singular habits, shunning company and very seldom going out. His life was irregular, but in one respect he was regularity itself. Every evening, at the same hour, he walked into the consulting room, examined the books, put down five and three-pence for every guinea that I had earned, and carried the rest off to the strong-box in his own room.

I stared at him in astonishment.

"I may say with confidence that he never had occasion to regret his speculation. From the first it was a success. A few good cases and the reputation which I had won in the hospital brought me rapidly to the front, and during the last few years I have made him a rich man.

"So much, Mr. Holmes, for my past history and my relations with Mr. Blessington. It only remains for me now to tell you what has occurred to bring me here to-night.

"Some weeks ago Mr. Blessington came down to me in, as it seemed to me, a state of considerable agitation. He spoke of some burglary which, he said, had been committed in the West End, and he appeared, I remember, to be quite unnecessarily excited about it, declaring that a day should not pass before we should add stronger bolts to our windows and doors. For a week he continued to be in a peculiar state of restlessness, peering continually out of the windows, and ceasing to take the short walk which had usually been the prelude to his dinner. From his manner it struck me that he was in mortal dread of something or somebody, but when I questioned him upon the point he became so offensive that I was compelled to drop the subject. Gradually, as time passed, his fears appeared to die away, and he had renewed his former habits, when a fresh event reduced him to the pitiable state of prostration in which he now lies.

"What happened was this. Two days ago I received the letter which I now read to you. Neither address nor date is attached to it.

"'*A Russian nobleman who is now resident in England,*' it runs, '*would be glad to avail himself of the professional assistance of Dr. Percy Trevelyan. He has been for some years a victim to cataleptic attacks, on which, as is well known, Dr. Trevelyan is an authority. He proposes to call at about quarter past six to-morrow evening, if Dr. Trevelyan will make it convenient to be at home.*'

"This letter interested me deeply, because the chief difficulty in the study of catalepsy is the rareness of the

70

disease. You may believe, then, that I was in my consulting room when, at the appointed hour, the page showed in the patient.

"He was an elderly man, thin, demure, and commonplace – by no means the conception one forms of a Russian nobleman. I was much more struck by the appearance of his companion. This was a tall young man, surprisingly handsome, with a dark, fierce face, and the limbs and chest of a Hercules. He had his hand under the other's arm as they entered, and helped him to a chair with a tenderness which one would hardly have expected from his appearance.

He had his hand under the other's arm as they entered,
and helped him to a chair.

"'You will excuse my coming in, Doctor,' said he to me, speaking English with a slight lisp. 'This is my father, and his health is a matter of the most overwhelming importance to me.'

"I was touched by this filial anxiety. 'You would, perhaps, care to remain during the consultation?' said I.

"'Not for the world,' he cried with a gesture of horror. 'It is more painful to me than I can express. If I were to see my father in one of these dreadful seizures I am convinced that I should never survive it. My own nervous system is an exceptionally sensitive one. With your permission, I will remain in the waiting room while you go into my father's case.'

"To this, of course, I assented, and the young man withdrew. The patient and I then plunged into a discussion of his case, of which I took exhaustive notes. He was not remarkable for intelligence, and his answers were frequently obscure, which I attributed to his limited acquaintance with our language. Suddenly, however, as I sat writing, he ceased to give any answer at all to my inquiries, and on my turning towards him I was shocked to see that he was sitting bolt upright in his chair, staring at me with a perfectly blank and rigid face. He was again in the grip of his mysterious malady.

"My first feeling, as I have just said, was one of pity and horror. My second, I fear, was rather one of professional satisfaction. I made notes of my patient's pulse and temperature, tested the rigidity of his muscles, and examined his reflexes. There was nothing markedly abnormal in any of these conditions, which harmonized with my former experiences. I had obtained good results in such cases by the inhalation of nitrite of amyl, and the present seemed an admirable opportunity of testing its virtues. The bottle was downstairs in my laboratory, so leaving my patient seated in his chair, I ran down to get it. There was some little delay in finding it – five minutes, let us say – and then I returned. Imagine my amazement to find the room empty and the patient gone.

72

"Of course, my first act was to run into the waiting room. The son had gone also. The hall door had been closed, but not shut. My page who admits patients is a new boy and by no means quick. He waits downstairs, and runs up to show patients out when I ring the consulting room bell. He had heard nothing, and the affair remained a complete mystery. Mr. Blessington came in from his walk shortly afterwards, but I did not say anything to him upon the subject, for, to tell the truth, I have got in the way of late of holding as little communication with him as possible.

"Well, I never thought that I should see anything more of the Russian and his son, so you can imagine my amazement when, at the very same hour this evening, they both came marching into my consulting room, just as they had done before.

"'I feel that I owe you a great many apologies for my abrupt departure yesterday, Doctor,' said my patient.

"'I confess that I was very much surprised at it,' said I.

"'Well, the fact is,' he remarked, 'that when I recover from these attacks my mind is always very clouded as to all that has gone before. I woke up in a strange room, as it seemed to me, and made my way out into the street in a sort of dazed way when you were absent.'

"'And I,' said the son, 'seeing my father pass the door of the waiting room, naturally thought that the consultation had come to an end. It was not until we had reached home that I began to realize the true state of affairs.'

"'Well,' said I, laughing, 'there is no harm done except that you puzzled me terribly, so if you, sir, would kindly step into the waiting room I shall be happy to continue our consultation which was brought to so abrupt an ending.'

"'For half-an-hour or so I discussed that old gentleman's symptoms with him, and then, having prescribed for him, I saw him go off upon the arm of his son.

"I have told you that Mr. Blessington generally chose this hour of the day for his exercise. He came in shortly afterwards and passed upstairs. An instant later I heard him running down, and he burst into my consulting room like a man who is mad with panic.

. . . he burst into my consulting room like a man who is mad with panic..

"'Who has been in my room?' he cried.

"'No one,' said I.

"'It's a lie! He yelled. 'Come up and look!'

"I passed over the grossness of his language, as he seemed half out of his mind with fear. When I went upstairs with him he pointed to several footprints upon the light carpet.

"'D'you mean to say those are mine?' he cried.

"They were certainly very much larger than any which he could have made, and were evidently quite fresh. It rained hard

74

this afternoon, as you know, and my patients were the only people who called. It must have been the case, then, that the man in the waiting room had, for some reason, while I was busy with the other, ascended to the room of my resident patient. Nothing had been touched or taken, but there were the footprints to prove that the intrusion was an undoubted fact.

"Mr. Blessington seemed more excited over the matter than I should have thought possible, though of course it was enough to disturb anybody's peace of mind. He actually sat crying in an arm-chair, and I could hardly get him to speak coherently. It was his suggestion that I should come round to you, and of course I at once saw the propriety of it, for certainly the incident is a very singular one, though he appears to completely overrate its importance. If you would only come back with me in my brougham, you would at least be able to soothe him, though I can hardly hope that you will be able to explain this remarkable occurrence."

Sherlock Holmes had listened to this long narrative with an intentness which showed me that his interest was keenly aroused. His face was as impassive as ever, but his lids had drooped more heavily over his eyes, and his smoke had curled up more thickly from his pipe to emphasize each curious episode in the doctor's tale. As our visitor concluded, Holmes sprang up without a word, handed me my hat, picked his own from the table, and followed Dr. Trevelyan to the door. Within a quarter-of-an-hour we had been dropped at the door of the physician's residence in Brook Street, one of those sombre, flat-faced houses which one associates with a West-End practice. A small page admitted us, and we began at once to ascend the broad, well-carpeted stair.

But a singular interruption brought us to a standstill. The light at the top was suddenly whisked out, and from the darkness came a reedy, quivering voice.

"I have a pistol," it cried. "I give you my word that I'll fire if you come any nearer."

"This really grows outrageous, Mr. Blessington!" cried Dr. Trevelyan.

"Oh, then it is you, Doctor," said the voice, with a great heave of relief. "But those other gentlemen, are they what they pretend to be?"

We were conscious of a long scrutiny out of the darkness.

"Yes, yes, it's all right," said the voice at last. "You can come up, and I am sorry if my precautions have annoyed you."

He relit the stair gas as he spoke, and we saw before us a singular-looking man, whose appearance, as well as his voice, testified to his jangled nerves. He was very fat, but had apparently at some time been much fatter, so that the skin hung about his face in loose pouches, like the cheeks of a blood-hound. He was of a sickly color, and his thin, sandy hair seemed to bristle up with the intensity of his emotion. In his hand he held a pistol, but he thrust it into his pocket as we advanced.

"Good evening, Mr. Holmes," said he. "I am sure I am very much obliged to you for coming round. No one ever needed your advice more than I do. I suppose that Dr. Trevelyan has told you of this most unwarrantable intrusion into my rooms."

"Quite so," said Holmes. "Who are these two men Mr. Blessington, and why do they wish to molest you?"

"Well, well," said the resident patient, in a nervous fashion, "of course it is hard to say that. You can hardly expect me to answer that, Mr. Holmes."

"Do you mean that you don't know?"

"Come in here, if you please. Just have the kindness to step in here."

76

In his hand he held a pistol . . . .

He led the way into his bedroom, which was large and comfortably furnished.

"You see that," said he, pointing to a big black box at the end of his bed. "I have never been a very rich man, Mr. Holmes – never made but one investment in my life, as Dr. Trevelyan would tell you. But I don't believe in bankers. I would never trust a banker, Mr. Holmes. Between ourselves, what little I have is in that box, so you can understand what it means to me when people force themselves into my rooms."

Holmes looked at Blessington in his questioning way and shook his head.

"I cannot possibly advise you if you try to deceive me," said he.

"But I have told you everything."

Holmes turned on his heel with a gesture of disgust. "Good night, Dr. Trevelyan," said he.

"And no advice for me?" cried Blessington, in a breaking voice.

"My advice to you, sir, is to speak the truth."

A minute later we were in the street and walking for home. We had crossed Oxford Street and were half way down Harley Street before I could get a word from my companion.

"Sorry to bring you out on such a fool's errand, Watson," he said at last. "It is an interesting case, too, at the bottom of it."

"I can make little of it," I confessed.

"Well, it is quite evident that there are two men – more, perhaps, but at least two – who are determined for some reason to get at this fellow Blessington. I have no doubt in my mind that both on the first and on the second occasion that young man penetrated to Blessington's room, while his confederate, by an ingenious device, kept the doctor from interfering."

"And the catalepsy?"

"A fraudulent imitation, Watson, though I should hardly dare to hint as much to our specialist. It is a very easy complaint to imitate. I have done it myself."

"And then?"

"By the purest chance Blessington was out on each occasion. Their reason for choosing so unusual an hour for a consultation was obviously to insure that there should be no other patient in the waiting room. It just happened, however, that this hour coincided with Blessington's constitutional, which seems to show that they were not very well acquainted with his daily routine. Of course, if they had been merely after plunder they would at least have made some attempt to search for it. Besides, I can read in a man's eye when it is his own skin that he is frightened for. It is inconceivable that this fellow could have made two such vindictive enemies as these appear to be without knowing of it. I hold it, therefore, to be certain that he does know who these men are, and that for reasons of his own he suppresses it. It is just possible that to-morrow may find him in a more communicative mood."

"Is there not one alternative," I suggested, "grotesquely improbable, no doubt, but still just conceivable? Might the whole story of the cataleptic Russian and his son be a concoction of Dr. Trevelyan's, who has, for his own purposes, been in Blessington's rooms?"

I saw in the gaslight that Holmes wore an amused smile at this brilliant departure of mine.

"My dear fellow," said he, "it was one of the first solutions which occurred to me, but I was soon able to corroborate the doctor's tale. This young man has left prints upon the stair-carpet which made it quite superfluous for me to ask to see those which he had made in the room. When I tell you that his shoes were square-toed instead of being pointed like Blessington's, and were quite an inch-and-a-third longer than the doctor's, you will acknowledge that there can be no doubt as to his individuality. But we may sleep on it now, for I shall be surprised if we do not hear something further from Brook Street in the morning."

Sherlock Holmes's prophecy was soon fulfilled, and in a dramatic fashion. At half-past-seven next morning, in the first glimmer of daylight, I found him standing by my bedside in his dressing-gown.

"There's a brougham waiting for us, Watson," said he.

"What's the matter, then?"

"The Brook Street business."

"Any fresh news?"

"Tragic, but ambiguous," said he, pulling up the blind. "Look at this – a sheet from a note-book, with '*For God's sake come at once – P. T.*,' scrawled upon it in pencil. Our friend, the doctor, was hard put to it when he wrote this. Come along, my dear fellow, for it's an urgent call."

In a quarter-of-an-hour or so we were back at the physician's house. He came running out to meet us with a face of horror.

"Oh, such a business!" he cried, with his hands to his temples.

"What then?"

"Blessington has committed suicide!"

Holmes whistled.

"Yes, he hanged himself during the night."

We had entered, and the doctor had preceded us into what was evidently his waiting room.

"I really hardly know what I am doing," he cried. "The police are already upstairs. It has shaken me most dreadfully."

"When did you find it out?"

"He has a cup of tea taken in to him early every morning. When the maid entered, about seven, there the unfortunate fellow was hanging in the middle of the room. He had tied his cord to the hook on which the heavy lamp used to hang, and he had jumped off from the top of the very box that he showed us yesterday."

Holmes stood for a moment in deep thought.

"With your permission," said he at last, "I should like to go upstairs and look into the matter."

We both ascended, followed by the doctor.

It was a dreadful sight which met us as we entered the bedroom door. I have spoken of the impression of flabbiness which this man Blessington conveyed. As he dangled from the hook it was exaggerated and intensified until he was scarce human in his appearance. The neck was drawn out like a plucked chicken's, making the rest of him seem the more obese and unnatural by the contrast. He was clad only in his long night-dress, and his swollen ankles and ungainly feet protruded starkly from beneath it. Beside him stood a smart-looking police inspector, who was taking notes in a pocket-book.

"Ah, Mr. Holmes," said he, heartily, as my friend entered, "I am delighted to see you."

"Good morning, Lanner," answered Holmes, "you won't think me an intruder, I am sure. Have you heard of the events which led up to this affair?"

"Yes, I heard something of them."

"Have you formed any opinion?"

"As far as I can see, the man has been driven out of his senses by fright. The bed has been well slept in, you see. There's his impression deep enough. It's about five in the morning, you know, that suicides are most common. That would be about his time for hanging himself. It seems to have been a very deliberate affair."

"I should say that he has been dead about three hours, judging by the rigidity of the muscles," said I.

"Noticed anything peculiar about the room?" asked Holmes.

"Found a screw-driver and some screws on the wash-hand stand. Seems to have smoked heavily during the night, too. Here are four cigar-ends that I picked out of the fireplace."

"Hum!" said Holmes, "have you got his cigar-holder?"

"No, I have seen none."

"His cigar-case, then?"

"Yes, it was in his coat-pocket."

Holmes opened it and smelled the single cigar which it contained.

"Oh, this is an Havana, and these others are cigars of the peculiar sort which are imported by the Dutch from their East Indian colonies. They are usually wrapped in straw, you know, and are thinner for their length than any other brand." He picked up the four ends and examined them with his pocket-lens.

*Holmes opened it and smelled the
single cigar which it contained.*

"Two of these have been smoked from a holder and two without," said he. "Two have been cut by a not-very-sharp knife, and two have had the ends bitten off by a set of excellent teeth. This is no suicide, Mr. Lanner. It is a very deeply planned and cold-blooded murder."

"Impossible!" cried the inspector.

"And why?"

"Why should anyone murder a man in so clumsy a fashion as by hanging him?"

"That is what we have to find out."

"How could they get in?"

"Through the front door."

"It was barred in the morning."

"Then it was barred after them."

"How do you know?"

"I saw their traces. Excuse me a moment, and I may be able to give you some further information about it."

He went over to the door, and turning the lock he examined it in his methodical way. Then he took out the key, which was on the inside, and inspected that also. The bed, the carpet, the chairs, the mantelpiece, the dead body, and the rope were each in turn examined, until at last he professed himself satisfied, and with my aid and that of the inspector cut down the wretched object and laid it reverently under a sheet.

"How about this rope?" he asked.

"It is cut off this," said Dr. Trevelyan, drawing a large coil from under the bed. "He was morbidly nervous of fire, and always kept this beside him, so that he might escape by the window in case the stairs were burning."

"That must have saved them trouble," said Holmes, thoughtfully. "Yes, the actual facts are very plain, and I shall be surprised if by the afternoon I cannot give you the reasons for them as well. I will take this photograph of Blessington, which I see upon the mantelpiece, as it may help me in my inquiries."

"But you have told us nothing!" cried the doctor.

"Oh, there can be no doubt as to the sequence of events," said Holmes. "There were three of them in it: The young man, the old man, and a third, to whose identity I have no clue. The first two, I need hardly remark, are the same who masqueraded as the Russian count and his son, so we can give a very full description of them. They were admitted by a confederate inside the house. If I might offer you a word of advice, Inspector, it would be to arrest the page, who, as I understand, has only recently come into your service, Doctor."

"The young imp cannot be found," said Dr. Trevelyan. "The maid and the cook have just been searching for him."

Holmes shrugged his shoulders.

"He has played a not unimportant part in this drama," said he. "The three men having ascended the stairs, which they did on tiptoe, the elder man first, the younger man second, and the man in the rear – "

"My dear Holmes!" I ejaculated.

"Oh, there could be no question as to the superimposing of the footmarks. I had the advantage of learning which was which last night. They ascended, then, to Mr. Blessington's room, the door of which they found to be locked. With the help of a wire, however, they forced round the key. Even without the lens you will perceive, by the scratches on this ward, where the pressure was applied.

"On entering the room their first proceeding must have been to gag Mr. Blessington. He may have been asleep, or he may have been so paralyzed with terror as to have been unable to cry out. These walls are thick, and it is conceivable that his shriek, if he had time to utter one, was unheard.

"Having secured him, it is evident to me that a consultation of some sort was held. Probably it was something in the nature of a judicial proceeding. It must have lasted for some time, for it was then that these cigars were smoked. The older man sat in that wicker chair – it was he who used the cigar-holder. The younger man sat over yonder – he knocked his ash off against the chest of drawers. The third fellow paced up and down. Blessington, I think, sat upright in the bed, but of that I cannot be absolutely certain.

"Well, it ended by their taking Blessington and hanging him. The matter was so prearranged that it is my belief that they brought with them some sort of block or pulley which might serve as a gallows. That screw-driver and those screws were, as I conceive, for fixing it up. Seeing the hook, however they naturally saved themselves the trouble. Having finished their work they made off, and the door was barred behind them by their confederate."

We had all listened with the deepest interest to this sketch of the night's doings, which Holmes had deduced from signs so subtle and minute that, even when he had pointed them out to us, we could scarcely follow him in his reasoning. The inspector hurried away on the instant to make inquiries about the page, while Holmes and I returned to Baker Street for breakfast.

"I'll be back by three," said he, when we had finished our meal. "Both the inspector and the doctor will meet me here at that hour, and I hope by that time to have cleared up any little obscurity which the case may still present."

Our visitors arrived at the appointed time, but it was a quarter-to-four before my friend put in an appearance. From his expression as he entered, however, I could see that all had gone well with him.

"Any news, Inspector?"

"We have got the boy, sir."

"Excellent, and I have got the men."

"You have got them!" we cried, all three.

"Well, at least I have got their identity. This so-called Blessington is, as I expected, well known at headquarters, and so are his assailants. Their names are Biddle, Hayward, and Moffat."

"The Worthingdon bank gang," cried the inspector.

"Precisely," said Holmes.

"You have got them!" we cried, all three.

"Then Blessington must have been Sutton."

"Exactly," said Holmes.

"Why, that makes it as clear as crystal," said the inspector.
But Trevelyan and I looked at each other in bewilderment.

"You must surely remember the great Worthingdon bank
business," said Holmes. "Five men were in it – these four and
a fifth called Cartwright. Tobin, the care-taker, was murdered,
and the thieves got away with seven thousand pounds. This
was in 1875. They were all five arrested, but the evidence
against them was by no means conclusive. This Blessington or
Sutton, who was the worst of the gang, turned informer. On his
evidence Cartwright was hanged and the other three got fifteen
years apiece. When they got out the other day, which was some
years before their full term, they set themselves, as you
perceive, to hunt down the traitor and to avenge the death of
their comrade upon him. Twice they tried to get at him and

failed. A third time, you see, it came off. Is there anything further which I can explain, Dr. Trevelyan?"

"I think you have made it all remarkable clear," said the doctor. "No doubt the day on which he was perturbed was the day when he had seen of their release in the newspapers."

"Quite so. His talk about a burglary was the merest blind."

"But why could he not tell you this?"

"Well, my dear sir, knowing the vindictive character of his old associates, he was trying to hide his own identity from everybody as long as he could. His secret was a shameful one, and he could not bring himself to divulge it. However, wretch as he was, he was still living under the shield of British law, and I have no doubt, Inspector, that you will see that, though that shield may fail to guard, the sword of justice is still there to avenge."

Such were the singular circumstances in connection with the Resident Patient and the Brook Street Doctor. From that night nothing has been seen of the three murderers by the police, and it is surmised at Scotland Yard that they were among the passengers of the ill-fated steamer Norah Creina, which was lost some years ago with all hands upon the Portuguese coast, some leagues to the north of Oporto. The proceedings against the page broke down for want of evidence, and the Brook Street Mystery, as it was called, has never until now been fully dealt with in any public print.

The Locked-Room Mystery
by D.J. Tyrer

I have long had the privilege to assist my good friend Sherlock Holmes in his investigations and to record accounts of some of our more intriguing or unusual cases for the edification of the reading public. For a variety of reasons, I have been hesitant to put pen to paper concerning some of our earliest adventures together, but would like to rectify that deficiency a little by recounting one of the stranger examples that we encountered.

Now, I have always fancied myself a wordsmith of some small skill, but, at the time this particular case took place, had yet to write more than a couple of unimportant articles in minor medical journals and an alexandrine that had been printed anonymously in an obscure poetry journal. Thus, I was quite enthused and a little humbled to learn that this particular case had a literary dimension.

I was sitting with Holmes as he propounded his theory on the difference in texture between British and American cigarette ashes.

"It is due to the variation in the grain of the paper used to enfold the tobacco," he stated with the certainty of one who had examined the topic in depth.

As he spoke, a tap upon the door interrupted his flow. The boy in buttons entered, but Holmes waved him into silence before he could introduce the man who followed him in.

The man opened his mouth to speak, but Holmes interrupted him. "Allow me a moment to indulge myself and see what I can ascertain about you, dear fellow, from my observation of your appearance."

He looked the man over, who blinked at him, bemused, and coughed.

Although I had begun to grow used to my friend's ways, I had to allow myself a wry smile, for today, I suspected, I had him at a disadvantage.

The man was stooped and thin with a gangliness about him. His face was narrow with a high brow and a bushy moustache. He looked to be in his thirties and wore a suit that surely had seen better days, giving him an air of decayed respectability. He hacked another cough as he waited for my friend to speak.

Holmes gave a nod and said, "You are, I believe, a clerk." He glanced at me. "As you might observe, he has the callous upon his finger that is common to those who wield the quill on a regular basis. I would further hazard that, given the poor shape of his chest, that this fellow is a native of this metropolis, living in one of the more insalubrious districts, afflicted by the smoky air."

I laughed. "Sorry, but I have to tell you that you are quite wrong in the details, Holmes."

It is rare for my friend to ever show signs of surprise, and I assuaged him with the reassurance that his observations were not inaccurate in themselves.

"Holmes, may I introduce to you Mr. Robert Louis Stevenson."

"Please, call me Louis," he said, in a voice that carried a trace of a Scottish accent and a hint of another I couldn't place.

"He does, indeed, 'wield the quill on a regular basis', as you put it, for he is a writer – a rather successful one, in fact. You might have heard of him if you ever cracked open a journal other than *The Police Gazette*. He is particularly known for his *New Arabian Nights*, which includes his tales of "The

Suicide Club", first published in the *London Magazine*, if I recall aright."

"You do," murmured Louis.

I turned to our guest. "I saw your story in the *Cornhill Magazine* recently, the one written in Scots . . . ."

"'Thrawn Janet'?"

"Yes, that's the one. Most evocative."

Holmes sniffed.

"As for his chest, given that he is not a native of the city streets, I would suggest that he suffers from the effects of tuberculosis."

The author nodded. "Correct. I have only recently returned to this island after a period travelling in the United States in search of a climate better suited to my health."

"Warm and dry," I suggested.

"Yes. I spent some time in California. Although my health failed to improve, I did find myself a wife, which was an improvement of a different kind."

My friend looked dismissive. Whilst he could be tender, almost sentimental, to the fairer sex at times, the notion of love remained an alien one to him.

The world of literature was one just as alien. My friend would frequently proclaim to me that he paid no attention to subjects he considered to have no useful application to his studies. Thus, he might pronounce upon such obscure topics as the difference between the ashes produced by British and American cigarettes or the variations in clay from around the capital, yet something considered common knowledge might be a mystery to him. He once professed not to know that the Earth circled around the sun, a fact even the dullest of schoolboys must be aware of, claiming it had no relevance to him. Not that I believed him for, given his formidable memory, I doubted he could have missed learning, and retaining, the

90

fact. Besides, there was bound to be a time when such a knowledge was likely to be relevant to a case and he wouldn't dismiss it from memory in case it so proved.

"And, how is it that you come to know Mr. Stevenson, Watson?"

It was a fair question. Merely reading a man's fiction would not provide one with his image, and Louis was not of a stature or inclination to feature in the newspapers.

"I attended a talk he gave," I admitted.

Holmes was, at least, aware of my literary inclinations and gave a nod, satisfied that the minor mystery was resolved, and asked the author what brought him to us.

"Well, sir, I have followed your burgeoning career with interest. In fact, I based my mystery-solving characters of Prince Florizel of Bohemia and Colonel Geraldine upon you and Dr. Watson."

I am not sure that Holmes was best pleased to learn that.

Louis coughed and, then, continued. "I have been a victim of theft, Mr. Holmes. Theft and blackmail."

"Really? You do not seem the sort of man to blunder into scandal . . . ."

"Not a scandal, no. It is worse than that!"

I almost laughed. Only a man with an artistic soul might see the threat of scandal as a secondary one.

"You may not be aware of the tale that I currently have appearing in print, for it is published under a *nom de plume* better suited than mine to such a tale of derring-do featuring pirates. It is appearing in serialisation, but – Oh! – the remaining chapters have been stolen."

"Stolen?"

"Yes, Dr. Watson. A thief has purloined my pages and demands a payment of a hundred pounds for their return – an amount beyond my ability to pay." He shook his head. "After everything I have been through . . . ."

"It would seem," said Holmes, "that someone seeks to prevent your story from being published. Do you have any enemies who would like to see you embarrassed or who would profit from your failure? Or, could it be that someone has no desire for a sequel to *Penzance*?"

If Louis was offended by my friend's light-hearted retort, he showed no sign, but rather simply answered his serious question in the negative.

"But, there's more to it than that . . . ."

"Yes?"

"I am afraid you may think me given over to fiction, but this case is a veritable locked-room mystery."

Holmes, who, to this point, had displayed only slight interest in his predicament, looked at him with renewed interest. "A locked room, you say?"

"Yes, Mr. Holmes, although you may not believe me."

"On the contrary, Mr. Stevenson, I can see that you are speaking the truth – at least insofar as you know it. Please, proceed."

Louis coughed heavily for a moment, then continued. "I keep my manuscript in a locked drawer in a locked room. Yet, when I opened the drawer this morning, the manuscript was gone and a note was in its place."

"Two locks? Interesting. And were they still locked?"

"Yes. It wasn't until I opened the drawer I saw anything was amiss."

"And, nobody else had keys? Your wife, for example?"

"I am renting the place while I am in town, finishing my story for my publisher, but the landlord assures me that I have the only keys for the study and desk. Indeed, he made a point of admonishing me not to lose either, as there were no spares."

92

"I shall have to talk to him to confirm this, but you present an intriguing scenario: The thief appears to possess copies of these keys. He is a well-prepared villain."

He looked at Louis. "We will have to take a look at the scene of the crime. But first, might I see the note?"

"Yes." Louis took a crumpled, unsealed enveloped from the inside pocket of his jacket and handed it to my friend. His name was written upon the exterior of the envelope.

Holmes slipped a sheet of notepaper out from it and examined it closely.

"Both the notepaper and the envelope were taken from the supply upon my desk," said Louis.

"That's odd," I observed. "A well-prepared thief who paused to write the all-important ransom note during his theft?"

"It is possible," Holmes said, slowly, "that he wished to avoid carrying the incriminating note upon his person, or risk using paper to which he might be linked."

"Your ability to deduce such connections is becoming well-known to certain sections of the criminal fraternity," I acknowledged.

"Or it could be that he had prior intelligence that reassured him that he could write the note. Mr. Stevenson, had you noticed anything amiss in your study before today?"

He considered for a moment, coughed, then said, "Now that I think of it, yes, I have. Items on my desk appeared to have been moved, or the pages of my manuscript, neatly stacked, a little askew, although I dismissed that as no more than the effect of the motion of the drawer being opened causing them to slide a little."

Holmes drew in a slow breath and lowered the lids of his eyes, as if he were envisaging the scene. "So, it seems he may have scouted your study prior to the theft, yet chose not to act till now."

"The processes of the criminal mind are a mystery."

"No, Mr. Stevenson, they are not. A thief may be a fool or operating under the effect of some delusion or emotional disturbance, but once the motivation and methods are understood, the most convoluted and confused of criminal minds is an open book."

"I bow to your experience, sir."

Holmes nodded, satisfied, then showed the note to me. "What do you make of this, Watson?"

"It appears to be a ransom note," I said, "nothing more."

"Look more closely . . . ."

I did. The note read:

> *I have your precious ms., Mr. Stevenson. Should you desire your treasure's return, bring £100 in 10/- bills to Farley's Warehouse down by the docks at six o'clock this evening. On my honor, I shall return it to you, Mr. Stevenson.*

I am embarrassed to admit it took me a moment to register the obvious.

"'*On my honor*'!" I exclaimed.

"Exactly," said Holmes. "Our thief spelt the word without a '*u*'."

"An American."

"Precisely, Watson. As confirmed by the use of the word '*bill*' rather than '*note*', or the more-colloquial '*sheet*'." He nodded at Louis. "You mentioned a sojourn in the United States of America."

"That is correct, sir."

"Did you make any enemies on the far side of the Atlantic?"

"I believe not. Certainly none who would be driven to pursue me to England and take such elaborate revenge. The men amongst whom I moved were not given to such fanciful behaviour – a swift stab with a bowie knife or a bullet from a gun would be the likely resolution to any such serious falling out."

Holmes rubbed his chin, then took out his pipe and lit it. He proffered the match to Louis, who had produced a cigarette case from a jacket pocket and took from it a narrow cigarette with a silvery band. The author took a series of puffs upon it, the expectorant quality of the smoke helping to loosen the burden of his lungs. He took out a handkerchief and coughed into it.

"That's better," he murmured, voice clearer.

"So," said Holmes, "an enemy determined enough to cross an ocean and play a cruel game with you – yet one unknown to you."

"Could it be a proxy?" I suggested to him. "A hired thug sent by some enemy?"

"It could, but that returns us to the same conundrum: Mr. Stevenson is unaware of anyone who would be driven to pursue such a course, in person or by proxy."

"True."

"Still, Watson, it is possible that an examination of the study may reveal more."

Holmes and I pulled on our hats and coats, and then the three of us exited 221b Baker Street and hailed a passing hansom cab and had it carry us through the busy London streets to the apartment Louis had rented for his short stay in the city.

"This is my wife, Fanny," he said, introducing us to a woman who greeted us upon our entrance. "Honey, these are the detectives I told you about, Mr. Sherlock Holmes and Dr. John Watson."

"Pleased to meet you," she said with a curtsey. She had a pronounced, yet not-unpleasant, American accent. "I do hope you can assist my husband in his travails."

Holmes bowed low with an elegant motion. "Madame, I shall endeavour to do all I can for your husband."

I noted the hint of a glow upon her cheeks. Taciturn Holmes could, if he desired, produce a somewhat-archaic yet effective charm. It was, I suppose, the simplest of the disguises that he was inclined to wear.

"I will leave you gentlemen to it," Mrs. Fanny Stevenson said, retiring from the hallway.

Louis proceeded to lead us to the study which was quite unremarkable, save for the crime that had occurred within its walls. We later verified to Holmes's satisfaction that Louis held the only keys and, as the windows were locked and unbroken and there were no hidden doors behind the panelling, it seemed there was no way in which the thief could have entered the room.

"Might he have hidden within the room before you locked the door?" I suggested.

The author shook his head. "No – I am certain I didn't leave the room between unlocking and relocking the door. Indeed, I was only in here for a short period. I checked my manuscript, locked the drawer, emptied my ashtray, and left. Besides," he looked about, "there is nowhere that anyone could hide."

I had to admit that was true. "Could he have come down the chimney?" I asked.

Holmes, who had already examined the fireplace and its environs, shook his head.

"That was my thought, but there is no soot dislodged from the flue, not a spot, nor any between the fireplace and the desk, and no one can come down a chimney and remain clean. Besides, it is uncommonly narrow, and even a child or a trained monkey would struggle to pass down it. No, I believe we can rule it out as point of ingress."

He looked down at the desk and examined the contents of the ashtray without comment.

"Regardless, no matter the means of entry, we are left with the locked doors and windows. And, please note, even if the chimney were passable, it is impossible to exit through it and clean up after oneself.

"Having established a lack of places to hide in the room, the intruder couldn't have waited until after Mr. Stevenson's exit to effect his departure."

Shaking his head, he concluded, "No, he certainly exited through that door – which requires possession of a key."

"A copy – or, they stole the one Louis carries."

"Precisely, Watson." He turned. "Mr. Stevenson, has that key been out of your possession?"

"I keep it on my person all day. At night, my wife locks the keys into her jewellery box, and she wears the key to that upon a ribbon around her neck."

Holmes and I exchanged a look and I remembered his earlier query. "Did you recognise the handwriting of the note?" Holmes asked.

"No, I – wait! Are you suggesting my wife?"

Was his denial unconvincing? I couldn't be sure. "It has to be asked, Mr. Stevenson."

Despite his stooped posture, Louis attempted to give the impression of an indignant and straight-backed fellow.

"The point must be laid to rest," I said, as soothingly as I could. "Was the handwriting that of your wife?"

"No. I would recognise it immediately, and it was not hers."

Had the letters been deliberately distorted, I knew that Holmes would have noted the deception, so was unsurprised when he said, "Very well. Please excuse my question."

Louis huffed a little, but let it go.

There was, of course, another possibility. Had Fanny Stevenson handed the key to a co-conspirator? To me, it seemed the obvious answer, but I was wary about raising it and Holmes left the possibility unsaid, which I took as a sign that he had his reasons to remain silent.

With no further leads to follow, we had just the one course left to us: The exchange. Louis reminded us he lacked the resources to raise the necessary funds. "We could use bundles of newspaper cut to the size of a ten-shilling note," I suggested.

"The problem with that, Watson, is that a thief who has such a degree of access might become aware of the ruse and abandon the meeting. No, we need money."

"But," I said, "where can we come by so much in a few hours?"

Holmes smiled, wolfishly. "Luckily, there are clients of mine who are grateful to the tune of a hundred pounds. We shall have our money by six – and, then, we shall have our thief."

Louis looked relieved and Holmes had us prepare for the evening.

I had every confidence in him, of course, but things did not proceed as we wished after our arrival at Farley's Warehouse as the distant clocks of the City struck six times, their sound echoing down the Thames to us.

"Place the bag at the centre of the warehouse, then leave," Holmes said, handing Louis my old black-leather medical bag, which was stuffed with bundles of money. "Watson, you must watch the rear entrance." Holmes gestured with his cane.

"And, you?"

"I shall apprehend him."

Doing as he bade me, I slipped into a dark alleyway between two buildings from where I could watch the other entrance to the warehouse. I drew my old service revolver, ready for whatever would occur.

One may imagine that assisting the world's premier consulting detective is a glamorous and exciting business that constantly challenges one's wits and, to a large extent, that would be correct. I have met fascinating people in intriguing locations, and risked life and limb in pursuit of dastardly villains, and have been confronted by mysteries of devilish complexity, but a substantial number of the cases upon which I have helped have involved periods of tedium such as the time I spent in that alleyway, shivering a little in the evening chill, and staring at a door that refused to open.

A shout from within the warehouse made me start.

Holmes had told me not to leave my post for any reason. Yet he was apparently involved in some sort of pursuit or melee.

Drawing back the hammer of my revolver gave me the illusion I was doing something.

I continued to wait.

Another shout caused me to disobey my friend's injunction and I ran into the warehouse.

Crates and tea chests were piled within, the narrow spaces between them forming a maze of passageways.

Somebody slammed into me and I sprawled in an ungainly fashion upon the floor. My gun discharged with a bright flash and deafening bang.

"Watson, you fool!"

My ears were still ringing from the sound, but I heard the exasperated cry quite clearly and looked up to see Holmes standing over me.

He looked away from me and I followed his gaze to see the door that I had closed behind me was now open.

I had let him get away.

Retrieving my gun, I followed Holmes out into the narrow lane. It was empty. A moment later, Louis joined us. He looked at us, eyes wide and expectant. "Well?"

Holmes shook his head. "Sorry."

"The money? The manuscript?"

"He seized the bag and ran. He was ready for me. I doubt that he even had the manuscript with him. Still, I almost caught him, only he was nimble and strong. Next time . . . ."

"What next time?" I asked. "The fiend has the money."

"Does he?" Holmes asked in mock innocence. "He has a bag . . . ."

"Yes. I watched you pack the bag myself. I saw you hand it to Louis . . . ."

"Indeed. What you didn't see was a young lad place an empty bag in the warehouse this afternoon in return for two shillings, one similar in appearance to yours. It was the work of a moment to exchange the two before I took to my hiding place."

"So he didn't take the money?"

Holmes smiled his predatory smile and Louis gasped.

"If he wants the money, he must repeat the exercise – and, we must be better prepared."

We retrieved the case with the money from where Holmes had hidden it and took a cab back to Louis' rented rooms. "Tea?" asked his wife as he unlocked his office and went inside.

"Please," I said. I never got to drink it.

There was a sudden cry and we ran into the office to find Louis holding a sheet of notepaper. Newly written upon it were the words:

Pope's Passage. Seven.

I whistled at the daring of our opponent.

"How?" asked Louis, shaking his head.

Even with his head-start, the thief had taken a great risk. Was he desperate, or did he believe he could outplay us all?

"If he means the time and not a door, we had best hurry," I said, taking out my pocket-watch. We had but ten minutes to make the new rendezvous.

"I know the place," said Holmes. "One of the less-desirable corners of the city."

He looked at Louis. "Wait here with your wife. I cannot risk endangering you further. Our opponent knows we are in the game, so it should make no difference if I carry it thither. Do not despair, Mr. Stevenson. We shall return your treasure to you."

"Please do, Mr. Holmes."

"Trust me."

We took another cab, but first, Holmes had it halt at Baker Street. "Watson, place the money safely in your room."

I nodded, an understanding forming in my mind. "It is his wife, isn't it?" I asked as the cab bounced across cobbles towards Pope's Passage. "You didn't want her to know you intended to repeat your little trick."

"I would remind you that the thief was very definitely male, Watson." He rubbed at his arm, where he had been struck in the scuffle. I still ached from being floored.

"Yes, her accomplice, clearly. But, it is she who is behind it all – plotting, planning, like a spider at the heart of the web."

Holmes laughed. "Your reading habits appear to have disturbed your equilibrium, although like a pirate might be more apt."

"Amusing, Holmes. Amusing. But, I am right, am I not?"

"It could well be, Watson. It could well be. We will know soon enough, for here we are." The cab stopped and we climbed out, Holmes taking the empty bag from me.

Pope's Passage was one of those unsignposted, narrow alleyways set between decaying slum houses, black with shadows.

For a moment, I imagined that we would have the criminal trapped between the two ends of the lengthy alleyway, but was disheartened to see there were a number of doors and openings into yards along its length. Sighing, I said, "I believe we are defeated before we begin. They can come and go via many routes."

Holmes chuckled. "Trust in me, Watson. I have a plan that takes them into consideration." He said no more.

I took position at one end and, having deposited the bag, Holmes at the other.

I had to wonder if the bag would remain where it had been placed until the thief came for it. In an area like this, a dropped penny or a cane leant against a wall would disappear in short order.

Soon, if my friend was right, we would apprehend the thief, and then whomever had hired him. I had no doubts my suspicions were correct, although the motivation behind the theft remained unclear. I had heard rumours the Stevenson's wife had been married before and had children. Might she be planning to leave him? Perhaps she had naively assumed he could and would pay the amount she desired. Well, we would know soon enough.

Very soon . . . .

"Watson, now!"

The sound sent me running down Pope's Passage.

"In there, mister," I heard a child's voice cry.

I could see Holmes ahead of me, kicking a door. It yielded to his mighty blows as I reached him and I followed him into the building.

Another maze, this time of stairs and rooms. It was as if nothing were as it seemed.

There was a scuffle in the darkness ahead of me and I ran to it. There was the hiss of a match. Holmes stood in an empty cellar.

Once again, it seemed as if we had been thwarted, but Holmes held up a sheaf of papers tied with a loose ribbon. "I managed to wrestle these off of him," he said with a satisfied smile. "Most of the manuscript, I believe." He studied the pages for a moment, then handed them to me as the match's light died.

I followed him back to the waiting cab. "So, what do you think?"

Holmes nodded at the pages clutched in my hands. I glanced over them. "It seems exciting enough. It should prove popular with children."

"We're here," said Holmes, as the cab came to a halt outside Louis' rented rooms, not responding to my observation.

The front door was wide open.

"Hurry, Watson – the study!"

I heard a woman cry out and Holmes shout, "Stay up there!"

Running past him, I exploded into the room where our quarry waited, about to open the purloined bag upon the desk.

I stared in shock. "Louis?"

The author turned and threw the empty bag at me and, in the moment that I was distracted by catching it with both hands, he leapt at me and thrust his own hands about my throat with a cry of murderous rage.

It was definitely him, although his coat was turned inside-out, making him look more like a vagrant than a gentleman.

Holmes swung his cane and struck Louis upon the back. He yelped and let go of me, and then turned and snarled at Holmes. I slumped back against a bookcase filled with classics, gasping for air.

Louis seized a paper knife from the desk and lunged at Holmes, but he struck the man's wrist and, with a cry, Louis dropped it.

Leaping with surprising agility, Louis headed for the door. Holmes threw his cane with a spinning motion and it crashed into the author's legs, causing Louis to stumble and fall. My friend was upon him in a moment, pinning him in place until the mania left him and Louis looked about in bewilderment, demanding to be released.

Letting go of him, Holmes allowed Louis to stand. Louis stared at him in shock. "What? What? What!"

Holmes seized him by the shoulders and shook him.

"*You*, sir, are your thief."

"What are you talking about, sir? Are you mad?"

My friend showed uncharacteristic restraint in not throwing that back at him.

"There was only ever one person who could have taken your manuscript, and that was *you*."

"I don't understand . . . ." He coughed from his exertions.

"Oh, it might have been your wife, as Watson surmised, but that the cigarette-smoking man remained unaccounted for and, following the example of William of Occam, one should not multiply elements unnecessarily."

"Wait," I had to interrupt. "Cigarette smoking?"

Holmes nodded to the desk.

"Mr. Stevenson stated he emptied his ashtray, yet there was ash in it this morning – from an American cigarette of the sort he smokes."

"But you struggled with him . . . ."

"In darkness. Had I seen him clearly . . . ." Holmes shrugged. "Turning his coat inside-out was a simple but effective means of disguising himself in the shadows and to my touch."

"When did you suspect?"

Louis was blinking in confusion as we spoke.

"As I said, I was disinclined to add to the list of suspects without further evidence, and an 'inside job' seemed the simplest explanation, so I was considering him by the time we left for the warehouse. Only the lack of any clear motivation caused me to remain sceptical of my reasoning.

"Having spent time in America, Mr. Stevenson could easily have picked-up some bad habits or chosen to spell the words so as to create an illusion of another party's involvement. But, always, motivation . . . ."

Holmes shook his head. "I never should have doubted myself. The moment I seized those pages of the manuscript and looked upon them, I knew I was correct in my logic – the handwriting was identical to that of the ransom note."

Looking sharply at me, he added, "You really do need to be more observant, Watson."

"That as may be, but you keep mentioning motivation – or rather its lack. Why did he do it?"

"Yes, why?" Louis was shaking his head with the dazed expression of a man who had been awakened from a deep sleep and had no idea what was real and what was dream. "You say I did these things, but I remember none of it."

"Your exact motivation remains obscure to me, I admit – some deep dissatisfaction with the story, perhaps, or a bid to steal the money and resolve your financial difficulties – but, the nature of the force that compelled you to act so is quite clear to me."

He paused and waited as Louis coughed, horribly.

"Your health is as precarious as your finances, yet you are newly married to a widow with children. There is, I daresay, more – if I recall your words aright, 'after everything I have been through . . .'?"

Louis nodded and murmured, "My father," without further explanation.

"Indeed. Then, there was the pressure of ensuring your story was finished in time. Difficulties all round. "Now, I am no alienist, but I have read of cases where the mind of a man under such pressure might snap in twain like a twig. I would conjecture this is what happened to you."

Louis was shaking his head in denial, but there was a dawning comprehension upon his face.

"The part of you that was driven by a motivation to disrupt your completion of the story took control of your body in a manner similar to one who has been mesmerised and acted in accordance with its aims without your conscious knowledge."

"Goodness, that sounds . . . strangely plausible."

"Indeed. Now that you are aware, it is likely it will not happen again – although, as a precaution, it might be best to get that manuscript to your publisher right away."

He handed the pages over. More were dumped upon the desk.

"I . . . I will."

Holmes nodded, satisfied.

Louis blinked. "What happens to me?"

"To you? Why should anything happen to you?"

"I'm a thief."

"You cannot steal your own property."

"But, the money . . . ."

"Watson." I opened the empty bag and Holmes assured him, "It was never stolen."

"It wasn't?"

"No," I said. "Never."

"Given that no crime was committed," continued Holmes, "there remains nothing more for Watson and me to do. And, in the same spirit, and in gratitude for such a fascinating case, I shall be waiving my fee."

"Oh, thank you, thank you." Louis grabbed our hands, in turn, and shook them with vigour.

"Come, Watson. Our work here is done."

"Good luck with the story," I said, then paused and told Louis, "You know, a man divided against himself would make an excellent theme for one of your tales."

It is gratifying to know he took my advice.

The Adventure of the Missing Shadow
by Jayantika Ganguly

Since it is rather painful for me to recall my days after the supposed death of my friend Sherlock Holmes, I have, perhaps, never mentioned the thousands of letters, messages, and wishes that were sent to me during that period. When Holmes finally returned after three years, I was too pleased to see him alive to think of much else. Later, however, once we had settled down somewhat, I found the case where I had stored away those messages from people whose lives he had touched, directly or indirectly. After some deliberation, I brought it to him and handed it over silently.

He looked up at me curiously. "What might this be? More of your case-notes?"

I shook my head and sat down. Sensing my reluctance to speak, Holmes opened it gingerly and picked up the first envelope. His eyes widened at the date and glanced at me.

"My dear Watson," he said gently, sorrow etched upon his sharp features. "I really have been unforgivably unfair to you."

I shook my head again. "You are alive and well. That is what matters."

Holmes chuckled sadly. "I should have written to you . . . at least after you rose to my defence and wrote 'The Final Problem'. I have wronged you." He bowed his head in apology.

Such a gesture from this proud man would move even the hardest of hearts.

"Holmes," I said quietly. "I did not give you that box to make you feel sad or guilty. You had your reasons, and I am grateful for your return. I simply . . . wished for you to be aware how much you were appreciated."

He looked down at the letter in his hand, clearly embarrassed at my display of sentiment. "Oh," he said, looking at the return address on the envelope. "The Marquess of Lancaster". He opened the letter and laid it on the table.

May 31, 1891

Dear Dr. Watson,

I learnt today from a mutual acquaintance of the unfortunate demise of Mr. Holmes in a small village in Switzerland, and took up my pen to write to you. I could hardly believe it. How could one as great as he just be gone so easily?

It is indeed a great loss for England – no, the world. I cannot even imagine how terrible it must have been for you. If you permit, I would like to visit you as soon as I return to London. For now, please accept my deepest condolences on your loss.

My Shadow and I shall forever remember the debt of gratitude we owe to you and Mr. Holmes. Had it not been for your timely assistance, we might have met an ominous end, too. It pains me greatly that I shall never hear of Mr. Holmes's brilliance again.

Shadow has not been keeping well lately. The doctors tell me that his time is near, and I dread the day my best friend, too, will depart. He has ensured that I will be looked after by his three children and five grandchildren in his stead, but I cannot bear to think of his absence.

Please reply when you can. I shall be waiting to hear from you. We have been acquainted for almost a decade now, and I hope that you are aware how highly I regard both you and Mr. Holmes. So please, if there is absolutely anything that I can do for you, no matter how inane or otherwise, do let me know.

With deepest sympathies,
Adrian Lawson

Silence reigned for a few moments after Holmes read the letter.

"This brings back memories," Holmes said finally. "That was an odd case, wasn't it?"

"It was, indeed," I replied, remembering our early days.

"Did you meet him?" Holmes asked.

"I did. He came to visit a few months later. Shadow had passed away by then."

Holmes took a deep breath and returned the letter to its envelope. "I am sorry to hear that. Perhaps I should write to him."

"You should," I agreed. "He has grown up well."

I smiled as I recalled our first encounter with Adrian Lawson.

It was towards the end of the first year of my association with Mr. Sherlock Holmes – consulting detective, my flatmate and the man I later came to regard as my closest friend – that we had a rather unusual visitor at our humble abode in 221b Baker Street.

Holmes was in one of his hibernating phases. He had just concluded a matter successfully for Inspector Lestrade and retreated before the light of glory could reach him. I expected him to rest for a day or two and then chase his next mystery, but he had been surprisingly lax. It appeared that none of the missives that he'd received caught his interest. I was a little concerned, for I knew that if his *ennui* lasted for a few more days, he might resort to his favourite seven-per-cent solution. To be honest, his casual use of the potent drug nettled my medical sensibilities.

It was late evening and I was preparing to go out for dinner. I had attempted to persuade Holmes to join me, but he waved away my offer from his cat-like position on the couch.

"You are not working. You should eat," I told him unhappily. "You hardly touched your breakfast, and Mrs. Hudson told me that you refused lunch as well."

"Not hungry," came the response.

"You sound like a petulant child," I remarked.

"And you sound like a nagging nanny," he grumbled. "My apologies, Doctor. Please ignore my black mood."

With a sigh, I donned my coat and hat, picked up my cane, and made my way downstairs. I had barely stepped out of the door, however, when a small figure stopped in front of me.

"Are you Mr. Sherlock Holmes?" a boy, aged about ten, asked me.

"No," I replied, looking around for the child's guardian.

The boy appeared to be alone. He was rather well-dressed, so I assumed that he was from a well-to-do family.

"But he does live here, doesn't he?" the child asked, fixing round green eyes upon me. "It says 221b Baker Street." He waved a piece of paper.

To my astonishment, the paper, in Holmes's writing, said "*Sherlock Holmes, 221b Baker Street, London*".

"He does," I replied absently. "Are you here to see him?"

111

The boy sneered at me, the effect on his little face rather quaint. "Naturally."

Chuckling to myself, I led the child upstairs.

"Holmes, you have a visitor," I announced, not particularly surprised to see him now reclining on a chair in his dressing gown, looking a lot more presentable than the state in which I had left him in a few minutes earlier. His sharp ears must have picked up our approach.

To my amusement, the slight widening of grey eyes showed Holmes's astonishment at his unusual visitor. I knew that he had a soft corner for children, and I had seen his kindness to even street Arabs and beggars, to whom most men would turn a blind eye.

The boy rushed forward while I hung up my hat and coat, abandoning my dinner plans. My military instincts tingled. The game was afoot.

"*You* are Sherlock Holmes?" cried the child in an incredulous tone.

"Indeed," Holmes replied, a corner of his lips curling up.

The boy was not convinced. He eyed Holmes suspiciously. "You don't look old enough to be a detective," he complained.

Holmes chuckled. "If my age and appearance are unsatisfactory, perhaps your Lordship would prefer to visit a more suitable person. Besides, I am a 'consulting' detective."

The boy turned red.

Holmes wasn't done yet. "I am certain that even Scotland Yard can trace your Lordship's missing dog. Shall I refer you to some excellent officers?"

The child's demeanour changed immediately. His bright green eyes went wide and filled with admiration. He leapt towards Holmes and grabbed his hand in his two small ones.

"Brilliant! You are as clever as Adrienne said!" he cried excitedly. "How did you know?"

"There is a photograph of a rather exotic dog peeking from your pocket, your Lordship. Is it not a reasonable deduction that a distraught person seeking a detective while carrying such a photograph wishes for the detective to locate the subject of said photograph?"

The child jumped for joy. Literally.

"Incredible!" he cried, delighted. "How wonderfully clever!"

Holmes, I had noticed previously, was rather susceptible to genuine, wide-eyed admiration. The impact of a small child's guileless, innocent praise was probably much more forceful than an adult's. I could see him softening.

"Mr. Holmes, please, will you help me find my Shadow?" the child asked, a pleading look on his face. "Please don't be like the other adults and tell me to get myself another dog! Shadow is special! He is a Saluki. My uncle brought him back from Persia two years ago. He was a little pup then, but now he has grown magnificently big. He is my best friend and closest confidante." He pulled out the photograph from his pocket and showed it to Holmes, who then displayed it to me as well.

The dog – a Saluki, an exotic breed from the Middle East – was a beautiful creature indeed. This was the canine equivalent of an aristocrat. I had briefly glimpsed one from a distance during my unfortunate days in Asia, but my vague memory could not do justice to the regal creature in the picture. Shadow had pure white fur, fluffy ears, a long snout, powerful muscles, and an elegant bearing. His limpid, dark eyes shone with intelligence, even in the photograph. A magnificent specimen.

"He is beautiful," I said.

"Indeed," Holmes agreed, returning the photograph to the child.

The boy put it away carefully before speaking. "No one is taking me seriously. They said he must have run away, or that he's a foreign dog ill-suited for London. But that's impossible! He always protects me, and it's impossible that he would run away and abandon me!"

"How long has he been missing?" I asked gently. The boy's distress was affecting me, I realised.

"Nearly two days," the child replied. "Shadow always sleeps in my room, you see. But when I woke up yesterday morning, he was gone. That has never happened before! He is always within five feet of me! The only time when Shadow has left my side before was a year ago, when one of Father's enemies tried to shoot me during a hunting game. The man was twenty feet away, but Shadow sensed him aiming at me and attacked him. The man confessed to everything, and then the police came and took him away."

"A remarkable dog, indeed," I murmured, impressed. Even Holmes looked touched.

"Please, Mr. Holmes," the boy pleaded. "Please find my Shadow. He is dearer to me than anyone else. I've looked everywhere that I could think of, but he is nowhere to be found! He won't even eat without me. Why would he leave me? Something must have happened – someone must have taken him by force!" His bright green eyes welled with tears, to our horror. "Adrienne said that you are like a wizard, and that you helped her when no one else did. That you were the cleverest man in the room, and yet the only one who believed her bizarre story and didn't laugh at her, and even saved her!"

I eyed Holmes curiously, taking note of the name. If a chance arose, perhaps I could cajole him into sharing the tale of how he saved this Adrienne.

As expected, Holmes couldn't resist the dual force of a child in need and honest admiration. He caved in. "Very well, I shall attempt my best," he said with a sigh, and glanced at me. "Watson, would you like to join me?"

"Certainly," I replied.

Holmes then turned to me and said, "Watson, I have recognized that this is the Most Honourable Marquess of Lancaster, the son of one of my old school chums."

The boy pouted. "Pah! Forget that stuffy title, Mr. Holmes, Dr. Watson. I am Adrian Lawson. You may call me Adrian."

We heard a commotion downstairs and then frantic footsteps.

"Ah, it appears that your guards have located you," Holmes said.

The child – Adrian – frowned deeply and then looked at Holmes beseechingly. "You will help me, won't you, Mr. Holmes?"

Holmes smiled slightly. "I did say I would, your Lordship."

"Adrian!" the boy said, stamping his foot. "I told you to call me Adrian!"

"You must not do that, your Lordship," a gasping voice at the doorway interrupted. "It is inappropriate."

Holmes narrowed his eyes at the man who had just arrived. Behind him were a couple of other men.

Adrian's face turned cold immediately and, with a sombre expression befitting a noble twice his age, he said, "Who I bestow the permission to use my first name upon is my privilege, Douglas, and none of your business." He lifted his chin, the perfect picture of aristocracy, and announced, "Mr. Sherlock Holmes and Dr. John Watson shall henceforth address me by my first name, Adrian."

Douglas looked unhappy, but bowed. The guards behind him bowed as well. "Yes, your Lordship."

"Now go away," Adrian said, reverting to his actual age. "Mr. Holmes has agreed to help me find my Shadow."

I could see Douglas clenching his fists.

"Adrian," Holmes said quietly. "Would it not be better for us to return with them?"

The boy grinned up at Holmes. "You will accompany me?"

"With pleasure," Holmes replied.

Douglas spoke up again. "With all due respect, your Lordship, we cannot allow – "

"Be quiet!" Adrian snapped. "On whose authority are you allowed to bar *my* guests from entering *my* house?"

This vicious change in the child's temperament left me speechless, and I felt a little sorry for the man who was apparently in charge of him. I glanced at Holmes, and saw him fix his gaze upon the man named Douglas. Animosity shone in his grey eyes. Since I knew by now that Holmes cared for neither station, status, or wealth of a person, there had to be something suspicious about this Douglas.

The child's deep attachment to his pet aside, this was, I realised, much more complex than the simple case of a missing dog.

"Mr. Douglas Brown," said Holmes, his voice ringing with the masterful authority that, years later, I would witness when it caused the highest-ranked men and women to quiver. "Is it not time for you to release your master's Shadow?"

Instantly, with a look of shocked understanding, Adrian leapt up and threw himself at Douglas, kicking and punching and biting at the man.

"How dare you? Where is Shadow? What have you done to him?" the child cried, his voice getting louder with each word. His small was red with anger, and he was clearly putting all of his strength into the attacks.

Douglas, to his credit, did not retaliate against the child. Rather, he merely put up his arms to protect his face and let the boy attack him.

With a sigh, Holmes stepped forward and pulled the boy away. "Calm down," he snapped.

Adrian backed down with a scowl, but continued to glare at the man.

Douglas stood up straight and winced. Then he looked at Holmes and said flatly, "I'm afraid you have the wrong man, Mr. Holmes. My name is Henry Douglas, and I have no idea where Shadow is." He turned to Adrian. "If I knew, I would have brought him to your Lordship."

"Is that so?" Holmes asked mildly.

Douglas nodded without a word and winced again. Surely a small child couldn't have hurt him *that* badly?

"In that case, Mr. Douglas, would you mind explaining why you are covered in fresh dog hair and have an untreated dog-bite on the side of your wrist?" Holmes asked archly.

Douglas dropped his gaze, clearly in pain. I noticed a patch of blood soaking though his cuff. It was not very noticeable and well hidden by his greatcoat, but the scuffle with Adrian had apparently caused it to bleed anew.

The man shook his head stubbornly, even though his face was pale as death by now. "I am not injured," he insisted.

Adrian, who had gone rather pale as well, stepped forward quietly and tugged at his servant's coat. "You *are* hurt, Douglas!" he cried, spotting the bloodstained garments. He clutched my sleeve. "Dr. Watson! Help him! Please!"

"Sit down on the couch," I ordered, while Holmes silently fetched my medical bag.

Douglas was breathing rather heavily by now, and his face was pale and clammy. Adrian stood quietly by Holmes's side, watching carefully as I assisted the removal of the man's coat and rolling back of his soaked sleave in order to treat the man's wound. It was a vicious injury, and I realised that the dog was probably even more powerful than it looked. A bite like this, if aimed at the throat, would have killed Douglas instantly. And I knew how callously men dealt with vicious dogs, and that pets were put down for frivolous reasons. I wondered if Shadow would meet the same fate – or had already – and how it would affect young Adrian.

The two men who had accompanied Douglas murmured amongst themselves, but I made an attempt to ignore them, wishing that they would stop. There was an upset child in the room – no matter how mature he tried to act – and these insensitive adults were muttering about how his beloved dog should be treated! I nearly opened my mouth to reprimand them or to ask for silence – I didn't know myself – when they fell silent suddenly of their own accord. I assumed that Holmes must have glared at them.

I glanced at the child as I finished bandaging Douglas. His small face was scrunched up in distress.

The boy approached his servant as I stood up to wash my bloodied hands. He was clearly holding back tears.

"Douglas," he whispered. "Does it hurt very much?"

Douglas looked shocked for a moment. Then his face softened. "There is no need to worry, your Lordship."

"I'm . . . I'm sorry, "Adrian said. "That I hit you. That I hurt you."

"Your Lordship, it was not you that hurt me," Douglas replied. He looked up at Holmes, his face pale but his eyes steady. "It was a fox that bit me. Shadow chased after it, and I lost track of them."

The servant and the detective exchanged a meaningful glance.

"I see," Holmes said calmly. "My apologies, Mr. Douglas. I stand corrected."

"But why didn't you say so from the beginning?" Adrian cried. "You were hurt and then hid it!"

"Your Lordship, if I told you that Shadow chased a fox into the woods, would you not have followed?" Douglas asked patiently. "I did tell you that he had run away, though."

"Yes, and I have been extremely angry with you since then," the boy admitted in a small voice. "But you were hurt! Bites can get infected! I've read about it! What if you die?"

Douglas laughed softly. "I'm not that easy to kill, your Lordship."

"Do you promise?" Adrian asked quietly.

"If you wish," Douglas replied cheerfully.

It was apparent that these two were actually quite fond of each other. Adrian's viciousness earlier had been a result of his anger that Douglas had hampered his search for Shadow. But then, Douglas had clearly lied, and Holmes wouldn't be unnecessarily suspicious of the man. Besides, even though I didn't possess Holmes's keen sense of observation, I was still a doctor, and I could certainly distinguish between the bite of a dog and that of a fox. This was hardly be the first time that I had treated either. Douglas had been bitten by a dog, and I suspected that it was Shadow who had bitten him, but I couldn't fathom a reason. The man, while awkward, definitely cared for his little liege. Therefore, why would he abduct his beloved dog? But if that was the case, why did the man lie just now to protect the dog? And why had Holmes called him "Douglas Brown" instead of "Henry Douglas"?

Holmes caught my eye and shook his head slightly, clearly asking for silence.

After a few minutes, and with a lot of fussing from the flustered child, Douglas stood up and declared that it was time to return.

"Mr. Holmes, Dr. Watson, if you would care to accompany us, I shall be glad to show you where I last saw Shadow. Perhaps you will be able to find him quickly," Douglas said. He seemed to imply that it was necessary for us to join them. Then he curiously added, "I am glad that Adrian has made your acquaintance. I believe that you will be able to help correct a situation where I have failed."

Adrian looked up at him with shining eyes.

And thus, an hour later, Holmes and I found ourselves in a lavish study, facing a Duke, who insisted on accompanying us and his son into the woods.

Adrian stamped his foot impatiently and glared at his father. "You refused to help me when I was looking for Shadow, and now that I've hired Mr. Holmes, you want to come with us?" he accused.

The Duke, whose face was the adult version of Adrian's, smiled mischievously. "Of course," he replied, adding, "I haven't seen you since school, Holmes! Have you been well? Are you still practicing that business of observation?"

And then Adrian told about how clever his new friend Holmes was. The Duke retorted by pointing out that he had known Holmes before Adrian had been born.

I was greatly amused. Douglas merely looked tired, and Holmes appeared mildly annoyed.

Father and son continued arguing as Douglas led us through the woods, and then beyond the Duke's estate, into another more ancient forest, unkempt and clearly abandoned. Douglas seemed to know where we were going, and we walked for quite a while before arriving at a small, dilapidated cottage, cleverly hidden amidst the woods.

Indicating for us to stand to one side, Douglas said softly, "Gentlemen, forgive me for not explaining beforehand. I didn't have the courage. It's time to reveal the truth." Then, before we could question this most-mysterious statement, he nervously walked up to the door and knocked.

A large, filthy man with an eye-patch opened the door almost immediately. "You again!" he yelled as soon as he saw Douglas. "Have you got the rich brat yet? I'm telling you, I'll kill the girl and the mutt if you don't bring him by tonight!"

Douglas stepped to the side and gestured towards Adrian, standing with us to one side of the door. "I have brought him."

The man's eyes widened in shock as he realized that we were there. The Duke's faced showed puzzlement, and the beginnings of anger. "Douglas . . . ." he began. "What's going on here?"

The man with the eyepatch grabbed Douglas by the collar, hissing, "Do you want to die? Why did you bring the Duke *here*? And outsiders?"

"I told you there would be consequences if you persisted," Douglas said calmly, making no effort to defend himself.

The man thrust Douglas away and lunged at Adrian, but Holmes blocked him smartly.

"Why have you abducted Shadow?" Adrian demanded angrily, looking from behind Holmes. "Who are you?"

The man laughed. "Your dog was just a means to an end, Young Master," he said teasingly. "What I wanted was *you*. Unfortunately, your servant here is highly incompetent. Well, at least he was useful as a shield when that mad mutt of yours tried to bite me again."

"Why would you want to abduct me?" asked Adrian.

The man bared his teeth. "Why indeed. Perhaps you should ask your dear father here."

121

However, the Duke looked as puzzled as his son. "Did you want money? I'm sure that you did. What I don't understand is why Douglas didn't turn you in immediately. Douglas . . . ?" he murmured.

"Douglas *can't* turn me in," the man said, laughing heartily. "You see, I know of his greatest weakness. Yours, too, your Grace. None of you can do anything to me."

"What do you mean?" the Duke demanded.

"I'll show you," the man said, and led us inside. In the small, dingy room lay an unconscious child and an equally unconscious dog.

"Shadow!" Adrian cried plaintively, rushing towards his beloved pet.

The dog opened an eye groggily but didn't have the strength to stand. Adrian stroked his fur and cried into his neck.

The Duke, on the other hand, had frozen at the sight of the child. It was a girl, perhaps a couple of years younger than Adrian.

"Oh, Reggie . . . ." he murmured plaintively. He turned to Douglas. "Is this Reggie's – my late brother Reginald's daughter . . . ?" he asked in a trembling voice.

"Yes," Douglas replied simply.

"Why does this man – ?"

"He was married to the mother of that child. He adopted her when she was a baby. But he killed her soon after the child was born – temporary insanity, they said – and went to prison. He was released recently and came looking for the child to make some easy money," Douglas explained. "Legally, he is still her father."

"Where has she been all these years?" the Duke asked.

Douglas held his master's gaze. "There is much about me that you do not know – of my life before I entered your service last year. Mr. Holmes recognized me – my true name is

Douglas Brown. I have – secrets in my past. I've done my best to repay my debts, but . . . ." He glanced toward the girl. "She is my niece as well, the daughter of my late sister, who was . . . involved with your brother. After my sister died, I was unable to care for the child, Ariel, so I placed her with a good family. I didn't realize that this . . . man had been released from prison early and had taken her away. I wasn't told. He brought her here, and sent me a message to meet him. He threatened Ariel if I wouldn't help him in his plan to kidnap Adrian. He insisted that first I bring Shadow to him, so that he could take Adrian more easily later without Shadow's protection. But when we arrived here, Shadow sensed something wrong. He fought me. He bit me.

"I didn't know what to do. I would have done anything to protect Ariel – she is our niece. But I also wanted to spare you any of the shame that she might bring upon your family, my Lord. I didn't know where to turn. And then Adrian sought Mr. Holmes's help, and it seemed that I could shift the burden of my dilemma. I couldn't make myself reveal the truth, but I led all of you here to see for yourself."

"Did . . . did Reggie know that he had a daughter? Before he died?"

"I do not know, your Grace."

"I see." A look of sadness crossed the Duke's face.

Meanwhile, while Holmes prevented the man from coming any closer, I had examined both the girl and the dog and declared them to be safe. They had been drugged, but they would be fine when they awakened. Adrian clung to Shadow and eyed the girl curiously. He was an intelligent child. He realised that she was his cousin.

The brutish man clapped his hands, thinking that he could still find a way to turn this to his own benefit. "All right, then.

Are you going to pay me, your Grace, to keep your dead brother's dirty secret?"

"It is hardly a secret that Reggie was an amorous man," the Duke said flatly. "Go ahead, by all means let everyone know. After you are imprisoned, it will give me a chance to adopt the child."

The brutish man gaped at the nobleman in shock. "You – *What*?"

Douglas looked equally shocked. "Your Grace, you would . . . adopt her . . . ?"

The Duke blinked, looking just like his little son for a moment. "Of course. Why wouldn't I? She is my late brother's child – there can be no doubt. That face is the splitting image of Reggie when he was that age. Does she have our family's green eyes, too?"

Douglas nodded absently, still in shock. Then his face broke into a smile "Thank you, your Grace!" he said. "Please . . . take care of our niece."

And then he threw himself at his scoundrel brother-in-law, raining blows. Of course, he was no match for the brute, and yet he seemed to be fighting as if his life no longer mattered. The one-eyed man seemed happy to oblige him, spinning the smaller Douglas around and placing a dangerous wrestling hold upon his neck. He began to press forward, and in seconds Douglas's neck would have snapped, but Holmes was quicker, stepping forward and hitting the big man in such a way and with a single blow that he dropped immediately to the floor, completely unconscious.

Adrian gave a distressed cry and left Shadow to stand by Douglas, now on his knees and attempting to catch his breath. Then the Duke took a step forward and picked up his son in his arms. Adrian buried his face in his father's shoulder.

124

Douglas looked up. "Did you mean it? Will you adopt her?"

"Of course I will," the Duke replied, his voice firm. "She will be my daughter." Then he turned his stormy green eyes to the brute, who had climbed to his knees. "As for you, you cretin, I shall ensure that you never step out of gaol again."

Over the next few weeks, Holmes worked closely with the Duke's lawyers to make sure that the kidnapper – we learnt later that his name was Smith – was incarcerated for a substantial period of the remainder of his life for the attempted abduction of Adrian.

Ariel was promptly adopted by the Duke, and Adrian was delighted to have a little sister. Douglas remained with the family, helping to care for his niece and her cousin. Shadow, too, approved of his master's new sibling. It had been decided that Ariel would be told about the truth of her birth once she reached adulthood. She was a bright, lovely child – quite similar to Adrian – and thought the world of her big brother.

Pulling my mind to the present, I returned the letter to its envelope carefully. "We should probably get in touch with Adrian, now that you are back amongst the living."

"He exaggerates," Holmes complained. "There is no need for such dramatic words. I hardly did anything in that matter."

"You knew before we went in that there was more to the matter than we realized, didn't you? You recognized Douglas, and knew his real name."

"I did remember some of his past, and the circumstances that led to his earlier incarceration. He had started a new life under a new name, and I was curious as to how that was related to the circumstances of the dog's mysterious disappearance."

Before I could reminisce any further, Mrs. Hudson brought up a bundle of letters, handing them to Holmes. He promptly handed them to me.

I looked at the return addresses before picking up one in surprise. I could feel my lips stretch into a smile.

Holmes groaned. "It's him, isn't it? When is he visiting?"

The letter was indeed from Adrian Lawson, and it said he would drop by the following week.

A Diplomatic Affair
by Mark Mower

"We live in extraordinary times, Watson," said Holmes, placing his folded newspaper down on the table and stepping over to the window. "An American President assassinated and his killer sentenced to death. Charles Guiteau's insanity plea was never likely to succeed in saving him from execution, yet the man is clearly of unsound mind. A senseless act – and all because he believed he had played some small part in James Garfield's election victory and expected to be rewarded with an ambassadorial post. That a President can be slain at close quarters by a handgun in a railway station should give us all pause for thought. Is anyone really safe from the murderous intentions of a disturbed and determined assassin?"

I too had been shocked to hear the news of President Garfield's untimely demise the previous year and the recent trial of his murderer, but there was something about Holmes's very pointed remarks which sat uneasily with me. "Am I to take it that you are fearful for your own safety?"

"No, just alive to the possibilities. By its nature, my work brings me into contact with all manner of criminals, including hired killers. We must therefore be ever vigilant. So when I see an advertisement placed in *The Pall Mall Gazette* inviting assassins to act, you will appreciate why I say we live in extraordinary times. See what you make of it."

He turned back to the table, picked up the newspaper, and passed it to me, pointing at the piece in question with the long stem of his churchwarden. The advertisement ran as follows:

Notice

We gladly postponed tonight's dietary binge,
so hold onto fried nightingales.

SEFTEN

I read the piece three times before looking back towards Holmes with an expression of some confusion. "I can see no obvious threat. I'll grant you that the wording is cryptic, but why do you believe it to have a more sinister meaning?"

He reached for his favourite pen and took the paper back, laying it on the table once more and folding the broadsheet into a more manageable size. "I make it my job to scrutinise any odd notices that appear in the London press. It is often the means by which the criminal fraternity broadcasts its intentions." He began to underline odd letters in the notice before placing the newspaper back in my lap. "Is that any clearer?"

I looked again at the print, casting my eyes over the underlined words, but was still unable to discern any particular meaning.

Notice

We gladly postponed tonight's dietary binge,
so hold onto fried nightingales.

SEFTEN

Holmes eyed me with mock disgruntlement. "Come on, Watson! Do I have to spell it out? Consider just the underlined words. Is it not clear that the hidden message reads: '"*WE Gladstone to die in Soho on Fri night*'?"

I studied the paper afresh, seeing for the first time that my colleague was absolutely correct. The message did appear to be forecasting the death of the Prime Minister, William Ewart Gladstone. "How did you identify this?" I asked.

"I have trained myself to examine seemingly nonsensical advertisements in order to see what is buried within. With my experience, identifying this message was elementary."

"But why are the four central letters of '*SEFTEN*' underlined as well?"

"That may very well point us in the direction of the author. If I remember rightly, the rallying cry of the Egyptian rebels in the mutiny of 1879 was 'Egypt for the Egyptians!' The initial letters spell out '*EFTE*'."

"That is astonishing!" I cried, remembering that it had been reported in the papers only a day earlier that on Sunday, 8th January, Britain and France had delivered a joint declaration to the Egyptian government guaranteeing the autocracy of Mohammad Tewfik Pasha, the Khedive of Egypt. "So this may be a plot linked to the hostility around Britain's continued support for the Khedival regime in Cairo, in opposition to those who are calling for constitutional government?"

"That is entirely possible, although my knowledge of international affairs in that part of the world is not as good as it could be. Luckily, I have an exceptional contact within Whitehall who can provide us with a comprehensive analysis of any threats posed by Colonel Urabi and his military faction."

With no further explanation, Holmes announced that there was little time to waste. If the apparent threat to our Prime Minister was to be believed, we had but two days until his predicted death. Donning coats, scarves, and hats, we set off hastily from 221b in the direction of Whitehall.

It was exceptionally cold out on the street, the result of the rising air pressure which had gripped the country since the start of the year. While bright, the sky had assumed a pinkish hue, hinting at the possibility of further snow. I was thankful for the thick woollen muffler which sat beneath my chin – a Christmas gift from the ever-thoughtful Mrs. Hudson.

We hailed a passing hansom on Orchard Street as the icy wind continued to bite, the cabbie taking us on a circuitous route through Grosvenor Square and Mayfair, before heading off along a myriad of small thoroughfares that I did not recognise. Holmes seemed strangely quiet in the cab and markedly reluctant to say any more about his well-placed "contact", beyond stressing that "in any matters of information or intelligence across government, this man has no equal."

It was close to eleven o'clock that morning when the hansom finally came to a halt outside the grand white façade of a government building in Whitehall. Having paid the cabbie, Holmes waved him off before heading briskly towards the entrance. It was only when we were stood within the spacious foyer of the interior, before an imposing marble staircase, that he spoke once more. "Watson, it is not my intention to offend you, but you really must believe me when I say it is in everyone's best interests that I meet with my contact alone. I trust you will not mind waiting here for the short time it will take?"

While the pronouncement took me by surprise, I was not in the least bit affronted – trusting, as I always did, in the absolute integrity of my colleague's reasoning. As it transpired, I had but little time to sit, for it took Holmes less than twenty minutes to conclude his business. Shortly afterwards we were once again within the interior of a cab, this time heading towards Knightsbridge to meet with "an important French diplomat".

Holmes seemed more favourably disposed to discuss the nature of his enquiries back in Whitehall. "This affair appears to be far more complex than I first imagined." He paused to pull up the collar on his long overcoat and shivered momentarily. "My contact was very pleased to discuss the coded notice, which he had already spotted himself. As a result, he has commissioned us to take further action. You will be pleased to learn that we are now acting as unofficial diplomats for the British Government!"

"Really?" I said, bemused.

"Yes. It seems we were right to suppose that there may be some Egyptian link to this apparent threat to the Prime Minister. As you know, the nationalists within that country have been rallying behind their leader, Colonel Ahmed Urabi, since the uprising of 1879. In a bid to quell the revolutionary tendencies of the nationalists, Khedive Tewfik invited Urabi to join his cabinet. Since that time, Urabi has been reforming Egypt's military, financial, and civic institutions in a bid to weaken the Anglo-French domination of the Khedival administration. You might remember that since 1876 – when the Khedivate was effectively declared bankrupt – both countries have assumed a shared control over Egypt's economic affairs."

"Then Whitehall might have good reason to suspect that any attempt to assassinate Gladstone might be part of this resistance to Britain's foreign policy?"

"Indeed. Although in this case, I believe that the coded notice is merely purporting to be a death threat from the Egyptian nationalists. My contact also believes that to be the case and is keen for us to pursue that line of enquiry."

"I'm not sure I understand."

"Well, consider the nature and placement of the communication. The notice appeared in the liberal *Pall Mall Gazette*. Only those within government or in close diplomatic circles are likely to know that the publication is our Prime Minister's favourite. The '*EFTE*' sign off within the name '*Seften*' is a little too obvious and twee – particularly as it is written in English. Most assassins tend to leave their calling card *after* they have acted, not before. Their biggest fear is being discovered before they have completed their assignment."

I could see the logic of Holmes's reasoning, but raised one small objection. "Yes, but the would-be assassin also pointed to the likely location of the killing. Perhaps he is brazen enough to announce his intentions before acting and confident in his assertion that Soho will be the place where he can achieve his objective."

"A fair point, Watson – and one which I did consider. But my contact has assured me that Gladstone has no planned engagements in Soho, or indeed anywhere in London, on Friday evening."

"So that part of the communication was a red herring then?"

"Not as such. He believes that its inclusion was deliberate. In fact, he went further in postulating that it was something of a private joke at the Prime Minister's expense. In earlier years, as part of his evangelical sensibilities, Gladstone was often to be found walking the streets of Soho undertaking 'rescue' work with ladies of ill-repute. There has always been more than a whiff of suspicion about this supposed moral crusade."

I found myself more confused than ever. "But if the missive was not written by an Egyptian nationalist and poses no real threat, are you suggesting that it is, in fact, part of some elaborate hoax?"

"Far from it – the placement of the notice is a calculated act of brinkmanship and international diplomacy. I had my suspicions, but the trip to Whitehall has convinced me that I am on the right track. Let us consider the position Gladstone finds himself in. On the one hand, it is a matter of prestige that he wishes to retain Britain's influence over Egypt and preserve the Suez Canal route to India. On the other, he has, thus far, pursued a liberal non-interventionist approach, believing that if armed intercession is necessary, this should be the responsibility of the Turkish Sultan as Suzerain for the region. By attempting to posit the notion that Gladstone should fear assassination by the Egyptian nationalists, the author is really sending the message that our government should act more directly in suppressing the threat to the *status quo*."

I began to comprehend his meaning. "That being the case, there is only one country likely to want to push us into such an undertaking. I understand now why we are planning to meet with a French diplomat."

"Exactly. France is keen for Britain to honour its *entente* commitments and intervene more directly to suppress the nationalist threat. Its government is also resolutely hostile to the idea of Turkish intervention in Egypt, or, indeed, the interference of any other powers."

Our cab had, by this time, reached an impressive building at 58 Knightsbridge, close to Albert Gate and one of the entrances to Hyde Park. A light flurry of snow had begun to fall and looked as if it might settle. As we approached the building I had a final question for Holmes. "Who is it we are about to see?"

He looked at me and smiled broadly. "My contact has informed me that the former Prime Minister of France, Charles de Freycinet, is currently residing in the building and would be receptive to a visit. Our impending arrival should already have been communicated by telegraph. While we have no official capacity to act, I have been asked to investigate whether there is any evidence to support the notion that the coded message was placed deliberately by an agent working for the French government."

"That will not be easy to ascertain," I replied.

"We will see, my friend."

Some five minutes later, we were shown into one of the large suites housed within the top floor of the five-storey building. It was luxurious in both size and decoration and looked more like the interior of a French *château* than a London residence. A man stepped out from behind a large and ornate desk set before one of the windows overlooking Hyde Park. He was slim and elegant, dressed in an immaculately tailored black jacket, beneath which he wore a red velvet waistcoat and matching bow tie. His full beard and moustache, along with the hair to the sides of his thinning scalp, were as white as any I had ever seen, and lent him a striking, statesman-like, appearance. He approached us with a warm smile and shook each of us by the hand with an iron-like grip.

"Gentlemen, you are indeed welcome. Please take a seat." His English was impeccable and the timbre of his voice low and melodious. I noticed that he seemed to be studying Holmes very intently as we took to our seats. "So, you are Mr. *Sherlock* Holmes?" he said, more by way of observation than enquiry.

Holmes nodded, "Yes, and this is my close colleague, Doctor John Watson."

"Well, it is a pleasure to meet you. Now, may I offer you some refreshment? He pointed towards a baroque side-table, on which sat a large selection of wines and spirits. "Perhaps a glass of port, some Madeira wine, or maybe a small measure of Vin Mariani?"

I winced at the mention of the latter, knowing full-well that the lively mixture of Bordeaux wine and cocaine within the popular tonic had hastened the demise of many a poet, politician, and pope. While I opted for a small glass of sherry, Holmes surprised me by readily accepting a glass of the intoxicating cocktail.

We spent some minutes talking about de Freycinet's background before he entered politics. He had grown up in the southwest of France and had later studied engineering at the École Polytechnique in Paris. When he mentioned that he had undertaken several special scientific missions, including one to the United Kingdom, Holmes announced equably that he knew of the work. "A most competent study, sir. I recollect the notable paper you published in 1867, the '*Mémoire sur le Travail des Femmes et des Enfants dans les Manufactures de l'Angleterre*'." Our host looked incredulous. I could but marvel at my colleague's pronunciation. To that point, I had been unaware that Holmes could speak any French.

Our conversation moved on to a general discussion about European affairs and the growing influence of both Germany and Russia. We agreed that the *entente* between our two great nations was essential in protecting Anglo-French interests across the globe. It was at this point that Holmes directed the dialogue more specifically towards the subject of Egypt. This prompted something of a snigger from de Freycinet.

"Tut, tut, Mr. Holmes. You have let your guard down. I was curious to know the real reason for your visit, and now you have revealed it to me. I am taking it that Whitehall is keen to know how I might view the possibility of military intervention in that country. Would that be a fair summary?"

Holmes did not deny that Egypt was indeed the matter we wished to discuss.

"Why would my views be of interest to your superior back in Whitehall?" he then asked.

I saw a flash of annoyance cross Holmes's face. He prided himself on being the most unique of private enquiry agents and I knew that the reference to a "superior" had rankled with him. Regaining his composure, he replied, "I know that you resigned your position as Prime Minister in September 1880, but since that time you have continued to operate in the highest of diplomatic circles. In particular, you have been something of a trusted confidante for certain officials within the British government. Our soon to be announced 'Foreign Intelligence Committee' is well aware that you are likely to be reinstated as Prime Minister by the end of this month, and your portfolio of responsibilities will include that of Foreign Minister. So your views on the Egyptian dilemma are of particular interest at this time."

The Frenchman leaned forward and reached for a wooden box that sat on the front of his desk, offering up the contents to us. Holmes and I both took one of the long Panamanian cigars and watched as de Freycinet did the same. It was only when all three cigars had been lit that our host responded.

"Gentlemen, since you have seen fit to disclose such a sensitive piece of information, I will be candid with you also. Barring some unforeseen calamity on the sea-crossing back to France, I do expect to be asked by the President to take up my former position within a matter of weeks. As for my views on the Egyptian debacle, I believe strongly that some form of direct military intervention is now needed to put a stop to the ambitions of the nationalists and remove the threat posed by Colonel Urabi and his supporters. I would also prefer not to let Turkey gain any foothold within the country. It is a concern to me that Prime Minister Gladstone does not appear to share my enthusiasm for such an undertaking."

Holmes reached inside his jacket and retrieved the folded pages of the *Pall Mall Gazette* from an inside pocket. He laid the notice with its underscored message on de Freycinet's desk and looked directly at him. "Is that why you placed this coded despatch in today's newspaper?"

"*Mon Dieu!* Why would you believe that I wrote that?"

"Observation and supposition. I imagine that the construction of such a cipher would appeal to you personally and play to your talents. You are a gifted engineer by profession, with a mastery of mathematics and strong skills in both organisation and problem solving – credentials which helped to secure your election to the prestigious French Academy of Sciences. Your English language skills are first-rate, and through your diplomatic work you have become well-versed in the art of communication and subterfuge. In your position, you are likely to know that the *Pall Mall Gazette* is Gladstone's preferred daily newspaper and be aware of the intimations concerning his night-time activities in Soho."

Charles de Freycinet laughed with some gusto. "That is some supposition, sir! But do you have any evidence for your assertion?" He said this playfully, as if the whole exchange was nothing more than a parlour game.

"I have two small, but telling, observations which lend weight to my hypothesis. Firstly, there is a discarded copy of the *Pall Mall Gazette* in the wastebasket to your side. That it is opened to the exact same page as this advertisement cannot be a coincidence. More tellingly, the ink blotter on your desk testifies to your recent word games. While it is covered in a multitude of random jottings in both French and English, there are three words in the top right corner which tell their own story. You have written down both '*dietary*' and '*dietery*', suggesting that you were initially unsure how to spell the word

137

dietary. And beside them, is the single word '*rossignol*' – a translation of the English *nightingale*."

"I see I have significantly underestimated your talents, Mr. Holmes. And I must concede that you have outflanked me on this occasion. I did indeed compose the notice. It is not the first time I have used the London press to send a covert message imploring your government to change its foreign policy. Of course, I would never admit publicly to doing so."

Ever the diplomat, he said this as if seeking confirmation that the matter would not come back to haunt him. Holmes responded accordingly. "You may rest assured that I will never disclose your role in this affair."*

"That is kind of you. Of course, my bigger concern is whether I can genuinely persuade your government to change its stance on Egypt and back the idea of some form of joint intervention."

I was surprised by Holmes's response. "Given that we are speaking openly of matters which are not to be made public, I can share with you the views of my contact in Whitehall. He is of the opinion that the machinery of government will operate so as to force Mr. Gladstone's hand. It is only a matter of time before the Prime Minister will be pushed to lay aside his pacifist inclinations and authorise some form of British military action in Egypt. He suggests only that you hold your nerve until that time has come."

It was a most astonishing disclosure and I wondered at the likely ramifications of communicating this to the French at that time.

Our meeting ended not long after, with de Freycinet thanking Holmes for his intercession and indicating that it would do much to preserve the diplomatic bonds between the two countries. We left Knightsbridge as heavy snow began to fall on the capital. I hoped it was not a portent of things to come.

It was only later in the year that I was to realise just how significant our meeting had been in shaping world events. On Monday, 30th January, Charles de Freycinet was reinstated as Prime Minister, with additional responsibilities as the Foreign Secretary of France. He continued to press Britain to take a more direct approach in unseating the nationalists within Egypt. And despite the pacifist proclamations of the Gladstone administration, the country was to become embroiled in the Anglo-Egyptian War after the bombardment of the city of Alexandria in the July of 1882.

Holmes seemed content to talk down his involvement in the affair. His view was that the political and military events which unfolded at that time were largely predictable given the power and influence of certain officials within Whitehall. And it is only now, with the benefit of hindsight that I can begin to understand exactly what he meant. While assisting Holmes on the 1888 case I recorded as "The Greek Interpreter", I realised of course that his mysterious governmental contact was none other than his older brother, Mycroft Holmes.

NOTE

* This was something of a smokescreen, for Holmes's words did not prevent me from writing up the narrative which I now set before you. It was out of respect for Charles de Freycinet that I have waited a great many years before finally committing the story to paper. The French statesman and four times Prime Minister of the Third Republic passed away last week, on Monday, 14th May, 1923 – *JHW*.

139

The Adventure of
Stonehenge in London
by GC Rosenquist

With the recent passing of the ninth Earl of Rendlesham, I am confident I can finally document a strange case that Holmes and I tackled early on in our association. As the principals involved are now no longer with us, I see little harm in publicly addressing the case and revealing some of the sensitive secrets of Rendlesham.

In mid-1882, at about half past noon on a cloudy Monday afternoon, Holmes and I were summoned to the great mansion of Proudsmarch by Inspector Lestrade of Scotland Yard.

Proudsmarch was one of the tallest structures in London proper. Starting out as a modest castle dwelling for the first Earl of Rendlesham when he visited London, over the centuries its gothic architecture had been added to so that it resembled more a giant Frankensteinian church than a mansion. It had wings reaching out, pointing this way and that in no logical measure. It was rumored to have twenty-eight bedrooms, twelve bathrooms, and a dungeon. Weird angles and strange-shaped corners added a rather sharp feeling to the whole of the large structure, but the height of it took my breath away. It was hard to believe that any form of human ingenuity could devise of such a thing. Holmes and I constantly traded quips about its odd presence whenever we passed Proudsmarch, so it was a great day to be able to visit and see what it looked like inside. But the circumstance of our visit was a dire one.

The eighth Earl of Rendlesham had gone missing.

When we arrived in the late afternoon, we found Lestrade waiting outside its gate.

"I'm glad you could come, Mr. Holmes," he greeted.

"I hope I can be of service to the Yard, Inspector," Holmes countered and shook his hand.

"We've been at this for two days," Lestrade began. "We're flummoxed. I think that we've gone as far as we can. We've interviewed the help, as well as the people of the surrounding neighborhood, and came up with nothing. We need your services desperately."

"I understand, Inspector."

Lestrade cleared his throat. "Two days ago, the eighth Earl of Rendlesham, Lord Riverworth, disappeared. He's an old man and was bed-ridden with consumption, but somehow he left the building and is now missing."

"Why wasn't he at his dwelling in Rendlesham?" Holmes asked.

"He preferred living here at Proudsmarch. Apparently, he loved residing in London. His butler told me he thought passing his final days in the castle was too depressing. Rendlesham is dark, cold, and gloomy. The ninth Earl currently lives there, but is on his way here."

Holmes nodded. "Good. I will need to talk to him. Is there anything else I should know before I begin my investigation?"

"You are familiar with the missing seven Earls of Rendlesham?" Lestrade asked.

"Yes, of course," Holmes answered.

"I'm not!" I protested, demanding an explanation.

Holmes turned towards me. "A strange thing occurs to every Earl of Rendlesham at the end of their lives, Watson. They disappear. Starting with the first Earl, up until now, this most recent Earl, no trace of them has ever been found.

141

Many theories have been put forth, such as they're buried in some secret devil's graveyard, or fallen into a vortex, or being eaten by Nessie. I fear more ridiculous theories will abound with the eighth Earl. The prospects of this mystery fills my blood with fire."

I was heartened at Holmes's excitement, he was always at his best when clearly motived. Lestrade opened the rusty, squeaking gate and we went up the stairs and into Proudsmarch.

We were met by the butler and led inside. The interior was dark and full of shadows, and I gathered that no matter how many lamps were lit it would always remain dark. There were high ceilings with lit mushroom-shaped chandeliers dangling down, long maze-like hallways, and a giant, long stairway that led up to one of the supposed twenty-eight bedrooms. The foyer was wide and its wood floors were covered by an ancient worn paisley rug. The building smelled suspiciously like fruit-scented candle wax.

The butler, Gerald, led us to the left and into a massive room that I assumed to be a study because of all the books on the wall. In the middle of the room stood two rugged looking men and a woman who was dressed as a maid, in a single-file line, shoulder-to-shoulder. Gerald introduced us. The first was a tall round man with a bald head and a grey beard. He was wearing a stained apron. His name was Follkes and he was the cook. An elderly woman wearing an apron rushed into the room and stood next to him, quite embarrassed that she was late. She was his wife, Mrs. Follkes. The man standing next to Follkes was the groundsman, Mr. Blank. He was well-built, wearing a brown coat and black breaches, and his boots were muddy.

Next to him was the maid, a Miss Moonves. She sported curly red hair and a pale complexion, but she was a formidably attractive young lady.

"I will interview all of you separately," Holmes informed them, "beginning with Gerald. If you'll please excuse us."

They exited the room quietly then Holmes turned his attention on Gerald. He was a proper and respectful figure, dressed in a pressed suit-coat and tie. His hair was thick and brown, brushed back from an immaculately shaved older face.

"You may sit if you like," Holmes offered.

"I prefer to stand, sir," Gerald countered.

"How long have you worked for the Earl?"

"Thirty-one years, sir."

"Quite a long time," Holmes stated. "I am told that he was sick with consumption."

Gerald nodded. "He'd been fighting it for some months, sir."

"He was on his deathbed?"

Gerald nodded. Tears collected in his gray eyes.

"How long had he been incapacitated?"

"Two days, sir.

"Who had been tending to him?"

"All of us, sir."

"How do you suppose he got up out of bed and went missing?"

"I have no answer to that, sir."

"I see," Holmes mused and rubbed his chin. "He was a strong man, I assume?"

Gerald nodded. "Strongest man I ever knew, sir," he said.

"You were fond of him then?"

143

Gerald nodded.

"What do you suppose happened to him?"

After a subtle hesitation, he answered. "That is why you are here, is it not, sir?"

"Quite, Gerald," Holmes smiled. "You may leave. Tell Miss Moonves that she can come in."

I watched as Gerald nodded stiffly and left the room. The interview seemed rather short and limited on information for my taste, but Holmes appeared to be looking for something specific. When Miss Moonves came in, Holmes subjected her to the same questions and received the same answers, and then let her go. I was quite astonished at how similar in tone and replies her answers were to Gerald's. The Follkes were next, followed by Mr. Blank. Same thing concerning their answers. It was very late in the afternoon when Holmes finished questioning them. Lestrade was peevish, but luckily, the ninth Earl of Rendlesham stepped through the door.

Gerald introduced him. He was a blond-haired man in his fifties whose blue eyes were overflowing with intelligence. He reached out and shook our hands.

"I am sorry to meet you under such circumstances, my Lord," Holmes said.

"I am sorry too, Mr. Holmes," he said. "I am familiar with your work and have complete confidence you'll find my father."

"Thank you. What can you tell us about the history of the Earls of Rendlesham?" Holmes asked.

"You mean their disappearances? My father often spoke to me about it when I was younger. It has become rather mythical in our family."

"May I inquire about your mother?"

144

"She died when I was six. A horse ran her over in the street. She was so beautiful."

"Tragic, my Lord. I am sorry. You've no other siblings? Or an uncle or aunt?"

Lord Riverworth shook his head. "I am the last of the Riverworths."

"Your father never remarried?"

"No, Mr. Holmes. He loved my mother more than anything in the world, except for me. He was devastated when she passed."

"What kind of man is your father?"

He closed his eyes a moment, as if in thought, then opened them, fighting back a tear. "He is a great man, friendly to everyone, and generous to the poor. In fact, he's left a quite substantial gift in his will to an orphanage." He stopped here a moment, to gather himself. "He is funny, aloof, very light-hearted. But he is firm. You never want to cross him."

"How does he treat Gerald and the others?"

"He is beloved by everyone who meets him," he replied. "He has a natural way of instilling loyalty and respect in people."

"I'll do my best to find your father, but I warn you," Holmes added, "it may not end on the best of terms."

"I understand. If you have any more questions, I'll be here, tending to affairs and getting things in order."

"Fine. One last question, if I may, my Lord. Why don't you reside here with your father?"

"I prefer the woods and greenery of Castle Rendlesham, Mr. Holmes. And the people. I have no love of London or cities in general. As soon as I was of age, I left Proudsmarch."

"Thank you, my Lord," Holmes said, and Lord Riverworth left the room.

"So, Mr. Holmes," Lestrade began. "Did you find out anything that will solve the case?"

"More than you realize, Inspector," Holmes answered. Then his eyes wandered. "If you'll excuse me, I have some exploring to do. I won't be long."

And off like a hypnotized waif with a purpose, he hurried away.

I must admit that I was concerned when Holmes didn't invite me to join him in his wanderings, but I did understood that sometimes the process of investigation was much quicker when he was alone. So I waited on a couch in the study with Lestrade while Holmes explored. Gerald brought us tea and buttered toast. This made Lestrade very happy. Afterwards, Lestrade pulled a book down from the shelf. It seemed to be a volume of old maps. I managed to take a light nap.

After an hour-and-a-quarter, Holmes came in, followed by the ninth Earl, Follkes, Miss Moonves, Gerald, and Mr. Blank. There was a distinct, confident spark in his step, but I knew that something was amiss. He had them line up in front of the fireplace. Night had fallen outside and the house was even darker now. They all carried brass hand-held oil lamps that had been set alight.

Lestrade closed the book and we stood up.

"What have you found, Mr. Holmes?" Lestrade asked.

"I have cracked the case, Inspector," he replied.

"You mean that you've found the eighth Earl of Rendlesham?"

"I have, Inspector, and the rest of the other Earls as well." Then he focused on the natives of Proudsmarch. "I still have some questions, so I've gathered all of you here to join me in unraveling this mystery. Perhaps one or more of you will provide some answers."

Each of them traded worried, suspicious glances with each other.

"I can assure you, Mr. Holmes, that we know nothing – " Gerald began.

"Hold your assurances until I reveal to you what I've found, Gerald," Holmes said. He then turned and headed for the door. "All of you, please follow me if you will."

He silently led us up the main staircase to the first floor, the yellow glow from each of the hand lamps lighting the immediate area and throwing animated, dancing shadows on the walls. Then we went up the stairs on the second floor, then the third and fourth. On the fifth floor Holmes stopped at a blank space in the wall and turned to face us.

"Upon my exhaustive investigations, I stumbled across this. Where I'm going to take you, very few men and women have seen," Holmes said. "But I'm sure that all of you already know this. Come."

He pressed his right hand against the wall panel. It clicked and bounced out, revealing an unlit small room where a flight of stone stairs rose upward into the darkness. Holmes checked each of their reactions, and then turned and went inside.

The staircase was small and filled with cobwebs. It was cold and dank and went straight. About halfway, there was a large flat stone landing. Then, at the far side, the stairs went up again. So we followed them. After a protracted climb, there was another large flattened space and a door. It was made of thick, heavy oak, painted black, and was cracked in many places. Ancient in every sense of

147

the word, the face of a wolf was carved into it, welcoming us with what seemed like a tooth-filled, hungry grin. I imagined it growling and drooling.

Without a word, Holmes took the latch, lifted it, and then pushed.

When we went through the doorway, we found ourselves outside on the roof. It was as if we'd stepped into a completely alien world. What stood before us was immediately strange and mesmerizing. It was a circle of nine large, vertical gray stones taller than I, weathered severely. Their faces were pitted and discolored. The stones were set deep into the cement upon which we stood and resembled a smaller version of the great Stonehenge on the Salisbury Plain in southern England. In the distance beyond the stone sat the recognizable, dark horizon of London.

Holmes glanced at Mr. and Mrs. Follkes, Mr. Blank, Miss Moonves, and Gerald. "Can any of you explain what we're seeing here?" he asked.

None of them answered. They just exchanged worried glances again.

I silently wondered why Holmes had made it a point to ask them this.

"Where are we?" asked the ninth Earl.

"We are on the roof of Proudsmarch, my Lord," Holmes replied with his hands clasped behind his back. "Higher than the surrounding buildings, where none may see us."

"Yes, but what are these?" the ninth Earl continued. "Who put these stones here?"

"You seem genuinely confused, my Lord," Holmes stated.

"Why shouldn't I?" the Earl rhetorically asked. "I never even knew that this place existed."

"Just as I thought," Holmes said. "I invited you here with us so that Proudsmarch and all of its secrets are revealed to you. This stone structure was built by the first Earl, who was obsessed with Stonehenge and its enigmas."

"But why did he do it?" the Earl asked. "What is their purpose? Are there any important astronomical alignments?"

"No, my Lord," Holmes answered. "It is completely devoid of any alignments or science whatsoever. I know this for a fact."

Lestrade and I fit ourselves between the stones to get a closer look. There was nothing on or about them that would betray their true usage.

"How do you know this, Mr. Holmes?" the Earl asked.

"Because they are gravestones, my Lord."

"Gravestones? There are people under these?" I asked.

"If all of you will follow me, I will explain everything," Holmes said and disappeared back through the door.

Back down the steps we went, stopping on that landing built halfway down. On two sides we were met by ancient stone walls with crumbling mortar between them. Holmes stopped at the wall on the right and began feeling for something. He asked Miss Moonves to raise her lamp so that he could see. Around the height of his shoulder, he stopped, pressed in a stone, and the wall moved inwards, becoming a door, revealing another dark corridor ahead.

We followed him in.

The corridor was wide, its stone ceiling rounded, and it went straight for a short distance before veering to the

149

left, where it opened up into a vast room. The room was so large the light from the lamps barely cut through the darkness, but there was light enough to reveal a series of huge stone tombs laid in a circle, matching the arrangement above us. I could see the bottoms of the tall gray stones dropping through the ceiling, stopping on the floor at the far end of each sarcophagus. The first Earl had put in a lot of work.

"We're in a crypt!" stated the ninth Earl excitedly. "Full of old sarcophagi'!"

"Yes, my Lord," said Holmes. He took Miss Moonves' lamp from her and held it over an open, empty sarcophagus. "And this particular one is reserved for you."

The ninth Earl stepped forward and looked inside. "What about the others?"

"They are all filled, my Lord, by all the previous Earls of Rendlesham," Holmes answered, lifting the lamp over the sarcophagus next to them. Words and dates were carved deeply into the side. "Your father, the eighth Earl, lies here. Freshly interned."

"But how?" the ninth Earl asked. "Why?"

"Ask them," Holmes answered, motioning at Mr. and Mrs. Follkes, Miss Moonves, Mr. Blank, and Gerald. Lestrade subtly moved closer to them, his hand hanging near his revolver. They all stared at Holmes with looks of surprise.

"You are very clever, sir," said Gerald. "How did you find this place?"

"It was a simple process," Holmes replied. "It was your personal interviews that gave all of you away. Each of you spoke with me and, though careful with what you revealed, your answers were obviously rehearsed. There was conspiracy here and I aimed to find out why. Then I

150

realized that the Earl, in his sickly condition, could not have been removed from Proudsmarch without anyone seeing him. Lestrade's interviews with the neighbors confirmed this. The Earl had obviously perished, so my questions were where in this house is the Earl, and who put him there? Upon search of the house, I saw that the rug on the fifth floor led past the secret panel door in the wall. I noticed fresh wear marks on the rug ended there, so there must have been a secret entrance. Going through the secret panel and up the stairs, I stumbled across the stones in the roof. Noticing that they were installed through the floor, I wondered if I could see where they came from. Then I remembered the landing in the middle of the staircase. There had to be a secret door there, too. After some investigation, I found the crypt and when I read the names on the sarcophagi, I had my answer as to where the eighth Earl was located. Now the only question was, who put him there?"

Gerald stepped forward. "He asked me to do it, sir," he said. "And he made me promise not to tell anyone, except to inform the ninth Earl of everything when the time was appropriate."

"When was that to have been?" the ninth Earl asked angrily.

"A year from now, my Lord," Gerald answered.

Mr. and Mrs. Follkes, Mr. Blank, and Miss Moonves stepped forward as one group. "He made us all promise," they said in concert.

"We all loved him, my Lord," said Mrs. Follkes. She and Miss Moonves were crying. "We all took care of the Earl through his infirmity, and we were there with him at the end. We did everything he'd asked, even if we disagreed with him. Miss Moonves and I made him comfortable, bathed him, fed him. Mr. Blank readied the sarcophagus. Mr. Follkes cooked for him, even when the Earl's diet changed to bread and soup. Gerald organized it all, making sure you were notified that your father was missing and making sure the transition was smooth. Please don't be angry with us, my Lord. We were only doing what the Earl asked of us."

"But why did he want to keep his death a secret?" The ninth Earl asked incredulously.

Gerald's eyes stopped upon him. "Tradition, my Lord, and superstition," he said. "He did not want to be the one to end it and curse you. That's how much he loved you."

"Curse me?"

"Yes, my Lord. He believed your life would be shortened if he disrupted the tradition," Gerald said. "You see, all the previous Earls have had long lives. The youngest death was the fifth Earl. He was eighty-one."

"Nonsense! It's all superstitious nonsense!" the ninth Earl exclaimed, throwing up his hands. "This all began with the first Earl! Well, the tradition will end with me, I can promise you that, Mr. Holmes! It's time the Earls of Rendlesham live and die in the modern world."

"I wish you all the best, my Lord," Holmes said. "And a long life."

"Thank you," the ninth Earl said quietly. "Now if you all will excuse me. I wish to say my goodbyes to my father."

"Of course, my Lord," Holmes said and everyone filed out of the crypt. Later, as we stood at the bottom of the stairs in front of the front door, it was full night outside and I was, along with Lestrade, very hungry. Holmes assured Gerald and the others that what he'd discovered would remain in Proudsmarch.

152

"Thank you, Mr. Holmes," Gerald said. "Perhaps . . . perhaps the ninth Earl will have a change of heart and accept it for himself someday."

He didn't.

The ninth Earl of Rendlesham died of a heart attack at the age of eighty-three. He was interned in the last remaining sarcophagus, but he made sure the world knew about his passing and location and his son, the tenth Earl, duly took the reins, forever burying the tradition of the missing Earls of Rendlesham.

The Doctor's Tale
by David Marcum

Part I – The Crime

I entered our Baker Street rooms that evening with a certain sense of weary satisfaction. Through the day's efforts, I had crossed that line, ever crouching at the edge of awareness, wherein my finances would be sufficient to pay my portion of the rent for yet another month. In those early days of sharing rooms with my friend, Sherlock Holmes, our obligation to our landlady was always met, but there were some very lean months when sacrifices were made elsewhere.

In the middle of the previous year, it had been determined that my service to the Army was in truth at an end. I had suspected as much long beforehand, based on reactions from those in charge of such things whenever I would have scheduled appointments to discuss my situation. I had learned to recognize, within moments of meeting with the latest official to conduct another review of my condition, that both the sympathetic look of pity from some and the indifferent and impatient intolerance of others meant that the writing was on the wall for me. In mid-1881, I was officially deemed unfit for further military service, my wound pension was set on a more fixed scale, and therefore the need to supplement it became more urgent.

Thus I turned my skills, learned in London as a new physician and then honed on the battlefields of Afghanistan, toward more domestic directions, finding work as a *locum* for various doctors in need of temporary replacement, as well as making myself useful at Barts, where I had trained in those carefree days when I was a medical student living in

Bloomsbury and believing, as the young will always do, that I was indestructible.

On that particular day near the middle of February 1882, I had completed a week of the typical medical routine at Barts and, with my financial reward in my pocket, I had rather righteously come straight back to Baker Street, rather than making my way to Ships Tavern in Holborn, or any of the other tempting spots of my acquaintance, happy instead to have my obligation met and with a little left besides. In a few days, it would be time to begin the accumulation of the next month's payment, but for this day I could relax.

While the temperature was mild for that time of year, the daytime hours were still short, and I unlocked our front door in darkness. Light from the windows of our first-floor sitting room had faintly stained the pavement around me, but the rest of the house appeared to be in darkness. Only then did I recall that Mrs. Hudson was away for the evening, visiting her sister Mrs. Turner, who lived just a few blocks away. Inside, the hall was unlit, and I fumbled while hanging up my coat and hat. Then, medical bag in hand, I trudged up the stairs, my mood suddenly subdued from the self-satisfaction that I had possessed only minutes earlier.

Often Holmes would call out as I approached, knowing that it was me by the manner in which I ascended the stairs, in the same way that he could recognize different policemen. While the injury to my subclavian artery had been the most serious wound that I'd acquired during the Battle of Maiwand, other subsequent damage had been inflicted while I was carried, for the most part unaware, away from the slaughter. Only now, more than a year-and-a-half after the fact, was I regaining some of my previous mobility, and my limp presented itself only when I was most weary.

The door to the sitting room was half open, and when Holmes made no comments, I began to wonder if he was home at all, or if he had left suddenly, called out upon some urgent matter and leaving the gas-lamps burning. But he was seated before the fire, curled into position with several books wedged on each side between his body and the arms of his favorite chair. One was splayed upon his knees, and still another was held open in his left hand while his right held a yellowed document beside it. His eyes darted back and forth between the two, obviously comparing something almost letter-by-letter.

I recognized the paper. It was an old map that had been forwarded to him, along with a contemporary note of explanation, from a correspondent in America seeking his assistance. In those days, Holmes was much more inclined to perform his investigations from his armchair whenever possible. Only when all else failed would he rise and "move around" in order to view the scene of a crime in person, or to dash here and there verifying facts. Although it would be several years before I would meet his brother Mycroft, or even learn of his very existence, I was later to realize that Holmes was in some way trying to emulate the older Holmes, who carried out his secret and complex tasks in as sedentary a manner as possible from his Whitehall office, or just as often from the inner sanctums of the mysterious and curious Diogenes Club.

Holmes had been in deep study of the old document when I left that morning and, except for more books around him than there had been earlier, there was no sign that he'd moved from the chair. As he had explained to me when opening the envelope, it contained both an explanatory letter and a map – or at least part of one – to some old and probably mythical lost treasure mine in the southeastern portion of the United States. It had been in the family for decades, and every few years, one or another of the family members that owned it would stir and decide to take a crack at obtaining the lost fortune. In this case, the current relative who wanted a turn had met Holmes when he'd traveled to New York in late 1879, and had been of some assistance during the mysterious-sounding events of the copper cellar. I'd never been able to persuade Holmes to share the details of that case, but I had hopes that, on one of those days when he was in a communicative state of mind, I'd be able to record the details in the journals that I kept for just such a reason. Unfortunately, the list of these untold cases mentioned in passing by Holmes was growing by the day, and I feared that he would never have enough garrulous spells and reflective moods to relate all of them.

I poured myself a restorative whisky, stepping around the large and filthy river buoy that squatted in the center of the room. The smell of the thing had lessened over the last few days (although I feared that I was simply becoming accustomed to it), but I had a few concerns about the rug and floor underneath, in case the thing had somehow leaked without our knowledge. It had been delivered at Holmes's request after he agreed to investigate a series of mysterious deaths along the Thames, and through all of the conflicting testimony, he had somehow seen that this object was what he needed to clear the confusion. I, along with Inspector Lestrade, had been puzzled to say the least, and the policeman and I had shared a knowing look when the brace of constables worked it up the stairs and left it for Holmes to examine, wiping their hands as they departed. He had seen what he needed to see within a quarter-of-an-hour, and had sent Lestrade off with a name and a single question to ask. Then, the letter from America had arrived, and he had seemed to forget that the buoy was still blocking a sizeable square footage of our living area, even when Lestrade's message of thanks had arrived following a successful arrest. Worse, he had appeared not to hear me when questioned as to when it would be removed.

I dropped into my chair by the fire with a sigh. Only then did Holmes seem to notice me. He raised his eyes over the book and paper, and then lowered them both, closing the map in the volume, which I didn't recognize.

"From the Library?" I asked.

He nodded. "I sent them a list of titles last night, and they were delivered not long after you left this morning. As you know, I have an arrangement with them to borrow what I need." He looked at the books that were wedged into the chair on either side of him, as if observing them for the first time. Then he began to dislodge them, one by one, and create a stack which he then transferred to the floor in front of the octagonal table beside his chair. There was some story associated with that table, saved from his Montague Street days, and he was sentimental about it, but that tale, like all the others, was still unrevealed.

"I believe that I have the solution. A wire to my American friend should settle the matter of the family treasure once and for all." Then, changing the subject, he said, "Unfortunately, Mrs. Hudson is away for the evening, and even worse, she left cabbage for our dinner. What do you say to a more hearty and appealing meal elsewhere?"

Thinking of my newly acquired funds in my pocket, which had only this day satisfied my forthcoming basic responsibilities, must have caused a look of dismay to flit across my features, no matter how I tried to hide it. Of course, it didn't pass unnoticed by my friend.

"There is no need to dip into your recently earned payment from Barts," he hastened to add. "I've received a generous settlement from the Duchess, upon the return of those hideous earrings. I had feared that, upon learning that they were stolen by her husband, she might balk at making any remuneration, but she fulfilled her obligation, and with some to spare. It shall be my treat, and there will be enough left to cover my half of Mrs. Hudson's requirements as well."

By this time, I didn't feel the need to ask for an explanation every time he observed something about me that I hadn't mentioned first. His knowing that I had received my wages from Barts was no doubt easily explained, but hearing about exactly *how* he knew was unnecessary – especially on that dark night. And truth be told, he probably kept close tabs on my financial situation, and my ability to pay my share of the expenses, as much as I did his, since we both relied upon one another to maintain the rooms.

I was nodding with new interest at the prospect of something savory for the evening meal, even if it meant going back into the night. I was ready to stand and suggest that we decide where on the way when the doorbell rang.

Holmes smiled, and I couldn't tell if it was a look of pity for me and the likelihood that our plans were likely scotched, or with a gleam of anticipation for a new client – probably some of both. Like him, I understood that callers at this time of night were almost certainly for the resident detective, as Mrs. Hudson did not receive visitors so late, and that it was the wrong time of day for deliveries. Additionally, my reputation as a local physician didn't yet exist.

Holmes bounded past me and thundered down the steps – far more quickly than I ever limped along them. I heard the door open and subsequent murmured conversation, and then Holmes returned, leading someone else.

I was surprised to see Dr. Leland Smallwood enter the room, for it had only been an hour or so earlier that I had waved to him as I departed Barts. He'd been standing down a long hallway, talking with a nurse, and had thrown up a hand in return as I left the building. Now he was entering our sitting room, blinking at the light – dim enough, but still bright after traversing the darkened stairway. Or possibly he was instead taking in the curious layout of our quarters, with Holmes's many curios of crime laid here and there in a most haphazard arrangement. I should point out in all fairness that my own possessions were littered there as well – but who notices a casually laid-aside book or an unframed portrait of Henry Ward Beecher when faced with such storied detritus as a Maori spear, or a sizeable stack of dried and flattened snake skins, or clear glass jar containing a full gallon of human teeth?

I welcomed Dr. Smallwood with a false *bonhomie* as I hung his hat and coat behind the door while Holmes directed him to the basket chair before the fire. As I offered and then poured a brandy for our visitor, I considered why he might be here. I felt that, whatever the reason, it had the undercurrent of a bad resolution for me.

Smallwood had arrived at Barts during that period of time when I was out of the country, and had set himself up as something of an amateur dictator. In his mid-fifties, I'd heard that he'd worked for a hospital in one of the industrial cities before gravitating to London, lured there by an administrative decision within the hospital to "straighten things out" – an idea that surfaced every few years with little long-term benefit but a great deal of immediate pesterment. When I began to work at Barts on a part-time basis, as my health finally allowed in the middle of 1881, Smallwood had been there for nearly a year, and had already established himself, making a series of policy changes that – from my perspective – accomplished nothing except checking a box to satisfy change for the sake of change. There were various allusions in the corridors to the uselessness of some of his ideas, whispered to me during passing conversations with various colleagues with whom I was slowly becoming reacquainted after my years of absence, but no one would openly declare for certain that the man was both a martinet and a poser – both of which were quite obvious to me.

However, he had authority, and I was beholden to acknowledge it if I wished to continue working there. Still, I went out of my way to avoid him if possible, as he went out of his way to demean me whenever we met, however subtly he accomplished it. For the most part, he seemed to enjoy implying that I was a green beginner, instead of a fully qualified physician who had gained invaluable experience while serving in some of the worst conditions imaginable. He was constantly calling me out in front of the staff and patients as I carried out my duties, advising me to do what I was already doing as if I had somehow never thought of it, and prefacing every remark that I needed to learn this or that if I ever wanted to be a professional, or that "We'll make a doctor out of you yet, Watson."

And now this man was in our sitting room, sipping the good brandy that Holmes had received from a grateful smuggler after clearing his son of a murder charge.

Normally a rather arrogant fellow, quick to offer a comment or opinion, Smallwood seemed unusually diminished, with a nervousness to him that I'd never seen before. While many people visiting Holmes showed these same symptoms, I was surprised to see it from someone who was regularly quite abrasive. He cleared his throat, looked my way, and said, "Tried to catch you this afternoon before you left, Watson, but you got away from me. You move pretty fast for a cripple. No doubt you wanted to sneak away as fast as you could, instead of helping us finish up the shift."

Right away he set the tone. He certainly knew that I had departed a full hour *after* my scheduled time, having stayed to help another doctor set a broken bone. But it was his way – he could no more avoid making such a comment to me, even in his nervous state, than certain dog breeds can stop themselves from springing to a vicious attack – and the fact that he was a guest in my home and still wouldn't change his nature shouldn't have surprised me.

Holmes, however, missed nothing, and I noticed that he'd observed the tightening of my lips.

Smallwood turned away from me. I was dismissed now that I'd been put in my place. "I wanted Watson to play the delivery boy, Mr. Holmes," he said. "Relay a message – a question about a certain matter that's come up. I need some advice. But now that I've had to come find you myself, he isn't necessary." He glanced toward me. "If you'll excuse us?"

Holmes crossed his legs and settled back. "Watson is a valued partner in my little practice," he said, in an innocent tone, without the possibility that it might be contradicted. "He hears whatever business that I hear."

"Nevertheless," replied Smallwood, flicking his finger as if dispensing an insect, "he doesn't need to hear *my* business."

Holmes uncrossed his legs and stood abruptly, as he so often does, having apparently made the decision that continuing the current conversation was a waste of his time. Smallwood's eyes widened in surprise, and he jumped back a bit in his chair. Clearly he wasn't used to such abrupt transitions.

"Then there is nothing further to discuss, is there?" asked Holmes. "It is both or none." He then gestured toward the door, plainly dismissing the doctor. I winced a bit – this was going to come back on me somehow. I was sure of it.

Smallwood's face turned the color of brick. His lips tightened, and he glanced toward me angrily. I opened my mouth, intending to offer to leave, but Holmes must have anticipated it, for he interjected in a low voice, "Stay, Watson."

Smallwood made a noise, the start of some word abruptly terminated, and then he tipped his brandy to his mouth and crudely ran his tongue around the lip of the glass to get the last drops before handing it to me with a dark frown. Standing, he made his way to the door, where he took his coat and hat from the hook. I wondered what story he had to tell that would have shaken his normal confidence, and yet could not be shared in my presence. Never had I seen one of Holmes's potential clients depart so quickly, or an interview become so disastrous in such a short amount of time. The fact that this man had authority over me . . . . In that moment, the consequences were unfathomable.

"Just a word of advice," added Holmes. "You'll want to avoid making any more wagers while your judgment is impaired by laudanum." Smallwood's expression went as pale as a sheet – but no more than mine, as I pictured the further retribution that would be directed my way when he'd had a chance to consider just how Holmes had laid bare a sampling of his secrets in only a few words, in the same way that a corpse is opened under the bright lights of an autopsy.

Holmes opened his mouth to continue, for clearly he had more to observe, but he wasn't able. With a wide-eyed look, Smallwood stumbled back a step, bumping the door. Feeling behind him, as if wary of taking his eyes from Holmes, he turned the knob and slipped out. Then we heard him rapidly descend and slam the front door behind him.

I rose beside my chair, aghast. "Holmes . . . My God, what have you done? It only took you a few seconds to ruin my career."

Holmes took Smallwood's brandy glass, still in my hand, and walked to the dining table, seemingly placing it there for

Mrs. Hudson to retrieve at some later time. "I do not like the man."

"But . . . but he has the power to completely prevent me from working at Barts. He already seems to barely tolerate me. Without that employment, I may not be able to pay my half of the rent, based solely on *locum* work."

"Nonsense," said Holmes, returning to his chair. "You are well thought-of there, much more than you apparently realize. When we were introduced on New Year's Day of last year, and it was suggested that we share rooms, you don't think that I simply relied on Stamford's recommendation, do you? I asked several people at the hospital who recalled you from before your army days, and you were – and are – very highly respected. And don't forget, I have my own connections there too, and your reputation will still be secure tomorrow. It is this Dr. Smallwood who should tread lightly.

"Additionally," he continued, "I've had other chances to observe our recent guest upon various occasions before today, during my own visits to Barts, and he is *not* as well regarded, or as secure, as you seem to believe."

I began to feel a tiny sense of reprieve, as if I'd been suddenly tossed overboard and adrift in a cold sea, but I'd at least been spotted by men in the boat sent to find me. They hadn't thrown the rope my way quite yet, but the situation wasn't as hopeless as just a moment before.

I realized with relief that I wasn't scheduled to appear at Barts for several days, thus sparing me an encounter with Smallwood after this embarrassment. And yet, I wondered if presenting myself there on the morrow anyway wouldn't be better, if only to stake my ground, and assess and possibly mitigate any damage that might have been done.

"Now," said Holmes, interrupting my pondering, "I believe that there was some mention of dining out?"

164

Soon after, we departed to find our evening meal, agreeing that Simpsons suited us both to the ground. I still felt unnerved after the rattling that Holmes had given Smallwood, but there was nothing to be done about it that night. We enjoyed ourselves, Holmes keeping us both entertained as he made observations in a low voice about the occupants of the surrounding tables. Later we returned to Baker Street, and soon after I climbed to my room, while Holmes sat and smoked and peered into the fire.

The next day, my indecision as to whether to boldly make an appearance at Barts was settled when I received an emergency call to serve as a *locum* for a Doctor Batson in Jacob Street. I made my way in that direction, with passing thoughts of the hospital frequently coming to mind throughout the day, and wondering whether, after the previous night, I would ever be welcome there again.

Batson's practice was in a dingy neighborhood, and I wasn't filled with confidence when I arrived and saw that the building reflected its surroundings. The man himself, not quite forty and unexpectedly jolly, showed me what was what, and where the necessary books and documents were kept, while catching me up on the more interesting details of a few of his current patients. Then, explaining that he had some family business in Eastbourne that he was going to use as an excuse for short holiday, he departed.

That afternoon, I was surprised when Dr. Batson returned abruptly, several days earlier than planned. He'd been rather jovial when he departed, but now he was sour and curt, mentioning simply that his holiday had been spoiled by the usual family disagreements. He paid me for my time to that ponit – and as he did so, I was aware that I had counted on those additional days that had been contracted and were now removed. I would begin tomorrow considering where my next source of income could be located.

Holmes had been gone that morning before I'd awakened, and I hadn't seen him. That was not unusual. I assisted him on his cases when I had the opportunity, but often – especially in those early days – he carried out many more investigations without my presence, in spite of his statement to Dr. Smallwood about my being a valued partner in his practice. Still, I must admit that, for the most part, his activities were far more interesting than much of what I saw while filling in for the likes of Doctor Batson.

When I returned to Baker Street, I found Holmes in his chair, reading one of the many newspapers to which we subscribed and pinching his earlobe. He appeared to take no notice of me while I divested myself of hat, coat, stick, and medical bag, and only looked up when I asked if he wanted me to pour him a whisky to go with the one that I was fixing for myself.

"Hmm?" he said, ignoring my offer. "Have you seen the news?"

I shook my head and moved to my chair. "No. Batson takes no newspapers. What has happened?"

"You know," replied Holmes indirectly. "I really have to wonder if I should involve myself, as it's possible that my initial reaction was a contributing factor."

"Holmes," I sighed, sinking into my chair, "what on earth are you talking about?"

"I'm sorry," he said. "I'm leading to the revelation as if I were a dramatist, or perhaps in the manner in which you write up our little investigations in your journals, instead of in the factual and precise linear manner that I expect." He tossed me the newspaper. "It seems as if our friend, Dr. Smallwood, has been murdered."

166

My surprise was great, and the details were scarce indeed. That morning, in the early hours, Mrs. Stroud, a housekeeper who was described as the only servant and lived elsewhere, arrived early as usual to prepare the morning and evening meals (to be warmed up later by the doctor), as well as to do some light cleaning and laundry as needed. There were no other servants, and no other tenants besides the doctor who could tell what had occurred during the night. Mrs. Stroud unlocked the front door with her key, only to discover the downstairs in a shambles, as if some terrific battle had taken place. She had rushed upstairs to discover the same disarray, and the door to the bedroom splintered open with apparent great force. A window leading out to the rear roof of the downstairs floor of the house was thrown open and the room was freezing cold. Of much greater immediate concern were the bloodstains on the bedsheets and elsewhere in the room – described in the press account as *"massive amounts, as if a terrible attack had occurred."* And yet, there were no reports of sounds of violence from the neighbors, and there was no clue as to where the body had gone, other than the outrageous assumption that it had been carried out through the window and across the rooftops, rather than through the locked front door, the only entrance to the building. Inspector Bradstreet was reported to be investigating.

"Well, Watson," asked Holmes, who had watched me as I read the story. "What shall it be? A little supper tonight, and then resumption of tomorrow's dreary routine, or shall we set forth and see if our unpleasant encounter with the doctor last night has any bearing on this matter, and along the way possibly learn something?"

I thought of my chair, which I had just managed to reach, and of the meal that Mrs. Hudson was preparing downstairs even now. She had been rather tight-lipped the previous night when the cabbage had gone uneaten, and I feared that she might be even more unhappy if we absconded before this night's efforts could be appreciated. Additionally, I had very little desire to set out and traipse around London, asking questions that could just as easily be posed the next day. And yet, I felt some little amount of guilt – What if the reason that Smallwood had followed me home in order to seek Holmes's assistance was somehow related to his murder? Holmes was certainly asking himself the same thing. I sighed, even as I realized that my answer had been fixed before the question was ever asked.

Within a few minutes, we had made amends with our landlady as best we could and were on our way to the Bow Street Police Station. Just months before, I would have questioned looking for Bradstreet or any of the other inspectors that I'd come to know at such a late hour, but now I realized that the chances were quite good that we'd find him there. And we did, sitting in his little office, surrounded by stacks of papers and the other valuable litter associated with his profession.

He rose and shook our hands and, with a raised eyebrow, asked how he might assist us. Briefly, Holmes told him of Smallwood's aborted visit. He didn't do anything to hide his abrupt dismissal of the man, being quite honest about his own rather rude deductions concerning Smallwood's gambling and drug use following the doctor's refusal to tell his story in my presence.

"So you don't know what he intended to say, then," rumbled Bradstreet – rather obviously, I thought. "It might have been about something completely unrelated to what happened last night."

"Very possible," agreed Holmes. "And yet, something moved the man enough to journey to Baker Street at the end of the day to consult me without an appointment. And the nearness of that event to his violent murder must be considered."

Bradstreet nodded. "That it must. Frankly, I can tell you that I'm glad you're here. I'd intended to drop around to see you both about this anyway. Any advice that you can offer will be much appreciated." He leaned back. "Would you care to see the file?"

"Does it have anything more than what was in this afternoon's newspaper?"

"Not particularly. We have Mrs. Stroud's statement," said Bradstreet, pulling a sheet of paper from the clutter on his desk, "but I don't think that there's anything there. She barely knew the man, didn't seem to like him, and had practically no contact with him except in passing, when he departed in the mornings – usually without any conversation, unless he had some specific instructions about whether or not he'd be dining at home that night."

"Had he so indicated yesterday morning?"

"Not at all. She said that he left without comment while she was in the kitchen, and she prepared his evening dinner as usual."

"Had he eaten it?"

"He had."

"And that was the usual custom?" I asked. "He would warm up what she prepared that night?"

"It was. According to the landlord's records, he moved there at the same time he accepted the position at Barts, in September 1880, and he immediately hired Mrs. Stroud upon the landlord's recommendation. They established the routine from the beginning, and it's rarely varied. The rooms are small – a converted mews apartment, with a ground-floor sitting room and kitchen, and upstairs a small bedroom and study. To

169

her knowledge, the doctor never had visitors. He seemed to prefer staying in, and he only missed evening meals a few times a year for hospital functions – banquets and so forth." He laid down the sheet. "Do you need to speak to her or the landlord?"

Holmes shook his head. "Not at present, although there may be a reason to do so later." He stood. "I believe that it would be much more productive to proceed directly to Dr. Smallwood's residence."

Bradstreet, with long experience as a policeman, didn't allow his expression to change. And yet, I could see that he was surprised at Holmes's suggestion of immediate action at that time of evening. "Surely," he said, "it would be better to examine the scene in daylight?"

"I believe that the news account stated that the doctor lived in the north side of Gower Mews, just behind Store Street?"

"That's right," replied the inspector.

"And the report indicated that the doctor's bedroom window, through which the body was supposed to have been carried, opens toward the rear of the house – thus it is a north-facing room."

Bradstreet nodded.

"I have some little knowledge of that area," continued Holmes, "and I know that a room situated in that alignment, and especially one in that location, will get very little light, even in the daytime hours, and especially at this time of year. Waiting until tomorrow is very unlikely to provide enough additional facts to justify the delay. We all know, Inspector, that catching a murderer is much more apt to be successful in those hours immediately following the crime. Tarrying will only allow the trail to grow that much colder."

Bradstreet took a deep breath through his nose, nodded, looked around his small office to see if anything needed attending to, and then reached for his coat.

Outside we turned north, intending to hail a four-wheeler when one presented itself. However, at that time of night we were well up Bloomsbury Street before we saw one, and by that point we agreed that we could just as easily continue the journey on foot. We passed the Museum, and within moments had entered the warren of streets behind it. Bradstreet turned into the mews, walking confidently through the darkness before stopping at No. 9. I had expected a constable to be on duty at the door, but it was unmanned. However, Bradstreet's knock quickly brought the sound of heavy footsteps from inside approaching the door, and soon it was pulled open to reveal a massive officer, haloed by a dim light.

"Inspector," said the man. "Wasn't expecting you. It's been very quiet."

"No doubt," said Bradstreet. "Let us by. We're going to look around upstairs."

"Right." The constable, who had either just put on his helmet or – less likely – had been wearing it he whole time, stepped past us into the mews. When we went inside, he remained on post outside the door.

The building was as quiet as a tomb – a most unfortunate comparison, I thought, as we shed our coats and hung them on a rack by the door. Holmes stayed behind, pausing to kneel and examine the lock on the front door. When he was done, he closed it upon the standing constable and joined us, peering at what I had already seen: The two visible ground floor rooms – a barely furnished parlour through a wide door to our left and a small kitchen to the rear, seemingly torn apart. The parlour had a small table and a couple of chairs, but nothing else to indicate the man's personality – No shelves holding books. No magazines or decorative figurines. No artwork on the walls. Quite likely it never saw any use at all. The table and one of the chairs were overturned. I suspected that both had been tipped-over originally, but the constable had likely righted one of them in order to have a place to pass the long quiet hours waiting for something to happen. The upholstery from both chairs had been cut apart, with stuffing scattered across the floor. Turning to look straight toward the back of the house, I could see into the kitchen, where the floor was covered in tossed-aside utensils, as well as white powder, possibly flour or sugar, spilled and spread from their scattered cannisters.

Bradstreet and I remained by the front door while Holmes carefully made his way throughout the wreckage, paying careful attention to the various footprints shown in the spilled powders on the kitchen floor, some of which tracked into the parlour, the hall where we waited, and so on up the stairs. When Holmes had worked his way to the base of the stairway, he dropped to his knees, exploring in that unique way of his that would reveal more than either of us, Bradstreet or I, would ever see. He crawled up the steps, one at a time, leaning forward until his face was just inches from each riser and tread, moving his body from side to side as if reading a large newspaper. Sometimes he would pay particular attention to a certain spot with his magnifying lens. When he reached the top, he spent a moment looking around the landing in the same manner before standing and indicating that we could join him, but to refrain from proceeding into either of the upstairs rooms.

I looked to see Bradstreet's reaction to Holmes's actions, expecting to find impatience, or a hint of amusement or contempt, but there was none of it. His expression was intent, as if he were watching a magician and trying to see just how the trick was being accomplished.

We went upstairs and paused on the landing, staying out of my friend's way. The residence was smaller on this level. The entire apartment was a cramped space, typical of these converted mews rooms that had formerly been stables – a necessary adjustment as the capital continued to grow and housing became ever more precious with each passing year, while private individuals gave up the need to keep their own horses. As I looked around, I found it strange that Dr. Smallwood had chosen to live here. A man of his position – and associated income – could have found far finer digs, and certainly would have, unless something unusual caused him to choose differently.

Holmes went here and there, bending and crawling, pausing and then rushing from one spot to another as a thought struck him, while always making those low whistles, clicks, and mutters that were characteristic of such examinations. Meanwhile, Bradstreet and I conversed in low tones. He, unnecessarily, pointed out the door to the bedroom to our immediate right, where the great quantities of blood had been found. I couldn't see in from where we stood, but trusted that my curiosity would soon be satisfied. I shared with the inspector my surprise that a man of Smallwood's position had chosen to live in such meagre circumstances. Bradstreet grunted but didn't reply, instead staying focused on Holmes's concentrated investigation, much of it spent crawling along the floor, or walking in a bent position, always focused downward. Gradually we fell completely silent, both intrigued by Holmes's apparent enthusiasm as one mysterious discovery led to another. Once we heard a series of thumps from the bedroom, followed by Holmes's "A-ha!", but still we refrained from entering.

Finally his inspection seemed to be complete and he joined us at the top of the stairs. "This has become a much more interesting study than I had first expected. I still have no idea exactly *why* Dr. Smallwood has chosen to pursue such a course, but I can tell you *what* happened here last night, and that the doctor expected for it to happen, and had thus made his plans accordingly."

"'Chosen to pursue'?" rumbled Bradstreet. "Do you mean that he staged all of this?" He waved his hand to encompass the entire flat.

"Only partially," said Holmes. "Let me explain: As I have often declared, the area where a crime has been committed can provide a plethora of clues if examined properly. Thankfully, even as Mrs. Stroud has kept the table-tops tidy, she has completely neglected dust along the floors, allowing enough to accumulate and provide a fairly accurate record of the comings and goings of various individuals over the last few days. The spilled flour downstairs provided a medium for additional information in the form of further recorded footprints tracked throughout the house. As might be expected, there have been numerous individuals present after the crime was discovered – policemen tramping up and down the steps, with regulation boot prints that are easily identified and disregarded – yours among them, Bradstreet. Similarly, I found evidence of one woman, certainly Mrs. Stroud. I was able to identify the prints of Doctor Smallwood from the shoes in his wardrobe – he has unusually small feet, as I had previously observed when meeting him at the hospital, and then in Baker Street.

"But after these were located and identified, there was one other set of footprints that revealed themselves. They were tracked through the dust and the flour, underneath all the others – the policemen, the housekeeper, and even Smallwood himself. They are in the dust on the landing there, and outside the bedroom door as well. Their configuration indicates that it was this unknown man who broke open the bedroom door.

174

From his stride, he is a bit over six feet in height. His prints are in the dust downstairs *before* the mess in the kitchen was made, and they are both under and in the flour, indicating that he spilled it when searching the rooms.

"First, he came in by the front door after picking the lock, as seen from the fresh marks on the downstairs door. Entering surreptitiously, he crept upstairs. Finding the bedroom door locked, he proceeded to break in. His prints in the dust of the hall floor tell the tale, including where he braced himself against this sturdy door. He then entered the bedroom, walked around quickly, and then left the first time before looking through the rest of the house. Finding it apparently empty, as shown how quickly he entered and then turned and left, he began to search more thoroughly, causing the mess in the kitchen. He went back and forth, upstairs and down, tearing up the parlour, tracking flour throughout the house and sometimes crossing his own earlier prints in the dust, showing that the search came after his initial entry. Finally he left, probably without finding what he sought."

"You say that he broke into the bedroom but then left quickly," I said. "Why didn't he encounter Smallwood? Wouldn't the doctor have been behind the locked bedroom door?"

"And how," added Bradstreet, "do you theorize that he left without finding what he was seeking?"

"I believe that it can be inferred this way . . . ." And so saying, he led us into the bedroom, providing my first vision of the bloody scene. It was poorly-lit, with one hinged window that looked out onto a low rooftop. Holmes had lit a lamp when he first entered, and the dim yellow light only served to emphasize the horror of the bloodstains splashed about. Most of it was on the sheets, themselves half-torn from the bed. But

175

there was some thrown against the wall, as if an artery had been ripped open, with gouts of pressurized gore shooting forth.

I was able to direct my attention away from the most horrifying aspects and see that the room had nothing in it to reflect the doctor's personality. Like the downstairs parlour, there were no pictures or paintings, no books or magazines – nothing to give this room any more personality than if it had been in a low-class hotel, with a different occupant every night.

Holmes was speaking. "A quick examination of the window shows that nothing went out that way – and certainly not a bloody body. From careful examination of the footprints, one can see that they are overlain in places by small bare feet – certainly the doctor's. As these are on top of the intruder's prints, he was clearly here *after* the intruder left. For if the intruder had found the doctor, then it's likely that the doctor's body would have truly lain here, instead of this staged illusion of murder."

"Staged illusion?" exclaimed Bradstreet.

"When the stranger entered the house," Holmes continued, "he was obviously confident as to his destination – the bedroom – and that he wouldn't be disturbed by any live-in servants. This shows that he had previously gained some knowledge of the house. At the top of the stairs, he encountered the locked bedroom door – and we know it was locked, for why else would he need to break it open? It says much about Dr. Smallwood's fears, in that he felt the need to lock himself into his bedroom at night in an already-locked establishment – and rightly so, as it turns out, as he had a visitor up to no good who managed to get in so easily.

"Once this mysterious intruder entered the bedroom, he clearly found it empty, because his footprints show that he only spent a few cursory seconds here, looking behind the curtains and under the bed, before searching elsewhere in the house –

first for the doctor, and then, not finding him, for whatever else it was that he sought. That must be an item that would fit into the torn chairs downstairs, or the flour canister. He returned to the bedroom a second time to search for the object – see the flour footprints here and here, lying over the top of his others in the plain dust? Why, throughout all of this back-and-forth, didn't he find the doctor? Because the man was cleverly hiding."

He motioned us toward the small fireplace across from the bed and pointed at the floor. "Here – Do you see the doctor's bare footprints? And this line of them here through the dust?"

I bent forward and could just make them out in the dim light. They led toward the wall to the right of the fireplace, between the mantel and the outside wall near the window. It was a narrow panel, about three feet wide and covered with dingy paper, and there was seemingly nothing noteworthy about it. Holmes motioned toward the baseboard. Bradstreet and I moved closer and, making sure to stay out of the dim lamplight, we could see that the small prints seemed to end at the wall. In fact, the baseboard was above what appeared to be the back half of a print, showing only the bare heel.

"These would have been invisible in the middle of the night. The searcher couldn't have seen them."

"But what does it mean?" asked Bradstreet.

With a smile instead of a response, Holmes stepped forward and pressed a hand against the bare wall. With a thump and a click, it suddenly opened outward like a door, revealing a narrow space behind it.

Bradstreet made a noise, and Holmes gestured us forward. We could see that it was only a foot or so deep, and it held nothing except for a very narrow table, about three feet tall, pushed to one side. This was covered in thick dust, except for a bare rectangular shape on top about the size of a small doctor's case. The floor was also dusty, and was marked by a number of overlapping footprints made by small bare feet.

Holmes leaned toward the chamber's door and took a deep breath. "The wood used to construct the door to this hidey-hole still smells new enough to indicate that it was Doctor Smallwood himself who constructed it, probably not long after he moved here. One can see that the back wall of the cavity – the original wall that was next to the fireplace – has a much-faded and different wallpaper than what is in the bedroom. Smallwood certainly built this chamber in secret, most certainly on weekends or at night when he returned from the hospital. Then he repapered the entire bedroom with a similar old wallpaper to hide the changes.

"But surely Mrs. Stroud would have noticed the difference? Or the signs of construction?"

"Not necessarily. A man who knew what he was doing could have built this over a long weekend. Or perhaps he informed her that she wouldn't be needed for several days, giving him more time. I'd be willing to wager that if questioned, she will remember a period when the doctor told her that he'd be out of town, or some such story, allowing him to accomplish this task undisturbed. After framing and installing the door, he could hang the wallpaper and get rid of any wood scraps or other litter. When she returned, she would have no reason to notice that this area beside the fireplace wasn't quite as deep as it had been just a few days before. I imagine that she rarely came up here in any case."

"And the bare spot on the little table?" I asked. "Where there is no dust. He kept a case there?"

"I believe so," answered Holmes. "I think that was the mysterious item that the intruder sought – which goes to the point of exactly why Smallwood felt the need to construct this little pseudo-priest's hole in the first place. He feared something, and he was prepared. He had to work to earn a living, and he did so at a public location where he doubted that he would be approached or threatened. But here at home, alone, he felt much more vulnerable. He built this chamber for hiding, and he kept the case hidden there, to be carried away if he had to flee – which he has clearly done.

"From the evidence of the footprints, I believe this is what occurred: As he did every night, Smallwood went to bed, locking himself in. In addition to the multiple broken slide bolts on the door – and why would he have so many if not in fear of something? – one can see that the lock is much more sturdy than those usually found on a bedroom door. When the intruder revealed his presence and began to try and force his way in, Smallwood jumped up and entered the chamber – something which he would have practiced repeatedly and would take only seconds. Pulling the secret door shut behind him, using that handle mounted there on the inside, he waited while the intruder came in, only to find a seemingly empty room. I've entered the chamber, and there is a very small hole in the door at Smallwood's eye level which would have allowed the doctor to see out into the bedroom.

"Smallwood observed the visitor, and then he listened while the search was made through the entire house. Only afterwards, when he was certain that the intruder had departed – possibly after hours of fearful waiting – did he come out and ascertain that the house was empty. His movements at this time are confirmed in several places throughout the house where his bare footprints lay on top of the intruder's. He then dressed – as shown by his small shoeprints overlaying his bare prints – and made his escape, taking the case with him."

"But the blood?" asked Bradstreet, gesturing toward the disheveled bed. "There is so much of it. How do you explain that? And why?"

Holmes waved a hand. "Distraction. Diversion. Deception. Smallwood decided that it was time to flee. Whatever he has feared has tracked him here, and rather than face it, he has abandoned his life and job. I believe that he must have had a plan in place, in the same way that he built this place to hide. He knew that Mrs. Stroud would see the broken bedroom door, and the violence that it implies, and so, to add further confusion to the issue, he cut himself and bled onto several spots, primarily the sheets. The pattern of blood on the wall, initially seeming to be a spray, is actually what would occur if he had cupped a bit of his own blood in his hand and simply threw it.

"As a doctor, he could effectively tap a spot, most likely a small artery or vein in his arm, to obtain an effective quantity of blood without endangering himself, and you both know that a relatively small amount of blood can spread quite far, as we've all seen before when a murderer tries to hide its presence. He opened the window to imply that the body was carried out by way of the rooftops, further adding to the mystery, but as I've noted, there is no evidence of a body actually passing through. Then he dressed and departed by way of the front door, locking it behind him. You will note that his keys are apparently not present."

Bradstreet winced at that missed fact and rubbed a hand over his face. He then spent a few moments looking around the hidden chamber, the bedroom, and the hallway. On several occasions he leaned forward to inspect the floor, but he didn't indicate whether he truly saw what had been described, or if it still remained invisible to him. I knew to trust Holmes's interpretation rather than waste my own energy trying to confirm it.

Finally the inspector straightened and said, "What now, then? Where has he gone? How do we trace him? And what crime are we actually investigating? This isn't a murder any longer. Instead, some stranger has invaded this property and caused physical damage to the premises. We might prosecute several other minor charges should we find this intruder, but to what benefit? And Dr. Smallwood has fled – he cannot bring charges or swear out a complaint, and I doubt that he would, even if we could find him, because it seems as if he has some secret of his own that's so dear that he'd rather abandon his life and career than to seek help."

"But he *did* seek help," said Holmes. "From me. Or he tried to, at any rate. And he shall have it."

Bradstreet turned his head. "If you're sure that this is related to his visit to your rooms, you're welcome to it. There's nothing for the police here, after all – although I don't relish the press's reaction when they're told that a gory murder was simply the merest moonshine."

"Then don't tell them," said Holmes. "At least for a while. Give me a chance to locate Smallwood."

"How?" I asked. "He's clearly planned his escape as carefully as he prepared his hiding place. He could be anywhere by now."

"True. But if I can pick up a trail, it will either happen easily or not at all. Will you hold back what we've discovered here tonight, Inspector?"

I thought it was rather charitable for Holmes to refer to the story that he had revealed as *our* discovery, and clearly the expression on Bradstreet's face showed that he was in agreement. Yet he concurred. "I'll see that we don't waste any more time on pursuing a murderer, and I'll start a discrete inquiry or two into where the doctor might have gone, and any enemies that he has acquired."

"An examination of his background before his arrival at Barts would be most helpful too, and ideally suited to your vast resources, Inspector," said Holmes graciously. "With your permission, I'll return in the morning to make a further examination of the doctor's papers in the other room down the hall. Perhaps there's a thread to be found there."

Bradstreet agreed, and with that, we made our way downstairs and out to the street. The large constable returned indoors, shutting and locking the door behind him. We walked out to Gower Street and thence around to the Tottenham Court Road, where we found cabs, one to take Bradstreet to his home, and the other to carry Holmes and me back to Baker Street.

Holmes had been silent upon our return that night, and he was already gone the next morning when I came down for breakfast. I decided to take myself off to Barts, both to offer my professional services, and to get a sense of what was occurring there following the reported violent death of Dr. Smallwood.

Surprisingly, while there were some conversations held in hallways by small private clusters of two or three people, the reaction was not what I would have expected. Now, having the benefit of Holmes's declaration that the man wasn't as well thought of as I'd believed, I could see that, while curious as to the nature of the event itself, no one appeared to miss Smallwood very much, and there was no sense of grief. How sad, I thought, when the absence of a life, by violent means as far as any of these people knew, could provoke no stronger reaction. I'd once heard the death of a certain ineffectual soldier callously described as having no made no more difference than that of a hole left in the ocean when a man removes his hand from it, and Smallwood's seeming death appeared to matter about as much. Schedules were rearranged, a certain curiosity was evinced, and as time passed, it would simply be another anecdote among many in the life of the hospital – the friendless doctor who was killed in his rooms.

Of course, I thought, it was just barely possible that someone at the hospital knew more than they revealed, but I believed that Smallwood's enemy wasn't here. After all, he had walked these halls with cocky confidence, fearing nothing. It was at his modest home, where he was alone, that he had felt the need to construct his defenses.

I didn't see Holmes that night, but the next day, when I was again back at Barts, I observed him down a long hallway, conversing with Sir James Wheeler, a man deeply involved with the hospital's administration. Even as I watched, they turned and went into one of the offices. I had my own responsibilities and went a different way.

Over the next few weeks, Holmes and I were involved in a number of other investigations, and yet I was aware that he hadn't dropped the matter of Smallwood's supposed murder. However, as was so often the case, he seemed to prefer that we didn't discuss it without any new facts to exchange, believing that theorizing without data tended to make one gravitate toward a favored theory, and in turn seek out supporting evidence while neglecting other facts. Therefore it was rather unexpected when, one evening not long after I'd arrived back at our rooms and was getting comfortable in my armchair, Holmes came in, rubbing his hands briskly. Clearly he'd had a successful day.

"Are you free tomorrow for a little trip to Harrogate in regard to the Smallwood affair?"

I raised an eyebrow. "You have a lead?"

"More than that. I have located the man."

Part II – The Curious Story

The next morning found us leaving King's Cross Station. We had a private smoker and had arranged ourselves comfortably with a number of newspapers strewn about. At Holmes's feet was a small black satchel, but he hadn't bothered to explain its purpose. As a matter of fact, I knew nothing about our trip but our general destination. It was no surprise to me by that point in our friendship that Holmes hadn't provided any additional information. The previous night we had instead discussed another unrelated matter which he had peripherally discovered while conversing with Sir James Wheeler, regarding a patient being treated through mesmerism. While I cannot provide any specific details, the conversation with Sir James led to the prevention of an assassination of one of the highest in the land. Hopefully I will be able to reveal the details of that affair at some point in the future, but current strictures prevent it.

Before we'd departed, Holmes confirmed that I was carrying my old service revolver. By that time, I'd learned that it was unwise to leave home without it. One never knew when, in Holmes's presence, violence might be encountered, and he had many enemies. As I was his associate, and also becoming more known to the criminal element, I'd found that I was acquiring a few as well.

As the train left London, Holmes related his activities of the previous couple of weeks. "The morning after our trip to Gower Mews, I returned there, with Bradstreet's permission, and gave the place a very thorough examination. I found no new evidence about the intruder's identity or the events of the night of the supposed murder, but I did gain a better understanding of Smallwood himself, by way of his papers and the sparse reading material in his study. He has stayed current

184

on his medical studies. He has a fascination with India, and especially legends from there relating to the old religions. And for a man who never went anywhere – at least since he arrived at Barts – he had a small collection of British travel brochures. At the hospital, I was given access to his office by Sir James, who owes me a favor or two."

I was impressed, but didn't say so. Perhaps this was the influence at Barts that Holmes had mentioned several weeks earlier, when alluding to the fact that my position was more protected than I had known.

Holmes pulled out his pipe and continued. "Dr. Smallwood had a stash of clippings and brochures, similar to those found in his home study, in his office desk at Barts."

"Including, I'm thinking, one or more related to Harrogate."

"You progress, Watson. Indeed, while there were various documents related to several similar sites in England, there were more about there than any other location. He'd also accumulated several newspapers from that area, and one showed a circled advertisement seeking a physician at the Valley Gardens Spa – quite recent, as a matter of fact."

"Very timely, it turns out, if that's where he has found a new billet, just as he needed it – *if* that's where he went."

"Oh, it is. I wouldn't be dragging us there simply to confirm the fact. I sent a man named Barker, a private detective who has done some work for me before, there yesterday, after eliminating the other sites. He has seen a man who is certainly Smallwood, and he confirmed to me by wire this morning that the doctor is still there.

"While I still have no idea what led to Smallwood's departure," Holmes continued, "the fact that he doesn't want to be found gives us leverage. I expect that we can get an explanation from him, if for no other reason than to satisfy our curiosity."

I raised an eyebrow. "I had wondered about that. As Bradstreet explained, the police have no further interest in this from the standpoint of a prosecution. It seems that there isn't a single solitary individual at Barts who cares if the man ever comes back. You have no client, and I certainly doubt that Smallwood himself will offer you any reward for rooting him out. Why should you go any further, or put yourself to all this trouble and expense? What is the point?"

"Education, my friend. It never ends. This affair offers neither public credit nor reward, but it is instructive and I would see the end of it, if only to satisfy the artist in me. Besides," he added, "I perhaps failed to adequately define the duchess's generous settlement when I located her hideous earrings. 'Generous' is an understatement. I can afford to indulge myself and see through to the end of this matter."

As I had learned to expect, Holmes didn't feel the need to further explain his process for locating the doctor, or what he expected when we arrived. Our talk instead ranged from Holmes's recent exposure of the peculations of Lord C------ to the peculiar withering of Colonel Edington's left arm and, more quickly than I would have thought, we arrived at Harrogate. Securing a cab, we took a direct route along the Leeds road. I could see that in warmer weather, the place would be beautiful, but under late February's grim skies, and with the trees bare and skeletal, the immediate charm of the place was decidedly absent. And yet, there were a number of tourists here, undoubtedly drawn by the mineral springs, unchanging in their reputed benefits regardless of the passing seasons.

At the main building, Holmes looked around, possibly hoping to spot his man, Barker. However, no one who looked like a private detective was visible, and we went inside. At the main desk, we inquired as to where the new doctor, known here as Stafford according to Holmes's agent, might be located. We were given directions to the clinic. Winding through the grounds, we found a small one-story structure, set discretely away in one of the many gardens dotting the property. Stepping to the door, I was prepared to confront Smallwood as we entered, but my expectations were dashed by an anticlimactic conversation with a receptionist, who stated that the new doctor was taking a walk in the grounds, as the call for his services was very light at present.

And so we found ourselves ambling along meandering paths, near vaguely metallic-smelling pools, passing small groves and flower beds that would be breathtaking in the proper months, but were now brown and fallow. Here and there we encountered other people out for their own explorations, mostly women in groups of twos or threes. We would nod, as would they, and sometimes Holmes would touch the front brim of his fore-and-aft cap – although what method of determination he used to decide when and when not to do this escaped me. As I considered his reasons, we saw, standing perhaps twenty or thirty feet in front of us, a big man in a brown suit and curiously dark glasses. From Holmes's reaction, this was undoubtedly Barker. The man nodded, indicated the path beyond him, and then turned and departed the area by another way. We continued along the main path, rounding a curve, and it was almost a surprise when we moved past a growth of bushes and found Smallwood sitting alone on a bench, staring across the gravel path at one of the wider ponds.

He glanced our way, and initially he showed no signs of recognition. We were just two more of the resort's visitors. But then he seemed to refocus as both of us became familiar to him.

187

He made a huffing sound while taking a sudden breath. He sat up straight, one leg cocked back as if to arise and perhaps flee. Then, almost as soon as he had made the motion, he collapsed back onto the bench with a look of defeat.

"Mr. Holmes. Watson. This is no coincidental meeting, is it?"

We paused five or so feet in front of him. "Not at all," said Holmes. "A man who is planning his own disappearance should certainly be more careful about which brochures and clippings he leaves behind. A great deal can be inferred from a man's interests. Your visitor that night may have seen them as well."

Smallwood shook his head, as if annoyed by an insect. "It doesn't really matter, does it? Are you here to reveal to the world that I am not dead?"

"Not at all."

"Then why? What do you hope to accomplish, tracking me here?" Suddenly he stiffened and sat up straight, perhaps only then hearing what Holmes had said about his visitor. "Were you followed?"

"Of course not."

"How do you know?"

"If you knew me, then you wouldn't need to ask that question."

Smallwood frowned. "Are you working for *him* then? Did he hire you to find me?"

"I assume that you mean the man of slightly over six feet who broke into your rooms, causing you to retreat to the small cupboard that you'd constructed by the fireplace. If that is who you mean, then he did not hire me. We haven't encountered him, and we know nothing of his identity."

Smallwood looked dumbfounded. "You discovered the hidden space? How? Did I leave it partially open when I departed?"

"No. I observed your bare footprints in the dust leading to and from that seemingly empty wall. One was cut in half, with only the heel end of your foot showing at the edge of the floor molding, left there when you entered and then shut the door. Clearly you had been behind the wall. It was but the work of a moment to discover how to open the door – What one man can hide, another can discover."

"Not just any man, I'm thinking," muttered Smallwood. "Why are you here?"

"Watson asked me the same question. Education. Enlightenment. To hear your story. And perhaps to offer assistance – which you were going to request that night before I declined to help you."

Smallwood shook his head. "I've regretted that ever since. Perhaps if I had gone ahead and told you – But then again, I don't know what you could have done. Going to see you was born of impulse, and in the end, my current situation is probably as good a solution as I could have expected – for now."

"Can you tell us your story? Why you fear this man, and why you have fled?"

He covered his face with his hands and sat still for a long moment. Our arrival had clearly shaken him. That is the only reason, in hindsight, that seems to explain why he chose to share his story.

Then he sighed. "I suppose it will do me good to tell someone, and I owe you something for going to the trouble of finding me. And Watson – " he added. "I owe you an apology as well. I've had some time to see my errors."

189

I waved a hand, although I couldn't disagree that he needed to make amends. "Perhaps," I said, "we could return to your quarters, and we can speak in a warmer environment."

And so we adjourned back to his modest rooms, and within a few moments we were behind a closed door in front of a warm fire, enjoying hot coffee when Holmes spoke. "My research into your past reveals that it's rather shallow. For instance, while you *are* a doctor, your name *isn't* Leland Smallwood. Rather, you are – or were – Grant Daventry, raised near Northampton, and trained in Edinburgh."

I glanced at Holmes, wondering why he hadn't mentioned these facts on the train. We'd certainly had time to discuss them. It seemed to be simply another example of his tendency to retain information until it needed to be shared. Smallwood, as I continued to think of him, had looked at Holmes for a few seconds in amazement, and then started to protest before settling back with a shake of his head. "You're right, of course, although how you could have learned the truth so quickly is beyond me."

"You were careless, Doctor," responded Holmes. "I went through all of your private papers and found several old items related to Grant Daventry – military pay documents, for instance. Tracing the rest was easy. Obviously you thought that your new identity would never be penetrated deeply enough for anyone to study your papers, or to learn anything from them. You should have kept them packed for when you fled, but I suspect that over time you've simply forgotten that you had them as you carried the old papers with you from place to place.

"I researched your past as 'Dr. Smallwood' and came to a dead end five years ago, when you first showed up in Manchester, obtaining a position with the hospital there. It was with that reference that you negotiated a move to Barts. Before

Manchester, the trail to Dr. Smallwood faded away, and I switched to Grant Daventry, born in 1831, raised in the East Midlands, and trained at the Edinburgh Medical School, after which you joined the army and went out to India, where you served during the Siege of Cawnpore.

"Something happened there, or not long after, Doctor, that caused you to abandon the name Grant Daventry. I don't know what name – or names – you took then, between Daventry and Smallwood, and it doesn't matter. There may have been only one identity, or there could be many others, before you became Leland Smallwood. And then something happened to make you abandon that one as well, obtaining this position as Albert Stafford."

"True, Mr. Holmes. All true."

"You went to a great deal of trouble," Holmes continued, "to build that hidden cabinet, and obviously you knew that it would be necessary. I'm curious. You've had much time to plan, and you've apparently had encounters before with whomever it is that is hunting you. Not that I can condone it, but why have you not simply killed this pursuer? For instance, you could have laid a trap in your rooms the other night. You could have killed him and no one would have known. Doctors are always clever at the ways of ending another human's life. You could have hidden the body in the secret chamber until you had time to dispose of it – and you would have certainly known how. Then you would have been finished with all of this. Why continue to flee from this man?

"Because," answered Smallwood, "I am a doctor, and I do not kill. And more importantly, because this man who pursues me is my brother."

We were silent for a moment, considering what Smallwood has just related. Then he continued, saying almost beyond our hearing, "I must tell it." Then, louder, "It's time to tell it to someone." He took a deep breath.

"I was in Cawnpore in '57, when the siege began. When reading about it now, the history books would make one believe that it was a cut-and-dried thing with certain moments that broke the events into discrete units, but it wasn't that way. You know what it's like, Watson. Oh yes, I know more about you than you think. I've seen your record, and know about your Afghan service. You know how it is in battle – to be trapped within the limits of what you can personally see, hear, and tast and smell – and learn. Rumors fly every which way, with no way to separate the truth from the lies, or simply the despairing wishes of the doomed.

"On the fifth of June, Nana Sahib, who had turned against us, politely sent a note to General Wheeler announcing that he planned to attack the next day. Word spread like a wildfire, and we knew we'd never be ready in time. I was never sure why the note was sent at all, although our panic did as much to hinder us as if we'd never done anything to prepare, and what we did manage to accomplish clearly communicated to the enemy what our intended defense was to be – allowing his own response to be formulated while exposing what we had left undefended.

"In the midst of this, I received a message from my brother, seeking my help. He is a year younger than me, but in temperament he was much more immature. I have to believe that even now, with no direct conversation between us in twenty-five years, that he hasn't changed. He was always physically quite different than me, and I've come to suspect that we had different fathers, but my mother died when we were young, and I could never verify it – even if I could have summoned the courage to ask. As we grew up, he was always in trouble, and it fell to me to try and look out for him. When I

192

joined the army after medical school, our father – who was small like me, yet never questioned that Benjamin, my brother, was his own son – felt that it would be beneficial to him if he joined as well. He arranged for Benjamin to be assigned with me, so that I could keep a brotherly eye on him. From the first the plan failed. He was a malcontent, a malingerer, and in constant conflict with his superiors. But as the conditions worsened around us, he didn't receive the rebukes that he deserved, for every man was going to be useful when the inevitable fighting began.

"It was the morning that the battle was promised that I received the message from my brother, whom I hadn't seen in several days, asking for me to join him in a nearby village. I had no idea why he was there, and I half-feared that he had deserted. No reason for his message was given, and I had duties that should have kept me at my post, but this was my brother, and I had promised to look out for him. Knowing that the enemy forces that were building against us, I felt that I had to seek him out.

"I arranged to get away and found him at in a seedy tavern, built to cater to the soldiers. Stepping from my horse, I was met with glares of hostility from the locals and was reconsidering my visit when my brother stepped outside, dressed in local garb. He has always been so different from me – taller, with thick dark hair even as mine started to vanish while I was still in my twenties – and he could have almost passed for a local, except for his bright blue eyes.

"He frowned when he saw my uniform, but he couldn't rebuke me, as his message had said nothing about disguising myself – as if that would have been possible. I started to go inside, but he took my arm, pulling me instead away from the gathered onlookers. Then he walked to a saddled horse and pulled down a blanket. 'Wrap this around yourself,' he muttered.

"Without asking why, I did so. He motioned that I should remount my own horse, and then he led me out of the village at a slow trot to the northeast. Riding while wrapped to hide my uniform was inconvenient, but I saw its wisdom as we were able to get by various men and women walking toward Cawnpore, all seemingly indifferent to our passing. Several times I tried to ask him where we were going, but he simply replied that I would know when we arrived. When I complained that we needed to return to our camp, and the protection it offered, before the battle, and that we would both be missed, or possibly even be charged as deserters, he growled impatiently. I must admit that my willingness to let him lead me to wherever we traveled outweighed my good sense.

"Finally we arrived at the edge of a series of low rolling foothills, seemingly stretching unbroken into the distance towards the high mountains of Nepal. Only at that point did he pause by a rushing stream to allow the horses to drink. We'd been traveling for several hours by then, and the road had first narrowed to a path, and then a barely visible trail passing between scrubby trees. India is a crowded country, but it had been quite a while since we had seen anyone. The land around us had become more rugged, and with it there hung a loneliness that made me think that no one had ever lived there – as if it were cursed.

"But while we were paused, my brother pulled an old parchment map from his shirt and checked it. I expressed curiosity about it, but he ignored me. Seemingly satisfied, he led us back to the trail, and within ten minutes we had passed across a low rise and were approaching the base of a small mountain, surrounded by tumbled boulders and jagged teeth-like stones pushing up from the earth. Stagnant pools surrounded many of them, with reeds choking the water. Other places between the rocks appeared to be solid ground, wide flat spots of a very dark green, but even as I watched, these would sometimes quiver, as if something unseen had passed underneath, causing the thin lattice of vegetation on top to rise and ripple. There was an oppressive silence, heavy like a storm about to break, and interrupted only the buzzing of insects. The ancient trail, or what there was of it, was a thin and winding line, and I believed us to be safe from the surrounding mire, but to leave it would mean death.

"As we neared the mountainside, I could see that what had initially appeared to be just more of the tumbled stone was resolving into something of a geometric shape – and more specifically, it soon revealed itself to be the lintel of a squared stone doorway, though only three or four feet tall. I had the impression that it had once been taller, but the weight of the mountain itself, along with the softness of the ground before it, had served to push the door, and whatever it led to, down into the earth. At some point, it would certainly vanish entirely.

"My brother dismounted and I followed suit. As we tied the horses, I asked, 'What is this place?'

"'I won the map on a wager,' was his evasive answer. 'I doubt that the man who lost it was supposed to reveal anything about this spot. Some old temple from some old religion – long before anyone's memory. I rode out here yesterday, but I couldn't force my way in alone. I need your help.'

"So now I understood. I considered reasoning with him, or asking him what he hoped to find, but I decided that it would be easier to help him and simply get it over with, and then insist that we return to Cawnpore as soon as possible. He led me to the entrance, and I paused a moment to study it. The stone lintel was supported by a couple of matching columns, squared and several feet across each side. They were covered in hieroglyphs, birds and men with animal heads. It was all vaguely Egyptian, but I didn't recognize the symbols. Over the years, I've done research and tried to find out what they might have meant, but my memory of that day is fragmentary at best, and I've never been able to ascertain anything.

"After just a moment, my brother made an impatient noise and gestured toward the dark opening. We bent low and entered. There was a damp smell all around us, rather like peat, and I couldn't help but think that the tunnel into which we had entered must surely be flooded, considering the high water table that was all around the entrance. And yet, my brother said that he had entered the day before. A dark path stretched away before us, down into the mountain, and it seemed dry enough. The ceiling was high so that we could stand upright. Lying on the ground just inside the entrance were a pair of lanterns, along with a pick and a steel pry bar, apparently left there when my brother had visited the day before. I pondered that there were two lanterns, but didn't give it too much thought. The reason only became apparent later. Lighting the lanterns, he handed one to me. Then taking the pick for himself, and gesturing that I should carry the bar, he led me down the tunnel.

"We began to slope gently down to the left and, looking back, I saw that the light from the entrance had already vanished as the tunnel curved. The walls were damp, and in places I could see small puddles on the floor, some of which ran to others, where they joined. As we progressed, a small rivulet – only a few inches wide – formed to one side of the chamber, its flow revealed only by the tiny ripples reflecting on its surface from the passing lantern light. Soon a small groove appeared in the floor, serving to collect and direct the increasing flow ahead of us and into the deeper darkness.

"I began to be concerned about the weight of the mountain above us, but a closer examination of the walls revealed that they were formed from giant stones, several feet in width and height, that fit together so tightly that I couldn't press the end of my fingernail between them. I couldn't begin to imagine how many stones that we'd already passed, making up the floor and walls and ceiling, and there was no telling how many more lay before us. Who had made this effort? What was their purpose? And where had they gone? I knew nothing of the local culture, or any of their legends, but it seemed certain that this place was far older than any of the peoples that now lived in the region.

"As I would stop sometimes to examine this or that aspect of the tunnel, my brother would lumber on, steadily advancing while I would pause and then hurry to catch up. He never looked back, and never spoke. Although it can't have been for more than a few minutes, time was meaningless there, and I lost track of how long we walked, with the tunnel never getting any wider or taller. The sameness had a numbing effect, and it came as something of a surprise when we were suddenly faced with a tall flat stone blocking our path – a door of some sort. I could see fresh chips along one side of it where my brother had attempted to force his way past it the day before. He set down his lantern, took the iron bar roughly from my hands, and wedged the end of it into the newly chipped cavity. The bar's curve angled it toward us. Then he impatiently ordered, "'Help me, for God's sake! Why do you think I asked you here?'

"Setting down my own lantern, I moved beside him. Taking hold of the iron bar and leaning close, I began to pull when I felt him do the same. At first, nothing happened, and I thought that we were fools to try. But then, with my brother's hissed instructions to try harder, and with a number of his curses ringing in my ears as well, I redoubled my efforts. And after a moment of groaning agony, in which I feared that I might crack my teeth from grinding them so hard, we felt the massive door slip – just a little.

"Easing back, we wheezed for several minutes, trying to slow our racing hearts. Then Benjamin reached down and, using the side of the pick-head as a hammer, proceeded to drive the bar a little deeper into the crack outlining the door. Then we leaned into it again, feeling a bit more movement. This process was repeated several times until, without warning, the door suddenly gave way, falling backwards onto the stone floor behind it with a loud jarring force that shook us both.

"The sudden release caught us both by surprise, and we fell forward. I went down on my hands and knees, feeling a stabbing pain as my left kneecap intersected with the stone floor. I cried aloud, and though my pain, I heard my brother wail, and then stop abruptly. Squeezing my eyes tightly shut for a moment, I waited until the agony had subsided, and then forced myself to my feet, trying to find my footing. In the dim lantern light, a terrible sight was revealed.

"In falling forward, my brother had somehow been impaled on the iron bar as it fell from where it had been wedged in the door opening. In some freakish way, one end had fallen to the floor just as he tumbled over it, bracing itself as the other end pushed through the soft tissues of his abdomen. He had then collapsed onto the ground, with the bar passing completely through him from front to back.

"He was lying on his side and seemed to be dead. I took a step forward, very much in shock, but even as I did so, my eye was drawn to a flash of light, past him in the darkness of the newly opened chamber, showing just a wink, seemingly floating two or three feet off the ground. Another step revealed it to be coming from something reflective, catching the weak yellowish lantern light and returning it with a focused white glow that left a spot burned into my vision. I shifted a step to one side, letting more of the lantern light pass me, showing a narrow thin stone plinth, only a few inches around, rising from the floor like a rock needle, formed from the rock of the floor itself. It was black and reflected nothing – it was almost an illusion. I could only see it at all because it was a little less black than the void behind it. And resting on the flattened top was a jewel.

"But that doesn't begin to describe it. There has never been another like it – years of study has convinced me of this. It was larger than the size of my fist – a diamond, with a multitude of facets, some large, and others much smaller, filling in the geometric spaces between the intersections of the various planes. It seemed to have a blue fire within it, a fiery bursting star, and I could not look away.

"For that moment I had forgotten my brother, until he groaned. With all my will, I tore my gaze away and forced myself to look toward him, and when my eyes readjusted back to the darkness of the tunnel, I could see him, lying on the floor just outside the lintel of the inner chamber, trying to push himself into a sitting position against the doorway, his limbs scrabbling like those of an insect who has been partially trodden and gutted by a child's indifferent footstep, spastically trapped in its own juices. Blood was pooling around him, shimmering in the weak light, and I was certain that his injuries must be mortal. In spite of that, I had started to go to his aid when I saw that he had pulled a gun from within his garments, and that it was aimed at my heart.

"'It's mine,' he groaned. 'You won't have it.' And with that he fired.

"I don't know how he missed me. I instinctively dodged, and he must have been very weak, letting the gun sag at the last second. I should have died then, but I felt the bullet pass me by inches, and I heard the whine of it ricochet off the stone walls behind me and back into the dark void beyond the diamond. Then, without a sound, Benjamin's arm dropped, the gun making a weak clatter, and he passed out.

"I dropped to my knees and warily touched his throat. His pulse was thready and his breathing was ragged. I believed that he would pass very soon. And as I considered what I should do – irrationally wondering how to get him home for burial, and what my poor father would think – my eyes glanced up again, and the glow of the jewel, perhaps even brighter from this angle, found me again and took all of my attention.

"As if in a dream, I stood and, stepping away my brother's body – which I believed would soon be his corpse – and through his blood that was running ahead into the darkness, I reached out a hand. From beyond the plinth, in the black darkness unaffected by the weak lantern light, a cold breeze blew, seemingly stronger as my hand neared the diamond. I had the sense, with no evidence at all, that the darkness continued into a vast cavern, and that the door which we had opened should have stayed shut forever. As my hand nearly touched the diamond, I hesitated, as if expecting a sting or shock, or perhaps even a burn, but then – I closed my fingers around it and lifted it from its resting place.

"It had seemed magical when first observed, but there was no supernatural rush of power through me when I took it, and no heat or vibration of energy. It felt cold, as could only be expected from something discovered in that long-forgotten damp passage. And yet, I felt an odd satisfaction, a completeness, as I held it, filling an emptiness that I'd never known I'd had.

"The question of what to do about my brother seemed less important now. He had lured me here, needing my help to find the jewel, and I suspected that he had shot at me so easily only

200

because he'd already planned to do so in any case, dismissing me in his own mind after my purpose was served. I would have been executed, and he would have departed with the treasure to fulfill his own plans. My mind was made up then, and without bothering to check him any further, I pushed the diamond into my shirt, stepped over his still form and, picking up one of the lanterns, walked quickly away and up the passage. He never made a sound, and I thought that he was already dead.

"In hindsight, I should have checked him one more time. Perhaps it would have saved my soul. But I felt a compulsion beyond explanation, calling me to carry away my treasure and escape. I thought of nothing else. And yet, besides failing to check and see if Benjamin still lived, I've always regretted that I never thought to retrieve the map that he'd carried. Clearly it told something of the tale of the jewel, and possibly its history. It certainly related to my brother the knowledge of what was behind the stone door so that he would know to search there.

"I don't know who originally made the map, or who lost it to my brother, or anything about the people who put the jewel there and made such an elaborate construction to conceal it. Knowledge of them has vanished forever – if it ever existed at all. In all the years since, in all my researches into the legends of that area, there has been nothing that I could find to explain what the stone represented to those lost people, or the tunnel, or how they gained such skills to build it, or even any of the legends that one would have expected to grow up around it.

"I can't say if I still might not have changed my mind and gone back to check on my brother, my compassion and my medical oath reasserting themselves after initially being suppressed. But outside, when I reached the horses, I happened to notice a mound of stones a few dozen feet to one side of the trail. Around it were a number of pock-marks in the soil, where the cobble-sized rocks had been dislodged to place onto the stack, leaving fresh muddy scars and holes in the earth. The stones which had been removed were obvious – half of their surface was discolored from having been so long in the earth – and I wondered what was hidden there under that pile, and apparently recently.

"It was only the work of a minute to uncover a body – a native, shot once in the back of the head. This, then, was the explanation of the second lantern that had awaited us in the tunnel. The man was in his fifties – rather elderly for the area – and small – even smaller than me, and quite thin and sickly looking. He had surely been lured there the previous day by my brother to assist in opening the door, but his strength hadn't been equal to the task. To tie up a loose end, my brother had apparently killed him before returning to civilization to enlist my aid. What I had suspected in the tunnel now seemed more certain: Like this man, some anonymous fellow whose connection or loyalty to my brother would now never be known, I would have been eliminated once my assistance was given, and most likely buried in a similar stone-covered grave – possibly even this same grave, reopened just long enough to tumble my carcass onto its first occupant.

"Whatever remorse I might have felt about failing to aid my brother seemed to vanish at that moment – although I was to find in years later that it never truly departed from me. I've agonized in the time since. Perhaps that will be worth something when I'm finally judged.

"I replaced the stones over the dead man's body and walked over to the horses. In the fading daylight, I pulled the diamond from inside my shirt where I'd stuffed it. Even there, in that empty and desolate place, I felt a fear, as if someone was hiding nearby and might see it and take it from me. But I couldn't resist turning it this way and that, watching the glimmer deep within it. It was like a small star, winking brighter and dimmer, and something seemed to hold my gaze, making me work to find the spot where the reflection would be at its peak. I noticed with distaste that when held a certain way, my fingermarks marred the surface, stained from my brother's own blood, still on my hands from when I had leaned down to check him.

"I was considering washing the stone in the nearby stream when the first cool puff of night breeze seemed to bring me back to myself. With a start, I realized that it was later than I'd realized. Hiding the stone once more in my shirt, and untying both horses, I wrapped myself in the blanket given to me as a disguise earlier that day and made the long trek back to Cawnpore. I reached safety to learn that I hadn't been missed, and the siege played out as history records it. However, I was always aware of that fist-sized stone hidden on my person. I fashioned a clever sling for it, and took to walking in a bent way, telling people that my back was injured, so that the bulge in my uniform would be hidden. The thing obsessed me more and more, and soon after the siege ended, I applied to return to England.

"My passage home was uneventful. I mustered out, as many did, and found employment in Edinburgh. My father passed away soon after – I always felt that it was from grief due to my brother's death. Following the siege, he had been listed as missing, but somehow it was recorded as a battle-related death rather than a desertion – although whichever way it had been listed made no difference to me. My father believed that his other son died a hero, and I didn't dispute it. My inheritance left me moderately comfortable. I was smart enough to recognize that my obsession with the jewel might overwhelm me. I couldn't think of parting with it, either to sell as a whole or to break into smaller stones. It would make me a fortune if I chose to dispose of it illicitly, but I couldn't lose it. In a practical sense, I knew that there was a good chance that if it were revealed, it would probably be confiscated by the Crown, with more questions about it than I could answer. I couldn't release it, but I also knew that if I didn't master it somehow, I'd be lost. I constructed a hiding place for it in my home and weaned myself so that I could go to work each day without carrying it on my person, constantly fearful of some attack that would take it from me. Yet it never quite left my thoughts.

"And then one day, less than a year later, I was told that I had a visitor. It was just luck that I was able to see a face through a window that I'd never believed would appear again. It was my brother, of course – somehow alive. He had traced me to Edinburgh, and was in the very hospital in which I was now employed! There was never a question that I'd speak with him. He'd tried to kill me, after all, and the call of the jewel for him was as strong as it was to me – I was certain of it. It had likely kept him alive, against all odds.

"I walked away from my life in Edinburgh at that moment and never looked back. I returned to my small lodgings and gathered the jewel and a bag of necessities that I'd kept prepared in case I ever had to flee in order to protect it – although I never guessed that it would be from my supposedly dead brother.

"When my father had died, I'd immediately sold the inherited property, converting all that I received into transportable funds, just in case I ever had to depart suddenly. I vanished from Edinburgh, went to Ireland without being followed, and set myself as a village doctor under another name. There I stayed for quite a while, having prepared once again a hiding place for the jewel – in my younger days, I'd become quite proficient as an amateur carpenter – until I began to sense that I was being watched. Whether it was true or not I couldn't say, but I realized that being in a small village had boxed me in – a tactical mistake. I had nowhere but the empty countryside in which to hide. I vanished again, changing venues to York, where I repeated my efforts, before moving again in a year or so. Over the years I had tried to alter my appearance, just in case, but there was really nothing that could be done to disguise me from my own brother, so I gave up that effort and relied instead on my instincts. I eventually ended up in Manchester, where I lived peacefully for quite a while with no sense that I'd been followed. Had my brother died in the meantime? I didn't know, but I felt that I was finally safe enough to pursue a better position in London.

"Upon arrival, I found a small set of rooms in Gower Mews and made my usual alterations – I may have felt safe, but old habits die hard. I grew comfortable in my new position. And then, on the day that I came to see you, Mr. Holmes, I believed that I might have seen my brother yet again.

"It was only in the distance, and just for a few seconds, but I've come to trust myself. For the first time, I thought about staying and fighting him. I'd heard of you, and Watson here, and sought your help. But my . . . my arrogance poisoned the well, as it has so often for me before. I left your rooms without sharing my story and returned home, wondering whether to stay or flee.

"I began to hope that I'd imagined it, but that night, after I went to bed, locking the bedroom door behind me as usual, I heard someone enter the house. He quietly climbed the stairs, and I knew it, being aware of every creak and groan that the stairway might possibly make. While he reached my locked door, and then tried to force his way in, I stepped into my hidden chamber – the door of which I left open every night in preparation – and closed myself inside.

"Through a tiny peephole, I saw him as he broke in, illuminated by the faint light from the window. His features were blurred, but I knew the shape and movements of my brother, even all these years later. I have no idea how he survived his wounds, or the blood loss or peritonitis that surely must have gone with them. He must have dragged himself from the tunnel and found a native healer. I don't know how he has since supported himself over the years, or where he has been or gone. I was afraid to seek the answers – doing so might have brought me to his attention when I would have remained otherwise hidden, and satisfying my curiosity wasn't worth bringing him down upon me, with the risk of losing the jewel, along with my life.

"I heard him search the house, moving up and down, becoming more frantic, tearing and knocking things to the floor. Finally I heard him leave. But had he really? I waited for quite a while, until nearly morning, thinking that his departure might be a trick and that he could have remained hidden inside. Finally, however, I became convinced that he'd truly gone, and I came out, dressed, and retrieved my bag with the diamond, some clothing, and my spare funds.

"Seeing that the house was wrecked, and that there was no concealing what had happened, I decided to lay a false trail – as a way to confuse my brother more than anyone else. He would certainly know that *he* hadn't attacked or killed me, so if there was evidence that someone else had done so after he left, he might believe that I had returned and been murdered. I opened a vein in my forearm and proceeded to let my own blood pour forth onto the sheets. I probably spilled a pint or two – you both undoubtedly know that a man can spare that much without any real discomfort – and tried to spread it as artfully and widely as possible. I believe that I left an effective picture, as it looked like an abattoir when I was done. Then I slipped out and, having made sure that I wasn't followed, went to a place of temporary safety that I'd long ago prepared. From there, I contacted the spa and arranged for an interview, based on forged documents I'd devised. Then I made my way here, where I was able to present myself and apply for the job. I was hired on the spot – I've spent plenty of time over the years preparing my next identity, and I can certainly demonstrate that I'm a physician."

He coughed. His throat must have been incredibly dry by then, and poured himself some brandy. Then he asked, "How did you know?"

"The footprints told me a great deal," said Holmes, and then he elaborated upon the rest of it, including how he had learned of the man's past and current destination by analysis of the documents in his desks, both at home and at work. He reached down and opened the satchel at his feet. "I've brought all of that documentation with me. I felt that you wouldn't want to leave it lying around for someone else to interpret."

Smallwood took the papers with a nod, but he didn't speak. "We are fascinated to hear your story," continued Holmes, "but I must ask: Why? Why tell it now, to two strangers? You could have simply acknowledged that we found you without ever admitting the existence of the diamond, or relating the fantastic way in which it was discovered. It seems unlikely that you would share a secret with two strangers that you have spent decades to protect."

Smallwood was very quiet for a long time. I almost thought that he'd chosen not to answer at all, but then he spoke without looking up. "I'm getting older," he said. "I'm tired. I look back at my life and see that, from the moment I first laid eyes on the diamond, it's consumed me – though not in the sense that a drug addict will burn himself up from within. I've always been able to maintain a functional possession of the jewel. But it has robbed me of a proper life.

"When I returned home, I had my name, my profession, and an inheritance. In spite of the events under that cursed mountain, I believed that it was a secret that would never be known. I could have lived a normal life. I could have married by now, had children, a real home. I believed that my brother was dead, and for all I knew, nothing would have ever disrupted a steady future.

"But even before I had the first hint that my brother had survived, I realized that something was wrong. My fear of the jewel being found on me in India, and of it being taken away, was the first indication – a sour note of dissonance that swells and grows. Even when I returned home, I could not relax. As I told you, the call of the diamond was strong, leading me to formulate more and more creative measures to protect it. That saved me when my brother arrived, but even as I fled my life, I knew that I was ceding more control to the stone.

"I know about you, Mr. Holmes. And you too, Watson. I don't think that you will try to take the jewel from me – or at least I believe that as intellectually as I can. Even now, deep in my mind, there is a gibbering shrieking child that urges me to flee, to attack you both and try and silence you before you can tell my secret. But I'm still enough of a rational man to understand this compulsion. And I suppose I can see the end of this long road – if my brother doesn't eventually find me and kill me and take the stone, I'll lose my mind for it anyway."

Then he looked up, first at Holmes, and then at me. "So that's why I'm telling you. So that someone will know the truth, someday, when I'm either murdered or mad."

The silence between the three of us stretched then. Finally, Holmes nodded, and asked, "Do you wish for us to help trap your brother? Or perhaps, would you like to be free of the burden of the diamond, leaving it to us to convey it anonymously to the proper authorities?"

At that, Smallwood, as I shall continue to think of him, sat up as if he'd been stabbed. A terrible look that I hope never to see again passed across his face. It was there but a moment, but I felt that a small window into hell itself had cracked open. I was very glad when he told us no, shaking his head for several seconds before he found the words.

"I cannot," he said. "The diamond is mine." He licked his lips. "It's hidden."

"Have you already constructed a hidey-hole in your new rooms?" Holmes asked. "I doubt that you would have had the time." At that, a look crossed Smallwood's face, regret and anger. I could see that he was already rethinking his statement of faith in our character. He now believed that we were going to steal his talisman.

Holmes must have seen it too, but he tried again, apparently making one last effort to save the man's soul. He leaned forward, his hands clasped between his knees. "Let us find a way to protect you and end this."

"No!" cried Smallwood, softly, and yet as if he was being burned. Then, leaning back and letting out his breath like a bellows going flat, he sighed and placed a shaking hand over his eyes, saying more softly, "No. It is my burden to bear."

We were silent then, for several long and awkward moments, with nothing further to say until – with a nod in my direction – Holmes leaned forward, snapped the satchel shut, and stood in that abrupt way of his. I found my way upright more slowly. Smallwood continued to slump in his chair, his expression hidden. Holmes and I looked at one another for a moment, and then we walked out, pulling the door shut softly behind us. We never saw him again.

On the train, I cleared my throat. We hadn't spoken since leaving Smallwood's presence. "He will run again, you know. He fears us now. He fears *you*. He's probably already raced to wherever he's hidden the jewel, certain that we're going to get there first, to seek it and take it from him. I wouldn't be surprised if he hasn't already taken to his heels."

Holmes frowned. "I started to have Barker remain on duty, to see where he goes, but it's really of no concern. It's bad enough that I've traced him here, and disrupted the fragile peace that he thought he'd found."

That thought surprised me, and Holmes noticed. "I was arrogant, Watson. It's a trait that I've noticed in myself before, and one that I shall have to work harder to avoid in the future. You asked my reason for pursuing this – no client, no fee – and I replied that it was for my own education – 'if only to satisfy the artist in me'. But I feel that, in my enthusiasm, I have done an injury here, of some sort or another. Once or twice in my career I feel that I have done more real harm by my desire to learn the truth, without taking time to learn the consequences. I need to learn caution – to refrain from acting just to know a little bit more."

He drifted into silence. Clearly this had shaken him somehow. But that was no surprise, as I felt the same way.

Then, as a number of miles has passed beneath us while we approached the capital, he asked, "Do you believe that there really *is* a jewel?"

The thought had already occurred to me. "Possibly. He certainly has something that he's hiding, and that he's willing to flee in order to keep for himself. His rooms *were* invaded, and he *did* flee, as he has before. Some other story might suffice to explain why, but I prefer this one as much as any other. You yourself showed us the evidence of the footprints, and that an object was kept hidden. And he did go to great trouble to construct the secret room."

"Yes, but did he also construct an elaborate story to cover up whatever it is that he's *really* hiding?"

I pondered that for a moment, and then said, "For now, that story of the jewel is as good as any other, I suppose. If he's simply hiding the loot from some old bond robbery, like Mr. Blessington in his house in Brook Street, I would be vastly disappointed."

Holmes smiled but said nothing. Much later, as we were well into the metropolis and slowing in our approach to the terminus, he roused himself, knocking his pipe out through the cracked window. "Assuming that it was real . . . do you wish that we'd seen it?"

"Hmm?" I sat up straighter, having been between wakefulness and uneasy dreams for many miles. "The jewel? I'm curious, certainly. But I think that I'm glad that I didn't – not that he would have let us. And you?"

"Possibly. I seek the path of logic and an intellectual perspective, but there is a part of me that cannot help but to respond to something like that. A massive jewel, with such a story to go with it. How could I *not* wish to see such a thing?"

"And yet . . . ." I drifted off, about to mention the fact that the thing seemed to have a corruptive power – at least if one believed Smallwood's story. Holmes would hold such a thought in contempt. But as usual he knew what I was thinking, and he surprised me.

"I agree, Watson. Perhaps it's best for both of us that Smallwood never showed us the cursed thing. After all, there must be a reason it for it being sealed up as it was."

I frowned. "It sounds as if you do believe him then – about all of it, including the tunnel, placed so impossibly by some ancient people. I must admit that I'm inclined to credit his story

211

as well, although there is no firm reason to. As you said, the whole thing might have been some story that Smallwood concocted in order to divert us from what really happened."

"I suppose. And yet, my friend, it's good to remember sometimes just how little that we really know. There are certainly even larger jewels in the earth than what was described to us today, and wonders achieved and then lost by the ancients that we'll never know or understand."

He set about relighting his pipe. "Let me while away the time in the few remaining minutes before we reach the station with the details of an investigation that I concluded a few years ago in the Preseli hills, in Pembrokeshire. I think that you might find it of interest."

And the story that he told, first on the train and then finishing in our Baker Street rooms, was nearly as unusual as that provided by Smallwood, and his unique and definitive solution to the problem helped to somehow make the world a little less mysterious – at least on that day.

The Finding of
Geoffrey Hobson
by David B. Beckwith

It was a mild spring morning, March the 7th, 1882. Holmes and I had finished breakfast and had taken up our accustomed chairs to read the newspapers, have a smoke, and finish our tea. I had been working as a *locum* with a Dr. Bogard, and I had settled into a steady routine. His consulting rooms in York Terrace were open from eight a.m. to seven p.m. Monday to Saturday. Dr. Bogard was an early riser, and always took the early shift, starting after Adelaide, our principal receptionist (and sometime-nurse) had opened the doors at half-past-seven. Bogard worked until noon, and that was when I commenced work, along with Caroline, our second receptionist. Bogard would take his luncheon for one hour, with Adelaide and Caroline conferring about what was needed to be ordered and other matters of the practice until Adelaide departed at one o'clock. Dr. Bogard would return and share duties with me until three, and thereafter I was in charge. The arrangements were working well. I had time for a leisurely morning every day.

The newspapers were all still full of articles about the attempted assassination of Her Majesty on the previous Thursday at Windsor Railway Station, and other associated articles about madmen, asylums, mental institutions, the police (in general), the Royal Household Police, and what the government should be undertaking about such matters.

The London Daily Metropolitan was no different, but being a more sensational rag, Holmes found great interest in what he called its "Agony Columns". Today the newspaper attracted the reader's attention by a headline that read: "*Assassination Plot Was Deadly*". Only yesterday the newspapers had asserted that either the bullet used was a blank, or that the gun involved was a non-functional replica. So I read on.

"Holmes!" said I, "You must read this article, here . . . ." And I folded the page to put the article to the top, and passed the newspaper to my friend.

Today The Daily Metropolitan *can reveal new facts relating to the assassination plot of last Thursday. The Queen was not injured in the latest attempt made upon her life by Roderick Maclean, and Her Majesty is in excellent spirits.*

It may now authoritatively be stated that Maclean is no doubt insane. He had been confined at the Wells Lunatic Asylum until he was discharged last September. From that asylum he was committed to the care of the Somerset Asylum as an out-patient, with conditions to report daily in person. The Daily Metropolitan *has obtained his address in Weston-super-Mare.*

He fired a single shot at Her Majesty, but his aim was averted by schoolboys Gordon Wilson and his chum Charles Robinson. Wilson is the son of the Australian Wool Magnate Sir Samuel Wilson. The boys, Wilson and Robinson, are students at Eton.

It was reported incorrectly, until now, that the fired bullet was a blank, or that the gun used was a mock weapon.

The Daily Metropolitan *can today reveal that the police have re-enacted the scene and discovered a deadly bullet missed the Royal*

214

carriage and ricocheted off a railway lorry outside the Windsor train station. Aligning the probable location of Maclean and the lorry, it could be seen that our Gracious Queen was seated almost directly in line. The assassination attempt was a deadly one!

Bravo to British schoolboys! It is reported that the pair of boys jostled Maclean as he was about to fire, and one boy hit him about the legs with an umbrella.

Maclean had tried to fling away his weapon before he was arrested, but the weapon was secured and is with the police, and it can be categorically stated that reports that the weapon was a replica, or even a toy, as asserted by several tabloids, are completely false. The weapon recovered is a fully functioning revolver containing two more remaining live rounds.

The apparent insanity of Maclean was reported to Detective-Sergeant Fraser of the Royal Household Police, and he has conveyed this information to Her Majesty.

The Home Secretary, Sir William Harcourt, who was present when the assassination attempt occurred, expressed his horror to bystanders. He has confirmed that this was the eighth attempt upon the life of Her Majesty.

A spokesman from Scotland Yard has confirmed that Maclean is suffering from constant headaches, and has quoted him as stating "I believe that all the people of England are against me, I felt I must injure someone because they are all conspiring to deceive me".

When asked where and how did he obtain the revolver, Maclean had replied "From Geoffrey Hobson, my only friend in the world. He got it for me. He was with me at Windsor Station. We planned this together."

It transpires that Geoffrey Hobson is a nurse at the Somerset Lunatic Asylum, where he had contact with Maclean. Scotland Yard are now seeking this man.

"Fascinating!" said Holmes, "Illogical, and obviously insane. They will no doubt find Maclean 'Not Guilty, but Insane'. I see *The Metropolitan* is maintaining its usual standard of reporting. We shall have to wait for the final outcome."

We resumed our reading, smoking, and drinking the tea that was growing cold. Some minutes later we heard the creak of the seventh step of the stair.

"That will be Mrs. Hudson coming to collect the breakfast things." I remarked. Then a second creak was heard. "No! I believe we have a visitor!" I exclaimed.

There came a knock at the sitting room door, Mrs. Hudson entered. "Mr. Holmes, Dr. Watson, you have a visitor, a policeman."

"Show him in, Mrs. Hudson." said Holmes.

We both stood to welcome our guest, as a thin man of average height, straight dark hair, grey eyes, and sporting a thin moustache, entered. His hat and coat were damp.

"I am Sherlock Holmes."

"And I'm Doctor John Watson."

"Detective-Sergeant Gareth Russell of Scotland Yard."

"Pleased to meet you, Detective-Sergeant. Before we begin, may we offer you some tea or coffee?" responded Holmes.

"That would be muchly appreciated Mr. 'Olmes," answered Russell. I noted his Cockney accent. "It's quite nippy outside this morning. A cuppa tea, please,"

"Then please take a seat," said Holmes. "Mrs. Hudson – another pot of tea, and more milk, and a cup for our visitor if you please."

Mrs. Hudson loaded her tray with most of the breakfast things and departed. Russell looked around, his eyes lingering over Holmes's chemistry table with its apparatus. Then he gazed at the folded *Metropolitan* on Holmes's side table, obviously reading the title of its prominent leading article.

"Now Detective-Sergeant, how can we be of assistance to the Metropolitan Police?" asked Holmes.

"I am 'oping that you can 'elp us," answered the policeman. "Your activities 'ave been noticed by the police for the last couple of years, but more so in the last twelve months. Your methods differ to those of the regular police investigations, and this could be the approach that we need."

I got my notebook and pencil ready. I was pleased with myself as I thought on the words "last twelve months". That meant the period since I had met Holmes and commenced collaborating with him. I had taken to jotting down the key points of our cases, for one day I might publish the accounts of our adventures.

"I see from the folded newspaper on your table," Russell continued, "that you're taking an interest in this latest assassination attempt on Her Majesty. That's why I am 'ere."

"But you already have the man Maclean!" exclaimed Holmes.

217

"Indeed yes, we do. The Force 'as been working 'ard since last Thursday, and over the weekend we gained the information about the man Geoffrey 'Obson. We don't know 'ow *The Daily Metropolitan* got 'old of the story," said Russell pointing to the newspaper, "but it is partly in today's edition, there."

"Spill the beans then!" said Holmes. "Tell of Geoffrey Hobson. But first let me light my pipe."

I witnessed the surprised look upon the Detective-Sergeant's face when Holmes reached for the Persian slipper and proceeded to fill his pipe. Then, with a spill from the fire, he lit it.

"My manners! A cigarette?" And Holmes offered the maroon-and-gold box of Sullivans to the policeman.

"I don't indulge, Mr. 'Olmes, but thank you." responded Russell. I wanted a smoke, but I knew I couldn't and take notes simultaneously.

"This Maclean is a right nutter," said Russell, "and wot wiv Sunday being a full moon, I'm thinking that there's truth in wot they says about madmen and being affected by the moon. I personally 'aven't met the man, but I've read the transcripts."

Then the Detective-Sergeant recounted what the police had learned from Maclean.

"Let me first say, Mr. 'Olmes, that wot the newspaper 'as written is not entirely correct. Her Majesty and the Princess Beatrice had left the Windsor Train Station and boarded the Royal Carriage. As the carriage started to move, Maclean drew 'is weapon. It is unclear to all involved whether 'e fired before or after being jostled. Two Eton schoolboys, Wilson and Robinson, did the jostling, Wilson 'itting them with his humbrella. Maclean was overpowered by Superintendent 'Ayes of the Windsor Police and a local photographer, James

218

Burnside. The weapon was of German manufacture, a six-chamber revolver firing ball cartridges. Two were still in the gun. Fourteen more cartridges were found on Maclean's person."

Russell paused and took a drink of his tea before continuing.

"The next day, that is Friday, Maclean appeared before the Windsor Magistrates, where 'e was charged with attempted regicide and treason, and committed to the Reading Police lock-up pending a trial. The police surgeon 'ad declared 'im sane. Maclean 'as since been transferred to the Central Metropolitan lock-up following initial interrogations which raised doubts about his sanity.

"We now believe the man is mad, and wonder 'ow the Windsor Police Surgeon could 'ave thought otherwise. I 'ave seen the man. Sometimes 'e is coherent, and at others 'e simply raves. The exact motive for 'is actions is difficult to come to terms wiv. 'E is devoutly and passionately in favour of 'Er Majesty and all that she represents, but then 'e wants 'is revenge on her. It transpires that 'e is something of a poet, and 'e sent a poem to the Queen. 'E says it was an impassioned ode to her greatness as Queen and Empress and as Britannia incarnate. Why 'Er Majesty should deign to reply I know not, for it appears the poem was received as being deeply offensive, and yet 'Er Majesty did reply to Macleans's letter, and 'er reply did not please Maclean.

"In a more lucid pronouncement Maclean stated this." Russell took out his notebook and flipped through pages until he found the reference. "'*I found 'er reply an affront to my poetic sensibilities, and I resolved to be avenged.*'"

The Detective-Sergeant shut his notebook, and then continued. "It was more often the case that Maclean ranted about the state of Britain, and that 'ow all of England was conspiring against 'im, and 'ow 'e would be revenged. For a Scotsman, 'tis surprising that 'e equates Britain wiv England. 'e will say Britannia the Great, and then in the next breath 'e'll say wot all England is against 'im. We 'ave learned that 'e 'as a sister in Scotland, but as yet, we know not where. In other outbursts, 'e states 'e is all alone wiv no family."

Here Russell paused. He drank some more tea, and Holmes refilled and relit his pipe, again using the tobacco kept in his Persian slipper, which had a tendency to make the leaf dry and burn quickly. I lit a cigarette, hoping to be able to enjoy it and still take notes at the same time. Then Russell continued.

"That brings me to point of my visit today – that is, Geoffrey 'Obson. Maclean started by asking 'Where is Geoffrey? 'e should be 'ere with me' Eventually, we obtained the man's second name, and that it was 'e who obtained the gun and cartridges for Maclean. Amongst Maclean's rants, 'e frequently both admonishes the general populace as being 'against 'im' and 'out to get 'im', but also that 'Obson is 'is one and only friend'.

"Maclean admitted that 'e and 'Obson had travelled together from Weston-super-Mare, and it was in London that 'Obson 'ad acquired the gun and ball cartridges. 'E was most adamant that 'e would not reveal where in London they 'ad stayed.

"We tried to get a description of the man 'Obson from Maclean, but the best we obtained was that 'e is of less than average height, 'as fair hair, and is clean-shaven. 'E rarely wears a hat. In the process of interviewing many of the witnesses of the attempted assassination, the police ascertained that a man matching this description was seen 'urriedly pushing 'is way through the crowded entrance to Windsor Station. The next train to depart was bound back to London. In the long labourious interviews with Maclean since Saturday, we ascertained that 'Obson was, or is, a nurse at the Somerset Asylum in Weston-super-Mare where Maclean was required to report on a daily basis. It was 'Obson who obtained the revolver and ammunition for Maclean, and 'Obson 'ad clearly accompanied Maclean to Windsor.

"Yesterday this description of 'Obson was confirmed by the Somerset Asylum. Additional information is that 'is eyes are steel grey, 'is hair so pale 'tis almost white. 'E is thirty years old, 'is 'eight is five-feet-five, and 'e speaks with an educated accent. 'E smokes a lot of Marlborough cigarettes made by Philip Morris." *

"I don't know why the company does not advertise them as a woman's cigarette," I interjected.

"Pray continue." urged Holmes.

"I 'ave no more details to give Mr. 'Olmes. We know that 'Obson left Windsor bound for London on last Thursday. After that we know nothing." concluded Russell.

"Did those in Somerset report the man's financial situation?" asked Holmes.

"'E appears to have some savings," was the reply, "but 'is salary as a nurse is not large."

"You have not yet asked, but I presume you wish us to find this man?" stated Holmes.

"In a nutshell, yes," answered Russell. "Your name was raised, and the powers-that-be thought this problem to be right up your street, so to speak."

"Is he armed?" queried Holmes.

"Difficult to say Mr. 'Olmes," said the policeman. "Maclean could not be persuaded to say yea or nay, but it was 'Obson who obtained the revolver and cartridges for Maclean. Thus, Maclean's reluctance to speak of the matter tend to weigh on the side of 'yes'."

"I accept the case, Detective-Sergeant. If I need to contact you, I shall send a telegram to Scotland Yard. Then," said Holmes rising to his feet, "if you have nothing more to add, we shall bid you a good day!"

"If you need assistance, Mr. 'Olmes, you just 'ave to ask. Goodbye!" said Russell, and with that he departed.

"What do you think, Watson?" asked Holmes.

"I have no idea where to begin. London is a very large city. One man in some four-millions is a difficult task." I replied. I looked at my watch, "I have a couple of hours before I report to Dr. Bogard's practice, if there is anything with which I can help . . . ." I said.

Holmes rang the bell for Mrs. Hudson and, when she arrived, he said, "Find all the newspapers that are still in the house, those dated from Friday the third, if you please."

Our landlady departed, shaking her head.

"There may be some clue to add to our knowledge," stated Holmes, "something that we overlooked because it was not then relevant to us. A long shot I realize, but one never knows."

We found nothing before it was time for a quick early lunch, and then I set off to work in York Terrace. As I was leaving, I asked, "What will you do now?"

"I have the beginning of a plan," he replied. "I will set that in motion. Then I shall renew my acquaintance with some people who deal in illicit guns. I shall see tonight. Goodbye, Watson!"

That evening Holmes had no success to report. He had visited four armaments suppliers and gained no information, save the names and addresses of four more suppliers. His contacts had been reluctant to help him, but when he had explained his business, they had become true patriots. The criminal classes may be partial to preying on the aristocracy, but any harm to Her Majesty is a different matter.

"I've asked Wiggins to report here tomorrow morning with five others of his street companions. I've promised him and his colleagues sixpence per day to seek out Geoffrey Hobson. If they don't discover Hobson's whereabouts in three days, then I shall consider increasing the amount."

Next morning, at half-past-eight, Mrs. Hudson came to our sitting room.

"Mr. Holmes, those dirty and scruffy children that you call 'The Baker Street Irregulars' are below."

"Kindly show them up, Mrs. Hudson," replied Holmes.

Moments later, six street urchins were admitted to our presence. Wiggins was the tallest, Jude the smallest. O'Hara was almost as short. I was impressed that those with hats had removed them.

"Now listen carefully," said Holmes. He then explained that the Irregulars were to seek out a man, and he gave a succinct description of Geoffrey Hobson. He explained that Hobson could be anywhere in London, but since he was from out of town, that he would most likely be not too far from a railway station, and that by this he meant both the above-ground and the underground stations. Hobson had sufficient money to pay for a hotel, but it was unlikely to be an upmarket establishment. Hobson smoked Marlborough cigarettes and – as I had suggested that these were a woman's cigarette – I had asked that two girls be included in their ranks.

"A tobacconist selling mild cigarettes might be a woman herself," Holmes agreed, "and therefore more willing to talk to a girl. I suggest that you pretend that you're looking for your uncle from out of town," he continued. "Say from Birmingham. Say that Uncle Geoffrey has a bad memory and

223

isn't used to the big city, and that your mother is worried about him."

"Holmes! Birmingham is the second largest city in Britain! Hobson cannot be unused to cities," I exclaimed.

"To Londoners, Watson, there is no other city in the world," replied Holmes. "All others are 'towns' at the best. Even Paris has a population only a little more than half that of London." Addressing the Irregulars, he said, "Any questions?"

They all looked at each other, a little mystified if anything. Finally Wiggins spoke. "Mr. 'Olmes, 'ow does a Birmingham bloke speak?"

"Well, I can't imitate the accent, but it is a northerner's accent. Say something in Geordie, Watson." said Holmes.

"Holmes!" I protested, "Geordie is nothing like Brummy!"

"Do it anyway!" insisted Holmes.

"*Awa then pet lamb*," I said. "*Wud yur lark a cupper?*"

"Not bad. Birmingham is similar," explained Holmes, "but not as far 'up north' – nonetheless a northerner's accent."

"Guv'nor," asked Wiggins, "wot did 'e say?"

"'*Away then my dearest.*'" I translated. "'*Would you like a cup of tea?*'"

"No more questions? Good! Then be off with you. Report again tomorrow at eight-thirty, or sooner if you find Hobson." said Holmes, and he ushered the Irregulars to the door.

"Do you think they will find him?" I asked.

"I am hopeful, but I believe they stand to have a better chance than I have in finding him by questioning arms sellers." replied Holmes.

The next morning, the Irregulars arrived punctually and lined up before us. They didn't have any air of success about them.

"What have you to report?" exclaimed Holmes.

"Mr. 'Olmes," said Wiggins, "We 'ad a fink about it, 'an there are eight big railway stations, all wivin two miles ov 'ere. Wot wiv there bein' only six ov us, we decided to not try South 'Ampstead or West Brom – Bromwich that is, them being the furvest from 'ere. We split up, went to the six other stations, north to south they are: St. Pancras, Euston, Marylebone, Paddington, Waterloo, and Victoria. At the stations, no railway person could be ov 'elp. Fact, they got quite shirty being' axed. The kiosks at the stations were more 'elpful – well in the sense that they didn't just say take off, or scarper afore I call the cops. Rick, you tell the Guv'nor."

"At Waterloo," said Rick Welsh, "the old geezer wot sells papers and fags, 'e remembered a man. It were cos ov the colour ov 'is hair an' the eyes. He said as 'ow 'e couldn't forgit them eyes – they woz like ice, 'e said, 'an they could see right through you. But this man, 'e 'ad not bought no fags, just a newspaper. An' that's all I got to say. Long walk it is to Waterloo an' back!"

Wiggins spoke again. "Now you Jim. You tell."

"Mr. Holmes," related O'Hara, "I went to St. Pancras. I thought I might get lucky in that this Hobson bloke might have gone back to Birmingham. Same as with Rick – the porters were no help. But a man bought Marlboroughs on Monday. He was the right height, and he wore a hat, but the man at the kiosk remembered that the hat was took off, so the man could scratch his head. His eyes were not seen. I don't think it's him, guv'nor, cos the kiosk man said a train had just arrived from the north, and I thought that was not the right way about, what with arriving not leaving."

"Any more to tell?" asked Holmes.

"No, guv'nor." replied Wiggins.

"Well, in both cases, the man could have been Hobson, but we are still no closer. Let us hope for more progress tomorrow. Here is your pay." said Holmes as he handed out six tanners.

"We will see you again tomorrow. Goodbye!"

The next day there was a more exuberant group of children at Baker Street.

"I see by your faces that some success has been achieved!" exclaimed Holmes, "What is the news?"

"Go on, Dan. Tell Mr. 'Olmes." urged Wiggins.

Dan Jones stepped forward, clasping his hat with both hands to his chest. He took a deep breath and started.

"A bit west of Paddington Station, I found a corner shop. I told my story just like you said. The geezer in the shop was reluctant say anything, so I said 'Come on, Mister, me Mum's dead worried about her brother. Have you seen him or not?' And then he says, 'Yeah, I seen him yesterday, came in and bought twenty Marlboroughs, he did'. So I says to the geezer, 'How did Uncle look? So I can tell Mum.' He replied that Hobson looked a bit lost and uncertain of himself. Then he said that Hobson was carrying a small suitcase. He asked, 'That hotel down the road, can you recommend it? I need somewhere to stay and rest.' 'The Sunderland, y'mean? I suppose it's alright. Never stayed in an hotel myself. Put it this way,' he says 'I ain't heard nothing bad about the place. Take that as you will.'"

"Well done, Jones! Where was this?" asked Holmes.

"Dorchester Gardens," replied Dan Jones. "In Bayswater, sir."

"And what did you do next?" queried Holmes.

"I told the bloke my thanks, and said I'd be off to tell me Mum. I left the shop and set off east, then turned right, and doubled my way back to Dorchester so as to come the Sunderland Hotel from the west. Just in case anyone was watching me like.

"Then I had to think a bit. I couldn't go into the hotel and ask directly, for two reasons that I thought of. One, Hobson might not be using his real name, and two, what if they said 'I'll tell him you're here'. Difficult I thought."

"My word, you did well, young Jones. Excellent, in fact. What did you decide to do, pray tell?" Holmes asked, and he sat on the edge of his chair. Dan Jones shuffled his feet, and then replied.

"I went around the back, where the bins are, and the door to the kitchen. When this girl comes out with scraps, I asked her. I said 'I'm looking for my uncle', and I gave the description, and I said as he had had an argument with Mum, but that she wanted to know if he was all right. This girl, Rose was her name, right friendly and only couple of years older than me. She told me yes, he was here, but not calling himself Hobson. But she didn't think this was unusual – she said his name was Cody, and that he had left that morning. She knew because she had already cleaned his room."

"Superb! Bravo Jones!" enthused Holmes. "You've performed magnificently. Give the boy a clap, everyone! Excellent." Jones went red at his applause

"Now let me think," added Holmes, proceeding to light his pipe. Then his eyes were shut. Minutes passed, and the Baker Street Irregulars fidgeted about. At last Holmes spoke. "I believe that I have it. Of course, it had to be Paddington – that is where the train from Weston-super-Mare arrives, and where the trains to and from Windsor depart and arrive."

"If I were Hobson," said Holmes, "I wouldn't be using my own name, and I wouldn't stay in the same hotel every night. Hobson knows that Maclean will have talked. He probably believes the police are seeking after him for procuring the gun. Now this what I want you do next . . . .

"Go in pairs now. Six individuals all asking the same sort of questions in one area will be suspicious. If I am correct, Hobson will remain not too far away. I think he's waiting for some news to be printed about Maclean and himself, so concentrate on Hallfield Estate, Westbourne Green, Maida Hill, Ladbroke Grove, and Kensal Town. I believe the districts east and south will be too expensive for his tastes, and his purse. And don't forget Paddington itself. That's all. Wait – your pay, you have earned it!"

The Irregulars departed. Holmes relit his pipe a minute later he said, "Get Mrs. Hudson to bring more coffee please, Watson. I am devising a plan."

I went and requested some coffee. Holmes had his eyes closed, so I remained silent until he opened them. I lit a cigarette, and then spoke. "A plan?" I asked as Mrs. Hudson knocked on the door and entered with more milk and coffee. "You aren't gambling man, and you do not have anything concrete to proceed upon. What can you plan?"

"The plan involves you, Watson. Thank you, Mrs. Hudson. I do not gamble – indeed never – but in this case I have strong feelings, almost intuition that tomorrow will be the day, and I thought that you should be involved in the capture. So, if can you spare the time, it will be in the afternoon or evening. I'm aware you're usually at work then. If needs be, and if you wish to be involved, can you be available?"

"I can organise for someone to be on standby for tomorrow, and then send him a telegram if he's required." I replied.

"Good man! Then we shall await the report from the Irregulars tomorrow. They are certainly a powerful tool to have available. That Dan Jones showed remarkable skill and maturity, and Wiggins is proving a capable leader."

"Indeed yes." I replied. "Jones is older than his ten years in more ways than one."

Saturday the eleventh arrived. The mild spring weather was becoming colder, the sky ever overcast, and Mrs. Hudson's prophesy of snow seeming more likely. The Irregulars arrived punctually and lined up. They looked pleased with themselves.

"We've almost got 'im, Mr. Holmes." said Wiggins. "A shop in Eglin Avenue – that's between Maida 'Ill and West Kilburn. 'Obson was there yesterday morning. We found out late yesterday afternoon. 'E bought a newspaper and some Marlboroughs. Told the man 'e was looking for somewhere to stay nearby. 'E had his case wiv 'im. The shop owner told 'im that it was a shop, not a 'otel reservations office. This shop bloke were not overly friendly – told us to bugger off. So we figured that was the area to start wiv this morning."

"Describe the place, please." said Holmes.

"Nothin' special," replied Wiggins. "Like most places, 'ouses three or four storeys, streets wiv trees, a few shops and caffs."

"Then you had better be off and at work! Your pay . . . ." And Holmes gave them each a shilling.

When they had gone, Holmes lit a cigarette. "You see Watson, I told you today would be the day."

"You paid them more, I saw." I remarked.

"I promised Wiggins that after three days I would increase their pay. They have earned it. Now we will just have to wait. Did you find a substitute at Dr. Bogard's?"

"Yes, I did, Dr. Caversham is a good man. I just need to send him a telegram before noon."

Holmes paced about with a cigarette. Then he lit another when the first was finished. I thought, this is going to be a difficult day. But the waiting was not long. A little before quarter-past-ten, Wiggins and the two girls returned.

"Guv'nor, the girls 'ave done it!" Wiggins exclaimed, "Tell Mr. 'Olmes, you two."

"We went into this small shop," said Amy, "and told the tale."

"An' I said wot I was Amy's friend," said Jude, "'cos our Mums didn't like us being out on our own. An' this old lady says, 'Your Mums are right about that'. Well she ain't that old, I s'pose."

"Well, she tells this tale," added Amy, "how Hobson had come to buy his Marlboroughs first thing this morning. They'd got talking 'cos of the notice in the window."

"Notice? Tell me about it!" exclaimed Holmes.

"It says '*NSWS Meeting tonight. Guest Speaker Millicent Fawcett. 7.00 p.m. Presbyterian 'All, Chipperton Road. All Welcome. Tea and Biscuits 1d, proceeds to N.S.W.S.*'" said Jude proudly, "I read it carefully an' memorised it."

"Anyway," added Amy, "this lady and Hobson chatted, and he said that he would go to the meeting, and he thought it evil that men did not give women the vote."

"N.S.W.S.?" I asked.

"The National Society for Women's Suffrage," Holmes replied. "One of several organised groups that have been campaigning since before we were born. They started getting serious about in 1825, I believe, but fighting a long uphill battle."

"Now we should ascertain where Hobson is staying, to be certain that he does attend the meeting tonight." I said.

"Already done, Doctor Watson!" said Wiggins with glee, "You can tell 'em Jude. Go on!"

"So, I says to this lady, 'Did 'e say if 'e woz stayin' nearby?'" related Jude. "An' she says 'Funny you should ask that, cos that's what's I asked 'im, too, cos I hadn't seen 'im before.' Then Hobson had said 'Spose it can't 'urt, I am staying at the Lincoln, down the street, in 'Allows Road.' Then t'lady says 'Don't know what he meant by it couldn't 'urt'."

"Then we said our thanks and left," continued Amy. "We ran down the street 'til it comes to end at Hallows. Around the corner was the Lincoln Arms. So I says to Jude, 'You go an' find Harry or any of the others. I'll check if Hobson was telling the truth.' So Jude ran off, and I remember what Dan had done, so I thought I'd give it a go too."

Amy then told how she had gone around the back of the hotel. Moments after getting there a maid had appeared. Amy said she told the maid that she was looking for a job, but didn't want anywhere they didn't treat their girls well and pay them fair. The maid had said that the Richards, who owned the hotel, treated the staff well, that the pay wasn't bad if you worked hard. Amy had then told Betty – presumably the maid – that it wasn't the bosses that worried her, but the guests. She had told a tale that in her last position they had a guest, shortish man, young but with nearly white hair and scary eyes, and this man had only wanted a fondle and a cuddle, and in her words, "You know what" every time she had seen him. She didn't want to go anywhere that had guests that expected "You know" from the servants. Betty had told Amy "Oh No! We've got a bloke that fits that description, and I don't like the way he looks at me! Those eyes! He had booked in yesterday, and was staying at least until after tonight."

"So I told Betty, 'Thanks, but no thanks!'" said Amy. "I shan't be asking about a job here. You watch out for yourself, Betty!"

"Then I went back to Hallows Road and found Jude, with Harry and Rick. We left Rick to watch the place and came here as quick as possible. Fact is," Amy concluded, "we ran, Mr. Holmes!"

I looked at my watch – a quarter-past-eleven. Events were moving rapidly, exceedingly so.

"Watson, the game is afoot," said Holmes. "Are you with me? Yes! Good man!" He stood up and from his desk, produced a telegram form, and passed it me. "I presume Mrs. Hudson has delayed lunch because of our visitors, so you three, go downstairs and wait in the entrance. One moment. Wiggins. Take Dr. Watson's telegram as quickly as possible to the Post Office. I'm sure you know where it is, and then come back. Off you go."

I handed the telegram form to Wiggins. It was short and to the point, and I prayed Caversham would forgive the such short notice. Holmes gave the boy a shilling to pay for the telegram. The three Irregulars left, two sets of shoes clumping down the stairs, and the patter of one pair of bare feet.

Mrs. Hudson and Tess the maid brought our lunch. Mrs. Hudson was concerned. "Mr. Holmes," she began, "there're two bairns downstairs . . . ."

"Indeed there are," said Holmes. "I would like you perform two tasks for me: First, prepare six sandwiches for the children. Wiggins will return shortly, and they have three accomplices, as you already know. Second, please tell Wiggins to return with the girls to the hotel and keep out of sight. Tell him that Dr. Watson and I will see them after luncheon. Thank you!"

Two o'clock that afternoon found us in Hallows Road and, as we descended from the cab, we heard a sharp whistle. Looking around, we saw Wiggins waving at the entrance of a narrow alley. We crossed the road and entered the alley to find all six of the Irregulars.

"What news?" asked Holmes.

"'Obson went out about an 'our ago Mr. 'Olmes. We followed 'im to Westbourne Park Station, and 'e boarded a train 'eading east. We didn't dare follow no further. The likes of us would be a bit obvious on the Underground."

"Very wise." I commented.

"Well, this is what I propose," said Holmes. "Wiggins, you can show us the hotel and the Presbyterian Hall. The remainder of you are dismissed for the rest of the day. But I would have all of you report to Baker Street tomorrow as usual. Then Watson and I can tell you of the success or failure of tonight's activities. So off you go. Lead on Wiggins."

Wiggins showed us the way to the Lincoln Arms, and then into Chipperton Road to the Hall.

"One more thing," asked Holmes. "Did you notice a Post Office nearby?"

"Go back to 'Allows Road and turn right," answered Wiggins. "It's about three-'undred yards."

"Thank you," answered Holmes as we stood outside the hall. "That will be all for today' We'll see you tomorrow morning with the others. I suppose we can look within," he continued. "The doors are open, so they must be getting ready." And so we entered.

From a rather drab and boring exterior, the hall interior was surprisingly light and airy, with many high windows admitting light. People were busy hanging bunting and banners, while others were arranging chairs, and yet more were unpacking cups and saucers.

A woman approached us. She was about our age, quite pretty with light brown hair well arranged, and she wore a very dark red dress.

"Can I offer you gentlemen any assistance?" she said offering a hand to be shaken. "My name is Rowena Staplefield."

"I'm Holmes and this is Watson," replied Holmes. "No assistance is required, thank you. We were just checking that everything is going well for this evening."

"Can I count on your attendance tonight?" she asked.

"I am afraid not," he answered. "We have other business to attend to, Mrs. Staplefield, but you do have our support, I assure you."

"Then at least accept a brochure, and I shall get on with business." said the lady and, plucking a sheet of paper from a stack on a nearby table, she handed it to Holmes.

"Goodbye, Mr. Holmes. Mr. Watson." And she departed.

"How did you know she was married?" I asked.

"Simple, Watson," he replied. "A wedding ring. Let's talk as we walk.

"I am wondering how to go about arresting Hobson," he continued. "I do not like the idea of disrupting the meeting, but we have no guarantee that Hobson will return to his hotel before attending. Therefore, we'll have to arrest him before he enters the hall, since the only probable certainty is that he will honour his word to the shopkeeper and actually attend. We're going to the post office to telegraph Russell."

"It definitely will be better to arrest him outside," I responded. "It will make less disturbance in the street than in the hall."

At the post office, Holmes wrote the telegram form and handed it to me to check before sending it:

Meet me CNR Harrow and Chipperton Maida Hill
six tonight STOP Bring two men to arrest Hobson
STOP Holmes END

234

"That should be fine, I think," I said. "Send it."

Back at Baker Street, we told Mrs. Hudson that we would require a something to keep us going until dinner, for we would need to leave before six to meet Russell. She wasn't pleased, telling us that she had already had to buy an extra loaf for sandwiches for the Irregulars.

I lit a Sullivans and commenced to read the brochure we had been given by Mrs. Staplefield:

Propaganda Against Women's Suffrage

- *Only men should legislate for women because only men know what is good for women.*
- *Women would be over-excited by politics and would have nervous breakdowns.*
- *If women had votes, they would outnumber male voters. Parliament would become feminised and Britain become the laughing stock of the world.*
- *Politics is none of women's business. They know nothing, and indeed* should *know nothing about it.*
- *Women have no grievances, and if they have, these can be put right by men.*
- *Women are Conservative by nature, and the Liberals would lose the next election.*
- *Anyone can get up a petition and get ignorant women to sign it.*
- *Votes for women will inevitably lead to Socialism.*
- *Men are logical, stable, thoughtful, and strong-minded. Women are ornamental, quick-tempered, illogical, fickle, and emotional.*

- *It is a Trojan Horse: If you let women vote, soon they'll demand to become MP's, which is self-evidently absurd.*
- *Women are too dainty and delicate for the rough-and-tumble of politics.*
- *Women are already represented in Parliament by the votes cast by the men in their family.*
- *If women cease to be under men's protection, they will be in competition with men and, being weaker, they will be oppressed and eventually go under.*
- *Women already have a huge influence over men, and thus also Parliament. Giving them the vote will give them too much power.*

And so the brochure went on with many more statements of illogical thought. I gave up. I felt sickened that my half of the human race could be so stupid – less than half, in fact, for the last census had shown that women outnumbered men. I didn't know how many women would wish to enter politics, but I felt sure that they should have the right to both vote and become politically active if they desired. Holmes did have some misogynistic tendencies, but I knew that he too was in favour of suffrage.

At ten-to-six, we left 221b and took a hansom to Maida Hill. Holmes had asked me to take my service revolver, which implied to me that he thought Hobson might be armed. Russell and his men of course would not be armed, save for truncheons – not very effective against bullets.

As we arrived at the corner of Harrow Road and Chipperton Road, so did a black police van.

"Do you know, Watson, that in the United States they call these vans 'Paddy Wagons'?" asked Holmes. "A slur against

236

the Irish, suggesting that the occupants of such vans are often from Ireland. If the Fenians persist with their current acts of violence, I predict the use of Paddy Wagon here in Britain."

We greeted Detective-Sergeant Russell, and Holmes advised him, "Hide the van quickly! There's an alley fifty yards that way called Ashfield Way. We don't want Hobson getting a forewarning of what is to come."

"Good thinking, Mr. 'Olmes!" replied Russell, "See to it, Jenkins, and then make sharp and be back 'ere." Then he stated, "So you 'ave succeeded in finding the man? Excellent! What is the plan to happrehend 'im?"

"Hobson is staying at the Lincoln Arms, just up the road, but we do not know if he is in residence. However, we have information that he will attend a suffrage meeting in the hall in Chipperton Road. The meeting commences at seven, so I suggest we hide in Chipperton Mews, twenty yards up Chipperton Road, just before you get to the Presbyterian Hall on the right. When Hobson passes, we shall apprehend him. If he hasn't appeared by the time the meeting starts, we shall fall back to my second plan. We'll go to the Lincoln Arms and attempt an arrest there. Let's go!"

The five of us, Holmes and I, Russell, and his two constables, all went north twenty yards and hid near the entrance to Chipperton Mews. A few drops of rain fell and I hoped that it wouldn't develop into a shower or, as the temperature dropped, that it wouldn't turn to snow. I hoped the legendary long winters of a hundred years ago wouldn't return.

"Have your truncheons and handcuffs at the ready," said Holmes to the two constables, "Watson, ready your revolver. Now we wait."

The daylight faded, but there was still sufficient light to see, and the lamplighters hadn't commenced their rounds. In the dusk there wasn't enough light to read my watch. We waited.

"There!" exclaimed Holmes. "It's Hobson! Grab him!"

Hobson was completely taken by surprise. Two constables had him by the arms. I pointed my revolver at him. "Get the Darbies on 'im!" cried Russell.

Hobson was restrained. Clearly distressed, he had been taken completely unawares. His shoulders slumped, realizing that, with handcuffs on, his chances of escape were zero. A lamplighter appeared and started lighting the gas lamps. Nearby a clock chimed seven o'clock.

"Where is your gun?" demanded Holmes.

"In the hotel," was the reply. "I wouldn't take it to the meeting."

"One moment, Mr. 'Olmes," said Russell, "Geoffrey 'Obson, I arrest you on the charges of treason, and aiding and abetting a person in treason. I must warn you that anything you say may be used against you. And I'll be adding a charge of possession of firearm when we find it. We can't be having an unattended gun lying about."

At the hotel, we stood in the small reception area, a space not built to accommodate so many persons easily.

"Room number and key please." commanded Russell.

"Seven, first floor," answered Hobson. "The key is in my left waistcoat pocket."

A constable went to find the gun.

"Why did you do it?" asked Holmes, "You realise that treason carries the death penalty. You will hang for this."

"Roddy was so gullible," replied Hobson. "He was so easy to manipulate. At first, I thought that he'd kill the Queen and that would be that. I hoped that he'd shoot, and that he too would be shot, and that would be the end of the matter. But it

238

all went wrong. I counted upon his lunacy that any tale he gave of me wouldn't be believed."

"But why kill the Queen?" I asked.

"Because she is the epitome of the suffrage problem. Even if women had the vote, she as Queen could not use it. All her life, she has been manipulated by men. That German conniver of a husband, and now whomever is Prime Minister. She does not and cannot understand what suffrage is about. She is a symbol of subjugated women. Removing her would show the world that."

The next morning, the Irregulars arrived and lined up in our sitting room.

"This time it is I who reports to you," started Holmes. "I have good news. Geoffrey Hobson was arrested last night, entirely due to your efforts. But you already know that, don't you? I saw you lurking, Wiggins. You must have seen Detective-Sergeant Russell and constables take Hobson away."

"Sorry, guv'nor," said Wiggins. "Mr. 'Olmes, I mean. What will 'appen to 'im?"

"He will stand trial for conspiracy to treason, be found guilty, and will be hung by the neck until he is dead." replied Holmes grimly. "Now here is your pay, one shilling each."

Wiggins shook Holmes's hand when he received his. Amy performed a little curtsy when accepting her pay. Then they turned and left, and at the door, Wiggins turned to face us.

"At your service, Mr. 'Olmes. Dr. Watson." He gave little bow, and then he too left.

So ended the case of Geoffrey Hobson. Hobson and Maclean came before the courts and both were convicted. Hobson was found guilty as charged, and sentenced to death by hanging. Roderick Maclean was found "Not Guilty, but

Insane" and sentenced to life imprisonment. Queen Victoria objected to Maclean's verdict. "I want the law changed," she said. "He *was* guilty. The verdict of such matters should now be '*Guilty*, but Insane'.

And so it was.

NOTE

*   Phillip Morris started selling Marlborough cigarettes in 1847 from his factory in Great Marlborough Street. In 1885, Morris finally did market the brand as a Lady's Cigarette. In 1902, the company opened in New York, and registered "Marlboro" as a brand in 1908, although no cigarette was marketed under that name until 1923. In the 1930's, it was advertised as "Mild as May". The product was eventually re-packaged for men, and the famous Marlboro Cowboy was used in advertising, beginning in the 1950's.

The Adventure of the
Last Laugh
by Tracy J. Revels

Looking back over my notes of many decades, I am struck by how seldom I recorded the more comical adventures of my friend Sherlock Holmes. Often this was from discretion, to protect those involved from further ridicule or embarrassment that publicity might bring. At other times, Holmes did not feel the cases were serious enough to merit being committed to posterity. However, upon retrieving the records of our adventure at Waterlynn, which concerned the rather bizarre self-portrait of the late Eustis Lacey, I feel compelled to offer my faithful readers a glimpse into a moment in 1882 when a peculiar client and his most unprecedented problem took us into the realm of both high art and low comedy.

"I have no means of compensating you for your efforts, Mr. Holmes," my friend's newly arrived client said. "I barely have two farthings to rub together, but I promise that if you unravel this mystery, I can make you rich beyond your wildest dreams."

Holmes turned from his perusal of the sketch above our mantelpiece, lit his pipe, and considered our rather extraordinary visitor. The young man, who had introduced himself as Ambrose Burnside Bartley, was a spectacle of an aestheticism run amok. He was perhaps thirty years of age, and his long blonde curls, each carefully oiled, trailed down over a purple frock coat and a ruffled cravat that would have made a Regency dandy proud. His crane-like legs were encased in pink silk breeches, paired with checkered stockings above green patent-leather slippers. Every item of his ensemble was spotted with stains, or patched and mended with no great skill. He was fortunate, however, to have been blessed with a handsome face and, despite his odd appearance, a genuine and pleasing manner.

"Indeed, Mr. Bartley?" Holmes asked. "While my work may be its own reward, I am intrigued by your proposition. What mystery could I solve that would elevate me to the aristocracy of wealth in such a dramatic fashion?"

The young man appeared not to hear the mocking tone that I clearly discerned, and plunged forward with painful earnestness. "Why, if you could unravel the clues in Eustis's self-portrait, and direct me to the location of the combination for his safe, which contains a trio of the world's greatest masterpieces, we would both be richer than King Midas in an instant!"

Holmes waved his guest to the sofa. "I consider myself something of a connoisseur of art, though Watson claims my knowledge of the subject is flawed and my tastes border on the crude. However, this is nothing but jealousy on his part, so let us have your problem from the beginning, Mr. Bartley."

The young man eagerly launched into his tale.

"Eustis Lacey was a dear friend of mine at Oxford, where we both studied art, with an emphasis on the works of the High Renaissance. Eustis's prospects were excellent, as he was the only child of wealthy parents, connected on his mother's side to nobility and on his father's to some of the greatest entrepreneurs of our age. But Eustis was a rebel, always at odds with his class. He broke every rule, and I have no doubt that some of his more scandalous behaviors drove his godly mother to an early grave. He was sent down twice and finally expelled for activities that are best left unspoken – only to say that a goat, a pair of lady's drawers, and an intoxicated sexton were involved.

"For a time, my friend was disinherited by his father, and forced to make his own way in the world. Fortunately, Eustis had a knack for discovering lost masterpieces in out-of-the-way shops and the homes of impoverished baronets. He regularly received commissions to travel to Italy, Spain, and France to purchase pieces for wealthy patrons. But Eustis's great goal was not merely to be an expert for hire – no, he wished to be a master himself, and to be accepted by the arbiters of taste.

"And there, Mr. Holmes, was the problem – Eustis could paint with great technical precision, but he lacked originality in his work. He was rejected by every academy to which he applied – the French were particularly insulting, and the Germans replied that he would do better to take up house painting. Even the Americans – the Americans! – refused to display his works in any of their shows. I should add that he had a real skill for drawing caricatures – you should have seen the funny sketches he used to make of our deans – but he made the mistake of getting one of his little 'wistful studies', as he called them, published in *Punch*. The Home Secretary was not the least forgiving, and after that incident there was even less chance that anyone in the British Isles would do anything except denounce him as a 'talentless amateur'. I am sad to say that my own artistic success – quite modest I must add, and mainly in portraiture of spoiled brats and aging dowagers – caused a cooling in our friendship, as Eustis experienced continued disappointments in his bid for acceptance.

"And so my friend began his sad decline. He had been restored to the bosom of his family, and his father had recently died, but the fortune he inherited could not buy him the one thing he desired: A reputation as an artist. He took to drink, and when he was sober (which I fear was not often), he amused himself with his other pastime from his college days – building all sorts of strange mechanical devices that, inevitably, involved explosives. Half-a-dozen times he nearly burnt down Waterlynn, his ancestral manor, with his little toys that caught themselves on fire.

"Then, just over a year ago, I received an invitation to a dinner party at Eustis's home. I was astonished by the guest list, which was made up of a dozen or more of Eustis's greatest critics and foils, including Professor Peter Schmitt, the sneering old instructor of art history from our college, and Miss Karen Blisschild, who has made a name for herself writing criticism for artistic journals, along with a number of other self-proclaimed experts and connoisseurs. Knowing my friend's utter contempt for these individuals, and their disdain for him, I could hardly see the purpose in the assembly. I halfway expected a brawl to erupt before the coffee was poured. Conversation was strained, to say the least, but at the conclusion of the meal Eustis rose, dramatically cleared his throat, and began a speech.

"'I am dying,' he said, without any preamble. 'I have a tumor which the doctors inform me is inoperable. Therefore, I must put my affairs in order. I will have little to leave to the world, for as some of you know I have led a profligate and wasteful life, and most of the money left to me by my sainted parents has been squandered. However, this treasure remains.'"

"He went to a large easel which had been covered with a cloth. He threw back the drapery, revealing three small paintings. One was a Madonna holding an apple, the other a still life of bread and wine, and the third a head of Zeus. An electricity ran through the room, as everyone recognized, even from our places at the table, the distinctive styles of Da Vinci, Rembrandt, and Raphael. Eustis allowed us all a moment to gape.

"'You surely see what I have accomplished – I have located three lost paintings of the greatest masters the world has known, paintings that have often been described but never found. Tonight, I will lock them a safe. The combination I will secure in a hidden place. To find the combination, you must look in my self-portrait, recently completed, which will be unveiled on the occasion of my funeral. He or she who successfully opens the safe may have what is found inside, along with Waterlynn as well! But have a care, dear friends . . . have a care!'

"At this point, Eustis replaced the drape on the pictures. He then walked over to the corner of the room and removed a second covering from a green metal safe. The squat, ugly box was wrapped with metallic wires, which in turn were attached to a strange clockwork mechanism atop it. Eustis grinned at us – I'll never forget how unnerving that grin was. I still see it in my nightmares!

"'Should you try to force this safe open,' Eustis said, 'or attempt to unlock the safe with the wrong combination, an incendiary device within the safe will activate, destroying the masterpieces! Now, fellow art lovers . . . shall we retire to the drawing room for our dessert?'"

"He herded us from the chamber, and within an hour we were all unceremoniously packed into our carriages and sent away. I was astonished, of course, and intended to appeal to him, as a dear friend and fellow aesthete, to at least allow me to gaze upon those beautiful pictures and commit them to memory. But it was not to be. A week later, his housekeeper found him expired in his bed. Eustis had left an account that would fund the maintenance of the property for a year after his passing, and, following his funeral, at the reading of the will, the strange situation he had explained to us over dinner was made even clearer."

Our guest fumbled in his pockets, finally drawing out a much folded piece of foolscap. Another round of searching produced half-moon spectacles, through which he peered.

> *To all interested parties, I declare that my greatest treasures lie secured in the green safe in my library. However, one must take note that I have devised a trap for the unwary. My safe is rigged with one of my special devices, and should anyone attempt to open it without the proper combination, the artwork inside will be incinerated. To find the combination, one must look in the self-portrait above the library fireplace. He or she who finds the combination and opens the safe is the owner of the masterpieces within, along with Waterlynn.*

"What a bizarre arrangement!" I said.

"Mr. John Lindley, who was Eustis's solicitor, was further required to open the library to guests on the first Saturday of each month, from one until four in the afternoon, to study the portrait and hunt for clues. But this funding will soon run out. The final provision of Eustis's extraordinary will stated that if no solution was reached in a year's time, the contents of the house would be auctioned and the money given to the Bethlehem Royal Hospital – better known as Bedlam, the lunatic asylum!"

Holmes smiled. "Your late friend's sense of humor was rather pawky."

Mr. Bartley ignored the comment. "I suppose that once everything is put up for sale, some wealthy individual will purchase the safe and try to open it, without having the combination in hand." Our client's agitation returned as he wiped away a sudden tear. "I have seen these paintings, and I

246

know of Eustis' remarkable ability with explosive devices. I fear these irreplaceable treasures will be destroyed in greed and haste! Please, Mr. Holmes! Tomorrow is the final day the portrait may be inspected – I must have your assistance!"

Holmes's thin lips quivered, then abruptly turned down, giving him an expression of exaggerated solemnity.

"I presume you have rivals for this challenge?"

"A year ago, almost a hundred artists and experts descended on Waterlynn, but as every clue has been followed without success, now only three of us remain: Professor Schmitt, Miss Blisschild, and myself."

"Has either of your competitors expressed an intention to purchase the safe once the year has expired?"

"Neither of them could afford it, I suppose. They are not penniless, but they are far from wealthy."

Holmes nodded thoughtfully. "If they are truly as obsessed with obtaining the artwork as you state, then they may not let such a handicap as pecuniary difficulties stop them."

"You think they would try to steal the safe?"

Holmes put his fingers together. "I think many things are possible. By any chance would you have – ah, I see you have anticipated my request. Watson, observe – Mr. Bartley is an ideal client."

The young man had removed a rolled paper from his moth-eaten carpet bag. Holmes rose and began clearing chemical apparatus from his table.

"You have my word, Mr. Bartley, that we will be at Waterlynn at one tomorrow. I do not believe your problem presents any great difficulty."

The client's jaw dropped. "You mean – you know where the combination to the safe is?"

"I do," Holmes said. He considered the picture he had unrolled across the table. It was clearly a copy of Eustis Lacey's self-portrait. "In fact, I can state with some certainty and no false modesty that I knew the location before I ever saw this facsimile. It is an exact reproduction?"

"Yes, to every line, but – you know where the combination is?"

"I do."

"Then tell me!"

Holmes shook his head. "To do so now might tempt you to folly. Have patience, Mr. Bartley. All will be clear tomorrow afternoon. A good evening to you now, and we will see you at Waterlynn." Holmes waited until the man had made a quivering exit. "Come, Watson, what do you make of this image?"

I moved to Holmes's side. My immediate response was one of bafflement. My secondary reaction was annoyance.

"He could not have been serious! It must be some type of jape!"

In the picture, the subject faced the viewer, but the subject's eyes were crossed and his teeth locked in a disturbing rictus of a grin. The scrawny, unattractive man appeared to be clad in a strange blue toga, with a laurel wreath in his long ginger hair. In his right hand sat a monkey, while his left hand grasped a golden key. Behind him was a window, and beyond was a landscape of blasted trees and cragged peaks, with lightning striking out of a sky filled with boiling black clouds. I leaned forward, attempting to make out three figures on the horizon. They appeared to be older women, cavorting around a cauldron.

"Are those witches?"

"So they appear."

"And is that . . . a bust of Shakespeare just to the side, peeking through the shadows?"

"What a keen eye you have, Watson. It is indeed the immortal bard, lurking in the darkness at Lacey's elbow."

I grimaced. "What a hideous picture. If this is a true sample of how he painted, no wonder every gallery rejected him."

"Yet it is done with a certain level of technical precision. One cannot fault his use of perspective, or his choice in colors."

"So where is the combination to the safe in all this?" I asked. Holmes merely smiled at me, then tapped his temple.

The manor of Waterlynn was but a short train journey from London. We arrived early and enjoyed a pleasant ride from the station to the manor. The massive iron gates were locked, and our client paced nervously before them.

"Mr. Holmes and Doctor . . . ."

"Watson," I said. Our names were not so clearly linked in those early days.

"I've heard a rumor, sir. It's hideous! It's – why, I can barely believe it. To gain money this way – it is shameful!"

Holmes paid our driver, then made a show of brushing the dust from his travelling cloak. "So which one has made the marriage," he casually asked, "Professor Schmitt or Miss Blisschild?"

Mr. Bartley clutched his chest. "Sir! Are you a wizard, to know such things?"

"Calm yourself," Holmes said, "it takes no great leap of logic to deduce that if both of your rivals remain obsessed with acquiring the safe, then – lacking the location of the combination from the portrait – they will attempt to obtain the funds to purchase said safe and attempt to force it open. I spent

249

last evening looking up their credentials, and found that they were both unwed. The easiest way to acquire sudden wealth is to marry it."

"Or kill for it," I said. Holmes smirked.

"What a devious mind you have, Watson. Clearly, I must watch my step around you."

The client ignored our banter. "Professor Schmitt is married – to Edwina Lucretia Talbert. Do you know the name?"

I snapped my fingers. "The opera singer!"

"*Aspiring* opera singer," Holmes corrected. "She has given a number of London galas, funded by her family's wealth, to underwhelming reviews. She was made for roles that require a sizeable voice, which she possesses – unfortunately she does not also possess the requisite ear for tune. But here comes the happy groom now."

A miserable little trap had pulled up, discharging a thin, sallow man with a wild mane of grey hair and a face set in a perpetual scowl. His shoulders were hunched and his coat looked worn and shabby. He peered at us through tiny spectacles, then sneered and failed to offer a hand as Bartley made introductions.

"A detective, are you? There was hardly any call for that – it is an academic matter, pure and simple. Tell me, what do you do, Mr. Holmes? Track down runaway maids and pilfering butlers? Or is your specialty finding lost dogs?"

I wondered how such an unpleasant man could have snared a wife of any description, much less one who came with a substantial dowry. Holmes calmly congratulated him on his nuptials.

"Yes, yes, she's a fine woman. Former opera singer, you know. Soprano. Still in voice. Can hit notes to break glass." He barely suppressed a shudder. "I'm used to a quiet bachelor life. Still, I suppose I will adjust."

Another vehicle approached. This one carried a lady in bright blue dress, with blonde hair and icy eyes. She waited until the driver could assist her, descending from the carriage with the cool dignity of a queen. Her profile was striking, but as she drew close I could see that most of her appearance was artifice, that paint and powder were waging a mighty war against time. Her hair was shot through with gray, and there was much of the disappointed spinster in her haughty expression. She approached us with an upturned nose, as if we were a pack of dirty farmers just returned from the field.

"Hello, Karen," the professor said, showing her none of the courtesy one would expect him to adopt toward a lady. "Where's your garish trinket?" he demanded. "First time I've seen you without it."

"What I do with my jewelry is none of your business, Peter!" she snapped, even as her hand strayed to her collar and toyed nervously with a piece of floppy lace. Bartley leaned close and whispered in my ear that Miss Blisschild had previously flaunted a golden broach bearing a yellow diamond, said to have been a family heirloom.

"Sold it, have you?" the professor cawed, ignoring her distress. "How much did you get for that piece of paste?"

"I assure you, my jewel was real, and worth more than you have earned in your entire miserable, undistinguished career," Miss Blisschild hissed, turning her attention to our client. "Ambrose, I see you have brought along friends. They couldn't be Peter's friends, as we all know he has none."

"I have a wife now," Professor Schmitt muttered.

"So I have learned," Miss Blisschild said, with bite. "It was no doubt a *weighty* decision for you to make. Let us hope the furnishings of your miserable rooms can *support* her."

251

Fortunately, we were spared any more barbs by the arrival of a manservant, who opened the gates and bid us to follow. The grounds of Waterlynn were thick with trees and choked with overgrown grass and weeds. Through the tangled, unkempt landscape I spotted a substantial folly, the artificial ruins of an antique temple. My mind leapt back to the painting, and how the subject had been portrayed in the garb of some type of Greek or Roman god. As we came up the gravel drive, I also noted that on the lintel of the solid Georgian home was a frieze depicting three women standing around a large pot. I seized Holmes's sleeve.

"Do you – ?"

"Yes, I see."

We were admitted into a gilded foyer by Mr. Lindley, the solicitor, a small, ferret-like man who clearly wished to be done with his duty. Despite the house's outer magnificence, inside it had an air of being stale and dusty. Boards had been pulled up in the hallway, and in places there were gaping holes in the walls. Carpets and tapestries were ripped, marble-topped tables overturned, glass cabinets shattered, their contents scattered across the scraped and damaged floors. It looked as if barbarians had arrived to sack the place, but given up on their quest midway through their pillage.

"You all know the rules, of course," the solicitor said, with the air of a bored tour guide. "The portrait remains in the library. You may study it for three hours, and seek the combination anywhere you like, but you must not touch the safe without the combination in your hands."

We were escorted into the library. It was filled with hundreds of books, though many of them had been knocked to the floor and loose pages were scattered about. A pile of broken plaster marked where some unfortunate artwork had met its demise. My eyes were drawn to a funny bit of sculpture

252

on a high shelf. It was a golden monkey, its tail held between its teeth. A large volume of Shakespeare's plays was tucked beside it.

Much to my surprise, Holmes merely settled into a chair. The three art experts began to consider the painting, and quickly seemed to forget that Holmes and I were in the room.

"It is clearly an allusion to the folly," Miss Blisschild said. "The toga and the victor's wreath tell us that."

"And how many times have we dug up that damned folly?" Professor Schmitt muttered. "It has nothing to do with the combination! The clue is in the bust of Shakespeare!"

"Which you broke, last month," Bartley said. "We sorted through all the pieces, broke them into dust, as if we were looking for a pearl. It was a dead end."

"The toga is blue," Miss Blisschild continued, her voice suddenly sharp. "The robe of the Virgin Mary is often blue. This could be an indication of a religious tie, a direction to the combination being in a place of worship. Was Eustis a Catholic?"

"The brat was a damned pagan," his former professor snapped. "And I hope he's burning in Hades now, for all the trouble that he has caused us. If I have to listen to one more aria –"

"Have you considered the monkey?" I asked, caught up in their speculation in spite of myself. "Perhaps Eustis is saying that the monkey sculpture holds the key to this conundrum."

All three of them turned and glared at me. Even the solicitor, who had been slumped in a window seat, let out an annoyed sigh.

"That was the first thing we thought of," Bartley said.

"I'll give Eustis credit, he was more subtle than I imagined," the professor grumbled. "Perhaps the clue lies in his smile, or his gaze. He seems to look both ways at once . . .

as if misdirecting us." The professor thumped his cane on the floor. "He used to cross his eyes like that in class, just to make me stumble in my lecture."

The lady folded her arms. "And he was certainly no saint. I have never forgotten that time when he asked me if I would – no, I will not speak of it! But perhaps that is also a clue – he wishes to be what he is not, so the combination must be in some place where we would not expect it."

A loud yawn took us all aback. Holmes leaned forward in his chair, elbows on his knees.

"The Scottish play."

The academic pair frowned in unison. "Yes. What about it?" Professor Schmitt demanded.

"*Macbeth* is referenced three times in the painting – in the bust of Shakespeare, the three witches, and the blasted heath beyond the window. Your deceased friend was, as the lady points out, far from a saintly figure – one who was perhaps, as his image suggests, often intoxicated to the point of ludicrousness. He is also clearly 'monkeying' with the key to the safe, casting a spell of sorts to keep you from igniting the lightning within the device, just as lightning strikes within the picture. I would suggest that the combination might be found not in a private spot, but in a public place like a public house. Correct me if I err, but I believe there is an establishment in the nearby village named 'Macduff's' and – "

Professor Schmitt and Miss Blisschild both whirled at the same time, running for the door. There was an unsightly collision at the portal, with the lady demanding to go first and the professor uttering some oaths that would have gotten a lad sent down from school. Mr. Bartley started to go after them, but Holmes seized his cane and barred the young man's exit. We heard the outer door slam in the distance.

"But you said – "

254

"I said a great deal of nonsense, Mr. Bartley. And, unlike Professor Schmitt, I do not wish your late friend in the nether regions. Indeed, I hope he looks down from heaven and is enjoying this moment."

"What do you mean, sir?"

Holmes rose from his chair. "The correct answer is usually the simplest. Allow me to demonstrate."

Holmes pulled a large rag and a dark bottle from his coat pocket. He poured out some liquid onto the cloth and then, before any of us could raise our voice to object, he drew up a small ladder and reached above the mantel, swiping the rag across the painting. Instantly, the gaudy image of Eustis Lacey began to dissolve in a riot of blended colors. Holmes plucked the canvas down from the wall.

"Behold. When you friend told you that the clue was in his painting, that is what he meant."

Indeed, the paint had blurred and streaked, revealing a set of numbers that were carved into the canvas. Bartley began to tremble.

"My God . . . he always said . . . critics made too much of symbolism."

"Your rivals have been led astray by their own insistence that their academic expertise outweighed Eustis's very words. Will you try opening the safe now?"

"I'm too nervous. What if I make a mistake? No – you do it, Mr. Holmes!"

The solicitor cleared his throat. "By law, the contents of the safe belong to whoever opens it. You will have no claim on the paintings if Mr. Holmes does the work."

Mr. Bartley twitched so violently I feared my medical services would be necessary. Holmes shook his head.

"I hereby give all my rights to the contents to my client. Yes, I will sign a paper to that effect. Please, sir, do sit down.

I would like this task completed before your erstwhile competitors return."

We watched, holding our breath, as Holmes knelt and deftly spun the dials. There was an instant of hesitation and then a sharp and clear click. Holmes turned the handle. The green monster opened its jaws.

Within, a collection of copper wires dangled.

"Why, they're not attached to anything!" Bartley cried.

"Of course not. It was all a blind."

"But . . . why?"

"A final bit of fun, perhaps? Do come here, Mr. Bartley, and claim your prize."

The man fell to his knees and fished inside the safe. He pulled out three small but magnificent paintings. One was clearly by Da Vinci, the others I could not vouch for. Bartley began to weep.

I suddenly felt sorry for my friend. He had given up a treasure, and to a man I was not sure was deserving of it. Yet a knowing smile played across Holmes's face.

"Perhaps we should retire and leave our client alone with his masterpieces. There may be some amusement in checking to see if his rivals have torn Macduff's public house apart at the seams. Do be careful, Mr. Bartley. I would not put murder beyond either of your competitors, especially as one has parted with a favored jewel and the other has said goodbye to the peace and freedom of bachelorhood."

"You will hardly succeed in your line of work if you continue along this pathway," I told Holmes, as we arrived back in Baker Street.

"Whatever do you mean, Watson?"

"I mean, you did not even present your client with a bill – and he is now perhaps one of the richest art collectors in

England. Imagine what those three lost masterpieces will go for at auction! You could certainly acquire better lodgings than these had you claimed at least one of the paintings as payment for your services."

"Ah, but I like this picturesque pile," Holmes said, as he hung his travelling cloak on its peg and took up his pipe. "It has already seen the beginning of a few adventures, and I suspect many more intriguing clients will pass through its doors in the years to come. Indeed, when you write your little tales, you may one day make this address famous."

"But the money!" I protested. "The paintings, by right, belonged to you."

"Great art belongs to the world, Watson. No, no," he scolded, as I settled at my desk with my notebook. "Do not think of writing up this little adventure. It is hardly a worthy example of my skills, and, quite frankly, lends itself more to the humorous than the deadly or dangerous, or even the bizarre."

"Perhaps you do not wish the world to know that you work for free," I snorted.

His smile was enigmatic. "Perhaps."

Three months later, upon returning from some errands, I was surprised to find Mr. Ambrose Burnside Bartley once again perched upon our sofa. He was a much changed man. Gone were the oiled curls and purple frock coat and checkered hosiery. Instead, he could have been mistaken for any dour London businessman in his black suit and high collar, with a proper leather bag at his feet.

"I had to sell it, of course," he was saying to Holmes. "That wretched manor was sinking in debt. I was lucky to get out with my shirt by the time the thing was done. Oh, hello Doctor. I've come to settle my account with Mr. Holmes."

My friend waved the suggestion aside. "You owe me nothing."

"I think I owe you everything. You see, even before I came to you, I'd made up my mind that if I couldn't discover that combination on the last day, I was going to sell the one thing of value I possessed – a miniature of Charles II by Samuel Cooper – to try and outbid the others for the safe. This miniature was given to me by my mother – its sentimental value alone – well, even now, just to think about losing it, all for nothing, makes me sob!"

He demonstrated, plucking a handkerchief from his vest. Holmes shook his head.

"I take it that both of your rivals have come to regret their hasty decisions."

"Oh, sir, if you could see the old professor! He's a ghost of himself, and gone half-deaf from all the shrieking, he says. Miss Blisschild – well, I hear she's under lock and key, awaiting trial. When she learned what happened, she tried to steal back her diamond from the fellow who bought it. No, there's been nothing but misery that has come of this – misery you saved me from."

"And the paintings," I asked. "Have you had them appraised?"

The man gave me a sour look. "I did. They are worthless."

"What? How can they be worthless?"

"Because they were painted not by Da Vinci, Rembrandt, and Raphael, but by Eustis Lacey," Holmes said with a chuckle. "Recall, Watson, what Mr. Bartley told us about his friend – Lacey was a painter of great technical ability, but no true originality. I had every reason to suspect the paintings with which he tempted his foes were forgeries, his interpretation of paintings described in books but lost to time."

"It was a grand joke," Bartley grumbled. "I suppose if there is an afterlife, as the spiritualists claim, then he is enjoying my discomfort. So be it. I've learned my lesson, given up on art and on being an esthete. I've gone into business with my uncle, learning the trade in gentleman's woolen undergarments. Perhaps I will make something of myself after all." He turned back to my friend. "If you will not accept a checque from me, sir, perhaps souvenirs of this strange adventure will suffice?" He reached into his leather bag and pull out the three small paintings. "I am sure that Eustis would want them to belong to someone who shares his sense of the absurd. I fear I have lost my taste for any type of 'wistful studies'."

"You are certain you wish me to have them?"

"Indeed, sir. You do me a favor to remove them from my sight."

The men shook hands and Mr. Bartley departed. Holmes settled into his chair, holding the false "Head of Zeus" that had been attributed to Raphael. I asked him some insignificant question and received only silence for an answer. So it was for the rest of the evening, until at ten I left Holmes bent over his table with his lenses, examining the paintings in detail. Unable to grasp his purpose, I retired.

The next morning, I found Holmes at the breakfast table, looking like the proverbial cat that had dined upon canary. He directed my attention toward the sofa and three paintings resting upon it.

"Where did these come from?" I asked. They were the same size as Lacey's work, but each depicted Biblical characters and each was done in a distinct Renaissance style.

"It is most helpful to have insight into the character of a dead man, Watson. Think how Eustis Lacey was described by his dear friend: An artist, a prankster, a man determined to have the last laugh on a society he felt had unfairly ignored his talents. And what were his talents? Beyond his ability to paint unoriginal pieces and construct ridiculous machines, he had an eye for hidden masterpieces and a knack for concealment. It occurred to me, as I examined the forgeries in great detail, that Eustis spoke of having wasted his fortune. On what, I wondered, beyond alcohol and, one presumes, the proverbial 'riotous living'? What would have prevented him from purchasing artwork for himself to enjoy, once he had the money for it?"

I blinked. "You're right. There was certainly nothing to stop him from becoming a real collector."

Holmes inclined his head toward the sofa. "And so behold, Watson, what hid beneath the paint that Lacey applied, and which I spent last evening carefully scraping away – these are small samples of the work of Masaccio, Titian, and Caravaggio. By creating false masterpieces atop real ones, Eustis Lacey played a game of wits with his colleagues. He doubtless imagined that once the safe was breached and his forgeries discovered, the disgusted winner would hurl the spoils into the fire without ever checking to see what lurked beneath the modern pigments. Just as the combination to his safe was within his portrait, his real treasure laid within his forgeries. Dear me, Watson, you look rather pale. Should you not avail yourself of your medicinal brandy? I look forward to having these paintings appraised, and then I believe that Mr. Bartley will be surprised to find that his future is not quite so bleak after all."

The Penny Murders
by Robert Stapleton

"I see you have discovered something of interest in the morning newspaper, Watson," said Sherlock Holmes as he surveyed me through the smoke of his early morning pipe.

I looked up from scrutinizing the pages of *The Times*. "How can you tell?"

"Simplicity itself, my dear fellow," came his rejoinder. "Whenever you come across an article worthy of note, you invariably shift in your seat and furrow your brow. Your entire expression grows decidedly studious."

I raised my eyebrows in surprise.

"What is it this time? Another bizarre death, like the one reported two days ago? A pig farmer in the Fens, I seem to remember, who was trampled to death by his own herd."

"Your memory serves you well."

He laughed.

"But you are quite right," I told him. "Today's article tells of a man, in rural Leicestershire, who has been killed and partially eaten by a Bengal tiger."

"In Leicestershire? Now that is indeed remarkable."

"It seems he was employed as a groundsman at the country house of a prominent peer of the realm. The article explains that his Lordship maintains a small menagerie in the grounds, and that this man somehow fell victim to the animal when nobody else was around. A singular coincidence, do you not think?"

"Two incidents too similar to dismiss as coincidence. I sense something darker in this matter."

It was a fine late spring morning in 1882, but I could already sense the shades of human tragedy invading the day.

"Your imagination is proving as agile as your memory today, Holmes," said I. "But what possible connection could there be between these two events?"

"It is too early to tell, but if there is one, then we shall undoubtedly hear from Scotland Yard when they finally admit themselves at a loss. Then we shall see."

A sparkle in my friend's eye displayed an appetite for action. I too can read expressions.

Holmes stood up abruptly and glanced toward the window. "Look sharp there, Watson. We have a visitor."

I put down my newspaper and turned my attention to events unfolding downstairs. I heard the doorbell ring, and then two female voices, one of which I instantly recognized as our landlady, Mrs. Hudson, but the other, sounding urgent and pressing, was unknown to me.

By the time the knock came upon our sitting room door, Holmes had changed out of his dressing gown and was standing before the unlit fireplace, dressed and ready to receive our visitor.

The door opened, and Mrs. Hudson announced, "Mrs. Elsie Horchester to see you, Mr. Holmes."

A woman in her mid-thirties hurried in. She stood approximately five-feet three-inches in height, wore a dark blue bonnet pulled down over graying-brown hair, and gazed at the world from brown eyes animated with urgency. Without a word of explanation, Mrs. Horchester hurried across the room to the window, from which position she looked down onto the busy thoroughfare of Baker Street.

Whilst I watched on in alarm at such an abrupt entrance, Holmes surveyed the woman with serene and dispassionate curiosity.

"They're still out there," exclaimed Mrs. Horchester.

"Who are still out there?" demanded Holmes.

"Why, those three men, of course. Can't you see them?"

We both joined her at the window, standing back slightly in order to make our surveillance of the street less obvious from below. On the opposite side of the road stood three men. They appeared bulky and robust, dressed in dark clothing, and all were watching our window with singular attention.

"A man of the sea, together with two London thugs," observed Holmes calmly.

Our visitor turned from the window. "How can you tell?"

"In the one case, mere observation, my dear lady," replied my friend. "He stands as though swaying with the rolling of the waves, whilst the others I recognize from previous encounters with London's criminal underclass. Those two ruffians go by the names of Withyburn and Smith."

"They sound like a firm of solicitors," I commented.

"Quite the opposite, I can assure you," replied Holmes drily.

"I have no knowledge of their names," said Elsie Horchester, "but I think you must be close to the truth, Mr. Holmes. You *are* Mr. Sherlock Holmes, I assume."

Holmes laughed. "Kindly take a seat, Mrs. Horchester, and tell us the nature of the predicament that has brought you here on behalf of your husband."

The woman sat down, and looked up at him in amazement. "You know about my husband?"

Holmes took the chair facing her. "No, but the ring on your hand proclaims that you are married," observed Holmes, "and the urgency of your visit is only such as a troubled wife might make concerning her spouse."

Clasping her hands together, as though in urgent supplication, she began. "As you already know, my name is Elsie Horchester. And you are right, Mr. Holmes. My husband, George, does appear to be in some kind of trouble."

"And what does this misfortune have to do with those men out there?'

"My husband believes they are intent on killing him."

"For what reason?"

Elsie Horchester shook her head doubtfully and let out a deep sigh. "The full nature of that predicament has not yet been made clear to me, Mr. Holmes, but it has to do with the tragedy of the *Henrietta Baldersby*."

"A ship?"

"A fishing boat. Her home port was a famous fishing town on the east coast of England. The incident took place ten years ago, and was reported in all the newspapers at the time."

Holmes stood up and searched through his extensive and mysterious filing system. After several minutes, he returned, holding up a dog-eared and badly foxed newspaper cutting. "Here we have the contemporary report from *The Times*," he declared. "It tells of a certain fishing vessel breaking up in heavy weather and stranding the crew on an island in the North Atlantic."

"That is quite right, Mr. Holmes," said Mrs. Horchester.

"And you think this present business has something to do with that tragic incident?"

"It was certainly the reason why my husband came to London, but that was before we met and were married, so I am ignorant of the details."

Holmes steepled his fingers thoughtfully. "Am I to understand that your husband has sent you here to request me to visit him?"

Mrs. Horchester's look of embarrassment was as good as a nod. "But what about those men? They followed me all yesterday, though I managed to lose them in the end. They followed me again this morning, and they are out there now. I believe they are intent on following me home, in order to discover the whereabouts of my husband. And George is fearful for his life."

"Then we must evade them once again." Holmes slapped his knees decisively, and stood up. "I am intrigued by this story. Come, we must leave at once."

Immediately we were outside in the street, Holmes flagged down a cab, and we all climbed aboard, with Mrs. Horchester between us, concealed beneath the folds of her coat. But our subterfuge failed to outsmart the watchers, for as soon as we were rattling toward the far end of Baker Street, they bundled into their own vehicle, and were soon in hot pursuit.

Animated by the chase, Holmes called to the cabbie, "Lose them, and I'll give you another sovereign."

We all held on as best we could, as our cab rolled from one side to the other along the busy streets of central London. By the time we reached the street-end closest to our destination, the other vehicle was nowhere to be seen.

Holmes paid the cabbie and, staying alert to any sign of our pursuers, we followed Mrs. Horchester down the narrow alleyway adjacent to where we had alighted.

She stopped at a darkly-stained door, pushed it open, and led the way inside, slamming it firmly shut against the world.

The gloomy building held the smell of mildew and decay, and a thin ray of daylight, filtered in through an upstairs window, lit up motes of dust floating in the chill atmosphere of the hallway.

We followed Elsie Horchester into the parlour, where we discovered a man of approximately forty years of age, lounging in a badly upholstered armchair at the far end of the room. He looked up as we entered, an expression of suspicion showing in his dark eyes.

Holmes removed his hat but retained his coat. "Good morning, Mr. Horchester," said he, addressing the seated figure. "We have come at your wife's invitation. And at your own behest, I believe."

The seated man leaned forward in his chair. "Ah, yes. You must be Mr. Sherlock Holmes. People tell me you are a man who can be trusted."

"Trusted to uncover the truth, Mr. Horchester," he replied.

Then, as Horchester turned his gaze upon myself, Holmes added, "And this is my colleague, Dr. John Watson. He has my full confidence, and you can rely upon his absolute discretion."

"Very well, Mr. Holmes. Kindly take a seat." George Horchester pointed to two upright chairs standing in the middle of the room.

"Mr. Horchester," said Holmes, "your wife has told us a little of your present situation, and we have come here post-haste. I would be obliged, therefore, if you would please now come to the exact purpose of this meeting."

George Horchester sat back in his seat. "Then allow me to unfold to you my tale, Mr. Holmes – a story which takes us back ten years."

"You and your crew were castaways on an uninhabited island, I believe," said Holmes.

"Indeed. The place was known to the Viking seafarers as Dragon Island. Or so our Icelandic rescuers later informed us."

"Very interesting. Pray continue. Watson, take notes."

"I was skipper of the sailing trawler, *Henrietta Baldersby*, one of a fleet owned by our father, but managed and partly manned by myself and one of my two brothers, William. At this particular time, we were fishing in Icelandic waters. The weather was bitterly cold, and the North Atlantic was proving a particularly hazardous environment that season. Other boats had been lost, and our vessel suffered badly from the mounting waves, losing rigging and spars. Then, through the gloom, between the menacing sky and the mountainous sea, we saw a dark shape emerge. An island. A black rock, rising from the ocean waves, akin to a whale emerging from the depths. Massive in height, and rugged in appearance, with waves breaking white over sharp rocks where the island met the ocean. We fought with the helm, but the rudder was too ineffectual against the power of the water to direct us away from that approaching menace."

George Horchester looked around at us with wild eyes. "Mr. Holmes, we struck those rocks with such force that we were all cast overboard into the boiling ocean. The last I saw of my vessel, she was being smashed to kindling by rock and waves. We all gave ourselves up for dead."

"But you managed to reach the island."

"And a most accursed place it turned out to be, Mr. Holmes. At first, I was glad to discover gravel beneath my body, and to touch the security of solid land. But every stitch of clothing was soaking wet, and the cold Atlantic wind was set to chill each of us to the bone, and leach both heat and life from our miserable bodies. The high cliffs and jagged rocks kept us restricted to one small section of the island. From the gravel beach, we climbed to a ledge some five feet above, and there we discovered the entrance to a cave. It wasn't much, but at least it provided us with shelter, and a chance to take stock of our unenviable situation. We discovered that we had next to nothing in the way of resources. I had, however, managed to rescue the ship's papers, together with useful items including a clasp knife and a box of matches."

Horchester paused, staring fixedly into space, as though, for a moment, he had returned to that island.

"Pray continue," Holmes encouraged him. "How many of you had managed to reach shore?"

The man who had been unfolding this tale looked at us with haunted eyes. "We had lost two in the sinking, never to be seen again, and we remained a crew of four. Harry Winter, Jack Shelton, my brother Bill, and myself. As skipper, I was the one in charge, and it was my responsibility to do whatever had to be done in order to save the rest of my crew. We needed to light a fire, so I set the others to gathering together as much driftwood as they could find. The majority of it was wet, and we had to allow it to dry. So the wood came with us into the cave, as we sought what little shelter it might provide."

"You were fortunate to find such shelter," I told him.

"Indeed, Dr. Watson, we were extremely lucky. As I told you, it was an island known to the Viking seafarers a thousand years before we landed there."

"Dragon Island," recalled Holmes, with a knowing nod.

"And well named," said George Horchester. "The interior of the cave was dark, but when some of the wood had dried, I lit a brushwood torch and discovered that somebody had indeed been there before us. Along the wall, incised deeply into the rock, we found the depiction of a dragon. Its mouth began as wide as the entrance, and the carving ended with the tail at the far end of the cave, as though deliberately indicating where a small spring of fresh water trickled from the rock. We had water, we had shelter, we had the beginnings of a fire, but we needed nourishment. We were fishermen by trade, but we had neither nets nor line with which to feed ourselves. It was outside the breeding season for seabirds, so we took what little we could access, together with limpets we wrenched from the rocks, and concocted a few meagre meals."

Holmes nodded slowly. "Did you find any further signs of human habitation?"

"Indeed we did. Toward the far end of the cave, we discovered, huddled together in the darkness, the skeletons of three people. There was no way of telling how long they had been there, or by their shreds of clothing whether they were men or women, but they must have been there for some considerable time. The discovery came as a profound shock to us all, as it suggested that we might never be rescued from that ill-fated island."

"Loss of hope can have a terrible effect upon people," observed Holmes.

"That is the only explanation for what occurred next."

"Pray continue."

George Horchester's face turned a deathly pale. "We were dying, gentlemen. And even though we managed to light a fire, its heat brought us little in the way of comfort. For several days, we sat and merely existed. We very soon became nothing more than skeletons, every bit as pathetic as those we had discovered inside the cave. We now considered ourselves unlucky to have survived. The other three men looked to me for leadership, and for some way of escaping or even surviving this unenviable predicament."

Our story-teller stood up, turned to face the corner of the room, and continued his tale. "I put into words the thought that had been haunting each one of us. We would need to kill and eat one of our number. Perhaps more than one. Until a single man remained, to die there alone. None of us wished to be that final survivor. But neither did anyone want to take the lives of his companions."

"Great Heavens!" I exclaimed. "Whatever did you do?"

He turned, glared down at us, and shouted, "I was the skipper! I was the one to do the filthy deed. My responsibility. My job. My burden to carry for the rest of my days."

Hardly knowing what words to use, I asked, "How did you decide which one of the crew should be the first victim?"

George Horchester sat down heavily, and once again looked blankly into space. "We tossed a coin," he told us in a small voice.

"A coin!" I exclaimed. "That sounds damnably cold and heartless."

He glared defiantly at me. "How else should we have done it?" he demanded. "Drawing lots? That too is a horrible way for a man to learn his fate. No, I had to be seen to be scrupulously fair, otherwise they would never have accepted the outcome. There was no choice. It had to be done that way."

"Quite," said Holmes, leaning forward in his seat. "Then, pray tell us exactly what occurred."

"I had a penny. It was enough. The fact that it carried a picture of the Queen perhaps gave it added legitimacy at that moment. I don't know. But they agreed that I, as captain, should conduct the selection process." The man sitting in front of us looked around, as though requesting our acquiescence in what was to follow. In this he failed. "I decided that I would toss the same coin in the same manner for each man in turn. It seemed the fairest method. Each time the coin fell 'heads' upwards, the man would be saved. But the very first time the coin fell 'tails' upwards, that man would be our victim."

"Not a pleasant situation," muttered Sherlock Holmes.

"Not for any of us, Mr. Holmes," replied Horchester. "Despite our personal differences, I decided to give my brother the best chance of all of us to survive, so I commenced with Harry Winter, a particularly valuable member of our crew. His eyes held a deep fear as he watched me. I tossed the penny into the air, and we all watched it fall to the ground. The image of Queen Victoria saved Harry, at least on that occasion. He was a lucky man. Jack Shelton was the next to face the ordeal. I tossed the coin, and saw it fall to the ground. Once again, 'heads' showed. Then I tossed for myself. Again, the coin fell so that I was spared."

"That was unusual," I commented. "Three out of three tosses falling the same way."

"Not necessarily, Watson," said Holmes. "If all other things are equal, then each toss has an identical chance of landing either way up." Holmes gave Horchester a questioning look.

"I had done my very best to spare my brother, Bill," said Horchester, "but it was now his turn to face the toss of the coin. And it fell showing 'tails'. Chance had selected my brother to die, so that the rest of us might live. I would willingly have been the one, but fortune had dictated otherwise."

"Horrible!" I exclaimed.

"Indeed," added Holmes. "Pray continue."

George Horchester sat back, and looked around. "There is little more to tell, Mr. Holmes. As skipper, it was my job to kill him, so that we could all eat and live. I do not wish to relive the details of that dreadful day, save to say that I killed my own brother. When we had eaten enough to make us all sick, we buried his remains on the beach below the cave. Several days later, as we were beginning to consider who might be the next to die, an Icelandic fishing boat saw our fire and came to our rescue."

"It must have been awkward when you returned home."

"Indeed, it was, Mr. Holmes. I stood trial for murder, and was initially sentenced to death. But the power of the Press was on my side. Through the strength of public opinion, I was fortunate to serve only three years in prison, before being quietly released. My family, on the other hand, were less forgiving. The news of what had happened to my brother went down badly with them, and undoubtedly contributed to the death of my mother only a few months after my return. My other brother, my sister, and my father all blamed me for her death – perhaps with some justification. They ostracized me and, when I left prison, I was forced to leave home and build a new life in London."

"And what happened to the other members of the crew?"

"They were both forced to leave home as well. One found employment at a country house in the Midlands. The other went to work on a farm, feeding pigs – just like the Prodigal Son. I found work in London, as a jobbing longshoreman, picking up whatever work I could find along the river. I became like Cain: Cast out from home, with a mark upon my character, doomed to wander the earth as a man who had killed and eaten his own brother. Then I met Elsie, who agreed, in spite of knowing something of my past, to become my wife."

"How long ago was that?" asked Holmes.

"We have been together for five years. I imagined that, by now, the horrors of those days might have blown over, and that the painful memory of my sins might have diminished with time. Instead, it seems they are now catching up with me. They have already caught up with the other two."

"Those two recent deaths reported in the newspapers were your other men, were they not?" said Holmes.

"Indeed, they were. Even though it seems they both met with accidents, I am certain that they were both murdered. And that I shall be the next to die. You must help me, Mr. Holmes."

On our return to 221b Baker Street, Holmes and I discovered that we had another visitor. The moment we walked through our sitting room door, we were greeted by the sight of Inspector Lestrade, standing before the hearth, fingering his hat in an agitated manner.

"Ah, Mr. Holmes," he exclaimed. "I am very glad to see you."

"Why, Lestrade," replied Holmes genially. "To what do we owe the pleasure of this visit?"

We all sat down, with Holmes leaning back in his chair, and the inspector inclining forward, with an earnest expression upon his face. "Mr. Holmes, we need your assistance."

"Those two unusual deaths reported in the newspapers, I have no doubt," replied Holmes. "Jack Shelton, eaten by his pigs, and Harry Winter, eaten by a Bengal tiger."

"Indeed. Both extremely nasty. Both men were crushed and disfigured by the animals that attacked them."

"A coincidence?"

"I think it must be more than that, Mr. Holmes."

Holmes nodded. "Then there has to be something you are not telling me, Lestrade."

"You are quite right, Mr. Holmes. One detail which seems to clinch the matter, and which has not yet been released to the Press, is that each corpse was discovered with a coin pushed into its mouth."

"A coin?"

"A penny."

"So, two deaths, which might otherwise have been dismissed as unrelated accidents, are deliberately manipulated to raise the suspicion of the police," mused Holmes. "And to be publicized as such by the presence of those coins. And you naturally suspect murder."

"The evidence points that way. We need your assistance to help us sort out what is going on here. Are we definitely dealing with murder? And if so, what is the meaning of the coins? Are we dealing with a killer who wants to be caught? Or somebody with a decidedly perverted sense of humor?"

"And your next step, Lestrade?"

"I should like you to come with me to examine the bodies, Mr. Holmes, and see what you can make of the matter."

273

"Then we need to begin by visiting the scene of each of these tragedies."

"I have already arranged for the sites to be secured, but it might be more convenient to visit the estate first. The site of the latest death."

Holmes turned to me. "Come, Watson. Pack yourself an overnight bag, and we shall be off."

A train journey, followed by an uncomfortable five-mile jog in a rickety four-wheeler, brought us to the Leicestershire country house mentioned in the newspaper report.

The estate manager, dressed in tweeds and carrying a shotgun, greeted us at the main entrance to the grounds.

"This is indeed a distressing incident, gentlemen," said the manager. "I hope we can have this matter dealt with as quickly as possible. His Lordship is extremely upset at having the police swarming across his land, and asks that we should have the matter sorted out before his guests descend upon the place for a banquet this Saturday night."

"In that case," said Holmes coldly, "kindly escort us to the site of the death, and explain to us exactly what occurred there."

The manager showed us the place where the body had been discovered. A fence of iron bars bounded an area of grass, with a tiger glaring out through the bars of a brick-built animal house. The smell took me back to my days in India.

"The matter is simply told," said the manager. "Somehow, Harry Winter gained unauthorized access to the tiger pen. The animal attacked him, mauled him, and partially consumed his flesh."

"Has the site of the attack been left as it was?"

"No. The police surgeon who certified the death at first said it was nothing more than a tragic accident."

"What made him change his mind?"

"The discovery of the coin concealed in the man's mouth."

Whilst the manager kept his eye on the tiger, and his shotgun at the ready, Holmes stepped into the enclosure, and examined the area carefully. All the while, he was grumbling that the tiger had trampled the scene as clear of useful evidence as any number of policemen.

He finally joined us outside and shook his head. "I have seen all I wish to see here," he declared. "Now I should like to examine the body."

The corpse had been removed to the local police station, and the police surgeon was already waiting in a back room for us to arrive.

"We are being pressed to release him for burial," said the surgeon, as he pulled back the sheet to reveal the body. "But this has now become a coroner's matter."

"What exactly killed him?" asked Holmes.

The surgeon stared at Holmes with incredulity. "Man, can you not see? It's obvious to even a blind man what killed him. His flesh has been torn and partly eaten, and many of his bones have been broken. His life has been literally crushed from his body."

"And a coin was found in his mouth."

"True. But that was not what killed him."

Holmes looked to me, and I stepped closer in order to make my own examination of the corpse. "He is badly bruised, and a number of the bones have been broken," I reported. "The animal's claws and teeth have caused extensive injuries, but strangely with little consequent loss of blood. Mr. Winter's body is in a poor way, Holmes. He could never have survived such a mauling."

Holmes looked from me to the surgeon. "Gentlemen, I would be obliged if you would now kindly turn him over."

275

The surgeon looked to me. I shrugged, and together we turned the dead man's body onto its front.

"I fail to see anything new," I announced. "Apart from the dislocation of the fourth and fifth cervical vertebrae."

Holmes leaned closer, and lifted the hair at the nape of the man's neck. "Now, do you see it?"

"Ah, yes. A fragment of metal embedded in the base of the skull."

The surgeon leaned closer. "Good gracious! I completely missed that." He collected a pair of surgical forceps from the instruments on the side-table and, with some difficulty, grasped hold of the protruding metal. As he pulled, we saw a length of steel slowly emerge from the base of the man's skull.

"What is it, Holmes?" I cried. "It reminds me of a carpenter's nail, but it measures no less than ten inches in length."

"A nail of that length is not unknown among shipbuilders," said Holmes. "But I suspect this is not one of those."

"And what on earth is it doing inside this man's skull?"

"This object is undoubtedly the cause of his death," declared Holmes. "Thrust up into the brain from the base of the skull. But before I pass further judgement, I shall need to consult someone with expert knowledge of maritime matters."

"If this is what caused his death," I added, "then we must conclude that he was killed before the tiger launched its attack upon him. But why?"

Lestrade broke into the conversation. "In order to cover up the crime, of course, Dr. Watson. Somebody wanted us to believe that the tiger was the cause of his death."

"In that case," interposed Holmes, "why was the killing publicized by the coin inserted into the man's mouth? No, gentlemen, this was a carefully staged murder. And the man who committed it is telling us something."

"Granted, Mr. Holmes," said Lestrade. "But what exactly is his message?"

"That is what I intend to discover," concluded Holmes. He turned toward the surgeon. "Thank you for your cooperation in this matter, Doctor." Then, stepping toward the door, he added, "And now we must continue to the site of the second death."

On the map, the pig farm was not far away, but the journey led us along rough and unkempt country lanes and took a further couple of hours. All the way, Holmes sat with his hands resting on the head of his cane, and his thoughts lost in a world that I could hardly imagine.

The pig farm, where the body of Jack Shelton had been discovered, lay at the end of a long and rough farm trackway. The sound of unusual squeals and grunts, coming from somewhere beyond the farm-yard, greeted us as we reached the buildings.

After stepping down from the carriage, I followed Holmes and Lestrade toward the farmhouse. There we were greeted by a woman who appeared to be deeply distraught – and naturally enough, I thought.

"Good afternoon, Mrs. Shelton," said Lestrade, with genuine sympathy in his voice. "I have brought a couple of gentlemen with me this time, to examine the scene of this most tragic incident."

Mr. Shelton's widow nodded and then led us across the farmyard and between the farm buildings to a paddock of churned-up mud. This was obviously the site of the tragedy, and was identified as such by the presence of a uniformed police constable standing guard at the gate. But the paddock itself was empty.

"We had the animals moved," explained Lestrade, "in order to allow us to retrieve the body. The pigs are now in an enclosure on the other side of the barn."

The constable stepped aside, allowing us to enter the area. The lingering smell of the pigs might have proved too much for some people, but I was determined not to appear weak. Mrs. Shelton seemed not to notice. Only Lestrade's face turned a shade lighter in color.

"Please explain what happened," said Holmes.

"Late yesterday evening," said the widow, "I heard a terrific commotion coming from this paddock. With my husband out here, I assumed it was feeding time, and thought nothing of it. But after it had lasted for some time, I came outside to investigate. At first, I could see nothing untoward. Then I saw the figure of my husband, lying in the middle of the paddock. The animals must have trampled him to death. They had even started eating him." The poor woman shivered at the thought.

"The situation is clearly very different now," said Holmes.

"We could hardly leave the animals in there," said the constable, defensively.

"Quite." Holmes examined the paddock, and then the area around the outside. "Too much has been disturbed here to allow me to make out much of value." He turned to Lestrade. "Except that one set of footprints appears to have been made by a man wearing sea boots."

"Sea boots?"

We all looked toward Mrs. Shelton for elucidation, but she shook her head.

"Interesting," said Holmes, without explaining the significance of the boots to the inspector. "We must now examine the body."

The mortuary at the police station proved to be little different from the one we had visited earlier in the day – a bare room with tiled walls and floor. The police surgeon had already laid the body out in advance of our arrival. On a side-table, close at hand, lay the surgical apparatus that had been used to carry out the *post mortem* examination. Alongside those, in a white enamel bowl, lay two distinctive objects. One was a penny. The other, a nail-like object, the twin of the one I had seen removed from the head of Harry Winter.

The surgeon, Dr. Blackstone, gave us his opinion. "Gentlemen, as you can see, the deceased suffered extensive physical injuries, which are consistent with his being trampled to death by a herd of swine. Their hoof marks are clearly visible on the skin. In addition, the animals had begun to eat away at the flesh, particularly at the extremities: The fingers, the nose, and the ears."

"Ghastly," I exclaimed.

Dr. Blackstone nodded, and pointed to the penny. "The corpse had this coin pressed into its mouth, almost certainly placed there *post mortem*. However, death was caused not by the animals, but by the insertion of that long object. I found it pushed up through the base of the skull, severing the spinal cord, and penetrating the brain to a depth of some ten inches. Although people have occasionally survived similar head injuries in the past, with the spine being severed, death in this case must have been almost instantaneous."

"Thank you, Doctor," said Lestrade.

"Indeed, a thorough and professional examination," added Holmes. He turned to Lestrade. "Now you have evidence of your connection, Lestrade. Both men were killed before their

279

bodies were crushed. Each man was killed by having one of these nail-like objects driven deep into his brain. Both had their spinal cords severed. Each man had a coin of the realm pressed into his mouth. And it seems nobody saw anything, or can give a description of the murderer."

"That is indeed how it appears, Mr. Holmes," said Lestrade. "But where can we proceed from here? How can we find out who killed those men? And why?"

"The fact that both men were partly eaten by the animals that attacked them is suggestive. But I think the real breakthrough in this case will come when we identify the origin and true purpose of those nail-like objects that were used to commit the murders. Allow me to keep one of those instruments, Inspector, and I shall make every effort to answer your question."

"Very well, Mr. Holmes." said Lestrade. "The hour is late, and I have to contact the coroner before returning to London. Is there anything else that you need?"

"Only the name of a local inn, located close to a telegraph office," said Holmes. "We shall need an early start in the morning."

After smoking pensively late into the night, Sherlock Holmes was up with the sun, and roused me from sleep with news that he had received an answer to his telegram of the previous evening.

"The police have furnished me with a description of the third Horchester brother – the one called Albert. It confirms the identity of the third man we saw outside our window in Baker Street."

"How does that help us?"

"With his identity certain, everything now comes together."

"Well, I cannot can see it."

"Get dressed and find us a Bradshaw. The game is afoot, Watson, and time is extremely short."

We took the train and reached the hometown of the Horchester family by early afternoon. I stepped down from the railway carriage onto the main platform and accompanied Holmes out into the town. We found the place bustling. Fishing boats were coming and going from the harbor, and the smell of fish pervaded the air.

Holmes stopped a man in the street and asked if he had heard of Mr. Horchester.

"Heard of him? Of course I've heard of him," the man replied. "Everyone in the town knows the Horchester family. They own a large number of the fishing vessels that sail from this port. I reckon half the town depends on that family for their livelihoods. Jimmy's getting on a bit nowadays and, with the boys all out of town, people are wondering about the future of the firm and the security of their jobs."

"Then you will be able to direct me to where I can find Mr. Horchester senior."

Only a few minutes later, we were standing before a splendid front door, in a street of high-class residences. Holmes rapped the large brass knocker which adorned the middle of the door.

Presently, it opened to reveal a housemaid standing on the threshold.

"Good afternoon," said Holmes, handing over his visiting card. "I am here to speak to Mr. Horchester."

"You mean Miss Horchester."

"Perhaps I do," said Holmes. "Is she home?"

The maid invited us inside, and asked us to wait in the front reception room. A moment later, a woman in her middle years came in. She stood prim, and held her head with an assertion of pride.

Holmes removed his hat. "Miss Horchester, I presume."

The woman merely nodded.

"Good afternoon. My name is Sherlock Holmes, and this is my friend and associate, Dr. John Watson."

"And how may I help you, Mr. Sherlock Holmes?"

"We are currently assisting Scotland Yard with their investigation into a couple of recent deaths, and I was hoping Mr. Horchester senior might be able to help us with our inquiries."

The lady looked doubtful.

"He does live here, does he not?" asked Holmes.

"Indeed, he does."

"Then, may we please speak with him?"

"I don't see how you expect him to help you, Mr. Holmes. He is elderly and very frail."

"Even so. This is a matter of the greatest urgency."

The woman paused, as though deep in thought. Then she nodded slowly. "Very well, but we need to talk before you meet my father."

"So, you are the sister of George Horchester?" asked Holmes.

"Oh, you've been talking to George, have you?" she asked with a sneer in her voice.

"We fear that his life might be in danger."

"Huh! I'd be surprised if it wasn't. Did he tell you what happened all those years ago? Did he tell you what he did? He killed and ate my brother."

"But that was many years ago now."

"Not so many that I'm likely to forget. Please sit down, gentlemen."

We sat down, and Miss Horchester continued. "Mr. Holmes, you need to understand one or two things which have not yet been made clear to you. My name is Elizabeth Horchester. Since the day that our mother died, struck down by the news of her son's murder on that dreadful island, I have been holding together what remains of our family. My parents had one daughter and three sons: Myself, George, William, and Albert. Being the eldest of the four children, and with none of us having married, I was the only woman left in the family, so it was up to me to take control of the situation as best I could."

"I have heard of George and William," said Holmes, "but please tell me about Albert."

"Albert is the youngest. He took over all the hard work when we lost William, and after George was sent to prison. For many years now, Albert has shown himself to be the most valuable and reliable member of the family. Until recently."

"What happened to change him?"

"Albert took it into his head to visit Dragon Island, the place where our brother was killed. He didn't tell me what he found there, but whatever it was, it turned him into an angry and resentful man. He focused his bitterness onto those who had survived that ordeal all those years ago – the men who had killed and consumed our brother."

"Might he perhaps have discovered William's body?"

"I think he must have done, Mr. Holmes. There can be no other explanation for his change in personality."

"I have gained the impression," said Holmes, "that there had been some tension between the two older boys, George and William."

"Tension?" Elizabeth Horchester paused, as though choosing the right words to use. "Yes, you are right, Mr. Holmes. You see, they were both in love with the same girl. Evie Carstone, as she was in those days. But George and

William were both wild for her. It caused bad feeling. Rivalry. Bitterness."

"Bad enough to kill?"

"You mean, on the island?"

"As one example."

"No, Mr. Holmes. Whatever happened there, it was the toss of a coin that took one of my brothers, and alienated the other from his family."

"And what became of this Evie Carstone?"

"When news of the events on that island were made public, she left town. The last I heard, she was happily married to a shopkeeper in Birmingham."

"Is there anything else you can tell me about your brother George?"

"George possessed a great many talents, Mr. Holmes. He was an illusionist, and was in great demand to entertain the children. He could tell stories, perform conjuring tricks, and loved to make the children laugh. He has been greatly missed, at least by them."

"Thank you, Miss Horchester," said Holmes. "That was most helpful. Now I need to meet your father."

"As you wish, Mr. Holmes," replied Elizabeth. "But try not to upset him too much."

We found Mr. James Horchester sitting in a wing-backed chair, gazing out of a bay window toward the harbor. He turned to face us when he heard us enter. He was thin and wiry, with a mop of white hair above a face alive with character.

"Father," said Elizabeth Horchester, "you have two visitors who would like to ask you a few questions."

"And about time too," grouched the elderly man. "Come along in, gentlemen. I don't like people hovering in the doorway. Find a seat, and tell me the nature of your business with me today. As if I cannot make an educated guess."

After Miss Horchester left us, my companion began. "My name is Sherlock Holmes, and this is Dr. John Watson. We are helping Scotland Yard in their investigations into a couple of recent deaths."

"And you thought these new deaths might be connected with that incident many years ago, the one that took away one of my sons, and ruined the lives of the rest of us."

"That is what we are investigating, Mr. Horchester."

"Then perhaps you are on the right track, Mr. Holmes. At the time of the tragedy, my other son, Albert, took the matter extremely badly. As did we all. Which is why George wisely decided not to return to his family home and business. Albert took on more and more responsibility for running the fishing fleet, and helped manage the company that I own. Then, recently, matters came to a head once more."

"What was the cause of that?"

"I decided to alter my will." The old man glared out from his piercing gray eyes, as he looked around the room. "I am growing old, Mr. Holmes, and I must make provision for the future. I decided to bring George back into the family firm, so I made legal provision in my will for the fishing business to be shared equally between my three surviving children – my two sons, and my daughter. Well, I have to tell you, Mr. Holmes, Albert took the news extremely badly. The bitterness he had bottled up inside him all spilled out. He told me he had recently discovered something significant about the death of William, and he said he was going to take revenge on each one of the survivors. Every one of those men who had killed and consumed his brother. I am horribly afraid, Mr. Holmes, that somehow those two recent deaths that I read about in the newspapers were the work of my boy, now in the grip of some insane spirit of revenge."

Holmes reached into his coat and drew out the steel object that had been used to kill one of the victims. He handed it to the old man. "Mr. Horchester," he said gravely. "Can you please identify this object for me?"

Mr. Horchester took the proffered nail-like object, and nodded. "It's a type of marlin spike, Mr. Holmes. It's commonly used by sailors, for a variety of purposes. To open knots, separate fibres, and repair rigging."

"So I thought. That confirms my suspicion."

"Wherever did you find it?"

"It came from the dead body of the man who had been trampled by his pigs. This is the object that killed him."

"And the man eaten by the tiger?"

"Killed in a similar manner."

The old man sighed. "That settles the matter. This is undoubtedly the work of my son. All three of my boys knew how to use these things. They were all marlin spike seamen."

Holmes retrieved the spike and stood up once more. "Thank you, Mr. Horchester," he said, decisively. "I shall leave you in peace now."

The old man hadn't yet finished. "Mr. Holmes, I have lost one son to the sea, and another will undoubtedly meet the hangman's noose. You must prevent any harm from coming to my other son, George. He may have done a horrible thing in the past, but a reasonable man can hardly refuse him forgiveness. And he is my son. Promise me that you will bring him safely back to me."

"I promise that I shall do everything in my power, Mr. Horchester," said Holmes, "but I fear that time is short, and we must leave immediately if there is to be any chance of rescuing your son."

Before we left the fishing port, Holmes sent a telegram to Lestrade, requesting that he find and hold the two men, Withyburn and Smith, who, with Albert Horcester, had initially followed Mrs. Horchester to Baker Street, suggesting he might discover them in the vicinity of George Horchester's residence.

On arriving in London, we drove directly to Scotland Yard, where Lestrade greeted us on our arrival.

"We have those two men, Mr. Holmes. Withyburn and Smith. Two of the most notorious thugs in London."

"Have they told you anything to help with the current murder inquiry?"

"Nothing at all, Mr. Holmes. I was hoping you might assist us with the interrogation."

"Very well. Lead the way."

We found the two thugs slouching in an interview room, with faces of stone turned defiantly upon the world. As we entered, I saw their eyes immediately show that they recognized Holmes. They had encountered him before.

"Now, gentlemen," Holmes began, as he sat down facing them across a table. "The police are investigating two murders. And they suspect you two of being involved."

Withyburn glared back at him. "We didn't kill nobody, Mr. Holmes. And that's a fact."

"And we've got nothing to say," added Smith.

"Then allow me to tell you want happened," said Holmes, sitting back in the chair. "A certain fisherman called Albert Horchester hired you to help him commit three murders."

"He might have done," growled Smith, "but we're admitting to nothing."

Lestrade leaned forward, and laid a drawing on the table before the two men – an artist's depiction of Albert Horchester. "Is this the man who hired you?"

Withyburn clearly recognized the man and seemed to realize that he was caught. "That's the cove. He told us what to do, and we did it for him. He promised us each a hundred quid when all three men were dead."

"But we didn't kill them," added Smith.

"Maybe not," said Holmes, "but you physically held down the farmer, Jack Shelton, whilst Horchester thrust a spike up into the back of his head. I have seen the bruises on his arms. Then you threw his body into the paddock, to be consumed by the pigs. You did a similar thing with the groundsman, Harry Winter. Again, I have seen his bruises. However, things failed to go so smoothly on that occasion. Winter failed to die as easily as you imagined, so you broke his neck before feeding him to the tiger."

"That was Horchester," said Withyburn.

"But you two did all the preparation, so that makes you guilty of assisting with those murders."

The two men glowered back at Holmes.

"Now we come to the third man," said Holmes. "Horchester's brother, George."

The two men looked back at him. One shrugged. The other nodded.

"Where is this third killing to take place?"

"Go down by the docks," said Smith, "and you'll find a warehouse owned by an old man called Schultz."

Lestrade rubbed his chin. "I've heard of it."

"But did you know that the place conceals a rat-baiting pit?"

"If it's hidden, how do we find the pit?"

"Go through to the back, pull up a trapdoor, and you'll find a flight of steps leading down. That's where you'll find them two brothers. And one of them's due to end up dead. Eaten."

288

"How do you know?"

"Because, Inspector Lestrade, we supplied the rats. Thirty or forty of the filthy vermin."

"When is this to take place?" demanded Holmes.

"Any moment now."

Leaving the two thugs in custody, Holmes and I, together with Lestrade and a couple of constables, took carriage toward the docks. The men had been right about the warehouse, and soon we were climbing down into a void beneath the building. There we were met by the lingering smell of dogs and stale human sweat, together with the enduring stench of rats. We found ourselves in a room with gas-lamps illuminating a rectangular pit almost twelve feet across. An unearthly squealing arose from the pit, and the squirming multitude of rodents it contained – the rat-pit. Here was the site of a cruel but popular blood-sport, which pitted dogs against rats, with bets placed on how many each could kill within a given time period.

A figure stepped into the light – the man we had seen in Baker Street with Withyburn and Smith, holding in one hand a marlin spike glinting in the gaslight, and in the other the woebegone figure of George Horchester, his hands tied behind his back.

"You must be Albert Horchester," observed Holmes.

"Quite right, Mr. Holmes. But you're too early for the main event of the evening, so we must make do instead with the death of just one rat." He gave his brother a violent shake.

"I think not!" shouted Lestrade, indicating his two constables. "Albert Horchester, drop that spike, and accept the fact that you are now under arrest for murder."

Instead, Albert pushed his knee into his brother's back, and thrust him over the edge of the rat-pit. With a shriek, George tumbled face-downward among the rats.

Whilst the constables took Albert in hand, I grasped hold of my Malacca and jumped down into the pit, where I pulled George to his feet, and beat off the rats which had already sunk their teeth into his flesh.

"Watson!" I looked up to see Holmes's hand outstretched toward me. A moment later, I had joined him on the rim of the pit, where Lestrade had also lifted George to safety.

Only now did we have a chance to inspect our murder suspect. It was evident that Albert and George Horchester were indeed brothers. There could be no doubt about their relationship – except that Albert's face was distorted by bitterness. He sneered at Holmes. "You have been very clever, Mr. Holmes," he said. "I would happily have swung for my brother, as well as for those other two. But somehow I was afraid that you would come along at the very last moment and rescue him."

Albert Horchester was hanged for the murders of Harry Winter and Jack Shelton, and for the attempted murder of his brother, George. The matter was widely reported in the press, and Inspector Lestrade basked in the fame of having solved the crimes so rapidly. The incident initially passed without comment from Sherlock Holmes.

A few days later, Holmes invited me to join him on a visit to the abode of the Horchester family, to which George had removed with his wife and household.

George welcomed us enthusiastically and invited us to sit down in his newly decorated parlour. "I must thank you, Mr. Holmes, for saving my life, and for bringing justice to my family."

"Justice?" demanded Holmes, with a sour note. "Is that what you think I have brought?"

"Why, certainly."

Holmes sat back, and fixed his gaze upon the newly-reinstated fisherman. "Indulge me for a moment, Mr. Horchester, by listening whilst I tell you a story. There once was a fishing boat which struck a rock and sank. Four members of the crew survived and managed to reach an island. As time passed, the crew began to starve. Eventually, it was decided that one of the men should die, in order to provide nourishment, and indeed life itself for the other three."

George Horchester's gaze remained riveted upon Holmes.

"The skipper took it upon himself to decide which one of the men should die," continued Holmes. "He decided to appear openly fair to all of the crew, and to leave the decision to the toss of a coin. The first to flip 'tails' would die. The skipper tossed the coin for the first man. It came down 'Heads', as indeed it did for the next man, and for the skipper himself. This was hardly surprising, since the skipper was using a two-headed coin."

Beads of sweat appeared on the face of George Horchester.

"When it came to the fourth man," continued Holmes, "the coin came down 'Tails'. Which is again hardly surprising, since the skipper, who was known for being adept at sleight of hand and illusionary tricks, had switched the two-headed penny for a coin with two 'Tails'."

"Of course," I gasped as the truth hit me.

"This is all pure speculation," growled George Horchester.

"Indeed it is," replied Holmes. "I told you, this is merely a story, and I have no way of proving that this is what really happened. But, allow me to continue. The man chosen to die was the skipper's own brother, and he wanted to be as merciful as possible in taking the young man's life. Consequently, instead of using his blunted knife, the skipper used a method which he considered more humane: A marlin spike. This he drove deep into the back of his brother's skull, bringing about what he hoped would be instant and painless death."

"Which we hope it was," said I.

I could see pain now haunting George Horchester's eyes. "This is all very interesting, Mr. Holmes," he said. "But you almost make it sound like murder. If so, then what possible motive might there have been for anybody committing such a terrible crime?"

"Jealousy," said Holmes. "The skipper in the story knew that one man on that island had to die, and who better than his rival in love, even if it was his own brother?"

George Horchester sat grim faced and silent.

"If I am correct in my interpretation of the facts," continued Holmes, "then the skipper was indeed guilty of the deliberate, premeditated murder of his brother. Years later, when the dead man's other brother discovered the body, and saw the cause of his brother's death, he flew into a vengeful rage. This was made all the more bitter when he discovered that the man responsible for the other brother's death would inherit an equal share of the family business and fortune on their father's death. Now, to pile one crime on top of another, when this younger brother confessed to a charge of murder, rather than admitting to what he had done, and providing mitigating circumstances which might have saved the man from execution, our fisherman remained silent. Now, to my mind, that is as good as murder."

"You have no evidence to identify this hypothetical cold-hearted villain with myself, do you, Mr. Holmes?"

"None at all," replied my companion. "It is all circumstantial. And as your brother has already pleaded guilty to the charge of murder, we shall never know what a trial judge might have made of my little story."

"Don't forget, Mr. Holmes, I have already been tried for the murder of William, and have served my sentence. If you could prove any of this new theory of yours to be true, and if you could convince the police of its importance, then you still could never have me tried for the same crime a second time. That would place me in double-jeopardy, and would be in violation of an Englishman's rights under Magna Carta."

"You seem to know your rights, Mr. Horchester."

"Ten years ago, I discovered that a man accused of murder had to be certain of where he stands in law, Mr. Holmes."

"Quite so. And that is the point of my tale. You could have saved Albert. But since he had discovered your secret, he had to die. Now, if the police were to hear of my story, and were to search the house of the man in question, they might come across those two incriminating coins. That would transform my tale from a hypothetical theory into an accusation with just ground for investigation. You may not be tried for the same crime twice, but if my suspicions were made public, then I can promise you, Mr. Horchester, that your life would quickly be ruined for a second time, but with no hope of ever returning to civil society. However, I promised your father that I would do my best to bring you home alive. That I have done, even if I find your actions on Dragon Island and since to be repulsive and uncivilized in the extreme. But be assured, one day the facts will be made public. One day, the story will be told."

It was on the day following this encounter with George Horchester that Holmes received a parcel. It was small but carefully wrapped. On opening it, he paused, and allowed an expression of satisfaction to cross his face.

"Well now, Watson. What make you of this?" He passed me two coins, which I examined with care. Both were copper coins of the realm. Pennies. Each measured one-and-a-quarter inches in diameter, but neither was like any that I had ever encountered before. One carried the design of the Queen's head on both sides. It was evident that two coins had been filed down flat, and sealed together by the application of intense heat. The second coin was different, in that it carried the figure of Britannia on both sides. The one had two "Heads", whilst the other carried two "Tails", just as Holmes had suggested.

I expressed my amazement, and passed the coins back to Holmes.

"I am assembling my own Black Museum, Watson," he told me. "And I shall add to it these two coins – the instruments of a man's deliberate killing of his brother."

"Whilst I gather together my notes."

"Have a care," cautioned my companion. "In view of the hurt it might cause, it might be wise to delay publication. As I suggested to George Horchester, the time for such revelations has not yet come."

"Very well. I have a box where it can be stored for the time being."

Holmes sat back, smoking his pipe. "The title is of course entirely up to yourself, Watson, but I might suggest, 'The Penny Murders'."

I mulled over my friend's wise and considered suggestion, nodded, and bent to amend my notes.

The Adventure of the Disappearing Debutante
by Stephen Herczeg

It was late spring in 1882 when a knock at the front door of 221b Baker Street presented my good friend Sherlock Holmes with an unexpected opportunity.

The caller was a simple messenger boy who delivered an expensively embossed invitation to Holmes on behalf of his old university friend, Roderick St. John-Smythe. I was the one to answer the door, partly to relieve our landlady, Mrs. Hudson, of the chore, and also because of a slight case of boredom.

I brought the envelope to Holmes, who proceeded to withdraw the card within, accompanied by a single-page handwritten letter. He began to smile a little as he read to himself, before explaining the details to me.

"It's from Roderick. It seems that we have been asked to attend a coming-out ceremony."

I was a little surprised, as it didn't seem the type of occasion in which Roderick or Holmes would have shown an interest.

"Any idea why?"

"No. There's no mention of a reason. I believe that Roderick may be trying to introduce me into polite society, or perhaps to pair us up with young ladies to take us away from this bachelor life of ours."

"That may be worthwhile then," I said. "I don't intend to stay single all my life."

"And good for you, Watson. I myself would need to meet someone extremely special before I shrug off my bachelor ways."

"Indeed," I answered with as healthy a dose of cynicism as one word could allow.

"Regardless of the bevy of young ladies on display, I believe that the event may prove useful from another front altogether."

"Such as?"

"There will no doubt be many affluent gentlemen at this event. Some there to display their eligible daughters, others there to examine the goods on offer."

I was a little put out by Holmes's graphic description of such a time-honoured event as a debutante ball.

"That's a little harsh, isn't it?"

He noticed my expression and smiled.

"I do apologise, but I find these sorts of evenings little more than a few steps above a slave auction in medieval Arabia. But I'll still go. It may be amusing. It may even be beneficial. I hope to make the acquaintance of some of the gentlemen there and, when next they are in need of services such as I can provide," he finished, "my name will spring to mind."

Three nights later, I stood in our sitting room, dressed in my finest black-tie ensemble. I was a little put-out, as I'd hoped to be allowed to wear my dress uniform and show off my medals. Ladies of all stations have always been drawn to the trappings of service, but Roderick's invitation and a follow up telegram stated that the men must be attired in simple black-tie. Something about not taking the attention away from the debutantes, and especially the guest of honour. Who this guest was to be was a question to which I would seek an answer on arrival.

Holmes stepped out of his rooms resplendent in his own ensemble and immediately I felt rather frumpy. The long black suit highlighted the tall, slim stature of my friend, and even accentuated his aquiline features so that he appeared even more devilishly handsome than usual.

"Ready then, Watson?" he asked.

"Er, yes. Ready."

"Good, good. Let's be on our way then, shall we?"

Downstairs, we found that the night had set in, as the invitation was for nine o'clock, well after the dinner hour. Luckily, Mrs. Hudson had provided a sumptuous feast to keep us going. She had hinted it was to forestall any effects of the champagne that would certainly be on offer.

A hansom sat outside, ready to whisk us to our destination. We didn't have to travel far, as after a quick trot through Marylebone and Mayfair we arrived at St. James's Square. Before us stood Cleveland House, the London townhouse of our host for the evening, Harry Powlett, the fourth Duke of Cleveland.

Cleveland House is a lovely four-storey Georgian mansion overlooking St. James's Park. My understanding is that it was used only rarely on such occasions, as the Duke spent most of his time in County Durham, at the family home of Raby Castle.

Our hansom was greeted by a footman and we followed the red carpet to the front door, where we handed our invitation to a doorman who announced us as Mr. Sherlock Holmes and Dr. John Watson.

A few heads amongst the assembled guests turned towards us, but failing recognition returned to their own conversations.

We stood on the small landing for a moment, peering across the assembled guests. I noticed a lovely melody creeping across the room from a string quartet nestled on a balcony above the main ballroom.

As Holmes and I stepped into the throng of people, one well-presented guest made his way over. I thrust my hand out to greet Roderick.

"Thank you ever so much for inviting us," I said.

"My pleasure. It was mostly as a favour to the Duke. He had asked for an assemblage of the most eligible bachelors in London."

"And you think we are included in that group," asked Holmes.

"I didn't really care. You two just happened to come to mind."

Roderick stopped talking as a tall, elegant man in full dress uniform, complete with feathered headdress, a line of medals, a ceremonial sword, and a blood red sash across his chest, stepped into the room. I was a little miffed at seeing the man, as I would have liked the chance to wear my own uniform.

The doorman announced, "Presenting his grace, Baron Sebastian Von Steurer of Bavaria."

"A German," I retorted out loud, receiving a slightly reproachful look from Roderick.

He waited until the Baron and his coterie had moved away before answering. "Yes. Another reason the Duke wanted so many eligible bachelors here," he said, "All will become clear in a few minutes."

I kept an eye on the Baron as he made his way through the crowd, stopping from time to time to make the acquaintance of someone he obviously knew. I myself had never heard of him, but admit it was probably due to the fact I rarely circulated in these sorts of social circles.

Eventually the Baron stopped before an older but very proud and upright man who sported a healthy shock of silver-grey hair and an impressive lion's mane beard with no moustache. He was dressed in a tail suit, with a single pin on his left lapel showing three swords leaning in with their points almost touching. I assumed it was the family crest or arms.

Roderick noticed my fascination and spoke up. "Ah, you've spied our host then," he said.

I was a little taken aback. "That's the Duke?" I asked.

"Yes. This entire affair is to introduce his young daughter, Elizabeth, into noble society."

I then noticed a woman standing demurely behind the Duke. She was small and a little diminutive, but attractive. She appeared to be around twenty years younger than the Duke.

"The woman is his wife, Lady Catherine Stanhope. They married late, as the Duke was engaged with his business affairs abroad for much of his early life. The child was a surprise to both of them, I think, but now the Duke wants only the best for her."

"To a point," Holmes piped up. "She has been promised to the Baron, has she not? Not something I would prefer for my own child, if I had one."

Roderick harrumphed under his breath.

"Well, yes. That is partly why I am here, after all. The engagement was coordinated by the Home Office, along with the blessing of the Duke, who will benefit remarkably from the business opportunities between the two countries that this match will bring about."

I was flabbergasted. "You mean to tell me that poor young girl is just a pawn in some diplomatic and business coup?"

"Well, if you put it that way," said Roderick, "yes. It's not any different to the proposals made between Royal families of old. It will be of great benefit to her family and to the country as a whole. The British and German governments have been negotiating a trading pact for some time now. The Baron here is a senior member of the Emperor's cabinet. We wished to open up channels of communication between our two countries. The Baron will receive a one-off payment of fifty-thousand pounds, and the marriage between himself and Lady Elizabeth seals the deal."

It was my turn to harrumph. Holmes simply smiled. "Fear not, Watson," he said. "Some things have a way of working themselves out,"

A loud voice rang out from across the room. We all turned to find a footman in full Georgian dress standing before a doorway and reading from an unfurled scroll of parchment.

"My ladies and gentlemen, if you would give me your attention please."

I realised this was the moment that the debutantes were to be introduced, and joined the group around me in forming a small open circular area for them to enter and parade around.

The Duke and the Baron were accommodated with positions at the front of their group.

Two doormen opened a pair of ornate brass doors and a line of beautifully attired young ladies could be seen stretching off down the corridor. Each was attended by a maid servant, making final touches to their hair, makeup, and dress.

The footman began, "May I present Lady Josephine Swann."

A tall, slightly gangly girl strode into the room. She appeared quite embarrassed, probably because she was the first to be introduced. She found her confidence and made her way past the assembled guests, her eyes meeting each in turn and stopping on one fellow across the circle from myself. I imagined this was her particular favourite and would be afforded the first dance in short time.

The footman continued and presently announced the arrival of ten other girls who followed the tall girl into the room and milled around in the circle under the calculating gaze of all and sundry.

I noticed the footman peer over at the doorway as he was about to announce another name. The lack of a further debutante stopped him short. He strode across and checked with the doormen. They both shook their heads. One marched down the hallway but returned quickly shaking his head and speaking in hushed tones to the footman.

The footman's face flushed red and sweat popped out on his forehead. He resumed his position and addressed the gathering one last time.

"My ladies and gentlemen, the band will now strike up for the first dance," he said, peering up at the band leader, who nodded to the footman and then to the other instrumentalists. Soon a lilting melody filtered over the crowd and young men approached each of the debutantes in turn to ask for their hand in a dance.

The rest of the crowd withdrew to the edges of the room to allow the courtship ritual to continue.

I noticed a new commotion erupt near the entrance-way and caught sight of the Baron and Duke in animated conversation. The Duke's face was flushed red – possibly with anger, probably with embarrassment.

I realised that his daughter was not among the young girls introduced previously and that this was the cause of the Baron's protestations. I continued to watch as they both made their way from the room, through the debutantes' entrance.

I turned back towards Holmes and Roderick to see a young man approach from a side doorway. He stepped up to Roderick and whispered in his ear. Roderick nodded several times and waved the man away. He closed in on Holmes and me and spoke.

"If you would both be so kind to accompany me, I think your services would be of valuable assistance," he said.

We followed the young man and quickly made our way out of the ballroom and down a nearby corridor. He stopped outside of another doorway and indicated for the three of us to enter.

Inside, we found the red-faced Duke and the even redder-faced Baron, still embroiled in a heated conversation.

"I do not understand why you would embarrass me in such a way," the Baron said, his voice thick with a German accent.

The Duke was obviously trying to defuse the situation but failing miserably. He held his hands out in placation, but the Baron did not seem to want any consolation.

"Sebastian, I have no idea what Elizabeth is up to. I don't know what could have happened, but can only think of the worst. Do you think I would expend so much money on this event if it was only to embarrass you?"

The Baron looked long at hard into the Duke's eyes and a slight hint of calm crossed his face.

"No. Not unless you wish to do yourself an injury. What do you intend to do about it, then?"

The Duke looked across at Roderick and sighed in relief. "Roderick, thank goodness," he said, and indicated the three of us to the Baron.

"Yes, I know this Roderick," said the Baron then continued. "These two," as he indicated Holmes and myself, "I do not know."

Roderick quickly introduced the two of us and added, "I invited them along tonight simply as they are eligible bachelors, but Sherlock Holmes is also a renowned consulting detective and, by chance, can add a level of investigation that would be problematic due to my position within Her Majesty's government."

Holmes quickly took the lead, turning to the Duke and saying, "Can you please explain what has happened, from the start, and do not leave out any details, no matter how small."

The Duke pursed his lips and regarded him for a moment before starting. "My daughter, Elizabeth, has recently come of age. A pivotal time in any woman's life, but more so for Elizabeth, as it makes her eligible for wedlock. In this case, I negotiated her hand in marriage to the Baron."

The Baron stood prouder and puffed out his chest slightly, no doubt assuming to affect more of a presence. Personally, I was unimpressed and hopefully hid my views from those around me.

"And in return . . . ?" prompted Holmes.

"In return, there would be a discreet change in the way Bavaria exchanged business with my companies – a benefit to both my family and to England as a whole."

"The reason that Roderick was involved," he said.

"Yes, precisely," said the Duke.

"Was your daughter accepting of this arrangement?" Holmes asked.

"What does that have to do with anything?" the Duke replied. "She is of noble stock, and that has been an expected part of her future – to accept the contract of marriage as negotiated by myself."

I could hold my tongue no longer. "But surely in these enlightened times, such a forced proposal would be rejected by the younger members of even the most noblest of families."

The Duke blanched at my suggestion. A tiny smile crossed Holmes's lips.

"That is immaterial," he answered. "The arrangement was made. It is Elizabeth's duty to accede to it."

"That may well be so," Holmes countered, "but we should investigate all facets of this mystery. There is the *why*, plus the

303

how, the *when*, and naturally the *where* to determine before we can close this case. Also," he added, "the *who*."

"The *who*?" I asked.

"Yes. *Who* stands to benefit from Lady Elizabeth's disappearance? *Who* does it most affect? *Who* could be responsible? Even *who* is the root cause?"

I nodded.

"I don't understand," said the Baron.

"Well, sir, we simply must establish various facts," Holmes continued. "Was this a kidnapping?" The Duke's face dropped in shock. "Is it an attempt at ransom? Or is it simply a sign of cold feet on behalf of the young woman? All ideas are relevant until we dismiss them one by one."

Holmes stepped towards the entrance to the parlour, and then turned back. "First, shall we retrace young Elizabeth's steps?"

The Baron followed us for a while but decided to return to his lodgings. It turned out that he had been offered rooms within Cleveland House as a guest of the Duke, a fact that I found interesting in itself, and I noticed that it also piqued Holmes's curiosity.

The Duke led us to the first-floor bedrooms, and we stopped outside of Elizabeth's room. Holmes turned back to the Duke. "Do you know if anyone has examined this room?" he asked.

"I have no idea," he said. "I can only assume that one of my servants came here to confirm that my daughter was missing."

Holmes actually smiled. "Good," he replied. "That means it should remain almost exactly as it was when Lady Elizabeth left it."

He opened the door and peered in. The gaslight was still burning, casting a yellow pallor. It was a large double room with a free-standing four-poster bed along the centre of one wall. A wardrobe and tallboy sat opposite, with a dressing area complete with mirror beside it. Nestled against the opposite wall sat a small dressing table and writing desk.

Holmes entered and glanced around. I followed close behind, not wanting to miss any of his investigative techniques. However, I purposely stopped in the doorway to restrict entry by the others in our party. A harrumph from the Duke greeted my actions. I stood my ground until he spoke. "I say, Doctor, if you wouldn't mind moving aside so I may enter," he said.

Holmes spun and held up a hand. "If you would be so kind and please do not enter until I have finished my initial investigation."

This was greeted with another harrumph and an audible sigh. Holmes ignored both and continued to peer around, not touching anything while he perused the scene in its entirety. Finally, he moved across to the writing desk and peered down. I noticed a folded piece of parchment sitting in the middle of the desk.

Holmes reached for a small pencil and gently pushed the folded page open until he was able to read it. His expression was one of intense interest. I noticed a small smile play on his lips for a moment before being replaced by a more serious look.

He dropped the pencil onto the desk and reached inside his pocket for a kerchief. He used the small square of cloth to smooth open the parchment, then picked it up and brought it across to the doorway.

"What have you there?" asked Roderick.

"The first clew in this mystery," Holmes said, "though it may be all that is required for now."

Roderick withdrew a pair of gloves from his jacket and took the proffered note in hand. He read aloud for the benefit of the rest of us.

"*To the Duke of Cleveland,*" he said. "*We have your daughter. There will be no marriage between a Bavarian prince and the non-Teutonic spawn of the Englander.*" Then he added, "It is signed by The Sons of Bavaria."

He handed the note back to Holmes before turning to the Duke. "I am so sorry, your Grace," he said. "It would seem that your daughter has indeed been kidnapped, and by some German resistance group. I've never even heard of these 'Sons of Bavaria'."

The Duke's face was a mesh of anger and fear, and glowed bright red with it. "We must talk to the Baron, immediately," he said, "And have the local constabulary search high and low. My daughter must be found."

The Duke, Roderick, and the Duke's valet left at high speed, leaving Holmes and me alone. I was slightly mystified. It was then I heard Holmes chuckling to himself. I turned to find a grin across his face.

"You find the kidnapping of this young girl funny?" I asked.

Holmes opened the note which was the first chance I'd had to have a good look. The writing was a delicate flowing script. It occurred to me straight away that this was a woman's handwriting. When he saw that I'd finished, Holmes moved back to the writing desk and began to search the drawers. He finally found the object of his search and straightened up, holding a small diary. He opened to the first page and read the name inscribed there.

"Lady Elizabeth's journal," he said.

He placed it on the desk and opened to a random page full of a similar flowing script. He put the note above and compared the two writing styles.

He let out a little sigh of anguish as I noticed that the two scripts didn't match as he would have first imagined. He flipped through several pages until one particular passage stuck out from the rest. The writing on this page was almost identical to that of the note.

"What do you surmise?" I asked.

"Well the diary is most certainly Elizabeth's – it has her name on the first page. I assume that the lighter, more-delicate script is hers. The single passage that matches the note must have been made by another."

He flipped through the diary and found two more passages in the same style. "I would say these were written by a very close confidant of Miss Elizabeth. A close friend or . . . ."

He stood up and smiled at me.

"Or?" I asked. "A maid servant. Somebody that would be as close as a friend and always be with Lady Elizabeth."

He read one of the passages and another laconic smile grew on his face. "Yes. This passage follows on from the previous one, but that was written in Elizabeth's hand. I would say that it was dictated to somebody whilst she was predisposed, possibly while she was in the bath."

He checked the pages closely and then showed it to me. His finger pointed to two small discoloured circles at the top of the page. "Water droplets," he said.

"Extraordinary," I replied. "But what does it mean?"

"Our young Elizabeth has either staged her own kidnapping, or this maid-servant was responsible."

"That seems unlikely."

"Indeed," he said. "I would think that there is something more that has triggered Lady Elizabeth's actions. We must ensure that she left of her own free will, and then determine why."

"Should we tell the Duke or Roderick?" I asked.

Holmes grinned. "Why would we do that? They have their investigation to pursue, and it will keep them busy and out of our hair long enough that we might even solve this case without them."

I nodded in agreement.

Holmes moved across to the wardrobe and opened it. The wardrobe was half full, with several bare hangers dangling from the rack. A couple had fallen to the base and lay abandoned. The remaining clothing was of a very high quality, suited to a woman of Elizabeth's station in life. Satin and silk dresses for formal occasions, plus several cotton dresses for day-wear.

Holmes closed the door and moved to the tallboy. He opened and examined several drawers, finding a similar result with two of them being only half-filled with clothing and essentials. There was a drawer dedicated to Elizabeth's smalls, which I was a bit embarrassed that we were investigating, but Holmes in his wisdom simply opened it to check its emptiness before closing it once more.

Another held several exquisite silk scarves, neatly rolled up. Again, several were missing, not something that would require laundering all at once.

He closed the last drawer and stared at the four hat stands arrayed on the top. Only three held hats, and those were of the delicate type used for formal occasions.

"What do you think, Watson?" he asked.

"Someone has packed for a trip, perhaps," I replied, "or it's washing day, though given that there are scarves and a hat missing, I would be surprised if those items are located in the scullery."

One of Holmes's eyebrows raised. He moved across to a small wicker basket and glanced inside. I checked as well. It was empty.

"Could still be washing day, I suppose," Holmes said as he headed for the doorway.

"Where to next?"

"The laundry, of course. Not just to check on the young lady's clothing, but below-stairs is always a good place for gossip and hearsay."

As we descended the stairs to the basement, the noise of suppressed conversation was palpable. It was obvious that word of Lady Elizabeth's disappearance had reached the underground world of Cleveland House.

As we stepped out of the stairwell shadow and into the dimly lit passageway, two maids, engaged in a deep conversation, immediately straightened up, almost dropping their loads of plates and towels. They scurried off before we could even apologise.

We made our way down the long passageway towards the bowels of the basement. Tiny snatches of conversation ceased as soon as we were in eyesight of the speakers.

Finally we reached the kitchen and stepped through into the scullery. A large, formidable-looking woman was busily running a tablecloth across a washboard. A large red stain spoiled the appearance of the normally crisp white linen and seemed to be drawing its own ire from the woman.

After a moment of patient waiting, Holmes let out a small cough. The woman jumped and dropped the cloth into the bucket in her fright. She turned around, a hint of anger on her face which disappeared as soon as she saw us.

Immediately she stepped down from her stool and wiped her sudsy hands against her apron. "My word," she asked. "Are you two gentlemen lost?"

"Not at all," replied Holmes. "We seem to have found the person we were seeking."

"Me?" she asked. "Why?"

"If I am not mistaken, you would be the person most skilled in the laundering of this household's clothing."

Her chest puffed up at the slight compliment. "Why yes, that would be me," she said. "What can I do for you then? Have you soiled your lovely suits?"

Holmes smiled. "No, nothing like that, but thank you for offering. We are investigating the location of the Duke's young daughter."

The woman's face dropped. "That poor dear. If those Germans harm one hair on her head, then they'll have to deal with me."

I felt that I wouldn't want to be in the kidnappers' shoes – if there were kidnappers.

"And that is a sentiment shared by me and my associate here, Dr. John Watson."

"Oh, a doctor, aye. Well, I'm Mrs. Havsham, if you have a mind to know. Been in this house for nigh on twenty years. Seen that lovely lass grow up, and would never wish any harm to her."

"Quite so," said Holmes, "You are the perfect person then to help our inquiries. Would you know if young Elizabeth has any clothing that has been brought here for laundering?"

"That's a very personal question," she said, tensing a little before smiling, "But you seem to be a lovely gentleman, so I will tell you. No. I'm surprised, but there's nought been brought down here for a day or so."

"Interesting," said Holmes.

310

Mrs. Havsham was about speak when a very loud voice cut through from the folding room next door. We turned to see an attractive flame-haired young woman dressed in a kitchen hand's uniform float down the stairway into the room carrying an armload of tablecloths. She directed her speech to a straight-backed man who stood at the shoe bench, polishing a pair of knee-high boots.

"Hello, Fritz," she said. "What's up with your master this evening? I haven't seen him since before luncheon."

The man stopped working, a look of intense hatred bordering on fury crossing his face. "My name is Friedrich, not Fritz," he said in a very thick German accent before diverting his attention back to the boots.

"Doris," said Mrs. Havsham. "Leave the Baron's man alone and get those over here."

Doris smiled, walked into the scullery, and across to the washing barrel. She dumped the tablecloths onto the ground and clapped her hands together, releasing a cloud of white powder.

"Don't know why they needs me to go up and get these. Those maids upstairs are just lazy good-for-nothings."

Mrs. Havsham face showed a look of indignation. Her reply was a little sharp. "The maids have guest rooms to prepare and beds to turn down. You were asked to help out, so there should be no argument."

"I have pastries to bake for the morning," she said, turning around and heading back to the kitchen.

Mrs. Havsham shook her head. "Don't know what gets into their heads nowadays."

We bid her a good evening and Holmes stepped into the folding room, with me close behind. Friedrich was busy with his boots and ignored us. He was wearing a starched white shirt with a dark tie with a vest, matching his black trousers. I

311

noticed a small red-and-white pin in the lapel of his vest. It had the look of a pin given for having been in military service.

Meanwhile, Holmes was scrutinizing a nearby pile of laundry, topped by a jacket that clearly belonged to the Baron. He leaned in and pulled a long red hair from the shoulder. It was then I noticed a small smear of white powder on the arm. My eyes grew wide.

"Can I help you?" came Friedrich's voice from behind us.

Holmes turned towards the valet and studied him for a moment. The valet began to become very agitated before Holmes spoke to him in German. "*Sie sind der Mann des Barons?*" he asked. (You are the Baron's man?)

Friedrich straightened. I spied a military background just by his posture. "*Ja. Seit vielen Jahren bin ich mit ihm zusammen,*" he said. ("Yes. For many years I have been with him.")

Holmes returned to English, much to my happiness, and continued. "Ah, born in Saxony, I think?"

Friedrich's eyes opened wide as if he had seen Holmes perform an unexpected magic trick. I was growing used to the way that Holmes could pick apart a person's life solely through observation.

"Yes, but how?"

"And from your posture, I would say Army – First Royal Saxon Corps, perhaps?"

Friedrich's face softened slightly. He appeared intrigued by Holmes's remarks. "Yes, but – ?"

Holmes cut him off. "Is this your first time to England?"

"No. Ve have come here a number of times. The Baron has interests in this country. He keeps a close eye on them."

"And the Duke?" Holmes asked.

"Yes. The Duke and the Baron have long known each other. The Duke has companies that deal vith the Baron's as vell."

"Interesting. And the Lady Elizabeth? She has known the Baron for a while?"

"Not really." He stopped and put the boot brush down. An exasperated look appeared on his face, and he looked like one under some internal torment. He stared off into space and began to speak more to himself than to us. "It's these Englanders. They have changed the Baron. He vas never interested in politics, just business. Then they arrange this marriage to the young Lady Elizabeth. The Baron has always liked the ladies. Especially the young ones. He has never vanted just one, so I don't understand it. It does not make any of the sense."

He suddenly caught himself and realised what he'd been saying. He remembered his chores, picked up the boot brush, and began polishing the boots once more. "If you'll excuse me, I am the busy," he said.

Holmes turned and moved back into the scullery. He stepped up to Mrs. Havsham again.

"I beg your pardon again, madam," he said.

Mrs. Havsham stopped her washing, happy to have Holmes's attention once again, and dried her hands on her apron. "Not a problem, sir."

"The young Lady Elizabeth, and the Baron?" he asked.

Mrs. Havsham's face went very serious. She checked on Friedrich, then looked from side to side before leaning in closer to us.

"All arranged without young Elizabeth's consent. The Duke has sold her off to further his business interests, and that old lech just wants to get his hands on a young filly, if you know what I mean. He's never been able to keep his hands off them since he's been coming here."

She stopped herself when she realised what she'd said. She started to turn, but Holmes asked one more question. "Lady Elizabeth would have needed a maid servant, would she not?"

Mrs. Havsham nodded, "Yes, that would be Caitlin. Caitlin Brown."

"Where could I find her?"

"She should be around, unless she's gone for the day. She has family over in Lambeth. Since we've come back to London, she's been going home regularly to see them. Check with Mrs. Scunthorpe, the housekeeper, just down the hall," she said pointing off down the corridor.

Holmes smiled and said, "Thank you, Mrs. Havsham. Sorry to have taken your time."

"It's all right," came her reply as she turned her attention back to the washing.

Holmes took my arm and led me away. We moved through the kitchen where Doris was busy making pies, her arms dusted in flour up to the elbows. She noticed us and smiled coyly. I nodded in reply as we moved on.

Luckily for us, Mrs. Scunthorpe was in her room, readying herself for the servants' evening meal. Our appearance brought an interested look to her face. "Are you gentlemen lost?" she asked. "The party is still going upstairs. I can take you back if you wish."

"No, that will be quite alright, Mrs. Scunthorpe. I am Sherlock Holmes, and this is my associate, Dr. John Watson. We are assisting with determining the location of young Elizabeth, and were hoping that you could help us."

Mrs. Scunthorpe sat down heavily, almost in a faint. She put a hand to her forehead in anguish. "Oh, my, this has been

314

a night. I think we've kept it from most of the guests, but it won't be long. I'm happy to provide any help to find that young girl, and soon."

"I understand that her maid's name is Caitlin Brown," Holmes said.

"Yes."

"She would probably have been the last person to have seen Elizabeth, and presumably would have been helping to ready her before the introductions. Has she been around since then?"

Mrs. Scunthorpe thought for a moment, a quizzical look on her face, and then shook her head. "No. I haven't seen her since earlier. The guests finished dinner around seven o'clock, and the young ladies went back to their rooms to prepare for the ball. Elizabeth and Caitlin went past me as I was coming up stairs to supervise the removal of all the dinner dishes, but since then I haven't seen hide nor hair of her." She sat bolt upright. "You don't think that she was kidnapped as well, do you? Or worse, that *she's* the kidnapper?"

Holmes held his hands up to calm the housekeeper. "No, no, nothing like that, I assure you. We just need to retrace Elizabeth's steps and talk to Caitlin. Could you give us her home address?"

"Certainly," she said and quickly pulled out a piece of paper and a pencil, jotting down a Lambeth address.

Holmes smiled and took the paper.

Mrs. Scunthorpe looked up at him, her eyes full of anguish. "Please find our young Elizabeth. She's a good girl. She doesn't deserve any of this."

"You mean the kidnapping?" Holmes asked.

"Oh, and that as well," she said, his question drawing a look of surprise.

As we climbed the stairs back to the ground floor, I had to ask Holmes a question. "The First Royal Saxon Corps? It was the pin on Friedrich's vest's lapel, wasn't it?"

"Why, yes, it was. Well done."

"Is that how you determined his accent?"

Holmes smiled. "Actually, no. I met a fellow student at University who was born and raised in Leipzig. I polished my very basic German by conversing with him from time to time. Some of his pronunciation was vastly different to what I'd learned, and we decided that it was because of the local dialect influences."

"Outstanding," I said. "Where to next?"

"Well, I believe a short trip is in order," he said, holding the small scrap of paper in his hand. "I feel that the current occupants of this address will reveal a lot more about this mystery than anything else."

We walked a short distance down the corridor before hearing stern voices coming from a room nearby. We stopped and crept up to the doorway. They belonged to the Duke, the Baron, and Roderick. From the tone and volume, the Baron was enraged.

"This disappearance is a ruse! You are just trying to humiliate me. What more do you want? More money? More business contacts? I'm very close to forgetting everything and returning home. The Emperor will not be amused."

Roderick piped up, "I assure you, your Grace, there has been no intent by either the British Government or by the Duke himself to undermine this deal. For all we know, Lady Elizabeth has been kidnapped and is in great danger as we speak."

"The police have been informed," said the Duke. "The Government has dispatched agents to search as well. I am at my wits end. This is my only daughter we are speaking of here.

I can only assume that we will receive a ransom note soon. I will pay whatever they ask to get Elizabeth back."

"That may be so," said the Baron, "But what if the Lady Elizabeth is soured by this experience? What if she returns damaged? I was promised a young beauty. If that is no longer the case, then where is my recompense? In fact, I may simply walk away from this deal altogether. It seems very slovenly for the British Government to have let these brigands snatch the Lady from under their noses."

We could hear the Duke simply bristling in rage. "See here! That's my daughter you're talking about!" he said, his voice rising in volume along with his anger.

Roderick stepped up and diffused the situation. "I'm sure that Her Majesty's Government was not responsible for this act, and I'm also sure they would be happy to provide compensation, or indeed improve your situation, should anything untoward arise."

"Very well," said the Baron. He suddenly appeared at the doorway, causing us both to jump back in surprise. He had a wry smile on his face which didn't fade when he came upon the two of us. He quickly looked each of us in the eye and continued on down the corridor. I felt that he would have been quite happy to whistle a jaunty tune as he did. I started to have severe doubts about his innocence in all this.

Roderick appeared at the door. "There you are. Anything new?" he asked. "We need to find this lass as soon as possible. The favourability of this deal for the Government is degrading by the minute."

Holmes replied, "I understand your concern, but there was nothing new in her room. We questioned a few of the staff and nothing either. I plan to journey home and contact my Irregulars. They have an ear to the street and may have come across these so-called 'Sons of Bavaria'."

317

Roderick thought for a moment and then nodded. "Agreed. I have men working on it as we speak, but they don't have as close an insight into the criminal underbelly as your urchins do." He pulled out a pocket watch and we realised it was well past eleven o'clock. "Hmm. I daresay there will not be much sleep gained in this house tonight, but that will only lead to more anger and indecision. Meet us back here in the early morning – say eight o'clock. Hopefully there will be more information by then. With any real hope, we may have even found the Lady Elizabeth."

"Indeed," said Holmes.

With that, Roderick went back into the room to inform the Duke. We turned on our heels and proceeded to the front door.

As we alighted from the hansom that dropped us in front of 221b Baker Street, Holmes stepped to the side of the footpath and spied up and down the street. He focused on a shadowy spot a couple of houses away, held up his hand, and clicked his fingers. I swore that the shadows dissolved and a figure moved quickly away.

The hansom drew away and I turned to enter our house just as a young boy in filthy clothes ran up to Holmes. "Wiggins," Holmes said.

The boy, Wiggins, removed his flat cap and addressed Holmes. "'Ello Mr. 'Olmes. Sorry I took so long. What can we do for you this fine evening?"

"Small job for you. I need someone to keep a watch on Cleveland House at St. James Square. Pay particular attention to a German called Baron Von Steurer – tall, fifty, grey hair, moustache. I want to know what his movements are." He turned towards me, "Watson, do you have a crown on you?"

I fished around in my purse, drew forth a silver coin, and dropped it into Holmes's hand. He turned and gave it to

318

Wiggins. It disappeared into a pocket as quickly as it appeared in his hand.

"Here, this should cover any expenses you'll have. Whoever goes will be there all night. Stay out of sight and send word if the Baron leaves"

"Is the prize on offer?" Wiggins asked.

Holmes smiled, "Naturally. Anyone who brings me a vital clew will receive a guinea, as always."

Wiggins gave a mock salute, placed his hat on his head, and said, "Right you are Mr. 'Olmes. We are on the case." He turned and hightailed it down the way he'd come with increased speed.

"I'd hate to say it," I commented, "but I think that the police will still be putting their boots on by the time your Irregulars have come up with solid clews."

"Quite so. It's amazing what can be achieved with an eager force of invisible urchins and a little cash incentive. Now let's change. We have another address to visit before this night is out."

By the time the hansom dropped us outside the Lambeth address supplied by Mrs. Scunthorpe, it was well into the wee hours of the morning.

There was a light still burning in the front parlour window – a good sign for us and one that bode well for a quick conclusion to our search.

Holmes stepped up to the door and rapped lightly with the knocker, trying hard not to cause too much ruckus for the neighbours.

For a moment there was an immediate hive of activity inside the terraced house, before a shuffling could be heard just inside, and the bolts were drawn on the entrance door.

A grey-haired, stoop-backed man opened it and peered up at Holmes's tall imposing figure through watery eyes.

"Yes?" he asked, "Do you know what time it is?"

"I do apologise, sir. I assume that you are Mr. Brown? Father of Caitlin?" Holmes said.

"Grandfather actually," the old man said.

"Ah, good. I am Sherlock Holmes, and this is my associate, Dr. John Watson," Holmes said.

The old man looked Holmes up and down then repeated the gesture with me. "What's that to me?" he asked.

"Well, your granddaughter was in the company of Lady Elizabeth Powell, the daughter of the Duke of Cleveland, earlier this evening, and now both have disappeared. We have been tasked with ascertaining their whereabouts," Holmes added.

The old man looked us both up and down again. He seemed very determined to stop us from entering his house.

Suddenly, a softer voice came from within. "Father, let those gentlemen in. It's cold and you'll pay for it tomorrow, I tell you."

The old man turned for a moment and then looked back at us. He shuffled backwards to allow us to enter.

It was much warmer inside. While we divested ourselves of coats and scarves, The man wandered back into a nearby sitting room. I looked for somewhere to hang my coat and noticed that there were no free hooks. All four were taken up with coats, all of which had scarves draped over them as well.

In the end, Holmes and I simply folded our coats over our free arms and stepped into the parlour.

A woman of about forty years of age sat in the warmth of the little room. A cooling pot of tea was in the middle of the room on a small table. A quick scan showed a total of four teacups distributed on either the middle table or the two other side tables.

Holmes sauntered up to the woman. "Mrs. Brown, I assume? As I mentioned, I am Sherlock Holmes, and this is my associate, Dr. John Watson."

"Yes," she said. "I'm afraid that you've wasted your time, Mr. Holmes, Caitlin hasn't been home for weeks. We are so proud of her. She's fallen on her feet with Lady Elizabeth. The two are inseparable."

"That is my understanding as well," said Holmes, "So much so that in such a time as this, when young Elizabeth has been driven to her wits end, she seeks solace in the only other place available."

Mrs. Brown's face creased up in confusion. "Where would that be?" she asked.

"Why, *here*," said Holmes, "Amongst the family of her closest friend."

"But I just told you, Caitlin is not here, and Lady Elizabeth has never visited before."

"I admire your audacity in protecting the young lady," he said, "as well as your daughter, but we both know full well that they are within,"

Mrs. Brown's face showed a distinct flash of anger. "I said they aren't here," she said, her voice rising in volume. "This is my house, and you should believe what I say."

Holmes paused to let the irritation in the air dissipate for a moment, before continuing. "And that would be fair, except for the evidence."

"What evidence?" said Mrs. Brown.

"Four coats hanging in the entranceway – one with an exquisitely expensive looking silk scarf. No offence to you or your father, but I would think such an item to be quite an indulgent addition to your wardrobe. Plus there's the matter of the four tea cups scattered around this room," he said.

Mrs. Brown looked deflated by the simple logic. "Come in here, Caitlin," she said, not even needing to raise her voice.

A door at the other end of the room opened and two shamefaced girls in their late teens entered the parlour. Elizabeth was immediately recognisable by her more opulent attire.

"Sit," said Mrs. Brown.

Holmes and I shifted around to allow the two to take their seats.

Lady Elizabeth sat straight backed and stared up into Holmes's eyes. "I do not think we've had the pleasure, sir."

Holmes bowed slightly and said, "No, we haven't, Lady Elizabeth. I am Sherlock Holmes, and this is my associate Dr. John Watson. You may have met Roderick St. John-Smythe. He works for Her Majesty's Government and has been assisting your father broker the deal with the Baron regarding your hand in marriage."

At the mention of the Baron, Elizabeth stiffened and drew in a sharp breath. "Something that brings you concern, it seems," Holmes added.

Elizabeth was close to tears, Caitlin, sitting next to her, took her hand and tried to console her. Elizabeth regained her composure before continuing, her voice slightly shaky. "Are you here to take me back?" she asked, her tone tingling with nervousness.

"I believe that you are of age. Therefore I, and no other person in authority, has any right to do so. I am also happy to keep your secret until you are prepared to return. I would say, however, that your father is extremely worried. They believe the story that you and Caitlin fabricated regarding your presumed kidnapping."

322

"But you didn't," she said. "Otherwise you wouldn't be here."

"True. I generally look beyond the obvious. My purpose here is to establish *why*. Why would you steel yourself away at the instant of, perhaps, the most important moment of your life so far?"

At this Elizabeth lost her control. Tears flowed freely down her cheeks as Caitlin pulled Elizabeth's head to her shoulder and allowed her friend to weep. She turned her head towards Holmes and spoke, her accent much broader than the gentle speech of Elizabeth.

"It's all because of that rotter, and that red-haired tart," she said.

Holmes smiled at the descriptions. "The Baron and – I presume – Doris, the kitchen hand?"

Caitlin nodded. "Yes. She's been gettin' above her station with the Baron. It started with a little flirtin', and then suddenly she goes missing late at night and slopes in just before dawn. I knows she ain't been out the house. You can talk to Friedrich – he knows all about it. Poor lad. He has to keep a lid on it. And then she parades around like she owns the place. Sayin' she's gonna move to Germany and work in the Baron's house and all that." She turned back and patted Elizabeth's head, cooing softly to her.

With her head still buried in Caitlin's shoulder, Elizabeth sobbed. Caitlin patted her head and continued, "I takes her back to her bedroom and we worked out a way for Elizabeth to disappear."

"Did you plan to go back at any stage?" Holmes asked.

"We hadn't thought that far ahead," she said.

Holmes turned towards me and spoke. "Watson, I think we can leave these people in peace. We shall retire for the night and return to Cleveland House in the morning." He turned back to face Elizabeth and Caitlin. "Lady Elizabeth, I will not reveal your whereabouts until I have resolved this matter. I feel that there is a lot more to the Baron's activities than a simple tryst with a servant girl. I wish you luck with the future, but I feel by nine o'clock tomorrow everything will be in order."

We bid *adieu* to the four, replaced our coats, and stepped out of the house, closing the door behind. Moments later the bolts were drawn.

On Holmes's instructions, I made my own way back to Cleveland House the next morning. He said he would be leaving early and would meet me there.

As I stood outside the grand mansion, another hansom arrived, depositing Holmes and Roderick to the footpath beside me. Roderick was in a less-than-hospitable mood, but contained it behind his normally stoic façade.

Holmes greeted me and we made our way into the house. We were shown into the drawing room where the Duke and Baron were having a stern conversation. It finished as soon as we entered, and the atmosphere remained business-like. I then noticed Friedrich standing to one side, not far from the Duke's own valet.

Roderick withdrew two sets of papers from his satchel and placed them on the desk, along with a beautifully crafted fountain pen, laid at the head of each contract. The Duke and Baron immediately set about poring over the documents. The Baron then turned towards Holmes and Roderick. "No word on my beautiful Elizabeth?" he asked.

Holmes and Roderick shook their heads and dropped their gaze.

I noticed a slight smile cross the Baron's face before he removed it. He turned his attention back to the contract. "One-hundred thousand," he said. "Well, this should more than compensate my broken heart for the loss it feels." He picked up the pen, signed both contracts and pocketed the pen in one fell swoop.

He turned to Friedrich and spoke in German. "*Mach die Taschen fertig,*" he said. "*Je eher wir uns von diesen Engländern und ihren blöden Frauen trennen, desto besser.*" ("Get the bags ready. The sooner we get away from these Englanders and their stupid women the better.")

Friedrich looked shocked at the Baron's words. He shot a furtive glance towards Holmes, knowing full well his grasp of German. Holmes simply smiled back and nodded. Friedrich's eyes grew wide and he quickly left the room.

The Baron was oblivious to everything and hovered over the Duke, waiting for him to sign.

"If I may be so bold, your Grace, you may wish to read the contract a second time to be clear on the terms," said Roderick. The Duke regarded him for a moment and went back over the details of the contract.

Suddenly a shrill voice entered the room from the doorway. "You pigeon-livered flapdoodle!" it cried.

We all turned to find Doris, her angry face almost the same colour as her flaming hair. Her eyes stared daggers at the Baron. He stood up straight and was taken aback by the vitriolic delivery of the young kitchen maid.

She stepped into the room and headed straight for him. "You used me! All that sweet talk about taking me with you was just bollocks!"

She walked up to the Baron and slapped him hard across the cheek. He was left stunned and unsure how to continue, his hand going to his jaw.

She continued to yell into his face, punctuating each word with a finger jab to the chest, "I'm not just some common strumpet looking for some well-heeled johnny to sweep me off

325

my feet! I got talents, I do, and I'm not gonna waste 'em on some foozler like you!"

She stared deep into his face for a moment before letting out an enraged howl and storming from the room.

The Baron stood, stunned. The Duke placed his pen on the unsigned contract, turned towards the Baron and asked, "Would you care to explain?"

The Baron stammered for a moment before Holmes interrupted. "I believe the Baron is trying to apologise. It seems that ever since this deal began to be brokered, he has been playing the field, as it is called, with your staff. The primary reason has been to undermine his relationship with your daughter."

The Baron began to grow angry. "How dare you!"

Holmes ignored him and continued, "The unfortunate Doris there was just the main player. My informants, who were watching the Baron, saw him leave your presence with a young blonde girl late last night. She was wearing simple brown street clothes with a brown bonnet. Her hair was quite long, braided into in a single plait.

The Duke's eyes lit up. "That sounds like Audrey, my chamber maid," he said. He threw a stern look at the Baron. "How could you, sir? She is barely sixteen!"

A voice with a thick German accent came from the doorway. "I know how."

We turned to find Friedrich standing there. He stepped into the room and spoke. "It vas always his plan. The young ladies who consented vere a bonus, but he only vanted to make the young Lady Elizabeth grow jealous and enraged so that she might do something silly and help the Baron change the deal in his favour."

"What are you doing?" yelled the Baron, stepping up to his valet and staring straight into his eyes.

"I am fed up vith this charade. I was born a man of honour. I am a Saxon. I vas an army officer. I cannot condone vat you had planned, and I vill not be a part of it. You bring dishonour to my country, and all for a little money. Your bags are packed. I quit."

The Baron's rage knew no bounds. He seethed at his valet and brought his hand up in a fist ready to lash out at the younger man.

The Baron's fist flew, but Friedrich simply stepped aside and the Baron tumbled to the floor. Friedrich looked down at him and shook his head.

"Baron, you really are a petty little man. I vish I had never come into your service."

The Duke stepped up to him and placed a hand on his shoulder. "You will always be welcome in my employ, dear boy. Go back to your room and I will find you later. We can discuss it then."

Friedrich nodded, said, "Thank you, your Grace," and left.

The Duke looked down at the Baron and shook his head in dismay, he then peered across at Roderick.

"Why didn't you know about this charlatan?" he asked.

"I do apologise, your Grace, I will be sending out some severe reprimands when I return to my office."

The Duke turned back to the desk, picked up both contracts, and tore them to shreds. He threw them at the Baron as he picked himself up and tried to regain his dignity.

"To think I almost let my daughter marry you," he said. "Get out of my house!" He turned on his heel and left the room.

The Baron started to move from the room. "Would you like a hand with your bags?" Holmes asked.

The Baron stared back at him with a steely gaze that could melt ice. He ignored the question and left.

"Obviously not," I said.

Back at Baker Street, we enjoyed a mid-morning repast of scones and coffee.

"I think that went quite well," I said.

Holmes took a sip of coffee, a pleased look on his face. "I'm not sure what was better, seeing the Baron's comeuppance, or watching Roderick embarrassed and grovelling to the Duke."

"Don't be too harsh on Roderick," I said, "He obviously doesn't have the quality of informants in his network like you do."

"Perhaps," he said. Then his face changed as he remembered something. "You wouldn't have a guinea on you, would you? I'll need to pay Wiggins for his information."

Grumbling, I reached once again into my purse.

About the Contributors

*The following appear in
Volume II:*

David B. Beckwith was born in the U.K. region of Cumbria. His family emigrated to Western Australia in 1969. He studied Mathematics, Middle English, Music, and Philosophy at the University of W.A. He is now a retired I.T. Professional. He started writing about Sherlock Holmes in 2010, he has now written twenty short stories and one long story, published three Holmes books, and a fourth book is in preparation. David lives in a rural region bordering to the metropolitan area of Perth where he and his wife grow vegetables and raise chickens for eggs.

Brian Belanger is a publisher and editor, but is best known for his freelance illustration and cover design work. His distinctive style can be seen on several MX Publishing covers, including *Memoirs from Mrs. Hudson's Kitchen* by Wendy Heyman-Marsaw, *Sherlock Holmes and the Menacing Melbournian* by Allan Mitchell, *Sherlock Holmes and A Quantity of Debt* by David Marcum, *Welcome to Undershaw* by Luke Benjamen Kuhns, and many more. Brian is the co-founder of Belanger Books LLC, where he illustrates the popular *MacDougall Twins with Sherlock Holmes* young reader series (#1 bestsellers on Amazon.com UK). A prolific creator, he also designs t-shirts, mugs, stickers, and other merchandise on his personal art site: *www.redbubble.com/people/zhahadun*.

Sir Arthur Conan Doyle (1859-1930) *Holmes Chronicler Emeritus.* If not for him, this anthology would not exist. Author, physician, patriot, sportsman, spiritualist, husband and father, and advocate for the oppressed. He is remembered and honored for the purposes of this collection by being the man who introduced Sherlock Holmes to the world. Through fifty-six Holmes short stories, four novels, and additional Apocryphal entries, Doyle revolutionized mystery stories and also greatly influenced and improved police forensic methods and techniques for the betterment of all. *Steel True Blade Straight.*

Jayantika Ganguly BSI is the General Secretary and Editor of the *Sherlock Holmes Society of India*, a member of the *Sherlock Holmes Society of London*, and the *Czech Sherlock Holmes Society*. She is the author of *The Holmes Sutra* (MX 2014). She is a corporate lawyer working with one of the Big Six law firms.

Stephen Herczeg is an IT Geek, writer, actor, and film-maker based in Canberra Australia. He has been writing for over twenty years and has completed a couple of dodgy novels, sixteen feature length screenplays, and numerous short stories and scripts. Stephen was very successful in 2017's International Horror Hotel screenplay competition, with his scripts *TITAN* winning the Sci-Fi category and *Dark are the Woods* placing second in the horror category. His work has featured in *Sproutlings – A Compendium of Little Fictions* from Hunter Anthologies, the *Hells Bells* Christmas horror anthology published by the Australasian Horror Writers Association, and the *Below the Stairs, Trickster's Treats, Shades of Santa,*

Behind the Mask, and *Beyond the Infinite* anthologies from *OzHorror.Con*, *The Body Horror Book*, *Anemone Enemy*, and *Petrified Punks* from Oscillate Wildly Press, and *Sherlock Holmes In the Realms of H.G. Wells* and *Sherlock Holmes: Adventures Beyond the Canon* from Belanger Books.

David Marcum plays *The Game* with deadly seriousness. He first discovered Sherlock Holmes in 1975 at the age of ten, and since that time, he has collected, read, and chronologicized literally thousands of traditional Holmes pastiches in the form of novels, short stories, radio and television episodes, movies and scripts, comics, fan-fiction, and unpublished manuscripts. He is the author of over fifty Sherlockian pastiches, some published in anthologies and magazines such as *The Strand*, and others collected in his own books, *The Papers of Sherlock Holmes*, *Sherlock Holmes and A Quantity of Debt*, and *Sherlock Holmes – Tangled Skeins*. He has edited nearly fifty books, including several dozen traditional Sherlockian anthologies, such as the ongoing series *The MX Book of New Sherlock Holmes Stories*, which he created in 2015. This collection is now up to 18 volumes, with several more in preparation. He was responsible for bringing back August Derleth's Solar Pons for a new generation, first with his collection of authorized Pons stories, *The Papers of Solar Pons*, and then by editing the reissued authorized versions of the original Pons books. He is now doing the same for the adventures of Dr. Thorndyke. He has contributed numerous essays to various publications, and is a member of a number of Sherlockian groups and Scions. He is a licensed Civil Engineer, living in Tennessee with his wife and son. His irregular Sherlockian blog, *A Seventeen Step Program*, addresses various topics related to his favorite book friends (as his son used to call them when he was small), and can be found at *http://17stepprogram.blogspot.com/* Since the age of nineteen, he has worn a deerstalker as his regular-and-only hat. In 2013, he and his deerstalker were finally able make his first trip-of-a-lifetime Holmes Pilgrimage to England, with return Pilgrimages in 2015 and 2016, where you may have spotted him. If you ever run into him and his deerstalker out and about, feel free to say hello!

Mark Mower is a member of the *Crime Writers' Association*, *The Sherlock Holmes Society of London* and *The Solar Pons Society of London*. He writes true crime stories and fictional mysteries. His volumes of Holmes pastiches include *A Farewell to Baker Street*, *Sherlock Holmes: The Baker Street Case-Files*, and *Sherlock Holmes: The Baker Street Legacy* (all with MX Publishing) and, to date, he has contributed many stories to the ongoing series *The MX Book of New Sherlock Holmes Stories*. He has also had stories in two anthologies by Belanger Books: *Holmes Away From Home: Adventures from the Great Hiatus – Volume II – 1893-1894* (2016) and *Sherlock Holmes: Before Baker Street* (2017). More are bound to follow. Mark's non-fiction works include *Bloody British History: Norwich* (The History Press, 2014), *Suffolk Murders* (The History Press, 2011) and *Zeppelin Over Suffolk* (Pen & Sword Books, 2008).

Sidney Paget (1860-1908), a few of whose illustrations are used within this anthology, was born in London, and like his two older brothers, became a famed illustrator and painter. He completed over three-hundred-and-fifty drawings for the Sherlock Holmes stories first published in *The Strand* magazine, defining Holmes's image forever after in the public mind.

Tracy J. Revels has been a Sherlockian from the age of eleven. She is a professor of history at Wofford College in Spartanburg, South Carolina. She is a member of *The Survivors of the Gloria Scott* and *The Studious Scarlets Society*, and is a past recipient of the Beacon Society Award. Almost every semester, she teaches a class that covers The Canon, either to college students or to senior citizens. She is also the author of three supernatural Sherlockian pastiches with MX (*Shadowfall*, *Shadowblood*, and *Shadowwraith*), and a regular contributor to her scion's newsletter. She also has some notoriety as an author of very silly skits: For proof, see "The Adventure of the Adversarial Adventuress" and "Occupy Baker Street" on YouTube. When not studying Sherlock, she can be found researching the history of her native state, and has written books on Florida in the Civil War and on the development of Florida's tourism industry.

GC Rosenquist was born in Chicago, Illinois and has been writing since he was ten years old. His interests are very eclectic. His twelve previously published books include literary fiction, horror, poetry, a comedic memoir, and lots of science fiction. His works include *Sherlock Holmes: The Pearl of Death and Other Stories* MX Books, and his Belanger Books children's novel *The Tall Tales of Starman Steve* and his adult novel *33 Tall Tales of Lake County, Illinois*. He has had his work published in *Sherlock Holmes Mystery Magazine* and several volumes of *The MX Books New Book of Sherlock Holmes Stories*. He works professionally as a graphic artist. He has studied writing and poetry at the College of Lake County in Grayslake, Illinois, and currently resides in Round Lake, Illinois. For more information on GC Rosenquist, you can go to his website at *www.gcrosenquist.com*

Robert V. Stapleton was born and brought up in Leeds, Yorkshire, England, and studied at Durham University. After working in various parts of the country as an Anglican parish priest, he is now retired and lives with his wife in North Yorkshire. As a member of his local writing group, he now has time to develop his other life as a writer of adventure stories. He has recently had a number of short stories published, and he is hoping to have a couple of completed novels published at some time in the future.

D.J. Tyrer is the person behind Atlantean Publishing, was placed second in the Writing Magazine "Local Reporter" competition, and has been widely published in anthologies and magazines around the world, such as *Disturbance* (Laurel Highlands), *Mysteries of Suspense* (Zimbell House), *History and Mystery, Oh My!* (Mystery & Horror LLC), and *Love 'Em, Shoot 'Em* (Wolfsinger), and issues of *Awesome Tales*, and in addition, has a novella available in paperback and on the Kindle, *The Yellow House* (Dunhams Manor) and a comic horror e-novelette, *A Trip to the Middle of the World*, available from Alban Lake through Infinite Realms Bookstore.
His website is: *https://djtyrer.blogspot.co.uk/*
The Atlantean Publishing website is at *https://atlanteanpublishing.wordpress.com/*

I.A. Watson is a novelist and jobbing writer from Yorkshire who cut his teeth on writing Sherlock Holmes stories and has even won an award for one. His works include *Holmes and Houdini, Labours of Hercules, St. George and the Dragon* Volumes 1 and 2, and *Women of Myth*, and the non-fiction essay book *Where Stories Dwell*. He pens short detective stories as a means of avoiding writing things that pay better. A full list of his sixty-plus published works appears at:

331

The following appear in
Volumes I and III:

Ian Ableson is an ecologist by training and a writer by choice. When not reading or writing, he can reliably be found scowling at a clipboard while ankle-deep in a marsh somewhere in Michigan. His love for the stories of Arthur Conan Doyle started when his grandfather gave him a copy of *The Original Illustrated Sherlock Holmes* when he was in high school, and he's proud to have been able to contribute to the continuation of the tales of Sherlock Holmes and Dr. Watson.

Deanna Baran lives in a remote part of Texas where cowboys may still be seen in their natural habitat. A librarian and former museum curator, she writes in between cups of tea, playing *Go*, and trading postcards with people around the world. This is her first venture into the foggy streets of gaslit London.

Derrick Belanger is an educator and also the author of the #1 bestselling book in its category, *Sherlock Holmes: The Adventure of the Peculiar Provenance*, which was in the top 200 bestselling books on Amazon. He also is the author of *The MacDougall Twins with Sherlock Holmes* books, and he edited the Sir Arthur Conan Doyle horror anthology *A Study in Terror: Sir Arthur Conan Doyle's Revolutionary Stories of Fear and the Supernatural*. Mr. Belanger co-owns the publishing company Belanger Books, which released the Sherlock Holmes anthologies *Beyond Watson, Holmes Away From Home: Adventures from the Great Hiatus* Volumes 1 and 2, *Sherlock Holmes: Before Baker Street*, and *Sherlock Holmes: Adventures in the Realms of H.G. Wells* Volumes 1 and 2. Derrick resides in Colorado and continues compiling unpublished works by Dr. John H. Watson.

S.F. Bennett has, at various times, been an actor, a lecturer, a journalist, a historian, an author and a potter. Whilst some of those things still apply, she has always been an avid collector, concentrating mainly on ephemera and other related items concerning Sherlock Holmes and British science-fiction of the 1970's. To date, she has written articles on aspects of The Canon for *The Baker Street Journal*, *The Sherlock Holmes Journal*, and *The Torr*, the journal of *The Sherlock Holmes Society of the West Country*. When not collecting, she can be found writing science-fiction and mystery stories, and has contributed to several anthologies of new Sherlock Holmes pastiches. Her first novel was *The Secret Diary of Mycroft Holmes: The Thoughts and Reminiscences of Sherlock Holmes's Elder Brother, 1880-1888* (2017). She is also the author of *A Study In Postcards: Sherlock Holmes in the Golden Age of the Picture Postcard* (*Sherlock Holmes Society of London*, 2019).

Thomas A. Burns, Jr. is the author of the *Natalie McMasters Mysteries*. He was born and grew up in New Jersey, attended Xavier High School in Manhattan, earned B.S degrees in Zoology and Microbiology at Michigan State University, and a M.S. in Microbiology at North Carolina State University. He currently resides in Wendell, North Carolina. As a kid, Tom started reading mysteries with The Hardy Boys, Ken Holt and Rick Brant, and graduated to the classic stories by authors such as A. Conan Doyle, Dorothy Sayers, John Dickson Carr, Erle Stanley Gardner, and Rex Stout, to name a few. Tom has written fiction as a hobby all of his life, starting with The Man from U.N.C.L.E. stories in marble-backed copybooks in grade school. He built a career as technical, science, and medical writer and editor for nearly thirty years in industry and government. Now that he's truly on his own as a novelist, he's excited to publish his own mystery series, as well as to contribute stories about his second-most-favorite detective, Sherlock Holmes, to *The MX Anthology of New Sherlock Holmes Stories.*

Chris Chan is a writer, educator, and historian. He works as a researcher and "International Goodwill Ambassador" for Agatha Christie Ltd. His true crime articles, reviews, and short fiction have appeared (or will soon appear) in *The Strand*, *The Wisconsin Magazine of History*, *Mystery Weekly*, *Gilbert!*, *Nerd HQ*, Akashic Books' *Mondays are Murder* web series, *The Baker Street Journal*, and *Sherlock Holmes Mystery Magazine.*

Emily J. Cohen lives in Rhode Island with her fiancé and her tiny dog. She received a Master of Fine Arts in Creative Writing from Lesley University and her work has appeared in *JitterPress Magazine* and *Outlook Springs*. A self-described geek, Emily enjoys Doctor Who, anime, and competitive video games.

Harry DeMaio is a *nom de plume* of Harry B. DeMaio, successful author of several books on Information Security and Business Networks, as well as the ten-volume *Casebooks of Octavius Bear – Alternative Universe Mysteries for Adult Animal Lovers*. Octavius Bear is loosely based on Sherlock Holmes and Nero Wolfe in a world in which *homo sapiens* died out long ago in a global disaster, but most animals have advanced to a twenty-first century anthropomorphic state. "It's Time" is Harry's first 100% traditional pastiche featuring Holmes and Watson, after his story "Doctor Bear, I Presume?" (*Sherlock Holmes: In The Realms of Steampunk*) featured the duo encountering Harry's ursine detective. A retired business executive, consultant, information security specialist, former pilot, and graduate school adjunct professor, he whiles away his time traveling and writing preposterous articles and stories. He has appeared on many radio and TV shows and is an accomplished, frequent public speaker. Former New York City natives, he and his extremely patient and helpful wife, Virginia, and their Bichon Frisé, Woof, live in Cincinnati (and several other parallel universes.) They have two sons living in Scottsdale, Arizona and Cortlandt Manor, New York, both of whom are quite successful and quite normal – thus putting the lie to the theory that insanity is hereditary.

Sir Arthur Conan Doyle also has stories in Volumes I and III.

Tim Gambrell lives in Exeter, Devon, with his wife, two young sons, two cats, and seven chickens. He contributed "The Yellow Star of Cairo" to *Part XIII* of *The MX Book of New Sherlock Holmes Stories*. Outside of The World of Holmes, Tim has written extensively for Doctor Who spin-off ranges. He has recently had two linked novels published by Candy Jar Books: *Lethbridge-Stewart: The Laughing Gnome – Lucy Wilson & The Bledoe Cadets*, and *The Lucy Wilson Mysteries: The Brigadier and The Bledoe Cadets* (both Summer 2019). He also has a novella, *The Way of The Bry'hunee*, for the Erimem range from Thebes Publishing, which is due out in late 2019. Tim's short fiction includes stories *in Lethbridge-Stewart: The HAVOC Files* 3 (Candy Jar, 2017), *Bernice Summerfield: True Stories* (Big Finish, 2017), and

Relics . . . An Anthology (Red Ted Books, 2018). Further short fiction will feature in the forthcoming collections *Lethbridge-Stewart: The HAVOC Files – The Laughing Gnome*, and *Lethbridge-Stewart: The HAVOC Files – Loose Ends* (both due later in 2019).

Richard Gutschmidt (1861-1926) was the first German illustrator of The Canon, providing over eighty drawings for twenty Canonical adventures between 1906 and 1908.

Arthur Hall was born in Aston, Birmingham, UK, in 1944. His interest in writing began during his schooldays and served as a growing ambition to become an author. Years later, his first novel *Sole Contact* was an espionage story about an ultra-secret government department known as "Sector Three" and has been followed, to date, by four sequels. The sixth in the series, *The Suicide Chase*, is currently in the course of preparation. Other works include five "rediscovered" cases from the files of Sherlock Holmes, two collections of bizarre short stories, and two novels about an adventurer called "Bernard Kramer", as well as several contributions to the ongoing anthology, *The MX Book of New Sherlock Holmes Stories*. His only ambition, apart from being published more widely, is to attend the premier of a film based on one of his novels, ideally at The Odeon, Leicester Square. He lives in the West Midlands, United Kingdom, where he often walks other people's dogs as he attempts to formulate new plots. His work can be seen at *arthurhallsbooksite.blogspot.com*, and the author can be contacted at *arthurhall7777@aol.co.uk*.

Paula Hammond has written over sixty fiction and non-fiction books, as well as short stories, comics, poetry, and scripts for educational DVD's. When not glued to the keyboard, she can usually be found prowling round second-hand books shops or hunkered down in a hide, soaking up the joys of the natural world.

Mike Hogan writes mostly historical novels and short stories, many set in Victorian London and featuring Sherlock Holmes and Doctor Watson. He read the Conan Doyle stories at school with great enjoyment, but hadn't thought much about Sherlock Holmes until, having missed the Granada/Jeremy Brett TV series when it was originally shown in the eighties, he came across a box set of videos in a street market and was hooked on Holmes again. He started writing Sherlock Holmes pastiches several years ago, having great fun re-imagining situations for the Conan Doyle characters to act in. The relationship between Holmes and Watson fascinates him as one of the great literary friendships. (He's also a huge admirer of Patrick O'Brian's Aubrey-Maturin novels). Like Captain Aubrey and Doctor Maturin, Holmes and Watson are an odd couple, differing in almost every facet of their characters, but sharing a common sense of decency and a common humanity. Living with Sherlock Holmes can't have been easy, and Mike enjoys adding a stronger vein of "pawky humour" into the Conan Doyle mix, even letting Watson have the second-to-last word on occasions. His books include *Sherlock Holmes and the Scottish Question*, the forthcoming *The Gory Season – Sherlock Holmes, Jack the Ripper and the Thames Torso Murders*, and the Sherlock Holmes & Young Winston 1887 Trilogy (*The Deadwood Stage, The Jubilee Plot*, and *The Giant Moles*), He has also written the following short story collections: *Sherlock Holmes: Murder at the Savoy and Other Stories, Sherlock Holmes: The Skull of Kohada Koheiji and*

Other Stories, and *Sherlock Holmes: Murder on the Brighton Line and Other Stories*. www.mikehoganbooks.com

David Marcum also has stories in Volumes I and III.

Will Murray is the author of over seventy novels, including forty *Destroyer* novels and seven posthumous *Doc Savage* collaborations with Lester Dent, under the name Kenneth Robeson, for Bantam Books in the 1990's. Since 2011, he has written fourteen additional Doc Savage adventures for Altus Press, two of which co-starred The Shadow, as well as a solo Pat Savage novel. His 2015 Tarzan novel, *Return to Pal-Ul-Don*, was followed by *King Kong vs. Tarzan* in 2016. Murray has written short stories featuring such classic characters as Batman, Superman, Wonder Woman, Spider-Man, Ant-Man, the Hulk, Honey West, the Spider, the Avenger, the Green Hornet, the Phantom, and Cthulhu. A previous Murray Sherlock Holmes story appeared in Moonstone's *Sherlock Holmes: The Crossovers Casebook*, and another is forthcoming in *Sherlock Holmes and Doctor Was Not*, involving H. P. Lovecraft's Dr. Herbert West. Additionally, a number of his Sherlock Holmes stories have appeared in various volumes of *The MX Book of New Sherlock Holmes Stories*, as well as the anthologies *Sherlock Holmes: Adventures Beyond the Canon* and *The Irregular Adventures of Sherlock Holmes* from Belanger Books. He is best known as the co-creator of the character Squirrel Girl for Marvel Comics with artist Steve Ditko.

Robert Perret is a writer, librarian, and devout Sherlockian living on the Palouse. His Sherlockian publications include "The Canaries of Clee Hills Mine" in *An Improbable Truth: The Paranormal Adventures of Sherlock Holmes*, "For King and Country" in *The Science of Deduction*, and "How Hope Learned the Trick" in *NonBinary Review*. He considers himself to be a pan-Sherlockian and a one-man Scion out on the lonely moors of Idaho. Robert has recently authored a yet-unpublished scholarly article tentatively entitled "A Study in Scholarship: The Case of the *Baker Street Journal*'. More information is available at www.robertperret.com

Roger Riccard of Los Angeles, California, U.S.A., is a descendant of the Roses of Kilravock in Highland Scotland. He is the author of two previous Sherlock Holmes novels, *The Case of the Poisoned Lily* and *The Case of the Twain Papers*, a series of short stories in two volumes, *Sherlock Holmes: Adventures for the Twelve Days of Christmas* and *Further Adventures for the Twelve Days of Christmas*, and the new series *A Sherlock Holmes Alphabet of Cases,* all of which are published by Baker Street Studios. He has another novel and a non-fiction Holmes reference work in various stages of completion. He became a Sherlock Holmes enthusiast as a teenager (many, many years ago), and, like all fans of The Great Detective, yearned for more stories after reading The Canon over and over. It was the Granada Television performances of Jeremy Brett and Edward Hardwicke, and the encouragement of his wife, Rosilyn, that at last inspired him to write his own Holmes adventures, using the Granada actor portrayals as his guide. He has been called "*The best pastiche writer since Val Andrews*" by the *Sherlockian E-Times*.

GC Rosenquist also has a story in Volume III.

Matthew Simmonds (with stories in both Volumes I and III) hails from Bedford, in the South East of England, and has been a confirmed devotee of Sir Arthur Conan Doyle's most famous creation since first watching Jeremy Brett's incomparable portrayal of the world's first consulting detective, on a Tuesday evening in April, 1984, while curled up on the sofa with his father. He has written numerous short stories, and his first novel, *Sherlock Holmes: The Adventure of The Pigtail Twist*, was published in 2018. A sequel is nearly complete, which he hopes to publish in the near future. Matthew currently co-owns Harrison & Simmonds, the fifth-generation family business, a renowned County tobacconist, pipe, and gift shop on Bedford High Street.

Annette Siketa is totally blind and lives in Adelaide, Australia. She first came to Holmes by accident – that is to say, someone "dared" her to write a Sherlock Holmes story. Since then, she has written over fifty Holmes stories, including the full-length novel, *Chameleon – The Death of Sherlock Holmes*. The books *The Failures of Sherlock Holmes* and *The Untold Adventures of Sherlock Holmes* will be released in early January 2020, and will be available through most online retailers except Amazon.

Kevin P. Thornton has experienced a Taliban rocket attack in Kabul and a terrorist bombing in Johannesburg. He lives in Fort McMurray, Alberta, the town that burnt down in 2016. He has been shortlisted for the *Crime Writers of Canada* Unhanged writing award six times. He's never won. He was also a finalist for best short story in 2014 – the year Margaret Atwood entered. We're not saying he has luck issues, but don't bet on his stock tips. Born in Kenya, Kevin was a child in New Zealand, a student and soldier in Africa, a military contractor in Afghanistan, a forklift driver in Ontario, and an oilfield worker in North Western Canada. He writes poems that start out just fine, but turn ruder and cruder over time. From limerick to doggerel, they earn less than bugger-all, even though they all manage to rhyme. He also likes writing about Sherlock Holmes and dislikes writing about himself in the third person.

A Special Thank You
to Our Backers

This book could not have been a success without the support of our Kickstarter Backers. We would personally like to thank the following:

Wanda Aasen
Charles C. Albritton III
Dean S Arashiro
Ron Bachman
Barak Bader
Howard J. Bampton
Chris Basler
Chad Bowden
Michael Brown
Rachel Burch
Alessandro Caffari
Mark Carter
Chris Chastain
Ivan Cobham
Gina R. Collia
Craig Stephen Copland
Terry Cox
Scott J. Dahlgren
Christopher Davis
Harry DeMaio
Michael Demchak
Edward Drummond
Derrick Eaves
Griffin Endicott
Fearlessleader
Rich Friedel

Tim Gambrell
Jacinda Gift
Brad Goupil
Richard L. Haas III
Paul Hiscock
Scott Jackson
Dave Jones
Melanie K
Miles L
Anthony & Suford Lewis
Debra Lovelace
Anthony M.
James J. Marshall
Scott Vander Molen
Mark Mower
Richard Ohnemus
Mike Pasqua
Robert Perret
Gary Phillips
David Rains
Mary Ann Raley
Michael J Raymond, PhD
Ray Riethmeier
Steve Rosenberg
Eric Sands
Steven Sartain
Scarlett Letter
Eric Schaefges
Evan Schwartzberg
Steven M. Smith
Danny Soares
Bertrand Szoghy
David Tai

Tom Turley

Ida Sue Umphers

Carl W. Urmer, MHS

Karly VK

F Scott Valeri

Douglas Vaughan

Sriranga Veeraraghavan

L.E. Vellene

David A. Wade

Joseph S. Walker

Michael Walker

Charles Warren

Deb "IGrokSherlock" Werth

Anton Wijs

Seow Wan Yi

David Zurek

Belanger Books

Made in the USA
Middletown, DE
01 January 2020